THE

LOST

ONE

A Russian Legacy

PENELOPE HAINES

For information contact;

www.penelopehaines.com

Published by Createspace 2015

ISBN ISBN-13:978-1508760306

ISBN-10:1508760306

This book is dedicated,

with a lifetime of love and thanks,

to Cavan

for his boundless support and encouragement.

PROLOGUE

Moscow, 1917.

IT WAS THE END OF WINTER. Late season snowflakes blew into his eyes, and the dark came early. There was good reason for Kyril Komarov to keep his eyes on the pavement and watch his step.

The man was almost invisible in the shadow of the door frame. Kyril, striding home, his mind on his own matters, was abreast of him, unheeding.

"*Merde*!" Kyril exclaimed, as a hand reached out and grabbed his coat sleeve.

"Quiet," urged the voice.

Kyril peered into the shadows to identify his accoster. It took him a few moments to place the man, recalling him as a minor government functionary who had once inspected the factory. Kyril sieved his memory for the name. "Sergei Petrovich," he whispered. "What in the name of Christ are you doing? You nearly gave me a heart attack."

"Follow me," returned the man, opening the door.

Once inside, Sergei released his arm. "Sorry, but I needed to stop you," he apologised. "You know they've arrested them?"

Kyril stared at him. All Moscow knew the Tsar had abdicated that day and the Bolshevik Army had put his family into 'protective custody'. He nodded. "So?"

"Word has it that you closed your factory in Petrograd Shausse today. Indeed, as we speak, your lovely wife, brother and son are all packing their bags to leave Moscow tomorrow. Many would say, given the current situation, that this is a wise move. I understand you have family in Great Britain?"

Kyril paled. It was true – one of the factory staff could have talked and mentioned the closure of the works, but no one was supposed to know the Komarovs were fleeing. He wondered who had opened their mouth, and to whom. Surely not his wife or his son.

It wouldn't be his brother, either. Ilya might be young and enthusiastic, but he was the least likely person of them all to talk about secret things.

Sergei watched Kyril's face and snorted at the expressions moving across it. "Don't worry, my friend. You have nothing to fear from me, but my boss would like to meet you. If you would be so kind as to follow me now?"

Kyril weighed his options. In these troubled times it made sense not to cross the secret police. Who knew where alliances were being formed? He shrugged his shoulders and indicated assent, receiving a wry half-smile from his companion.

"Thank you, my dear friend," Sergei murmured, before leading Kyril through a maze of narrow corridors and staircases.

They passed through a green baize door. Kyril hadn't had time to take note of his surroundings but knew he must be in a government administrative building. Once through the door, the corridors broadened, and the next flight of stairs was palatial.

Sergei paused beside a door, knocked and entered, drawing Kyril in with him.

The man seated behind the desk was unknown to Kyril, though clearly, given his surroundings, someone of importance. He raised his eyes as they entered and searched Kyril's face.

"General Mirov, may I present to you Kyril Gregorovitch Komarov."

The general nodded and gestured to Sergei. "You may leave us alone."

Sergei saluted and left.

Kyril may not have recognised the face, but he knew the name. Mirov, a highly decorated officer, was a war hero, praised in the press for his exploits at the front against the German aggressors.

Kyril studied the man in front of him. He was about the same age as himself but had a raw physicality and athleticism, which made him a commanding figure.

"Please sit." The general waved Kyril to one of the chairs. "Thank you for coming so promptly," he added.

Kyril blinked; surely he had been brought? Perhaps the general had the wrong man? He didn't like to correct him, so he stayed silent.

"I hope Sergei was courteous in his invitation?" There was a ghost of a smile in his eyes as he asked the question. "Sometimes he is a little enthusiastic in carrying out his duties."

Kyril nodded silently, wondering where this was going.

"I understand you and your family leave Moscow tomorrow and you intend to travel to Great Britain?"

Again Kyril nodded. How was it everyone seemed to know his business?

"I also understand you are a moderate, in your political views? I think your family business served the Tsar?"

Kyril drew a deep breath, wondering how best to answer. "We were appointed as official harness-makers to the Tsar, general."

The general grunted, stood up and paced across the room. "Good. Then I have a commission for you." He turned abruptly to face Kyril. "You must understand that in these complicated political times, while Mother Russia moves towards the future, much of the good from her past may be lost." He read Kyril's look of incomprehension. "I mean our cultural heritage," he added.

Kyril nodded uncertainly.

"There has already been looting. Even those charged to look after such things are not immune to political propaganda. Some of our churches have been desecrated and other artworks destroyed."

He came close to Kyril and leaned back against the desk, still facing him. "I am a historian, Mr Komarov, and a lover of Russia and of our heritage." He sighed. "If you study history … Do you know your history, Mr Komarov?"

Kyril nodded. "A little, sir, although my skills are those of a businessman, not an academic."

"Then you will know the course of events in all upheavals. So much was lost to France in their revolution. Most of their royal jewels were sold off as worthless at the time and ended up in the possession of the crown of England. Now France has no way of regaining her own heritage," he said morosely. I don't wish to see this happen to my country." He paused. "So much will be lost, but there is a little I can do to help save some of it."

Reaching forward he clasped Kyril by the shoulder. "You are a patriot, my friend. Your views are known to me. I also know you are an honest man, yet you're in danger because you are tainted by your association with the Tsarist regime. So you must take your family and go. Who can blame you?" he added. "But there is one last service you can perform for your nation."

He indicated a small crate on the floor against the wall. "I need you to take this with you in your personal luggage when you leave tomorrow."

Kyril turned to look at the box, and both men studied it in silence for a few minutes.

At last Kyril asked, "What's in it, sir?"

"I don't think you need to know that."

Kyril shook his head. "If you don't tell me what is in it then, with respect, sir, I'm not taking it with me. It could be anything, and it could put me and my family in danger."

"You may be safer, in fact, in ignorance," demurred the general.

Kyril Komarov had not been a trader for nothing. "General, either I know what's in that case, or it doesn't come with me. If it's valuable government property, I need to know about it."

The general shook his head and sighed. "It's not government property, Mr Komarov. It is private property, and I've been authorised by the owners to save and conceal it in the way that seems best to me in the circumstances." He looked at Kyril again. "Are you certain you need to know?"

Kyril nodded.

In silence the general reached down, lifting the crate onto the desk. Raising the lid disclosed a metal box, the type soldiers in the field have for their possessions. The general lifted it out and unlocked the top. Kyril looked inside.

Mirov moved the packing aside to reveal several wrapped parcels. Very carefully, almost reverentially, he unfolded the covering.

Kyril gasped at the opulent item that appeared. "What is it?" he whispered.

"One of the imperial family's Fabergé Easter eggs. The jeweller made one each year, commissioned by the Tsar. There is no safe place in Russia for them. Do you understand now, Mr Komarov?"

Kyril nodded.

"One day, if God wills, it will be safe for them to return to Russia. In the interim, harness-maker by imperial decree, I am appointing you their steward. My own position is under threat from various parties, and I cannot even guarantee my own survival over the next few weeks. I can't keep them with me. They must be saved for the future of Russia."

He paused for a moment before asking quietly, "Do you accept the charge?"

Kyril ran his hand through his thinning hair, a gesture he often favoured, so his wife told him, when his mind was troubled. He didn't want the responsibility, but he believed in what the general had said. He nodded reluctantly. "I accept."

Mirov looked at him soberly. "I know you don't want this charge, my friend. But if you can save these for Russia's future, you do us all a great service." He let out a sigh of relief. "Such service will not go unrewarded, or unsupported," he said.

He opened the drawer of his desk and pulled out a few small bags. "Take these as payment for services rendered, for help in the times you have ahead of you, and as my personal thanks."

He smiled at Kyril's questioning look. "There are diamonds, some other stones. Good quality. There is also gold and other coin, a couple of ornate eggs of no particular historical merit, but of some value. You will need to source a purchaser when you trade the stones or eggs, but for a man of your experience in business, that shouldn't be too difficult. Choose wisely, though. These are stones of the finest water."

He pushed the bag across to Kyril, who hesitated. "Take them, Mr Komarov," he said softly. "I know what you and your family have already lost." He smiled wryly. "These will provide a more than adequate recompense, I believe. Use them well."

Kyril looked at him squarely. "Thank you," he said at last. "I will care for this treasure, as you ask. I will always be a true patriot to my country." He picked up the bag and weighed it. "Thank you for your payment. It won't recompense us for what we have lost," he said, putting it into the inner pocket of his coat, "but I thank you."

"Go with God, Mr Komarov," said the general waving him away.

Later that night Kyril and Ilya sat in front of the dying fire. They had shared many evenings in this room. These last minutes in the family home were moments to cherish.

The brothers shared a fine-boned physique which, in Kyril, manifested itself as a sophisticated, trim figure, and in Ilya as a slightness that made him look younger than his twenty-eight years. Beyond that, the physical resemblance between the two was slight.

Kyril was dark. Immaculate grooming kept his trim moustache smart and his hair well cut, disguising the fact that his broad forehead owed more to a receding hairline than to the 'intellectual brow' he himself claimed.

Ilya's hair was longer and fair. His eyes sparkled with life and enthusiasm, and he moved with a dancer's slim-hipped grace. He had been a willing participant in the family business, but Kyril had sometimes wondered whether this was the result of Ilya's happy personality rather than a career choice made voluntarily.

The brothers complemented each other and had an easy rapport. Kyril was serious; Ilya the family clown and charmer. Kyril could be intimidating, and it was often Ilya's charm and easy manner that smoothed relations between employed and employer at the factory.

Twenty years separated the two brothers, the result of intervening miscarriages on their late mother's part. When their father died, Kyril had taken on the role of mentor and guardian to his younger brother, a role he believed he still occupied.

Kyril's wife Anna, dry-eyed and determined, had left them together an hour earlier. "I'll see you tomorrow, Ilya," she said heading up to bed. From time to time the brothers could hear the sound of her dry cough.

Both men were looking at the tin box.

Ilya had declined to view the Fabergé eggs. "The fewer people who see them, the better," he commented. "I don't need to see them. They were given to you and are your responsibility." He hesitated, squaring his shoulders. "Kyril, I was going to say this anyway, before you were handed this task, so don't think the two are related," he said, "but I'm not coming with you tomorrow, not to the West anyway."

Kyril stared at him, flabbergasted. "Of course you're coming. We can't leave you here. It's even more dangerous for us now, thanks to this box. Someone may connect us with this treasure. Sergei, for one, knows where I was tonight. Who knows who else does."

"I'm not staying in Moscow," Ilya said. "I want to go east."

Kyril snorted. "East is Siberia! That's nonsense. There's nothing there."

Ilya smiled. "Well, actually, there's a young student friend of mine from Yekaterinburg who waits for me. If that doesn't work out, I prefer the thought of being a trader in the East. I've read about Manchuria, Shanghai and other exotic places. I want to travel, just not in the direction that you, Anna and Charles are going."

Kyril frowned at him in dismay. "We'd never see you again! How could we travel between Europe and China? We would lose you, Ilya."

"I am sure that one day we'd travel and meet up – me with my central Russian bride, you with your English-speaking son. The world isn't so big nowadays, Kyril. Mail gets to every part of the globe. Ships and travellers can go anywhere." Ilya smiled. "This is a time of adventure for us, Kyril. Please don't make the parting hard." He held Kyril's hand. "Our world here has gone, big brother. We have to build a new one for ourselves. I fancy the East with all its exotic goods, spices, teas. I can be like Marco Polo!"

Kyril knew Ilya well enough to know once his mind was made up he wouldn't change it. Ilya might look slight and boyish, but he was tempered steel inside. Nor could Kyril really argue with him. He wondered fleetingly, if he didn't have a wife and child, would he too have taken the eastern road. "At least take some of this." He gestured to the pile of stones. "Maybe they'll give you start-up capital and help you on your way. That is, if you don't get murdered for them," he added.

Ilya grinned. "Trust me, big brother. I can look after myself."

Next morning the family assembled in the hall. They knelt in front of the family icon, and Kyril led prayers for the safety of them all.

"We will meet in Heaven, if not again on earth," prayed Anna, hugging her brother-in-law. She had tried tears and entreaties to change his mind but had failed. In the end, Anna sadly accepted the situation. She took a locket from around her neck. "Please, Ilya, take this. It has photos inside of Kyril and me, and a lock of Charles's hair. At least have some things from your family with you," she said as she put it on him, tucking the ornament down inside his shirt. "There," she said. "No one can see it, but it means your family will be close to your heart."

Ilya grinned, hugged Charles and embraced his brother one last time.

"Go with God," said Kyril.

"May God be with you too," echoed Ilya.

Both knew in reality they would never meet again. The pain

was so great; there was no point mentioning it. Neither brother knew what the future would bring.

Anna had decided that Ilya should take the icon with him as well. "You must have some family heritage with you," she declared. "You must remember your family, and your God."

Kyril and Ilya exchanged wry glances, and Kyril shrugged. "We'll both remember," he said obliquely to Ilya.

Ilya nodded, shoved his cap, which had shifted in their last embrace, back onto his head, and grinned.

The last possessions stowed, the family said goodbye to their servants and took the cab to the station, and the brothers parted to fulfil their separate destinies.

CHAPTER ONE

What's bred in the bone will come out in the flesh.
— late 15th-century proverb

London, Present Day.

THE LAST VISITOR LEFT. THE PRESS hung around long enough to report the funeral. Friends, work colleagues and staff had spent the afternoon in and out of the house, and most weren't there solely to comfort her in her grief, or to pay their respects to her late husband. They all had their own agendas.

Marguerite Dunning sank into the sofa in the drawing room. Without asking, Max poured her some Chablis. "Thank you," she smiled as she sipped her wine. "I need this. It's been a long day."

Max regarded her seriously. "You can rest up tomorrow."

She smiled. "Tomorrow, Max, we have a lot to do. There's a granddaughter to contact and a company to take control of." She laughed at his expression. "Don't look so dubious; you know

I've been planning this for years."

"So you are really going through with it, madam?"

"Don't turn all formal on me now," urged Marguerite. "Of course I am. I've waited a long time to right the wrong done to Tamara. Her daughter's place is with her family, and her inheritance. I've had to live a lie for so many years, Max, but the time has come to put the pieces back together."

Max scrutinised her fondly. "Some women might want to take it easy at your age, you know? It's not going to be easy, keeping control of Dunnings. You haven't been involved in the day-to-day running for a long time."

"No," replied Marguerite, "I've been a sleeping partner, but now the partner has woken up and is going to be heard. Don't fret, Max, I'm looking forward to it."

She sat up abruptly. Her back was straight, her knees and legs together, folded slightly to the side. She was a tribute to the values of her youth, thought Max. She could have been a textbook illustration from the debutante's yearbook of 1955. An ageing, elegant reminder of an era that was gone. Those standards and values were dangerous weapons in the hands of a woman like Marguerite. He sighed inwardly. There would be stormy water ahead.

He shared many of those values, so it was foolish for him to carp at her eccentricities. He thought Marguerite Dunning an admirable example of her age and gender. But while he respected her immensely, he wouldn't trust her one inch if they were enemies. He knew her to be capable of lies, evasion and treachery if she thought her cause could best be served by these means. He had, in a sense, always loved her and was fascinated by the energy that still burned vital and strong in her body.

"Get me Donald on the phone," she commanded. "We need to arrange a display for the masses after Eugene's will is read. We must have the press on board before Clive can work up enough bluster to try and spike my guns. At this point, speed and surprise need to be my weapons."

Max dialled the number. As Donald McCrae had been at the funeral, Max didn't expect the man to pick up the phone himself.

He was probably too busy totting up the account he could soon send through for professional services, Max reflected. He left a message with the secretary.

"Mr McCrae is not contactable at the moment," he announced in his most formal tones. "May I suggest you follow his example? I will get Cook to send you up a light dinner and then, with all due respect, Marguerite, get yourself to bed. If you want to go ahead with all this, you are going to need all the rest, health and strength you can muster over the next little while."

He laughed quietly at her when Marguerite curled her lip at him. "You know I'm right, even if you don't want to admit it. I'll go and organise Cook."

He left the room, and Marguerite looked thoughtfully after him. She saw Max as her friend, but there had been a time when she'd wondered whether he had betrayed her. She supposed now that she would never know the truth.

Tomorrow the real battles would begin. Old as she was, she could hardly wait. Her hunger for the day's chase was still there, and she allowed herself the luxury of a deep, self-satisfied smile.

CHAPTER TWO

Wellington, Present Day.

PURDIE SHOVED HER WAY THROUGH THE garden gate. It sagged on its hinges and dragged jerkily across the concrete path. With both arms carrying shopping bags, it took a complicated dance step to wedge it open far enough to get through and then kick it closed behind her. She was hot, her arms ached and she had finished a taxing shift in the Accident and Emergency department.

She glanced back up the street. Parked across the road was a shiny black car – the type of expensive vehicle that would belong to someone who never had to juggle front gates and shopping bags. It stood out in their quiet cul-de-sac like the proverbial sore thumb.

"Batmobile," muttered Purdie under her breath.

She was met at the front door by her flatmate Sophie who flung the door wide for her. "Da-dah!" she cried as Purdie pushed passed her.

"I've got the bread and milk," said Purdie, "and cheese, butter and mince. Plus a couple of broccoli that were on special, some tomatoes and courgettes. Hey, the flat looks clean!"

"I was in domestic goddess mode this morning," said Sophie proudly. "I'll help you put the stuff away. How was the day?"

"OK," said Purdie. "Just your normal shift, including a few early morning drunks, a couple of domestics, someone who had done something inappropriate with a Coca-Cola bottle, and a couple of cardiac arrests."

Sophie snorted. "Exciting stuff. I've got today and tomorrow off. No jobs to do, just time to relax with a book." Sophie was from the Catlins and rolled her 'r's in true southern manner. Blonde, pretty and slender, she was blessed with a warm, sunny nature. She and Purdie had met at Massey University while studying for their nursing degrees and had been friends ever since.

"The last time I saw you with a book was during the '*Harry Potter* phase'."

"Well, it's now the '*Shades of Grey* phase'," retorted Sophie. "I'm deeply in love with Christian."

"How you can like that stuff is beyond me," scoffed Purdie. "How can anyone make plastic electrical ties into an erotic fantasy?"

"You're just old and stuck in your ways," riposted Sophie. "You need to get out more and get a man, then you'd understand about yearning and desire. Also, if you know plastic electric ties are involved, you've obviously read the series."

Purdie sniffed. She wasn't getting out, didn't have a man and didn't have the energy required to make her want one. Something must have showed in her face because Sophie suddenly flushed.

"Oh, Purds, I'm sorry. I didn't mean that! I know you're still hurting over your folks' death. I didn't mean to get at you."

"It's OK."

"I wish you'd come to the UK with me in September, though," Sophie begged. "We could do our OE together. Just imagine London, the shops and hopping across to Paris for a weekend. Maybe get a job in Arabia somewhere, later. They're always looking for nurses, and we could make our fortune, just by not drinking alcohol for a year."

Purdie laughed. "You couldn't keep off alcohol for a week, let alone a year."

"I could, if they chopped my hands off, or whatever it is they do as punishment. It would be very motivational. AA should consider it. Anyway, you know what I mean." Sophie dropped her voice into a wheedling tone. "Please say you'll come with me. You've even got a British passport. You don't need a work permit or a visa or anything. You can just waltz into the UK like a native and stay forever. Plus you could always come back if you really hated it."

"Hm," said Purdie. "I'll think about it. I promise," she added hastily as she saw Sophie's eyes roll in exasperation.

"And that," said Sophie, "is that, I suppose." She put the last of the vegetables away. "Oh, and you've got mail."

The post was in a pile on the table. On top of the normal letters was a plain New Zealand Post envelope, addressed very clearly in firm black pen to Miss Perdita Davis, 32 Maxwell Close, Newtown, Wellington, New Zealand.

"Hey, there's no notification of who it's from," she called to Sophie.

"Yeah, I noticed that. I also held it up to the light, but it's one of those bubble-wrap jobs, so even though I felt it, shook it and tried to see through it, I couldn't get any information," said Sophie as she came into the room.

"Bloody cheek," said Purdie. She was trying to tear the plastic off the envelope and getting nowhere. "Stuff it, I need some scissors. I can't think of anyone who would be sending me things."

"Scissors," said Sophie, passing them over. "I knew you'd need them."

Purdie tipped the envelope up and slid out the package. It was a small, flat jewellery box. She lifted the lid. "Heavens," she said, "this can't be for me." Inside, on a gold chain, was a tiny gold and enamel book.

"Hey, it looks like an old-fashioned Bible," said Sophie. On the patterned front cover was a cross surrounded by flowers, with a border that had originally been blue enamel, but now some of it was missing.

"It's a locket," said Purdie. Midway down the long side of the book was a clasp, and the halves opened to display photo frames. On the left was a black-and-white photo of a woman, holding herself erect, smiling at the camera. Her dark hair was pinned up, her dress plain, long-sleeved and buttoned up the front, with a white bow collar. The effect was simple and severe. Behind her could be seen the blossoms and foliage of a garden setting. "She doesn't look like anyone I know."

The photo opposite was a headshot of a man in his thirties, with a broad forehead, moustache and dark hair parted in a firm, uncompromising line. He faced obliquely away from the photographer, leaning his head sideways and resting it on his left hand. What could be seen of his clothes suggested a dark suit with a white wing-tip collar. A line of white cuff showed against his wrist. It was a pose with little expression, but the face was pleasant in its formal presentation.

"That photo looks quite old," said Sophie, who was unashamedly looking over Purdie's shoulder. "Mum had one like that of her great-granddad. Are you sure you don't know who it's from?"

"Not a clue," replied Purdie. She shut the locket and looked at it thoughtfully. "It's a pretty thing, although not exactly something you'd wear nightclubbing. It's more a formal trinket to wear to church maybe?"

Sophie looked inside the envelope. "You're sure there's no note?"

"Nothing," said Purdie. She lifted the lining from the jewellery box. "Nothing in here, and nothing I could see in the envelope. It's got to be a mistake, because I don't know anyone who'd send me something like this."

Then Sophie said slowly, "This envelope hasn't been posted. There's no stamp on it. Someone dropped it off in our box, and it's addressed very clearly to you."

She grinned at Purdie. "I take back what I said earlier. You are obviously a mystery woman with a secret admirer."

"Yeah, funny," replied Purdie. "I suppose that's gold?" She

poked a finger at the locket.

"May I?" Sophie picked the locket up carefully and turned it over. "Well there's no obvious jeweller's mark that I can see. But then again, what would I know? All I know is what I've got from watching repeats of *Antiques Roadshow*. They'd look at it and tell you straight away that it's a late 20th-century fake from Taiwan or something."

"What on earth are you doing watching *Antiques Roadshow*? You live a sad, sad life."

"I watch because, when I get to England and meet Mr Darcy, I need to know my Limoges from my Lalique if I'm to be a creditable wife at Pemberton." Sophie struck a dramatic pose.

Purdie laughed. "Sweetie, the English probably think we all still wear grass skirts."

"They should meet Katy," said Sophie. "She'd fix them. Yeah, well maybe I'm an optimist." She indicated the locket. "Get it looked at by a jeweller and valued. Then you'll know how much it's worth."

"And maybe I should wrap it up again and wait for whoever dropped it off to come calling and apologise for sending it to the wrong address," said Purdie. "It's not mine, and I'm sure it's not intended for me."

She turned the envelope over again. "Still, it's funny there's no return address, stamp or postmark."

Sophie looked at her severely. "I hate to be a puritan, but you are sure you haven't been playing around on Internet dating sites, aren't you? This isn't some cyber-lover who is getting a little close?"

Purdie snorted. "Yeah, right. I have so much time in my life that I hook up with losers? I don't think so."

She ignored Sophie's muttered: "At least it would be better than nothing!"

"Piss off, sweetie, not a chance on winding me up on that one."

Sophie smiled. "Just a thought, darling. I know it's not your style, but really …" she tailed off.

"What's for dinner?" asked Purdie, changing the subject.

Sophie smiled. "I've played Sadie the cleaning lady all morning. It's your turn to cook, unless you can persuade Nick to do it for you." She leered suggestively at Purdie. "He'd do a lot more for you too if you let him, but now I know you're a woman of mystery I understand your reluctance to get involved with a mere doctor."

Purdie gave a slight smile and shrugged her shoulders. "I vant to be alone," she vamped. "Mind you," she added, "I'll text Nick and see if I can twist his arm."

The next few days passed quietly. There was no frantic visitor trying to reclaim their property, and by the end of the week the envelope resting at the bottom of Purdie's undies drawer had ceased to concern her.

Sophie's comment about being old and stuck in her ways had stung, although she recognised it was true. Since her parents' sudden death in a car accident 18 months before, she had been at an emotional standstill. Their death meant she was now the owner of the family home in Khandallah. Insurance paid out the mortgage, so she owned it freehold, and she had been able to pay off her student loan and put money aside into a savings account.

For a woman of 24 she was remarkably well off, but the circumstances leading to her inheritance gave her no joy. The family house was leased out and provided an income. The letting agency managed it very well, and if she occasionally drove past to indulge in a nostalgic moment, she didn't linger. She had clung to the familiar – her friends and her life in the Newtown flat. She didn't feel ready to make decisions about disposing of the property, or investments, so she allowed the days to drift by, pretending that the status quo would go on forever.

Sophie had reminded her it wouldn't. The girls had always meant to do their OE together and had made broad plans for this goal. There had been a time when Purdie couldn't wait to escape from New Zealand and start her life as an adventurer. The Labour Weekend road crash that took her parents' lives had stopped her in her tracks. Outwardly she coped, but her energy and initiative were missing. She felt no more capable of organising a year or so in Europe than she was of worrying about a mysterious gift. It was enough to get through each day.

The weather was magnificent as Purdie walked back to the flat. It felt wonderful to be up in the green belt enjoying the late autumn sun. Sophie's comments about Nick had caught her attention. Did he like her? He'd been full of kindness in the aftermath of the accident and Purdie was very fond of him. Was Sophie right to suggest there was more to it than him just being a good flatmate?

While mulling over these thoughts, she suddenly noticed the expensive car that had caught her eye a week or two before. She supposed the owner must be visiting relatives in the close, and she wondered who they were. She and her flatmates worked, and they didn't always keep up with the personal details of their neighbours.

She smiled. If there was anything worth knowing, Katy, the fourth flatmate, would know all about it. People liked Katy, and she liked them. She knew the ins and outs of the neighbours' lives, waved to them on the pavement, popped in for coffee, had cooked dinner for at least one old man – that Purdie knew about – when his wife went away. Katy might know who owned the car and who they were visiting.

It was impressive, its paint so deep, glossy and intense that it had to be expensive. The windows were tinted so Purdie couldn't see in, and a sun visor covered the windscreen. There was no obvious insignia that she recognised but her knowledge of cars was limited to the little Honda she drove. She found *Top Gear* amusing, but the technical details went right over her head.

The letter box was full of its usual clutter – junk mail, free local rags, bills – but on the parcel rack, a large package clearly addressed to her. Purdie felt her heartbeat quicken. The writing was the same as on the envelope resting at the bottom of her drawer. She felt the parcel gingerly. It was much larger than the previous one; a good A3 size bubble-pack with no return address. Inside she could feel something hard, like a book.

When she walked into the flat, the others were gathered in the kitchen. Their various shifts meant it was rare that all four flatmates had the same weekend free. Katy was still in pyjamas cooking brunch while Nick and Sophie were sharing the paper, seated at the kitchen table.

"Mail, guys," announced Purdie, "and it looks as if I've got another present."

Sophie looked up sharply. "Really? From the same person? What is it this time?"

"I don't know. Pass the scissors please, Katy."

Purdie slit the envelope open and slid its contents onto the table. Carefully she unwrapped the bubble wrap. "Ooh," she breathed.

On the table, shimmering in the morning light, lay an exquisite jewel of a painting. Richly decorated and enamelled, it framed a stylised depiction of two women, both with halos radiating behind their heads like sun rays.

"Bloody hell," said Sophie. "What is it?"

"An icon, I think," said Katy, unexpectedly. "I've seen pictures of them. I think it might be Russian."

Purdie lifted it up and turned it over. The back was wooden and surprisingly rough and primitive, just slats of wood with a couple of crosspieces holding it all together.

"It looks genuine," said Nick. "Or at least it looks old and delicate. Is there any note with it?"

Purdie ruffled through the packaging. "No, no note this time either. No return address. I don't know what to think. I can't see why this has been sent to me either."

"And it's been hand-delivered again," said Sophie. "Look, no stamp or anything. There's nothing to give any indication of where it comes from."

"If you ask me, it's kind of creepy," said Katy. "You must be being stalked or something."

"It's a funny kind of stalking," replied Nick. "What did you do with that other thing you got?"

"I'll go and get it," said Purdie.

She returned with the locket and placed it beside the icon.

"I suppose you could say they both have a religious theme going," mused Sophie. "Purdie, perhaps someone is trying to convert you."

"Yeah, very funny," muttered Purdie. "What do I do, guys? Should I take them to the police or something?"

"Well, it's clearly addressed to you. I don't imagine there are that many Perdita Davises around. It's not the most common of names," said Sophie. "I think it's meant for you all right. The question is, why? Are you sure you don't have a long-lost auntie who's left you something in a will?"

"If it was a will, the information would have come from a solicitor. There wouldn't be random presents arriving in the letter box without rhyme or reason," said Nick. "This looks as if it has some personal motivation behind it."

"Yes, but again, why?" asked Purdie.

"I don't know. You haven't saved a patient's life or something and their family are grateful? It might be something like that. Maybe they want to be anonymous."

"Maybe," said Purdie, "but I can't think of anyone." She paused to think. "No, no one at all."

"If the icon is Russian," said Katy, "do you think the locket is too?"

"Maybe that's it," said Nick. "Perhaps there's a Russian connection. Have you nursed any Russians in the last few months?"

"Not that I remember," said Purdie.

"Maybe someone saw them drop it off" said Sophie. "We could ask the neighbours."

That reminded Purdie of her earlier thoughts. "Actually, I was going to ask Katy if any of the neighbours know who owns the flash car out on the road. I saw it there a week or so back as well. Maybe Katy could ask them about our mysterious present giver as well."

"What car?" said Nick. "What do you mean by 'flash'? Do you mean a sports car?"

"Well, I don't know, it just looks expensive and out of place here," said Purdie.

"Well, for you to notice it, it must do," smiled Nick.

"You don't think it could be connected, do you?" asked Katy

suddenly. "You said the car was around a few days ago. Was that when you got the first present?"

Purdie stared at her. "I don't know. It could have been. I didn't really notice because I didn't put the two together. Maybe it was." She racked her brains. "The only thing I really noticed, apart from it being expensive, was that it had a really tacky sun protector across the windscreen."

"You don't think someone was watching you from behind it?" asked Katy. "That would be really creepy."

Purdie felt a shiver down her spine. She didn't like to say just how much that suggestion disturbed her.

"Well, let's see if the car is still there. Then, if we can find the owner and ask them, we can eliminate it as a possibility," said Sophie practically. But when they looked out on the road, the car had disappeared.

CHAPTER
THREE

Wellington, Present Day.

THE LITTLE ICON TOOK UP RESIDENCE on Purdie's dressing table. Even the locket was allowed to sit in her trinket box when she put it away that night. She studied the icon carefully. Its gilded intricacy fascinated her. It was elaborate, over-ornate and stylised, but a beautiful piece, glowing with a dull sheen when the sun touched it. She wondered about its provenance. Was it a genuinely old piece? Its relevance to a 21st-century flat in Wellington seemed as obscure as ever.

Purdie's family had left England when she was three. Her parents hailed respectively from Kings Langley and Cheam, neither of which were places likely to be the source of exotic gifts. She was adopted, but she always felt part of the family and had only a slight interest in her birth origins. The adoption had been good, and her parents' death had underscored how totally they were her only family. She had been their sole heir, their true daughter, in every meaningful sense of the word.

Sophie wandered past her room, saw her studying the icon, and came in. "You know, I was thinking last night that it was odd how specifically addressed these parcels have been."

"What do you mean?"

"Well, we're in a flat, right? We all have mobile phones, but no landline, so it's not as if someone could look in the White Pages to find Perdita Davis. How did anyone know where you live?"

"The Electoral Roll, I suppose," said Purdie vaguely. "I don't know. There's a lot of information out there, isn't there? People are always making a fuss on TV about how easy it is to get personal information."

"And that," added Katy, who had just opened her bedroom door, "is the bit that is truly creepy. Maybe we've had paparazzi going through our rubbish, just like they do with celebrities."

"Well, all they'll find in our rubbish is empty cans of V, Red Bull and wine bottles," said Purdie cheerfully. "I don't believe these things can be for me, because, try as I may, I can't think of any reason for them."

"No long-forgotten lover?" asked Sophie hopefully. "No maiden aunt, no grateful millionaire patient you saved from the jaws of death?"

"Not a one," replied Purdie. "If this is a genuine benefactor, then their anonymity does make it a bit of a problem. I can't thank them; and if they have any other reason that may be of a dubious nature, well they can't convey that either. It all seems a bit pointless to me."

Nick found Purdie sitting on the sofa later in the day. "I've been thinking about our mystery postman," he said.

"Well?"

"Just in case there is something inappropriate about these gifts, beyond the obvious query about 'why you', I don't think you ought to be wandering around the streets on your own."

"Pardon?" asked Purdie. She was inclined to be indignant. "I don't just wander about; that sounds like some sort of vagrant!"

"Well maybe, but you walk to work, usually alone. You walk home, sometimes late at night, again alone. Even yesterday, you were walking on your own up on Mount Vic."

"I like walking," said Purdie. "You know I like keeping fit."

"I don't care if you were imprinted by Sporty Spice at an impressionable age. All I'm saying is that, maybe, at the moment, you need to be more careful," said Nick. "Why don't you drive to work? At least you'd be less accessible shut in your own car. And if you want to walk on the weekends, why don't I come with you? At least it would put off anyone who has designs on your person."

"I don't think I'm in any danger, Nick," said Purdie. "After all, so far these presents have been to my benefit. Assuming they are meant for me after all."

"No one does things for nothing," replied Nick. "Sooner or later you are going to find out what they want from you in exchange for these gifts, and it might not be something you want to be involved with."

"Well, maybe. But I can always return the gifts if I don't like what I find. And frankly, I can't think of anything anyone would want from me."

"Hm," responded Nick. "At least be careful, though. Avoid walking alone, don't put yourself at risk. It's just common sense."

Something about the way he spoke annoyed Purdie. "Are you saying I'm short on common sense? Thank you. I'm well able to look after myself, you know." Heavens, she'd had nothing else to do since her parents died.

"I'm not saying you can't look after yourself," snapped Nick, "and I know you like to think of yourself as tough and independent. But you aren't quite as tough as you think. You just do a good job of hiding things. I'm saying that someone wants something from you for some reason. Be careful, and sensible. It's not just you, anyway. In case you haven't noticed, both Katy and Sophie are a bit rattled as well. They may laugh, but someone has been dropping things off here, where we all live. Unless Katy can get one of the neighbours to identify the car you saw, we have no idea what this person has been up to. We are all out most of the day, and anyone could have access to this property and no one would be the wiser."

"Well so far there hasn't been too much disturbance, has there?" shot back Purdie, annoyed. "I don't see that I'm putting the flat at risk, if that's what you mean. It's not as if anything horrible has happened; quite the reverse. But if you think it's too risky for you and the others, I suppose I could leave."

"Don't be stupid," snarled Nick, also annoyed. "I haven't said anything of the sort. I just said, avoid being alone, nothing else. The fact that you would even think of snapping at me like this shows just how jumpy this situation has made you. It's not like you to be twitchy and unreasonable."

Before Purdie could reply, he left the room.

She avoided him for the rest of the day. It was rare that temperament got in the way of good flatting relations, but she felt he was being overprotective, and she didn't like someone raising issues she was privately worried about herself.

They made their peace later that evening. Purdie cooked dinner and afterwards made a point of offering him a cup of coffee.

There was something disturbing about the way he cautiously raised his head to look at her when she entered the room. And something enormously rewarding in the big smile he gave her at the simple offer of a cup of coffee. She was startled to find Nick's good opinion was more important than she'd realised. She made a mental note to take his advice, while not giving him the satisfaction of being able to say, 'I told you so'.

Besides, for the next week she and Sophie were on duty at the same time, so the problem would resolve itself. She would simply walk down and back to the hospital with her friend, and there would be nothing to worry about. Without conceding anything to Nick, Purdie felt she was taking due care. She certainly didn't need someone telling her what to do, thank you very much.

She would be more careful how she behaved around Nick now. There had been a slight shift in the atmosphere in the flat. Nick had never criticised her before. He'd been in the flat when the news came of her parents' death and been part of the support team that held her together in the months after the funeral. It had been easy to take him for granted. His criticism of her, however mild, showed a side she hadn't noticed before. She wasn't sure whether she liked it or not, but it made her more aware of him.

It was noticeable that each flatmate now checked the letter box a couple of times each day, and each item was scrupulously examined. But there was no sign of any mysterious gifts, nor of the car in the street.

Katy had asked a few of the neighbours if they had seen anything. Apart from getting their commitment to keep a closer eye on the flat, no one could recall seeing anyone dropping off mail, and no one knew anything about an expensive car.

If it hadn't been for her own observation, the car might not have existed at all. Part of Purdie queried whether she had seen it. What did she know of vehicles anyway? Maybe it was a Mazda, or something ordinary, and there was nothing significant about it at all.

Ten days passed. No presents arrived; no suspect cars appeared in the close. The flatmates began to relax.

CHAPTER
FOUR

Wellington, Present Day.

WHEN THE LETTER ARRIVED, IT ALMOST BYPASSED the flat's scrutiny. Purdie arrived home to find the mail piled on the table, with an envelope addressed to her bearing the logo and imprint of a firm of barristers and solicitors.

She was distressingly familiar with lawyers' letters and didn't pay the envelope any attention, until she realised it was from a firm she'd had no dealings with. Purdie's parents' estate was long-since settled, and she felt no urge to open yet another missive from a legal firm. She took the envelope to her room to read in private.

Addressed clearly to Miss P Davis, it read:

Dear Miss Davis,

I have been asked by my client to contact you. While the situation is unusual, please accept my assurances this letter represents a genuine attempt by my client to introduce themselves through the reputable offices of our legal practice and involves an offer that would be materially beneficial to you. I request you phone me to make an appointment so I can present my client's information to you and inform you of the details of the offer I have been authorised to disclose to you.

Yours sincerely,
Peter Harris

Even though Purdie read the letter twice, the little information it contained was not much help. She carried it back out to the kitchen and handed it to Katy. "What do you think?" she asked.

Katy read it through. "Well, it probably explains the gifts. Someone wants to do you some good." After pausing she asked, "And you still have no idea who it could be, or why?"

"No," said Purdie. She turned the letter over, examining the letterhead. "Morrison and Maxwell, Barristers and Solicitors, The Terrace, Wellington. Let's Google them."

The glossy webpage showed that Morrison and Maxwell was 'a corporate and commercial law firm, providing a specialised range of legal services to business and personal clients'. The firm looked the epitome of respectability.

"Well, they look kosher," said Katy, who had been reading the screen over Purdie's shoulder. "They don't look like the sort of dodgy operation that would be promoting Nigerian scams."

Purdie looked up at her. "Is this what it sounds like to you, a dodgy scam? I suppose it could be, but so far I seem to be the one who has benefited."

"There's one way to find out," said Katy, pointing at Purdie's mobile phone. "Ring and make the appointment."

"Mm," murmured Purdie. "I'll think about it. I don't want to rush into it. Let's see what the others think when they come in tonight."

When consulted that evening, neither Sophie nor Nick could add anything very useful.

"I don't think you've got a choice," said Sophie. "It's either phone them, or die of frustration wondering what it's all about."

Nick agreed. "You've nothing to lose, and maybe something to gain. At least it would explain the two presents you received and put the matter to rest. Just make sure you don't agree to anything without thinking it through."

And that, thought Purdie, neatly summed up what she had already decided. She never doubted she would make a time to see Peter Harris. She wasn't particularly interested in any benefits, but the mysterious happenings of the last few weeks had whetted her appetite for an explanation. While she let her friends discuss the situation, she had been buying more time to make a decision. She felt manipulated, even if it was in her best interests, and resented the fact.

Her next day at work was particularly busy. A young victim of domestic abuse was brought in, the damage so severe it was unlikely the young woman would keep the sight in her left eye. Purdie knew she was good at her job and she conveyed quiet confidence and support in times of crisis, but she was deeply sickened by this case. She helped work on the victim and then had the mass of paperwork and reporting to process. She dealt with the girl's distraught family, police, social workers and Accident Compensation Corporation. It kept her occupied, giving her little time to think about the letter.

When she got home that afternoon, she focused on the phone call she had to make. She was put through to Peter Harris. "Hello, I'm Purdie Davis. You asked me to call you."

The voice on the other end of the phone perked up. "Oh, Miss Davis, thank you for calling. Would you be prepared to come in to my office and meet with me?"

"You haven't explained much in your letter," said Purdie. "What is the purpose of this meeting, please?"

Peter Harris hesitated. "I can't explain much over the phone. But I can assure you this is legitimate and will be of benefit to you if you accept my client's proposal. The choice to do so would always be yours, of course. I am afraid I really do have to meet with you to discuss this further."

Had she ever intended to do anything else? "What time would be convenient?" she asked.

"Whatever suits you. I understand you're a nurse? Make a time that fits round your roster. I must ask that you bring documentation to prove who you are."

"Pardon?"

"Sorry," Peter replied, "but I can't be too careful. I need to sight your driver's licence or your passport; whatever documentation you have to support your claim to being Perdita Davis."

"I didn't think I was claiming anything," said Purdie, bridling. "You contacted me, remember?"

"Yes, I do remember, but you do need to have some documentation to prove your identity. I'm sorry, but I have to insist on this."

Purdie gave a shrug. "OK."

"What time suits you?" he asked.

Purdie ran a mental review of her roster. "Would four o'clock tomorrow work? How do I get to your office?"

Peter supplied the necessary details, and Purdie ended the call.

She talked to her flatmates later. All of them agreed she had done the right thing. Sophie offered to go with her and Nick nodded approvingly, but he had reverted to what she described to herself as his 'strong, silent mode'.

She declined Sophie's offer, preferring go alone.

"But you can pour me a large Sav Blanc when I get home; I'm bound to need one."

Peter Harris was short, or at least shorter than Purdie's 166 centimetres. In his mid-thirties, he already had a receding hairline, was overweight and the complete antithesis of lawyers Purdie had previously encountered. Those who had wound up her parents' estate were grey, elderly and vampirish.

"Thank you so much for coming," he said, shaking her hand and showing her into his office. "Tea, coffee?" he asked. "No? Never mind. Please sit down. I'll come to the point."

Purdie politely sat down.

He took his place behind the desk and cleared his throat. "OK. Miss Davis, I have been asked by my client to contact you and provide you with certain information which may be of benefit to you. What you choose to do with this information is, of course, your decision, and not something that Morrison and Maxwell have any part in."

Purdie nodded.

He relaxed, leaned back and looked at her. "Miss Davis, I must ask you, what do you know of your natural family? I presume you know you are adopted?"

"Ahh," said Purdie. "I was beginning to wonder if that was why someone would take an interest in me. Is this my birth family trying to find me?"

"In a sense," replied Peter Harris. "You know nothing about them?"

"I thought that was normal," said Purdie. "That's the whole point of adoption, isn't it? Details remaining confidential, I mean. I know I could have gone searching, but I didn't think anyone could search for me. I thought I was protected."

"Well, the law has changed over the years and is more open nowadays. Anyway, your situation appears to have been slightly different, as it seems your adoptive parents may have known your birth family, at least to some degree. You weren't aware there was any contact?"

"No, not that I know of," said Purdie, rather surprised. "My parents never implied that they knew anything about my background. They just told me I was adopted, that they loved me and had chosen me. I once asked, when I was about thirteen, whether my birth mother had been a prostitute. I couldn't think of any other reason for a woman to give up her child". She laughed a little sadly. "Poor Mum, she was devastated. She couldn't reassure me enough that my mother was nothing of the sort. Still, she didn't imply that she knew anything more."

"OK. Well, I have been asked to give you a letter from your grandmother. That is, your birth mother's mother. Your actual birth mother died a number of years ago, so it's your grandmother who is making contact." He held an envelope in his hand.

"That's so sad," exclaimed Purdie. She might never have been concerned about finding her natural family, but somehow the thought of her mother being dead was distressing. This was the second mother she had lost.

"Your grandmother wishes to let you know that you are, by virtue of your birth and place in her family, the natural and only heir to her estate. Miss Davis, you must understand that in the UK your family's business is a household name. In the natural course of events, you would have grown up within that family, known of the family business, maybe even worked in it. Your grandmother has expressed the desire that, if you are willing, you visit her in England. She hopes she might persuade you to meet her, get to know her, spend some time with her and perhaps learn something about the business you will one day inherit."

Peter passed the envelope across the desk to Purdie. She looked at it, turning it over in her hands, while her mind tried to absorb what he had just told her.

"Can you tell me about this business? And my family surname?"

"They are both the same. Your surname is Dunning. The business is known as Dunnings, or perhaps better recognised as 'Dunnings of the High Street'. It's a chain of retail shops throughout Britain."

Purdie stared at him.

"I assure you, it's a well-known business. Even I've heard of it, and I am not really a shopper," Peter laughed sheepishly.

"No," replied Purdie slowly. "As it happens, I have heard of the shop. Gok mentioned it on one of his fashion programmes. So it's a family business? I have to say it seems unreal that I have anything to do with a business. I'm a nurse, not a business proprietor."

"I imagine there are perfectly good managers who run the business. After all, your grandmother must be a fair age, and I doubt she runs it all herself. No, this is an issue of inheritance."

He picked the envelope up, stood up, walked round his desk and handed it to Purdie. "Would you like me to leave you alone for a few minutes to read your letter?"

Purdie nodded. "Please."

When Peter left the room Purdie sat for a while, the envelope in her lap, gazing out of the window onto The Terrace below. After the last few weeks of strange happenings, she never expected anything as prosaic as being the heir to a string of shops. The locket and icon had been exotic, romantic and compelling items, suggestive of history and treasure.

She turned the envelope over and picked at the seal. It was a heavy paper, and in the absence of Sophie with her scissors Purdie had to pick and rip her way into it.

The letter was handwritten, something she hadn't expected. The writing was well formed, even and legible, handwritten or not.

Dear Perdita,

My darling girl, I have longed to meet you for all of your lifetime. That I have never been able to has given me a lot of grief. I have held the thought of you dear in my heart, particularly as I lost my daughter, your mother, my lovely Tamara. She would have been so proud of you.

I hope the news the lawyer will have imparted to you is not a shock, nor distressing in any way. I am also aware that your adoptive parents died recently. I am so sorry for your loss. Everything I knew of them told me they were good people. My heart goes out to you in your grief.

My dear, I would love to meet you, and if you are willing, I have asked the lawyer to organise tickets and transport to London for you. You have family who would welcome you and a place here should you choose to accept it.

If you are moved to accept my invitation, from curiosity or any other emotion, you would make me very happy. I can promise you a welcome fit for a princess, and you always have a place in my heart.

I remain your loving grandmother,
Marguerite Dunning

When Peter came back into the office Purdie was still sitting, staring into space, the letter held loosely on her lap.

"Good news?" he enquired.

"Unsettling news, certainly. I'm not sure how I feel about things yet. This is going to take a bit of time to get used to." She laughed suddenly. "When I was quite young I used to have fantasies about being adopted. I thought I might be a changeling or a gypsy princess or something. I certainly didn't envisage being a shopkeeper's daughter!"

"Well, that's a little like saying Paris Hilton is an innkeepers daughter – and about as relevant," remarked Peter drily. "Your grandmother is associated with a very large business empire, and you have a family who wants to meet you. I imagine you might find closure in meeting your birth family?"

Purdie felt her mobile phone vibrate. She hated ignoring calls, as it always seemed like bad manners, but this time she reached down and switched it off. "It might bring closure, or it might unsettle me further, I suppose. What's the next step?"

"Well, my brief, if you choose to accept your grandmother's invitation, is to organise all your travel arrangements for you. I take it you have a current passport?"

"Yes, but I'd like a couple of days to think this through. I'll call you back with my decision."

Peter nodded. "Very wise, don't rush into things." He smiled at her. "Actually, you've reassured me. It's good to see you have your head screwed on. Phone me when you're ready, or leave a message, and I'll set things in motion if that's what you would like me to do."

He showed Purdie out of his office and into the lift.

When she got to street level, she didn't feel like returning to the flat. Much as she loved her friends, she sometimes felt she never got enough time to herself, so she followed the road up, turned into Bolton Street, and without much conscious thought, climbed up the hill to the old cemetery where she followed the path to the nearest bench.

It had shaken her to hear that her birth mother was dead, and she was surprised by her depth of feeling. Never met, never known or loved, yet entirely part of her. Fifty per cent of her genes, all her history, was her mother's heritage. She was mourned only by her own mother perhaps, who had referred to her as Tamara, and thought of her as a cherished daughter. Purdie allowed herself a moment of self-pity. It seemed as if everyone important to her was dead, that she knew more ghosts than living people. She felt her adoptive parents press round her with their warmth, strength and love. What would they have urged her to do?

She was strangely shaken, now she had discovered her 'real' surname. She was firm in her identity, yet knowing her real name changed everything.

She read her grandmother's letter again. Should she explore her English family? Money didn't concern her. She had enough for her present needs from her parents' estate and from her earnings. Extreme wealth wasn't an ambition. She didn't desire a super yacht, had never needed expensive designer fashion clothing, and although she wanted to travel, she was perfectly happy doing so with a backpack. More compelling was discovering a family that was hers – a place where she belonged, where she could stand in her own right. She wondered if that thought was disloyal to her adoptive parents.

She sat back and looked at her surroundings.

Around her were trees and shrubs. Although the motorway ran only a hundred metres away, the place was green, shaded and quiet, the graves old, settled and restful. Birds flitted amongst the bushes, and sunlight dappled the ground. In the late-flowering flax a tui was drinking the last of the summer nectar.

She suddenly realised that all the gravestones in her vicinity were family ones – mothers, fathers and their children. Graves with two, three or more children buried together, their deaths sometimes mere days apart, a relic of colonial days when sickness could kill rapidly.

Her subconscious had led her here. Did she need this reminder of blood ties, of family togetherness in life and death? It was a vivid reminder that she was missing a part of her own identity.

The bushes on her right moved and she turned to look. A lone jogger came round the corner. A brief smile of acknowledgement between them as he passed her, then he was gone. The tui, disturbed by the intruder, fled to the top branches of the karaka, leaving Purdie alone. It was time to go. She stood up, grabbed her bag and suddenly remembered the phone that had vibrated earlier. She switched it on and waited while signal was resumed. A text from Sophie. She keyed into it to read: *anutha prcel arivd 4 U. WTF?* It reminded her that she had forgotten to ask the lawyer about the gifts. She'd ask him next time; and of course, by acknowledging that, she had conceded that she would be back in touch with him and the answer about the trip to England was going to be yes.

She was surprised to discover how much better she felt. Had the last few weeks really put such a strain on her? And were a few minutes 'away from it all' the cure she needed? She remembered Nick's comments about the insecurity they all felt.

Maybe it was time to get away. Easter was coming up, and she had put in for leave. She would phone Aunty Barbara and Uncle Tim and ask if she could spend the long weekend with them. They had a farm up the coast, at the edge of the Otaki Gorge, and if they were willing to have her it would provide the perfect place for time out.

She punched in their number and spoke to her uncle before she changed her mind.

"Yes, we would love you to visit. It is well overdue. You can join us for the muster up the gorge."

Purdie wasn't so sure about the last item; it had been some years since she had ridden, and at the very least she would be in for some very sore muscles. But she agreed, confirmed the time she would arrive and ended the call feeling she had made the right decision. Barbara and Tim had been her parents' oldest friends, and she could talk to them as surrogate parents. It would be helpful to get their point of view.

CHAPTER
FIVE

Wellington, Present Day.

WHEN PURDIE GOT HOME SHE FOUND an overexcited Sophie who had been circling the package on the kitchen table for two hours or more.

"It's exactly the same as the others," she exclaimed when Purdie walked in. "No return address, no postmark, no identifying features. I nearly opened it myself, I was so curious."

Purdie laughed. "I bet you shook it, weighed it and damn near X-rayed it. Still, it can wait. Let me tell you about today."

Over dinner she told her friend about the meeting, the letter and the request for her to go to England. She wanted to see Sophie's reaction as the tale unfolded.

Perhaps predictably, Sophie found it terribly romantic. She was sorry that Purdie's unknown mother, Tamara, was dead and would never meet her daughter, but otherwise felt this was the stuff of fairy tales.

"So, these presents come from your grandmother? I'm not surprised they're a bit exotic. Her name's Marguerite? It's hardly typically English, is it? You may have some European heritage you don't know about."

Purdie shrugged. "Nothing like that's been mentioned; not yet anyway. Let's look at the latest offering." She brought the parcel into the living room. It was a cube and hard to the touch.

"Please, Purdie," begged Sophie, "get on with it. I've already played 'guess the contents'. Just open it."

"I need scissors," murmured Purdie playfully.

Sophie groaned but went and got a pair.

From the parcel slid a cube of polystyrene packaging, which revealed a red, square box.

"Well it's not more jewellery," exclaimed Sophie. "What is it this time?"

Purdie opened the catch.

"Holy shit," exclaimed Sophie.

"Oh my God!" said Purdie simultaneously.

Sitting on the faded silk lining was a heavily jewelled egg of deep green enamel. Around its circumference was a band of gold worked in patterns of small flowers and leaves interspersed with a series of red stones. Each flower had a centre of tiny white stones.

"What do you think those stones are?" asked Purdie.

"I've no idea, but if you told me they were rubies, I'd accept your story. In which case, of course, the little ones would be diamonds."

"It looks terribly valuable. Not just a little expensive, but massively so," continued Purdie.

"And if you're thinking it's not the sort of thing that should be kept in a communal flat, I agree," said Sophie. "I guess this is a reward for you turning up at the solicitor's today?"

"Probably."

Sophie shrugged. "If that comes from Granny, then she didn't buy it in a shop for you, even if we're talking Harrods. That has got to be an antique."

Purdie carefully lifted the egg out of its case and held it in her hands. "It's heavy for its size."

"It's probably solid gold. Weren't decorated eggs important to the Russians? Easter eggs, I think."

"You could be right there, although I don't quite see the connection between my grandmother and Russia. I studied Russian at school and Marguerite sounds French to me."

Sophie shrugged. "Who knows? Your name isn't exactly a typical New Zealand one either, but you've still got it."

"Yes," objected Purdie, "but I was named in England by literary type parents."

"Maybe that's what happened to your grandmother as well," said Sophie.

"I think I need a drink," declared Purdie.

"I'll get the Sav Blanc."

Glasses filled, they looked at the egg.

"I'll google it," said Sophie. A few moments later she had some information. "It says here Easter eggs are a Russian tradition, and that a century ago, ornately decorated ones were made and exchanged as presents at Easter. The most elaborate ones were made for the Tsar by Fabergé. Why do I find that name familiar?"

"It's a perfume," said Purdie.

They stared at the photos of Fabergé eggs on the screen.

"Some of the most famous of them were on display last year," read Sophie. "It is believed that others may exist that haven't been seen in over a century – it could be a Fabergé egg, couldn't it?" she asked.

"This one isn't as elaborate as those pictured," said Purdie doubtfully. "What am I supposed to do with it? If it's a genuine antique, it probably ought to be in a museum or a private collection, protected by glass cabinets and a barrage of alarms."

"I don't understand why your gran is getting someone to drop these off to you here," said Sophie. "Surely it would be simpler to wait until you visit her in England and give this stuff to you then? I mean, how do you get it all through customs?"

"That," said Purdie, "is a very good point. Hard to see how you could get them through. I think historical artefacts have rules and so on."

The two girls were still staring at the egg when Nick walked in an hour later. He looked tired, Purdie thought, and was about to question him about his day when he noticed the egg.

"Whoa!" he said. "Maybe you guys should fill me in. That is a serious bit of, well, whatever it is."

Sophie, who by this time had drunk several glasses of wine while she googled, said "Yes, what you see here is a Fabergé egg. Also you are probably looking at a scion of the house of Romanov. Purdie's real name may be Anastasia. We are awaiting confirmation, but that could happen at any minute, thanks to DNA testing. She even speaks Russian."

Purdie flushed. "Not entirely. I studied it at college."

Nick looked at her curiously. "What made you study Russian?"

Purdie shrugged. "Our brother school, Scots College, offered Russian, and my parents thought I should do it. Said it might be useful."

"So learning Russian was your adoptive parents' choice?" asked Nick. "Did that never surprise you?"

"Well, no," replied Purdie. "Why should it? Parents are always forcing their choices on you, and this was no odder than any other."

"Still, in the light of this, it might not be a coincidence," murmured Nick.

"Is there any food?" he asked. "I'll grab something, and then you had better tell me the rest of the story. I take it this relates to the lawyer today, and it was all good?"

Once again, Purdie went through the day's events, this time with Sophie interjecting and adding drama at every opportunity, while Nick piled bread, salami, lettuce and cheese on to a tray. He came back with food and beer and sat on the floor between the girls.

"Well," he said. "The plot thickens. We have Granny who wants to meet you. She's rich and you might be the only grandchild, so she wants to resolve inheritance issues as well. You've got a family waiting to greet you with open arms. It sounds pretty good to me. Have you got your bags packed yet?"

He leaned back and drank deeply from his bottle of Mac's gold. "We'd better organise a going-away party, Soph."

Purdie smiled. "I still haven't decided." She intercepted the sceptical look between her friends. "Yes, I know that sounds wimpy, and I probably will go. But something about this is a bit odd. It's almost too good to be true. My grandmother could have got my attention in a simpler way, you know."

Nick, with his mouth full of sandwich, muttered something that sounded like: "Probably not, poor woman. It takes a nuclear blast to get your attention."

Sophie sniggered as Purdie glowered at him.

"The important thing here is that Purdie goes to the UK," said Sophie. "Maybe we can meet up when I get across and do our OE together anyway, Purds?"

"*If* I go," said Purdie, not wanting to be pushed into a declaration of intent. "Incidentally, I'm taking next weekend off and going to visit my aunt and uncle up on the coast for Easter." She noticed Nick's sudden stillness. "I'm going to talk to them, see what they make of this. They're the closest people to parents I've got now. I feel I'm getting caught up in the excitement of the last few weeks, and it's distorting my judgement."

"Probably a good idea then," said Nick lightly.

Eventually the others went to bed, and Purdie sat down at the computer to google Dunnings to find what she could about the business.

Dunnings, it turned out, was a very large British company. It had been founded at the end of the Second World War and had flourished, firstly in London, and later throughout the United Kingdom, finally opening branches in various European cities. A large mail order business further expanded their market. Dunnings were best known for their High Street fashion, offering designer outfits and styles at a price the average woman could afford.

Purdie checked out some of the clothes on offer and approved. Her lifestyle meant that, aside from work, she was a jeans and T-shirt type of girl. Still, she appreciated style when she saw it. As she had remarked to Sophie once, she intended to grow up into a stylish, older lady, she just hadn't got round to it yet.

Later, when Purdie climbed into bed, she looked across at the icon before she turned out the light.

"Thank you, Grandma," she messaged into space.

CHAPTER
SIX

Wellington, Present Day.

T HE THURSDAY HOLIDAY TRAFFIC OUT OF
Wellington was heavy, even at 11 o'clock in the morning,
and Purdie was stuck in a crawl through Pukerua Bay and
Paraparaumu before the traffic eased north of Waikanae. It had
taken her two-and-a-half hours to complete a trip that would
usually take one, but as she headed up into the gorge, she felt
her spirits lift.

Aunty Barbara and Uncle Tim both hugged and kissed her,
their pleasure in her visit warm and obvious.

They were not blood relatives of either Purdie or her adoptive
parents, but the two couples had met coming out on the ship
from England when Purdie was three. The resulting friendship
had flowered, and they had remained close over the years. The
honorary title had stuck, and they had filled in as aunts and
uncles for each other's children, replacing those lost because of
their emigration.

Purdie remembered many happy holidays as a child, visiting
Barbara and Tim. She had learned to ride, fish and swim in the

big, fast-flowing river that ran below the homestead. Twenty years ago, when her parents first took her to visit, Otaki had seemed like another world. There had been a perception of it being miles away, in both time and distance. Times had changed. In the last few years, dairying having done well for them, Tim and Barbara were in a position to enjoy life, and their 'trips to town' were just as likely to be to Sydney or London.

"So, you're here for the muster?" asked Uncle Tim. "I've got a nice gelding for you. Steady as a rock. You'll like him."

Barbara laughed. "Give the girl a chance; we've got a year or so of news to catch up on. The muster isn't until tomorrow. Make yourself at home, then tell us all your news."

Her searching eyes took in Purdie's thinness. "Country air, that's what you townies need," she said. "Now bring your bags in, and let's get you settled."

Over lunch Purdie filled them in on events. Uncle Tim had little time for chit-chat, but he listened intently and Purdie knew not much got past him. Aunty Barbara supplied the requisite 'oohs and aahs' as the tale was told and the locket, icon and egg revealed. Purdie had brought these with her, and they examined and exclaimed over them all. Purdie enjoyed watching Tim and Barbara's reaction, as it brought home to her again just how unique and extraordinary these items were and how curious the manner in which they had come to her.

"Tell me again how these were delivered," commanded Tim.

Purdie repeated the story of personal delivery, suspected involvement of a car, and the assumption they were part of her grandmother's contact with her.

"No," said Tom slowly, "these didn't come from your gran. I think you need to understand that."

"Why?" Purdie was surprised by his certainty.

"Because your gran, who sounds a nice person incidentally, has dealt with you straight up. She's done the right thing and involved a lawyer so you wouldn't be afraid. She's written you a nice letter, invited you to stay. She's talked about your real mum. If she was sending anonymous gifts, she'd have mentioned it. No, her dealings with you have been very simple. This is something else."

"How many people do I know who would send me gifts?" asked Purdie. "It can't be a coincidence that my gran decided to contact me, and the gifts started arriving at the same time. There has to be a connection."

"There may be a connection," said Tim, "but that doesn't mean the same person is involved in both things." He pointed his finger at the locket. "Suppose the person behind these only knew how to find you because your gran had finally contacted you. The only reasons I can think of for giving you gifts is to either catch your attention, or to get your support for something."

"You need to explain yourself, love," said Barbara.

"I was thinking about the elections. You know, the way in which someone gives money to a political party to ensure that the party does things in their favour. I was wondering if this were the same sort of thing. Only in this case Purdie is the 'political party'. You did mention that there was a good deal of money involved?"

"Well, yes, I suppose so," said Purdie. "But I can't see much point in someone 'buying my vote' before I have any idea at all of what the vote is about."

"I think that may be the whole point," said Uncle Tim drily. "Anyway, we have to get the horses up the gorge, so go and get your riding gear on, and we'll get them up to the overnight paddock. I'll see you down here in five minutes."

Aunty Barbara rolled her eyes at him but bustled Purdie out of the room to get ready.

Hours later Aunty Barbara welcomed her home with love, enthusiasm and Epsom salts. "Get yourself off to a nice hot bath, and add plenty of these before you get in. Soak for at least half an hour, then you'll feel much better."

Purdie may not have soaked for the full thirty minutes, but the bath she poured for herself was full of hot, bubbly water, and by the time she emerged, her aches and bruises had, at least temporarily, disappeared.

After the meal Barbara regarded her slumped form with amusement and said, "Get her up to bed, Tim. She's tired and needs to hit the sack. She can fill us in later on all the excitement. Poor kid," she said more quietly.

CHAPTER
SEVEN

Otaki, Present Day.

TWO DAYS LATER PURDIE WOULD HAVE sworn she was forty-eight. Every bone, muscle and ligament was screaming. She was knackered. The muster had been amazing fun, but her body was paying for it this morning.

Barbara laughed and offered Epsom salts, Voltaren gel, and pancakes with maple syrup, bacon and bananas.

Purdie acknowledged with all frankness that it was the last offering that prised her out of bed. But then again, who had time for pride when pancakes with maple syrup and bacon were on offer?

It took her a while, but after scoffing a few cakes and syrup, washed down with plenty of coffee, she was able to acknowledge she was still part of the human race.

Barbara was busy putting together ingredients for sandwiches. "We'll take lunch up to the guys in the shed later. If you'd like to come up with me, you're welcome, otherwise you could chill out here."

"No, I'll come with you," replied Purdie. "I'll help with lunch.

Do you need me to butter bread or something?"

They worked in comfortable silence for a while buttering and slicing piles of sandwiches, and filling rolls.

"Have you decided what you're going to do?" asked Barbara.

"Well, I suppose I will go to England, meet this grandmother and put the mystery to rest," replied Purdie. "I don't think there's much alternative. It's part of my heritage, so I'd be curious anyway, without all the extra stuff going on around it."

"What do you make of Tim's thought, that there might be someone other than your gran involved?"

"I don't know. My gran's made contact. I still feel it would be bizarre if two lots of people were doing the same thing."

"Didn't your solicitor imply that your grandmother had been in touch with your parents? Or at least that she knew them?"

"Yeah, but I don't think that's right. If my parents did know something, they never said, which would have been hard for them, especially when I was in my teens – when I started asking questions about my identity."

"Well, maybe they thought it in your own best interests not to tell you anything."

"They'd have had to be awfully committed to that idea," said Purdie. "They were totally honest, honourable people, and deceit wouldn't have come easy to either of them. And teenage girls have a real nose for bullshit, if you know what I mean. I think I'd have picked up if they were hiding stuff."

Barbara carried on grating cheese without comment.

After a few minutes Purdie continued. "Well, do you think differently? Did they know who I was and who my family was all the time?"

Barbara lifted her eyes to Purdie. "I don't know, love. I don't know any more than you, because you were their daughter in every sense of the word, but ..." She let the moment drag on.

"But?" prompted Purdie.

Barbara hesitated. "It was years ago anyway. I remember your mum saying something that stuck in my mind at the time. I don't remember the details but I do remember a reference to your name."

"What, Purdie?"

"Your name isn't Purdie, is it love? It's Perdita."

"Yes, and it comes from *A Winter's Tale.* I don't know why my parents picked it, but they did. My dad always had a Shakespeare thing going on. I should just be grateful they didn't call me Ophelia, or Cleopatra, or something really bad."

Barbara began, "Perdita means ..."

"Yes, the 'Lost One' but I don't see how that helps us. I wasn't lost to those who knew where I was."

"Perhaps that's the point," said Barbara quietly. "You were lost to anyone else."

"You can't leave it there," said Purdie forcefully. "What do you really think, or know?"

Barbara sighed. "It may not be much use, but I've always wondered if your mum knew more than she let on. We were on the ship over from the UK at the time, so we were both quite young. You know, young mums getting on with the business of rearing kids. You were just a toddler, and I think Matt can't have been more than four or five." She paused in her work. "Your adoption was mentioned, and I asked your mum how they had found you. By the 1990s it wasn't so common for white people in England to be able to adopt white babies." She looked shamefaced. "I don't mean that quite the way it sounds. But if you wanted to adopt in those years, and you were white and middle class, the chances were you would only be offered coloured babies, or ones with some physical or mental disability that meant they weren't wanted by anyone else. White girls were keeping their babies."

Purdie shrugged. "So?"

"Well, when I asked her she blushed and said you hadn't come through the usual agencies. That it had been a private arrangement. I expressed surprise, because that sort of thing wasn't common – it's not like there was an Angelina and Brad in those days. She coloured up and told me it was a private thing, but totally legal, and that was why your name was 'Lost', because your family had been forced to lose you. She sounded so sad for you, and I thought the story was sad too. Later, when I tried to bring it up once more, your mum always changed the subject. And it was never referred to again, not in all the years we knew your folks. I suppose, because of that, I wasn't too surprised when you said that family was trying to contact you. I always got the impression they had never wanted to let you go in the first place."

Purdie thought about things for a bit. "It must have been legal and binding, or else Mum and Dad could never have processed a passport for me, and I would never have been allowed to leave the country."

"Who knows? Maybe you're about to find out. At least your family wants to meet you."

"I suppose so," said Purdie. "It's very unsettling to lose one identity and find another."

Barbara smiled and shrugged her shoulders. "No doubt it will all work itself out, and if I may be frank, you need a new project." She smiled kindly. "It was awful for you to lose your folks when you did, but you have to move on with your life, love. I remember what an adventurous, confident little girl you were, always up to something. You took a hard knock, I know, but it's time for you to get up and going again."

"Yes," said Purdie, "I've been thinking the same thing too." The women smiled at each other. "One of the things I wanted to ask you, though, was if I could leave the egg and icon gifts with you to look after. I'll keep the locket. I can't travel with them, and I don't want to leave them in the flat because they're obviously valuable."

"Of course," said Barbara. "We've got a strongroom for the guns, so we could keep your treasures safe in there for you. I'll ask Tim. I can see why you wouldn't want to leave them lying around."

They took lunch up to the woolshed. Purdie felt a little sorry for the sheep as winter wasn't that far away and they would soon need all the warmth they could get. She hoped the wool grew back quickly for them. Tim, Matt and Ian, apparently unaffected by the ride yesterday, were hard at work sorting sheep, feeding them up to the shearers or organising the wool sorters. It was a cheerful, busy crowd of people.

Aunty Barbara's lunch was popular: rolls, sandwiches, big trays of Sally Lunns and a massive basket of fresh fruit. To finish, an enormous pound cake brimming with currants and cherries, all wrapped up in muslin cloth and kept cool in the back of the vans until laid out on the trestles. There were big urns of tea, and hot water for coffee. Purdie and Barbara were kept busy doling out food to the queue of workers.

Purdie spent the rest of the weekend shadowing Barbara as she did her chores. If Tim and Barbara were now comfortably well off, it was due to the amount of work they both did. Not only did Barbara provide food for shearing gangs or other labourers working on the farm, but she kept chickens, baked and among the other work that Easter weekend was bottling blackberry and apple.

The homeliness of the work soothed Purdie. When she left Otaki on the Monday, she was loaded with preserves and packs of meat for the flat. She had felt a slight pang when Tim had shut the egg and the icon in the safe. She took digital photos of both items to keep as a reference for herself. They were more secure, but she'd miss having them around to look at.

As she said her goodbyes, Tim hugged her and said, "Remember you always have a place to come to, girl. Don't forget that we think of you as our daughter. If you need help, whether you go to England or not, always feel free to call on us."

Purdie felt tears well in her eyes. "Thanks," she muttered.

Barbara kissed her. "Look after yourself, love." She waved as Purdie got into her car. "Keep in touch, and let us know what happens."

CHAPTER EIGHT

Wellington, Present Day.

PURDIE LET HERSELF INTO THE FLAT. It took several trips from the car to bring in all the provisions that Barbara thought necessary to send with her. When they were unpacked and stowed, Purdie took a cup of coffee into the living room and sat in the sun. A pile of mail waited for her. She flicked through it. There was a letter from Morrison and Maxwell, which she opened.

Peter simply confirmed the details of their meeting and expressed a hope that the writer would hear soon from Purdie, indicating her plans in regards to visiting her grandmother.

Purdie smiled. Yes, she was going to go to England. She'd phone Peter Harris tomorrow and get him to make the bookings. She was going to have to decide whether to take leave from the hospital or hand in her notice so there were no time limits on her travels. It was a nice irony that she would get an OE anyway, and be in the UK before Sophie after all. Sophie's suggestion that she come over to England and meet up with Purdie made sense. They could travel together and do all the things they had ever thought of. Grandma and her money wouldn't make much difference to her plans. She was flush enough with funds from the estate and could certainly afford to take some time off for travel and adventure.

Purdie looked at her watch impatiently. Where was everybody? Now she felt so re-energised she couldn't wait to start planning her trip.

She booted up the computer, and started googling. She looked up Dunnings again. There was a lot of material about the store and links to its website. It was harder to find specific information about her grandmother, although there were plenty of photos of her at various functions.

Next she returned to the Fabergé site and reread the information. There didn't seem any connection between a British retailer and a high-end Russian jeweller – certainly none that would concern a 24-year-old woman from New Zealand.

There had been many Fabergé eggs around before the Russian Revolution. The standard ones were given as gifts to visiting dignitaries, and as presents to other members of the extended royal family. The cream of the crop, and the truly rare, were the Imperial Eggs, made for the Tsar and his family. There were photos of some, sumptuously beautiful, jewelled and painted, each one a unique creation. Most had clockwork working parts, so that when opened, they moved, to entrance and entertain.

After the fall of the Tsar and the execution of his family, many treasures were lost, including a dozen or so of the Imperial Eggs. In the political changes that occurred post-revolution, everything imperial was regarded with contempt, or as dangerous, within Russia itself. The value of such trinkets was seriously diminished, and Western collectors managed to acquire them at devalued prices.

Nowadays these creations were recognised as the wonders they were, and their value had skyrocketed. Russia was now immensely proud of their place in her history. Many of them had been put on display the year before.

Purdie compared the photo of her egg to the ones on the site.

It seemed clear to her that this wasn't an Imperial Egg. It was nowhere near as ornate as those pictured.

It might have been anonymous, but it was certainly jewelled. She had no way of knowing exactly what the stones were, but she was pretty sure this wasn't a cheap Chinese copy. It weighed too much, and it looked valuable, which might not be proof but felt convincing to her.

She decided she'd better draft a reply letter to her grandmother but found herself unsure of what to say and, even worse, how to address the woman. It took her half an hour or so, but in the end she opted for the plain and simple:

Dear Grandmother,

Thank you so much for your letter. Yes, it has been a shock to receive it, but I hope that when we meet we will be pleasantly surprised by each other. I have asked Peter Harris, the lawyer, to contact you on my behalf and to say that I would be delighted to take up your offer of a visit with you, and to organise bookings for me. I don't know whether your invitation extended to my actually staying with you, or whether there is a convenient hotel close to where you live. In which case, if you can give him instructions, I will make accommodation bookings.

I look forward to meeting you and hearing your stories about my mother.

Yours sincerely,
Perdita Davis

She added the surname Davis as a deliberate statement that she was her own independent person.

She made another cup of coffee and returned to the computer. This time she decided to develop a wish list of places to go now she had decided to start travelling. As she researched, the list grew longer, and she was just working her way through Croatia and its attractions when she heard Katy come in. "At last," she said. "Here I am, dying of boredom. I need company."

Katy smiled. "It's nice to be needed. How was the weekend? Did your friends in the country help you get your head straight?"

Purdie detailed her decisions and her plans to go overseas and meet her family.

"Go, girl," said Katy. "I know I'd be pretty gutted if I didn't know my family. Mind you," she added, "not knowing them has got a lot going for it as well. If you go to England and get some closure with your nana, then good on you. If you come in to fame, money and fortune in the process, then shit, that's good with me too."

Sophie walked in an hour later to find Katy and Purdie busy making blackberry and apple crumble with Barbara's preserves.

"This is what home life is supposed to be like," Sophie declared approvingly. "Keep up the good work, guys; just make sure all my servings are small, calorie-free and yummy."

"Consider all of the above vetoed," chimed in Nick, who had come in 20 minutes earlier. "Large, high in calories, but of course, don't veto the yummy factor. How was your weekend, Purds?"

Purdie filled them in on the details. Her flatmates were able to pick out the important stuff, including that the treasures were no longer in the flat, and Purdie was going to England.

"Hallelujah!" exclaimed Sophie, rushing across to hug and kiss Purdie. "Does that mean we can do our OE together?"

"Heck, yes," replied Purdie. "I've researched heaps today. You have no idea of the places I've plotted to go to simply because I had to use the Internet to avoid terminal boredom."

Sophie looked at her in surprise.

"I'm buzzing with energy now I've made my decision, but there was no one here to talk to."

CHAPTER
NINE

B Y WEDNESDAY AFTERNOON, PURDIE HAD PHONED Peter Harris to confirm she would like to meet her grandmother, printed the letter she had written to her (no handwritten notes for her!) and forwarded it to him for posting on, handed in her notice at the hospital, checked with the management service that the Khandallah property would be looked after while she was away, and let the landlord of the flat know she would be leaving.

Of them all, the last chore was the hardest, as it had been a happy flat with a good group of friends sharing it. Purdie's trip was the first strand separating the thread that had held them together. Sophie was planning to leave in September, which left Nick and Katy effectively abandoned. Purdie could see them eyeing each other as they tried to work out whether to replace her as a flatmate, or alternatively, at least until Sophie left, share the additional rent between them to avoid adjusting to a newcomer.

Peter Harris had been pleased to hear from her. He seemed genuinely glad that she had decided to meet her family and assured her that he would forward her letter and organise all the tickets and transfers necessary. He promised to check whether she needed to book a hotel, or whether the invitation from her gran meant actually staying with her.

Purdie let Tim and Barbara know the news and organised mail from the flat to be redirected to them. She had been planning to put her few pieces of furniture into lockdown storage, but when he heard that, Tim said it could be stored in a shed up on the farm, to save her having to pay for it.

Suddenly events were moving very quickly. She decided to invest in a flash smartphone. "Just so you guys can keep in touch with me," she said to her friends. "I don't like being too cut off." She spent an evening setting it up, before realising the old phone hadn't transferred all her contacts and data across.

"Bugger," she said, deciding to keep the old phone as well so she could fiddle with the set-up at a later time.

Peter phoned. "I am just passing on your grandmother's invitation to stay with her in the centre of London for as long as you wish, and she looks forward to seeing you very much. She will organise someone to pick you up at Heathrow, so you don't have to bother with taxis."

"Thanks," said Purdie.

"As I had been waiting to hear from her about your accommodation, I hadn't sent off your tickets, stopover vouchers, or anything else. I'll get them in the mail for you later today," he assured her.

Two days later, a familiar style envelope turned up in the letter box containing a first-class Air New Zealand air ticket to London, with a brief stopover in LA.

Again, there was no indication of who had sent it, or more to the point, dropped it off, but as Sophie remarked philosophically, "It's unlikely more than one person wants to pay for Purdie to get to London. I think we can assume that dear old granny is back to her usual tricks."

Purdie thought the same and reminded herself once again that she must ask Peter Harris about the deliveries. He probably knew the story behind them.

It was hard to believe that within a week she would be in the UK. The movers were booked to come in on Monday morning, and Purdie would fly out early that afternoon.

They had agreed to have her farewell 'do' on Saturday night and just have a goodbye for the flatmates on Sunday. Purdie hated the idea of a prolonged farewell at the airport, when anything meaningful would already have been said. She was finding parting from her friends harder than she had realised.

She started the process of packing. There were some paperbacks, and a couple of ornaments that had belonged to her parents. She offered to leave the books but wrapped up the ornaments so they could go up to the farm with the movers.

She had an old family clock that sat on top of the shelves in the living room. Nick, who was helping her that evening, climbed up on a ladder to fetch it down. When he didn't hand it to her, Purdie looked up, and saw to her surprise that he had gone very still, looking at something beside the clock.

"What ..." she began.

He turned to her quickly, his finger to his lips, shushing her to silence. She watched as, with his careful doctor's hands, he picked up the object he was concentrating on, and climbed down the steps.

Still cautioning her to silence with his finger, he placed the object on the table. Purdie looked at it. It seemed like an electronic part from something. Maybe it had fallen out of an old stereo?

She watched Nick, completely baffled by his antics as he beckoned her across to the door and out of the room, and led her into the kitchen where he ran the tap, before finally turning to her.

"What is it?" she asked.

"Keep your voice down," Nick cautioned. "I'm no expert on these things, but I'd lay down good money that that little object is a listening device of some sort."

"You mean a bug?" whispered Purdie in amazement. "Oh, come on, Nick, I don't think so. Who would bug us?"

"More to the point," said Nick grimly, "who would bug you?

You're the only one with odd shit happening, Purdie. It may be that your gran and the gifts are only part of something more complicated. Maybe she wanted to hear what you were saying and doing about it all."

Purdie looked at him. "We don't even know if it is such a thing, Nick. What makes you so certain? I've never seen one before, and I really doubt that you have. *The Bourne Ultimatum* doesn't really count, you know."

"As it happens," retorted Nick, "I have seen them before. One of my holiday jobs when I was a student was with an electronics firm. You'll find that these little beasties are surprisingly common, surprisingly effective, and almost anyone bright enough can make them up from bits and pieces you can buy at Dick Smith's."

"Oh," said Purdie, deflated. "Well, what should we do about it then?"

"We need to search the rest of the flat, particularly your room, to see if there are any more," he continued. "I think we can assume the rest of us don't have a problem, so we don't need to check our rooms."

Purdie nodded.

"First of all," added Nick, "let's get that clock down so you can pack it, then we flush that little bugger down the loo."

"Shouldn't we save it for evidence?" demurred Purdie.

"Oh shit, you're probably right," said Nick. "But I think we should immobilise it by putting it in water first and then wrapping it up. It would also be an idea to talk to that lawyer you've been dealing with. This does cast some doubt on the motives behind everything that's been going on. Up until now it's been the heart-warming story of a girl about to be reunited with her family. This has turned it into something that could be interpreted in a rather darker light."

They searched the rest of the lounge and kitchen but didn't find another specimen. However, they met with success in Purdie's bedroom when they found another box taped behind her mirror.

They dealt with it in the same way, and Nick and Purdie stared grimly at the preserving jar and the two devices now covered with water.

"How do you think they got into the flat?" she asked.

"We have parties," surmised Nick, looking at the bug. "Perhaps someone wasn't here just for our good company."

"We aren't that free in those we invite," retorted Purdie. "Yes, we have people round, but they are all friends, most of them long-standing. I really can't see one of them planting this sort of stuff. Besides," she added, "I would have been very surprised to find a guest climbing a ladder to put something at the top of the bookcase, or in my bedroom."

"The alternative is that someone broke in while none of us were here," said Nick, "and that's a nasty thought as well. It's an old house, and none of the doors or windows fit tightly, but I thought the odd draught was the worst problem we had. I suppose it might not be that difficult to break in, and that's not something I really want to deal with right now.

"Purdie, you realise that bugging is illegal, don't you? I mean, unless this has a police warrant backing it up, it's not legal or legitimate. That means, by extension, whoever put it in here is prepared to work beyond the confines of the law. You might want to think about that quite carefully," he said, bringing the conversation to a close.

Purdie looked at her watch, it was seven o'clock. Peter Harris would have left work by now. She would call him tomorrow for an explanation. She was well aware there were only a few days left before she was on an aeroplane, heading into uncharted territory.

Katy and Sophie were understandably appalled at the invasion of their privacy, although both seemed rather more concerned about various amorous or embarrassing moments involving themselves than in any other risk the bugs represented.

Katy simply said, "How gross. Devon and I made out in that lounge." Sophie, Nick and Purdie's eyes swivelled to the sofa. "No, not in that way," exclaimed Katy, blushing as much as her dark skin would allow. "Just, we got quite friendly, you know? Before we moved to the bedroom," she added.

"Do you think we should go over that sofa with an ultraviolet light?" Nick murmured to Purdie, who choked on her dinner and scowled at him to express her disapproval. She couldn't hide the laughter in her eyes, though, and she thought Nick could read it there, because he suddenly looked a lot happier than he had all afternoon.

"Sophie," he asked, "what date are you going to the UK?"

"I've got an open ticket for September," she said. "I hope Purdie and I can team up together, because it would be fun."

"Does the thought of skiing in France over the winter grab you?" asked Nick. "I've got an old schoolfriend who's worked the last few winters in Les Gets. It's a mountain village in south-eastern France," he added, "and I've always planned to go over and spend the season with him. I wondered if you," he was looking at Purdie, "and you, Sophie," he added rapidly, "would be interested in meeting up there. Skiing together would be fun."

"I know we've all grown up on Whakapapa," he said as Sophie looked ready to interrupt, "but this is real, deep European snow. We could have a white Christmas."

Katy was inclined to be indignant. "Well, where does that leave me? On a back foot, thank you all very much, because I certainly can't just leave everything and go with you."

"I imagine it will leave you in the arms of Devon," murmured Purdie. She was suddenly taken with the idea of Nick on skis in France.

Sophie was nodding with enthusiasm. "We could all have Christmas together and catch up on each other's news from the year."

"Some of us may have more news than others," remarked Nick drily. "What do you think, Purdie?"

"I like the idea," she replied, delighted that giving up flat life didn't mean giving up her friends forever. She smiled. "It would be wonderful. All we need is for Katy to get away from her whanau and come and join us".

"Fat chance," replied Katy. "For one thing I'm just a poor student, not an affluent medical worker, and second, I can't begin to imagine the grief I'd get if I didn't turn up for Christmas. My nana would kill me."

"Well," said Purdie jokingly, "as long as my granny hasn't killed me by then either, it should be a great Christmas!"

She tried to contact Peter Harris the next morning but was told he had gone on leave. Assured that he would be back in the office on Monday, before she flew out, she left a message asking him to contact her urgently on his return.

The rest of the week rushed past, taken up with the formalities of goodbyes. On Friday afternoon Purdie took time off to drive up to Khandallah and say goodbye to her old home. She had asked the tenants if that would be all right, and they had agreeably invited her in for a coffee when she came through.

It was a bittersweet moment for her. The house was so familiar and filled with memories of her childhood that it seemed a desecration to find her tenants' possessions carelessly occupying what she still thought of as 'her' space.

Bill and Kate couldn't have been more welcoming. They kept the property in immaculate condition, and Purdie knew she was fortunate to have them as tenants. The house was leased out fully furnished, as she had no need for a household's worth of chattels. The private stuff had been locked away in the attic. One day, she supposed, when she felt less sensitive about the accident, she'd sort it all out. The lease could roll over should she need to stay away longer than she anticipated. Once she was assured that everything was as it should be, Purdie said her farewells.

CHAPTER
TEN

Wellington, Present Day.

THE FLAT PARTY WAS RAUCOUS AND happy. Katy was completely wrapped up with Devon, and Sophie's boyfriend Liam was cheerful and in good voice, playing songs on his guitar between other actions. Nick was everywhere, smiling, pouring drinks and being the good host.

The flat had organised a formal presentation of gifts, so an extremely embarrassed Purdie had to listen to speeches in her honour by her friends. The flatmates had clubbed together to give her a greenstone manaia as a farewell present. Nick hung it round her neck, and Purdie looked at herself in the mirror. The deep shade of the greenstone went well against her pale skin, and she felt exotic with the carving on her breast. "I feel like a Maori princess," she declared.

"A true export from New Zealand," asserted Nick.

Katy and Sophie kissed her.

"I love it," declared Purdie. "You guys," she exclaimed, tears coming to her eyes, "I'll miss you all so much."

"We love you too, Purds," said Sophie, "but we'll all be

together again in the next few months."

"You'll be gone but not forgotten," intoned Nick, but then he hugged her. "It won't be the same without you, girl; just look after yourself."

The party raged on round her. She danced a lot, drank a lot and swore with all her heart that these were her bestest ever friends, that she would miss them forever, that she was a fool to go.

It was later, a lot later.

Sophie and Katy had disappeared with their respective partners; late-night partygoers had been ejected from Purdie and Nick's bedrooms, and Purdie was washing up. She'd sobered up as the night went on. Dancing had made her thirsty but she had quenched it with water, so by three in the morning, she was sober. Nick was cleaning up the living room.

"Why would someone file a wine glass behind the stereo?" he growled at one point.

Purdie grinned. "Hand them over, and stop grizzling," she said.

For a while they worked silently together, Nick gathering up glasses as Purdie washed and dried them. The flat had grown quiet around them, and Purdie could hear the squeak of Nick's feet as he carried the tray into the kitchen.

"Purdie," said Nick.

"Mmm," she said, rinsing out red wine. It was a real pain the way it stuck to the bottom of a wine glass.

"Look at me, please," said Nick.

Purdie shot him a startled look. The last time someone had spoken to her like that, it had been her mother.

When he saw he had her attention, he gave a slightly self-conscious smile.

"Yes?" she said cautiously, watching him. She noticed his tension, that there was a muscle moving in his cheek. Her eyes widened a little. The flat suddenly seemed to fold into a space that contained only the two of them. She watched him put the tray down, watched his hands as he rested them on the kitchen bench. She had always liked his hands; they were strong, long-fingered and flexible. 'Musical' her mother would have said. 'Safe' would have been her own description.

He was looking at her with an intensity she found hard to sustain. Her breathing changed, lost its rhythm. "I don't want to let you go," he began, "without telling you just how important you are to me."

"I ..." began Purdie, but he drove on over the top of whatever she was trying to say.

"Yes, I know I've left it too late, but I didn't want to put pressure on you when you were grieving for your folks. And," – Nick looked a little self-conscious – "I also didn't want to disrupt the flat if you told me to piss off."

Purdie nodded.

"You must know I'm going to miss you horribly."

Purdie frowned. Was that all he was going to say?

He moved closer towards her. His hands shifted from the bench to her arms. Had he not noticed that her hands were deep in washing-up water? Purdie turned, looking round for a towel as Nick pulled her closer.

"Tell me it matters to you that you are leaving me. Tell me I haven't just been stupid hoping for you," he murmured.

By this time Purdie had dried her hands and was, much to her pleasure, held tightly by his arms. He put a finger under her chin and raised her face to his. It was a Mills & Boon moment, she thought – corny, but working for her.

She looked at him shyly. There was an exquisite moment: a hiatus, a pause drawn from the year or more's tension between them, before he lowered his face to hers. The kiss melted Purdie into him. She knew about kissing, liked it, and was good at it herself, but nothing had prepared her for the emotions raised by Nick's kiss. The tensions that had surrounded her for so long came to an explosive climax in that kiss. Without thought she melted against his body, opening her mouth and the whole length of her body to his touch.

She felt him shift his stance, spread his legs a little wider as he moved closer to her again. His hands shifted from her face, down her spine until his right hand cupped her buttocks. Held her tightly against him until she squirmed in his embrace, excited and yet embarrassed at how quickly and how naturally they had gone from friends to lovers in the few moments of an embrace.

She drew away at last from his kiss and opened her mouth to invite him to her bed, but he beat her to it.

"This isn't going to be a farewell fuck," he muttered with his lips close to her hair. "I want you so badly but I'm not going to start something the day before you leave. Go to Europe, but I'll be there in the winter to take you skiing. Don't forget that."

The next kiss was so sweet that Purdie later wished she could have preserved and bottled it. It contained pent-up frustration, Purdie's regret and sorrow at leaving, and Nick's drive and need for her. When they finally separated, she was on wobbly legs. She suspected Nick wasn't much better, as he controlled the situation by sending her to bed with a wry look, and turning off the last of the lights.

She went to sleep quickly; it was, after all, nearly four o'clock in the morning, but the memory of that exchange was to fuel her dreams for weeks to come.

The movers arrived at nine o'clock and packed her few pieces of furniture and possessions into their van. Nick and Sophie had said their goodbyes and were at work. Purdie stood in the hall and looked round. Her room was empty apart from her suitcase. There were a few dents on the carpet where her bed and dressing table had stood. She vacuumed the floor to leave everything neat and tidy.

She tried to reach Peter Harris on her mobile but was told he was in a meeting. The receptionist assured her he would call her back later. There seemed nothing left to do. She finished packing her case, checked and double-checked her passport and tickets were safe.

Katy, who was buying Purdie's car, gave her a lift to the airport. She offered to stay, but Purdie declined. Now that the moment had come, she didn't want to dwell on goodbyes. She hugged her friend, kissed her and watched her drive away.

She tried again to get hold of Peter. This time she was put right through. "Peter, I never asked you if it was my grandmother sending me presents. Do you know if it was her?" Then she explained about the flat being bugged.

"Are you sure?" asked Peter. "I can't see any reason why it should be your grandmother. I'll contact her now and see what she says. I'll get back to you as soon as I've something to report. Given the time difference, it will be the middle of the night over there at the moment. I'll have to call them this evening our time."

"Just remember, I'm running out of time," urged Purdie. "I really need to know now."

Peter assured her he would follow up her questions as soon as possible, but by the time she flew from Wellington to Auckland, she still hadn't heard from him.

She boarded the plane in Auckland later that night and was settled into her seat by the smiling stewardess. It was comfy, the service friendly and Purdie was just accepting an orange juice when her phone beeped and vibrated.

"Don't forget to turn that off before we fly," cautioned the hostess.

Purdie nodded as she retrieved the phone. She still wasn't familiar with the smartphone and it took a couple of seconds to find the text function.

The text read: *presents not from Dunning. No bugs either. Don't know who responsible. U shld call police. Peter H*

Purdie read the text through twice. What did it mean? If the presents had not come from her grandmother, and she assumed that was what Peter meant by 'Dunning', then who had sent them? Who had intruded into her life, and what were the implications?

Purdie wished there was someone to talk to, but it was too late to call anyone. As it was, the hostess was hovering to make sure she switched off the phone. She suddenly realised she didn't even know if the tickets she was using had come through from Peter.

She looked out of the window. The aircraft was already taxiing. One way or another she was committed to the adventure.

CHAPTER
ELEVEN

London, Present Day.

THERE WAS A BUZZ OF GOSSIP in the boardroom. A couple were reading papers, but the majority were speculating, talking shop and eyeing each other up.

"Did you see the piece Taki wrote about the old man in *The Spectator?*" asked Nathan Parsons of Tony Manners.

"No, I didn't see that one, but there were a few obits around: 'Mighty oak that's fallen', and all that kind of stuff. At least we're not publicly listed, so the old man's death can't affect share prices, but I guess it's going to be a relief for everyone when Clive takes over, and it's all confirmed, with i's dotted and t's crossed." He knew he was fishing with his comments, hoping someone else would recognise his own disquiet.

"Well, I guess it's just a formality," replied Nathan. "I hope they don't take too long this morning with all the ceremonial claptrap. I've got a bit of a crisis going on in my division. Half the staff are down with the flu, and it's not a good time to be short-staffed. I'd rather be there fighting fires than up here listening to formal speeches."

Tony grinned at him while he surveyed the other people present. He wondered how much arse-licking and cock-sucking would go on over the next few weeks, and how well established others were in Clive Hannah's camp. At best there would be a period of readjustment, at worst heads would roll, and he hoped his wouldn't be one of them.

Tony was proud of the work he had done in setting up the online retailing arm of Dunnings. He viewed e-commerce as increasingly important. It is hard to replicate, online, the customer service within a real store: the assistant asking to help you, the store layout, the ability to actually hold the product before buying – all of which help the customer make purchase decisions. It had been his ambition to create an equivalent experience online.

He had put a year and a half of his life into building the project. Eugene Dunning had belonged to a generation for whom the whole Internet world was anathema, and had been interested only in results. As Tony's work achieved measurable results, Eugene had given Tony a free hand in designing the project and Tony had grown and developed under a benign dictatorship. The old man had liked him and made him a bit of a protégé.

Every time he stuffed up, the old man gave him a bollocking, which Tony hadn't minded at all. If he got it right, Eugene Dunning had been generous in his praise. Without considering the consequences, Tony had become a servant to one man. Now Eugene's death had shifted the power structure in the company, and Tony wasn't sure he would emerge from the next few weeks very successfully.

He didn't particularly like Clive Hannah and had avoided him as much as possible. There was something about Clive that repelled Tony, and he had an uneasy feeling that maybe he hadn't taken the time to develop the relationship that he should have. Clive, unlike Eugene, was the sort of man it paid to 'butter up'.

Clive Hannah was someone who liked to be important. Tony had never heard Clive make a speech that didn't extol the virtues of Clive, or require others to recognise his importance and value. A greater contrast between Eugene, with his spare, intelligent, disciplined mind, and Clive, with his endless need for reassurance and self-aggrandisement, could hardly be found. Tony wondered if he could work with him at all. Maybe he'd be fired, or maybe he should get his resignation in before he got his pink slip.

The boardroom door opened and the official party entered. Everyone else stood up respectfully as they made their way to the table.

Leading them was the old man's widow. Donald McCrae, the company lawyer, escorted her, his arm solicitously held for hers to link with. Tony looked at her. She seemed to be bearing up okay so soon after her husband's death. Tony had seen her before, of course, at public functions, occupying the role of consort on her husband's arm, and less than a week ago at the funeral. No doubt she had come in today to wish everyone good luck: make a 'God bless all that sail in her' type of speech, and then let them get on with the show.

Marguerite Dunning was wearing a deep green suit. Dark enough to still signify mourning, colourful enough to set off her skin and hair, and sufficiently stylish to make every other woman in the room reconsider her outfit. Hell, she might be old, thought Tony, but she certainly had style. He watched as Samantha Merilees straightened her own skirt in response, and smiled to himself. He had plans in that department, and it was worthwhile finding out Samantha's weak spots. Not that she had many. Her sudden, involuntary vulnerability made her even more desirable.

Marguerite seated herself at the head of the board table, in the spot that her husband had occupied for so many years. After pulling the seat out for her and helping her with old-fashioned dignity, Donald sat down at her right hand.

Clive Hannah, who had walked in with them, seemed to pause involuntarily at their clear claim for territory but then shrugged and moved to his usual seat on Marguerite's left. It was clear to everyone he was humouring them, and amused by the situation. If you've just been given control of one of the foremost private companies in Britain, you can afford a little bit of indulgence.

There was a pause as everyone seated themselves at the table.

Donald set a number of papers in front of him. Marguerite sat with dignified poise and stillness while Clive shuffled, ran his finger round the inside of his collar and shifted in his seat.

Donald stood up. "Thank you, ladies and gentlemen," he opened. "For those of you who may not know me, my name is Donald McCrae. I am the corporate solicitor for Dunning Ltd."

There was a slight titter round the table. There would be very few who didn't know who he was, and few who weren't also aware that he'd been Eugene's friend and personal lawyer.

Donald continued, "My remit today is to inform you of the terms of Eugene Dunning's will, as it relates to Dunnings of the High Street, and to introduce you to your new CEO."

He smiled slightly. "As you all know, this is a family company, and it prides itself on that. When Eugene and Marguerite Dunning founded the company we know as 'Dunnings', way back in 1954, they always envisaged it would be a family-driven organisation. In a sense, theirs was a marriage partnership that gradually changed into a limited liability company. All shares in the company have been held by Eugene and Marguerite in their entirety."

He paused. "On Eugene's death, with the exception of a few minor bequests, Marguerite Dunning inherits all the shares of the company." He allowed the murmurs to travel around the table. "The future of the company therefore is totally in her hands." He glanced briefly at Clive. "I am very happy to inform you that Marguerite has consented to occupy the role her husband has so recently left, as CEO of 'Dunnings of the High Street'." He straightened his back and looked around the table. "I ask you to join with me in a round of applause as we all welcome her to that position."

There was a sudden surge of movement from Clive Hannah as he pushed his chair back and rose from the table. "Like hell we will!" he exploded. "This is my company now, and no geriatric is going to stop me. I've built it for the last thirty years. What has the bitch ever done?"

Tony was as startled as everyone else. He assumed Marguerite Dunning was in her eighties. If she was the heir, well, she was a welcome alternative to Clive Hannah, though he had his doubts. She might be stylish in designer fashions, but he'd never seen her tough it out at a board meeting. It was possible that if he supported her, he would be well and truly up the creek without a paddle. He looked round the table and saw the same thought mirrored on every face.

Clive Hannah was just hitting his stride in a monumental tirade. "I am the heir to this company," he snarled. "Not only by right of my birth, but by right of the years I have put into its growth. I will not let this crone ruin everything I have worked for." He realised, belatedly, there was an audience to his speech and turned and faced the other attendees of the meeting. "I call upon you all to recognise what I have done for Dunnings and my rightful place in its governance," he began, smoothly enough, but then he erupted again: "This bitch has no rights here. I will die before I let her wrest control from me! This is my company. I've worked for it!"

All of which, obscenities aside, was true, reflected Tony. No one was going to challenge Clive's achievements in the field. The trouble was, though, that aligning with a man as out of control as he was could count against you.

The murmuring around the table was building to a roar. Neither Donald nor Marguerite appeared affected, and both wore strictly neutral expressions on their faces. Clive was incandescent with anger. He was a big, solidly built man at the best of times, but under the influence of undiluted rage he swelled markedly. Every muscle in his shoulders and neck seemed enlarged. His face was swollen, coloured and best described as choleric. What a handy set of phrases Dickens had for situations like these, Tony thought.

Marguerite let the rage and surmises build. She couldn't have planned it better. Clive's uncontrollable outburst had only strengthened her position. She smiled deeply and rose to her feet.

The noise died down gradually. Marguerite was prepared to stand there until Judgement Day to get the effect she wanted. As the room quietened, she smiled again. "Thank you all for your input," she said politely, and turning to Clive, she continued, "and, my dear," (she allowed the phrase to hang there, open to interpretation as derisory or sympathetic) "I quite understand the shock it must be if you weren't aware of the provisions under which Dunnings was founded." The double implication of Clive's separation from the real centre of business, and of her own certainty and authority, was a masterly touch, thought Tony.

"With my husband, Eugene," she allowed her face a modicum of sadness, "I founded this company sixty years ago. I believe it has been moderately successful?"

There was a slight sycophantic titter around the room.

"Dunnings is a great company. And more than anyone, I recognise the mark my husband has put on this company." She paused for effect. They were all focused on her now. "It is, of course, a family-run company. The provisions of its founding are quite simple. Both Eugene and I had fifty per cent of the shares. If either of us died, all shares were to pass automatically to the other." She sighed. "I need hardly say how much I miss the man who was my lifetime companion."

There were sympathetic murmurs now from around the table.

"In essence, that now means I hold all the shares of 'Dunnings of the High Street'. However," she lifted her hands slightly in a conciliatory manner, "I cannot leave these shares to anyone I please. However attractive the man that cleans the swimming pool, I may not make him a gift of Dunnings."

She waited for the laughter to stop.

"Nor would I wish to," she added. "No. The founding documents are quite clear on this. The surviving partner, whether it be Eugene or I, inherits 100% of the shares. When he or, in this case, I die, then the shares must, in their entirety, pass to a direct descendant of Eugene's and my marriage, or, if such an heir does not exist, then it passes to any other direct heir of Eugene or myself that can be found. In other words," she paused again for effect, "Clive here, as a natural-born son of Eugene's, and long acknowledged as such, could be the natural heir of the company, unless," and here she smiled sweetly, "a direct descendant of Eugene and my marriage exists."

"As some of you know, many years ago, Eugene and I had

the tragedy and misfortune to lose our only child, our daughter, Tamara. You may have assumed that, in this situation, the heir apparent was Clive Hannah." She smiled broadly at Clive. "I am happy to tell you, however, that Tamara had a child, a child that I have been aware of since her birth. That child, my granddaughter, is now, under the terms of the company's foundation, the heir of Dunning's after me."

"I am therefore taking my place as head of the Dunning's empire. I am sure I can rely on all of you for your support. In due course, I will introduce you to my granddaughter."

She smiled again. "Thank you," she said simply. "If any of you have any questions, I am happy to receive them, or perhaps Donald can answer some of them."

She paused.

"You should know that Donald and I have already issued a press release which details these events, and which I imagine will hit the papers this evening." She sat down composedly.

Clive Hannah surged forward: A powerfully built man, his anger was impressive. "That is completely untrue," he challenged. "Tamara never had a child. I will testify to that in any court in the land." He glared at Marguerite. "Tamara had no child," he reiterated. He stared at Marguerite and repeated, "Your daughter had no child, and I know that."

Marguerite inclined her head towards Donald who shuffled his papers studiously. He let a few moments pass while Clive stood there fuming, then Donald stood up. "I can assure you that Tamara did have a child, that this child lives, is now twenty-four years old, and she is Eugene and Marguerite Dunning's grandchild," he said carefully. He looked directly at Clive Hannah. "It may be you would prefer further discussion take place in private? This must have been a shock to you," he suggested courteously.

"Like fuck I would," snarled Clive. "This matter is going to be a public scandal. Tamara had no child, so whatever mug you have put up for that role is a phoney and will be exposed as such. DNA tests are quite specific these days, I understand." He shoved himself out from his seat and marched round the table towards Marguerite.

She sat there composedly as he advanced on her.

"I assure you, you bitch, that I will slaughter you through the courts. You've dedicated your life to wrecking mine, but this is beyond compare. I've invested my life in this company. You won't dismiss me that easily."

"But I haven't dismissed you, Clive. Nor have I in any way demoted you." Marguerite smiled at him serenely. "Please return to your seat so we can carry on with this meeting. I'm sure you will continue, as you always have done, to work for the company Eugene and I founded. Your loyalty to my company goes back a long way, and I have always valued you for that reason."

Tony watched Clive. He was fascinated by the man's reactions. He had never seen anyone have an apoplectic fit, but Clive was certainly ticking every box on the symptoms sheet. Heavens, if he got any redder or more engorged, he would burst out of his suit.

"Fuck you!" he swore at Marguerite. "I don't know what you're playing at, but it isn't going to stop me taking the company for myself. I've earned it; it's mine."

And with that Clive Hannah sat down heavily in his place.

Donald McCrae winced overtly at the crudity of the expression.

Marguerite's expression remained, in contrast, as ladylike and remote as a duchess's at a tea party. She allowed a minute to pass in silence before she raised her eyes to the fascinated group around the table. "I think we should now move on," she said calmly. "I will be circulating around the stores and divisions over the next week, talking to you all and getting your input and feedback to various ideas and directions for the company that I am anxious to implement …" She paused. "Now, if we can just cover the essentials at this meeting: as Donald McCrae has indicated, I will occupy the position of Chief Executive Officer of the company. Donald himself will continue to be our legal representative and advisor."

She gestured towards Clive Hannah who was now sitting sullenly. "It was in my mind to continue Clive's position as General Manager. If today's exchange means you don't wish to continue in that position, Clive, then I am naturally distressed.

But no doubt we can have discussions on this subject in my office tomorrow."

She turned now to her right and addressed the man who sat beyond Donald.

"Seth Hampton is currently our Financial Controller; I intend to continue your service in that role, Seth. Now, more than ever, we need a clear, experienced and unbiased mind to guide us through the current recession."

Seth sighed in relief. He had fully expected to lose his position to a younger man.

"Mark Harmon, of course, is Seth's invaluable assistant. I propose that he continues in that position, because his advice is exemplary and he also provides youth and technical skills that are an important part of our movement into effective ownership of the twenty-first century."

Mark, who had assumed he would become the Financial Manager under a Clive Hannah-led company, swore quietly and viciously to himself. More years of toeing the party line loomed ahead of him. He smiled weakly at Marguerite and nodded his assent. He thought of the large mortgage on the house at Henley-on-Thames, and of his son at public school, the fees for which could cripple an empire. He knew Annie would be angry with him. She'd counted on his promotion and was already planning a holiday to Morocco. He hoped she would temper her ambitions for now.

Marguerite had already moved her attention round the table to the next candidate. "Samantha Merilees joined Dunnings two years ago as an intern on our 'fast-track to management' programme. Her presence here at this table is a testimony both to the success of that particular programme and to Samantha's own skills. I am pleased to announce that she will be extending her responsibilities to encompass the overall future design planning for Dunnings. I consider it of paramount importance that the company upgrades and updates its corporate image on the High Street, in its European operations and, most particularly, in its position in e-commerce."

Marguerite smiled at Samantha. "I will take pleasure in the

next few weeks discussing your role with you and seeing your work as you help Dunnings move forward to embrace this century."

For once in her life Samantha managed to be shy, *and* speechless. Tony enjoyed watching her in this situation.

Marguerite moved round the table, speaking to each person in turn, offering them their positions back, or modifying, downgrading or elevating their importance in the organisation. She spoke, apparently effortlessly, without notes, and remembering every single person at that table. Not once did she stumble or ask for help from her henchman Donald.

It was, thought Tony, a masterful performance (although he wasn't sure if that particular adjective was entirely appropriate, given Marguerite's gender).

Tony heard her confirm Nathan in his departmental sales manager role. Nathan's stunned but enthusiastic face broadcast that Nathan had moved up the ladder from sales manager in the main branch to managing the sales targets for all the London stores.

Soon it was his turn, and he was delighted to have his own position confirmed. Marguerite stated that a major focus over the next couple of years would be the development, profitability and market domination of e-commerce throughout the Dunning's range. Tony was now responsible for all of this, a role that would see him having to spend time working with Samantha Merilees. He sighed with satisfaction as he nodded his assent to Marguerite Dunning. Whatever the pros and cons of the situation, he was now and forever her man.

There were some at that table who had not done as well as others. Tony realised he would have to think about the implications of some of the decisions, but the majority seemed to feel reenergised and secure in their roles. They had started the morning assuming they were supporting a handover of power to Clive Hannah, and they had been wrong. By the end of the meeting it seemed there would be few who were very sad at the way the day had turned out.

Marguerite Dunning was accepted and praised as an incisive

and decisive leader. Clive Hannah had been significantly silent since his outbreak at the beginning of the meeting. Obviously he realised he had lost serious credibility. However, looking at the man's face, Tony felt certain Clive would regroup and be ready to fight another day.

There was such palpable hatred and malevolence in the look Clive threw at Marguerite that Tony rethought his opinion of the man as just a bullying thug. That look said Clive would willingly commit murder. A disturbing thought for the future of the company.

Tony watched the official party rise and leave the room, then turned to find Samantha and congratulate her. Inevitably, Nathan bailed him up before he could achieve his objective. Tony sighed.

"Well, what did you think of all that?" exclaimed his friend.

CHAPTER
TWELVE

London, Present Day.

AS MARGUERITE REMARKED TO MAX, IT didn't take very long for Clive to recover from the shock and start mustering his forces. Within the next few days Donald McCrae had received documents contesting Eugene's will and alleging it had been written whilst a dying Eugene was of unsound mind and therefore open to undue influence.

"Which," said Donald, "is utterly disprovable. Eugene's will remained substantially unchanged since the late 1950s, and any adjustments or minor bequests added later never changed the basic premise behind the inheritance of the company."

"Well, I suppose Clive feels he's got to try," said Marguerite philosophically.

They were taking tea together in Marguerite's drawing room.

"What news is there about your granddaughter?" asked Donald.

"I've organised a legal firm in New Zealand to make initial contact with her, and sent them a letter to be passed on to her," replied Marguerite. "I'm hoping she'll be sufficiently intrigued by the thought of her birth family to make her willing to meet with me. I can't force her, of course."

"You realise that Clive's next attack is going to be directed at her? That he will be looking for information to help him disprove that she is Tamara's daughter?"

"There won't be a problem there," asserted Marguerite. "There is clear evidence, well documented, that she is Tamara's child, given up at birth. Not only do we have birth records and so on that you can testify to yourself, Donald, but Nora Davis signed a statement at the time of the handover making sure her identity was well defined legally."

Max cleared his throat. "I understand Clive mentioned DNA tests."

Donald nodded. "Oh yes. I imagine when this gets really nasty, Clive will try every trick in the book. I don't know how your granddaughter is going to feel about this, Marguerite. She might find it very intrusive."

He rubbed his hand through his hair. "Of course, if she is interested enough in the inheritance, she may be prepared to put up with the inconvenience of being scrutinised." He smiled. "Money usually talks."

Marguerite shrugged. "I imagine most of this is going to be a paper war, isn't it, Donald?" She sipped her Lapsang Souchong. "I shouldn't imagine it's going to get to DNA or anything remotely like it." She smiled reassuringly at Max.

"The point is," said Max, looking at her significantly, "if it does come to DNA tests – and I imagine Clive could have it ordered by the courts – information may be obtained that would be very distressing for your granddaughter. You need to think this through very carefully, Marguerite, before you do irreversible damage."

Donald pricked up his ears and looked across at Max. "Is there something I don't know?"

Max didn't answer.

After a moment's silence Donald turned to Marguerite. "I ask again, is there something I should know? Marguerite, I'm prepared to run with this case as far as it will go. Eugene was my friend as well as my employer, and his will, and clear intention, will be honoured if I have to fight Clive through every court in the land. But you can't keep secrets from me. What is there about this girl's DNA that might prove distressing for her?"

Marguerite sighed. "It's all old history, Donald. I'm not sure we need to bring it up now." She glared at Max.

"Let it be sufficient, Donald, that Purdie is Tamara's. The daughter you organised legal guardianship for. I don't believe we need to discuss anything further than that."

From that position, she would not be moved, and Max refused to comment further.

Eventually Donald said, "My strong advice, Marguerite, is that you disclose everything to me now, and don't try and hide information that will only come out, more damagingly, later. But I can't force you to do so." He shrugged. "If that is all for today, I'll take this back to the office. Think about what I've just said, though."

He left and Marguerite stared at Max. "Was that strictly necessary?" she asked icily.

Max held her gaze firmly. "If I don't raise it, no one else will, or can," he said. "Modern technology means things once secret can now be revealed. I don't know enough about the science of these tests, but if they lead in any way to Perdita discovering who her father is, then you'll have ruined her life. Not to mention what the scandal could do to you and Dunnings."

Marguerite looked at him in silence. After a while she sighed. "It was all a very long time ago, Max."

"I challenge you to tell me your anger and hate has lessened over the passage of time. You need to think through the implications of your moves, Marguerite, and at what point you are going to be prepared to pull out of any action against Clive for the sake of this girl."

Marguerite set her chin. "It's because of past history that I will never give up on this particular battle."

Max shrugged and took the tea things out of the room.

Marguerite settled back in her chair, gazing across the room at her husband and her daughter smiling back at her from their silver frames. She wondered how they, especially Tamara, would have felt about her actions. Knowing exactly what Eugene would have thought was why she had kept her secrets for so long.

CHAPTER THIRTEEN

Poland, 1944.

IT WAS DARK, AND THE TRAIN was nine hours late. She stood beside her mother on the cold platform. Around them were piled their few cases – her sister, Katya, was sitting on one playing with her doll. Marguerite's father had gone to make sure their tickets were valid, leaving 'his women', as he loved to call them, to hold their place in the queue on the platform.

Everywhere she looked in the crowded station, other families were huddled, with pinched, shocked faces. Women clasped small children while wailing toddlers and crying babies battled to be heard over the hubbub of adult chatter. A few feet from her an elderly, well-dressed woman sat on her suitcase, rocking back and forth, a handkerchief clasped to her mouth to control her sobs, her face wet with tears.

Their mother was harassed and fretful. "Where is Charles? Why has he left us? We need him here."

"He's gone to get the tickets and papers. He'll be back soon. Don't worry."

Mother kept on commenting and complaining. "When is this

train coming? How do we know it's the one we need. I don't understand why we have to do all this so quickly and why we couldn't bring Anya with us."

Marguerite sighed. "We are fleeing the country, Mother. How could we bring a maid? We're going to be refugees." She could hardly get her own head around the situation.

Last week she had been celebrating her fourteenth birthday. Tonight she was standing on a draughty railway platform, bundled up so bulkily in three different layers of clothes that she could hardly move. Everything she had taken for granted – home, friends, pets and even Anya the maid – were gone. Of course, under German occupation, life hadn't been normal for a long time, but at least it was what she knew.

"It's not good for Katya," whined Mother. "She shouldn't be up this late."

Marguerite felt her temper fraying and was about to make a snappish reply when she saw her father pushing his way towards them through the people swirling on the platform. A tall man, Charles Komarov towered above others, his height accentuated by the homburg he wore. Like the rest of them, he was bulked up in his topcoat with all the clothes he now owned on underneath. The overall effect, thought Marguerite fondly, was of a great bear.

The Russian bear; she shivered suddenly at the thought. It was the Russian advance they were fleeing now, even though her father was Russian by birth. She knew he had left the country at the time of the revolution in 1917 and that he hated communists. She didn't understand why, but she had been reared to think of herself as Russian and to hate the communists even more than the Germans, although the latter were feared as much as they were hated.

The occupation had dominated her life. She had been nine when she learned to keep her head down, disappear and be quiet when the soldiers appeared. To be Polish under German occupation was a terrible thing, and her family had endured the situation with the rest of the population. Germany thought of the Polish people as slaves to serve the mighty Reich. There were rumours of terrible atrocities and murders. Father had remarked that their only consolation was that they weren't Jewish. Everyone knew empty houses where Jews used to live, empty desks at schools, empty shopfronts where Jewish businesses had once operated. The knowledge that they could share that fate kept the rest of the population subservient, even compliant.

Food disappeared, and hunger set in, with cruel results. Father and Grandfather had queued for hours in the cold for supplies, but Grandmother Anna died that first winter. Always frail, she developed a chest infection that wouldn't clear. Mother nursed her, but there was little she could do to ease Grandmother's condition at the end.

"What she needs is building up," Marguerite heard her say to Father helplessly, but warm chicken broth, milk puddings with sago, and all the old family standbys for convalescent food were no longer available. As winter deepened, Grandmother's life waned.

With her passing, Grandfather seemed to lose the will to go on. Living conditions got harder, and he took to sitting in one chair all day long, just gazing out of the window. Mother, whose sympathy for anyone was minimal, took to treating him with contempt, but Marguerite had memories of him playing with her when she was a little girl. If prompted properly, he would tell her stories of life in Russia before the revolution, about the time when her own father was a boy. He insisted they spoke Russian or English for these conversations.

"How else will you learn your heritage?" he asked, "and English is important for any educated person."

He wove wonderful stories about their old horses, about troikas in the snow and the harnesses his factory made. "Some were commissioned for the Tsar's own horses," he would tell her. There were tales of family trips into the country to the family dacha, and of the large family they had been part of. "For Ilya's fourteenth birthday we gave him a horse," the old man said. "We walked it into his bedroom on the morning of his birthday. He was so excited." Grandfather had smiled at the memory.

"But of course," he had added sadly, "there are no more horses and no mansions in Russia for ordinary folk. When we came to Poland we had to find work. Anna was so ill we couldn't carry on to England as we'd intended. A tailor's business was for sale, so your father and I became tailors." He smiled. "Charles picked up the skills easily, but I was always a little clumsy, so I did the bookkeeping."

Grandfather would speak with sorrow of his young brother, Uncle Ilya, who had gone east at the start of the revolution to escape the Bolsheviks and never been heard of again. "Your grandmother used to say we would all meet in heaven, but I never had her faith, God rest her soul."

"War," he told Marguerite, "is terrible. Not because it kills people, they at least are dead. It's the living whose lives are destroyed. Families separated, unable to reclaim their past. We lost so much when we fled Russia, your grandmother, Charles and I."

He had lingered for another couple of years and in the end passed very peacefully. "He wasn't so much ill," Marguerite overheard her mother once saying to their neighbour, "he just decided to stop being alive. And he succeeded."

The night of Grandfather Komarov's funeral, Father hugged Marguerite to him in sorrow. "I'm an orphan now."

It was a disturbing insight into the world of adults. Marguerite had assumed that only children became orphans. It hadn't occurred to her that her tall, strong papa would feel the same as a small child.

But now Germany was losing the war. There were rumours the Western alliance was advancing on Germany from the west, and the Russians were advancing from the east. This made Mother and Father grab the most important of their possessions and make their way out of Poland. Father had distant cousins in England, and he hoped to use these contacts to get admission.

There was no joy in Poland at the thought of yet another invasion. *Would Poland never be free?* thought Marguerite.

She sat down on her father's tin box. He was pacifying her mother, and Katya climbed over the cases and sat beside her. The little five-year-old looked up at Marguerite. Her pale face was white and pinched, the station lighting washing it out against her blonde hair; the big shadows under her eyes made her look like a baby giant panda. *She is too thin*, thought Marguerite – but then they were all too thin. Five years of hunger had left its mark.

"I want to go home," Katya whispered.

Suddenly Marguerite felt the misery of the last few days wash over her. "Oh so do I, darling, so do I." She pulled the little girl towards her. "Be brave," she urged, not knowing if it was Katya or herself she was encouraging. It seemed like good advice. Katya sat on her lap, snuggled against her, sucking her thumb, her tired eyes drooping.

I swear, thought Marguerite, *that if we get safely to England, Katya will never be hungry again. We'll make a new life.* She looked over at her father. He had succeeded in soothing her mother and had his arm round her protectively. Once upon a time, he had been a wealthy man. How must it be for him, she wondered, to leave behind his working life and start again in a foreign country, not just once but for a second time?

There was a sudden increase in the clamour. The train had arrived. A surge of people started towards the edge of the platform. Father grabbed some of the suitcases.

"Come on!" he shouted at them. "Quickly. Pick up the other cases." He turned to Mother. "Edith, take Katya. Come on, you can manage these bags as well."

Even Katya helped by picking up a small valise as Mother snatched her up protectively.

Marguerite gathered up bags and cases. It was even harder to get a grip on them all when she was so padded with clothing. Father grabbed the tin box she had been sitting on. It was an awkward shape to carry, but he looped a belt through its handle, loaded it over his shoulder and picked up another three cases. They joined the push to the train.

Getting on board was brutal. They used their shoulders, elbows and the sharp corners of their cases to shove and batter their way on. Even Mother was seen to hit out hard when someone else shoved in front of her. Katya was crying with fear as she was jostled and squeezed through the melee. The crowd was under no illusions – each one of them had to get aboard that overcrowded train or face an increasingly dangerous future from the Red Squad as the Russians invaded.

The Komarov family managed to find a place, which even had two seats, in the corner of the carriage. Mother sat with Katya on her knee, Father took the other seat and Marguerite sat on the bags piled between them. There was no room to move. The carriage was packed with people, standing, sitting, all claiming their tiny bit of territory.

The doors closed, but for half an hour, the train remained at the station, unmoving. The passengers, packed so tightly against each other, started to mutter. It seemed a real possibility they could be there for hours. Finally, just as they were beginning to get really restless, the train lurched into action, and slowly, so very slowly, pulled away from the station.

The passengers became quiet. Most were leaving home and family forever, and many had tears in their eyes. Marguerite glanced at Father, but he was smiling at Mother.

"It'll be all right, Edith," he said to her. "There will be a better life for all of us in England, you'll see."

Mother's eyes were teary and her lips quivering, but she smiled back at him wanly, cuddling Katya to her. Not for the first time Marguerite wondered at the nature of the love between her parents.

Marguerite, squeezed and pushed hard up against Mother's knees, felt she was boiling. The layers of clothes, worn because there was no place in the cases to carry them, were now unbearably constraining. She felt herself sweating, as a flush of warmth spread beneath her armpits and between her small breasts. Around her she could smell other bodies, all in equal conditions of misery.

Mother, who at least was beside a window, pushed it open, and the relief of the fresh air that entered the carriage was indescribable.

The train rattled north through the darkness. They were headed for the Baltic Sea, and the plan was, from there, to get on any available transport to Britain. Father had said they'd walk all around the coast on foot if they had to until they reached a place that would take them across the cold North Sea. Marguerite had very little knowledge of England. She fancied that King Arthur and Sir Lancelot came from there. She knew the country was at war with Germany. That one, simple fact made all English people their friends.

The train stopped once, five hours into the trip, to refuel. There was a rush as passengers tried to find toilets. Panicked at the thought of not getting back on in time, most simply urinated behind the platform. Marguerite envied the men who so easily disappeared behind the station shed and emerged a couple of minutes later looking relaxed. She, along with the other women, performed the necessary in a huddled group, trying to shield each other as best they could. All were so desperate that modesty was a lesser concern than relief.

Mother had elected to stay on board guarding their possessions and position whilst the others got off first. She had a hard time fending off ambitious families who were eyeing their spot, and she was shouting at a woman by the time they came back. When Father returned, the woman retreated, muttering angrily. Mother climbed over and made her own trip. She returned shortly and clambered back over them again. The woman who had challenged her place glared at her, but Mother looked away. She unpacked one of the bags. There was a tough loaf of bread and some pickles to eat. The dryness in Marguerite's mouth made the bread hard to swallow, and Katya simply refused to try.

"Come on, my darling," crooned Mother, but Katya turned her head away.

"You must make the effort," said Father. "We've got a long, long way to go. You will need to have food in your little tummy."

In the end, Mother chewed small pieces of bread into a soft, mushy paste and fed it to Katya like a little bird.

"Little bird," smiled Marguerite at her sister. "That's what I'll call you from now on, 'Birdie'."

Katya lifted her tired eyelids to look at her sister. The faintest of smiles crossed her face before she stuck her thumb in her mouth and curled back up to sleep again.

Marguerite dozed on and off. At one point she woke to see both her parents asleep, her father quietly snoring. Katya's eyes were open, but she stayed still, snuggled against their mother. Most of the other passengers were asleep or sitting quietly, keeping their own private fears and misery to themselves.

Eventually Marguerite dozed off again. When she woke, it was day, and the inside of the carriage was lit with cold, grey light. Other passengers were awake. Outside the window, the land stretched flat and featureless as far as she could see.

Father checked his watch. "It's supposed to be a nine-hour trip," he grumbled, "and we've already been going ten."

"Surely it must end soon," said Mother. Daylight seemed to have restored some of her courage and she looked more cheerful. She shifted Katya onto her husband's lap and stretched her arms out in relief.

"Katya, my darling," she smiled. "You're getting too heavy for your mama. My arms are all cramped."

Marguerite shifted, trying to get her mother's legs out of her back. She felt exhausted, dirty and hungry. Worse, she wanted to relieve herself again. Something of her misery must have shown on her face.

Her father smiled at her. "Well done; we've got through the first night, and we're all together and well. We just have to keep going."

Marguerite smiled and nodded back at him, grateful for his warmth and kindness. She loved him very much.

There was a cheer from the front of the carriage. Marguerite looked up. She could see so little from where she was sitting.

Other passengers were shouting, "We're here, we're here!"

Suddenly there were smiles on everyone's faces. The mood swung from misery to relief. They had all known there had been a real possibility of falling foul of the retreating German line; it had been an unspoken terror in the dark watches of the night. To arrive at their destination safe and well, if a bit grubby and tired, was a blessing.

"It's an omen of good fortune for our trip," said Father.

Even Mother looked happy. She smiled at the woman she had

harangued during the night, and she smiled back. The relief was palpable. "Good luck," the woman said to the Komarov family as they climbed off the train.

CHAPTER FOURTEEN

Poland, 1944.

THE JOY OF BEING OFF THE train was short-lived. As soon as they disembarked they discovered, to their dismay, that there was still a German presence in the town. A small, operational detachment remained.

They were scrutinised, processed and documented by an officious young guard with atrocious Polish. Marguerite felt her father sigh. Several years of occupation and both Poles and Germans spoke pidgin versions of each other's languages.

"Where are your papers?" As he scrutinised these he was asking, "Why have you come here? Where are you staying?"

Father answered calmly. Marguerite could see how stressed he was by the tightening of the muscles around his eyes, but Charles Komarov gave no other sign of tension. The young guard was frustrated by his composure but could find no reason to detain him.

There were a lot of other families to process, and the pressure of moving them on was growing. Finally, with visible reluctance, he released them and they were free to enter the town.

They stayed at a boarding house, down towards the sea. It was run-down, small and reeked of boiled cabbage. All four of them shared the room – Marguerite had a small trundle bed on the floor, and Katya was to sleep with Father and Mother. But they had a room to themselves, a bathroom to wash and clean up in, and food to eat.

The meal consisted largely of the cabbage they had smelled earlier, with a large loaf of black bread to mop everything up, but it was amazing how good food restored them. Katya was smiling, Mother relaxed and Father at his most urbane, chatting to the landlady.

Her husband had been killed early in the war, and she'd survived the intervening years by providing accommodation for the resident German troops. In return for her hospitality, they had treated her with abuse and contempt. Her life for the last four years had been that of a slave, she told Father. Now the Germans were going, and she rejoiced, but who knew what the future would hold? If the Russians got this far, she could be worse off.

The next morning, Father left early to go down to the docks to see if there was any transport to get them away. He made it clear they were not to leave the boarding house for any reason.

It would make for a long, boring day, thought Marguerite. Mother had become friendly with the landlady and was perfectly happy to spend the day helping with chores, caring for Katya and sharing experiences of life during the war. The landlady was equally happy with the company of another woman in the house and, more particularly, with Katya.

"I have never had a child myself," she said with regret, her eyes following Katya as the little girl played. "It makes a house joyous to have a child in it."

Left to her own devices, Marguerite sought out the sitting room. There were mementos of the troops that had billeted there. Initials had been carved into the wooden fireplace alongside the hated swastika, and most of the books on the shelves were in German. Marguerite sorted through the books. In the end she could discover only two in Polish. One was a trade manual, the other a novel.

She curled up in the big seat by the window and buried herself in the fiction.

The day dragged. The novel had particularly wooden characters, and Marguerite was growing restless. She joined her mother and the landlady, whose name she now discovered was Mrs Keppel, in the kitchen. Mother was helping Katya draw, and Mrs Keppel was darning. Her sewing basket was overflowing with socks, dresses that needed buttons, and skirts with ripped hems. It seemed she took in piecework from her neighbours. Marguerite's offer of help was accepted, although Marguerite could see Mrs Keppel was dubious about having a stranger darn her socks and stockings. Marguerite was handy with a needle and had been well taught. She was her father's daughter, after all. The group of women sat in harmony for a couple of hours as the pile of mending shrank in the basket.

When Marguerite finally pulled herself away from the work, she realised it was late evening. Mrs Keppel had risen to draw the curtains and put on the lamps. There was still no word from Father.

Mother immediately started fretting. "Where can he be? He shouldn't have been away this long."

Marguerite shared her anxiety. Father shouldn't have been away all day. He knew his family would worry.

"Something must have happened to him," whispered Mother. "Oh my God, what could it be? How do we find out?"

Mrs Keppel stood looking at the Komarovs. "You can't do anything tonight," she said. "It's already curfew, and you can't go out or the Germans will shoot you."

She started clearing up her sewing basket.

"It may be that he was delayed and has decided that he needs to stay where he is tonight. He cannot move round after curfew either."

Mrs Keppel looked at their frightened faces. "It will probably be all right," she added hopefully.

Marguerite and her mother spent a sleepless night, beside themselves with worry. This was an alien town. They assumed

Charles had gone towards the harbour, but neither knew where to look for him if he had an accident, or worse. Unspoken, but never far from their thoughts, was the German presence. Mother and daughter had seen enough atrocities over the last few years to have no illusions about what could occur.

When he had not returned in the early morning, they knew something terrible must have happened. Under no circumstances would Charles Komarov have left his family alone.

They got up, dressed silently and faced each other across the bedroom, Katya's small, sleeping body between them on the bed.

Marguerite waited for Mother to assume command, to say she would go and find Father, and that Marguerite must look after Katya while she was gone.

Instead, Edith looked at her daughter. "What are we supposed to do?"

Marguerite stared at her. "We've got to find Father," she said. "We've got to go and find out what's happened."

Still she waited for Edith to take control of the situation. "I can't leave Katya," she said. "You'll have to go."

Marguerite stared at her. She didn't want to go out on the streets of a strange town and ask after a missing man any more than her mother did. Up to that moment she had assumed she was the child in the relationship, her mother the adult who would undertake the difficult tasks. It seemed she was wrong.

"All right, I'll go, Mother," she said in a low voice.

"Wrap up warm."

Marguerite felt the inappropriateness of the comment. Mother was playing the role of authority, but not exercising it. Marguerite felt uneasy and unsafe. She'd never considered her mother as a person, rather than a parent.

She dressed warmly in a scarf and coat. With her hair in plaits she looked nearer twelve than fourteen, which was a great relief to her mother.

She nodded and let herself out of the house. It was still quite early, and people were heading to their work. No one paid attention to the girl. She was passed by several lorries loaded with troops and wondered if they were arriving in the town or were part of the retreat.

She walked down the cobblestone streets to the harbour. A few boats lay at anchor – some were military launches, but most were fishing smacks, rocking in the oily water. She smelt the sharp tang of sea air.

She assumed her father must have come down here, looking for a ship to take them out. A man was working on one of the fishing boats, coiling rope and washing the deck.

Marguerite walked over to him. "Excuse me."

The man, whose name was Gregory, looked up. He saw a slight, schoolgirlish figure looking down at him. He smiled up at her; he had young sisters of his own. "Good morning, sweetheart; what can I do for you?"

"I'm looking for my father. I think he came down here yesterday, and now he's disappeared. I wondered if you had seen him."

Gregory looked at her seriously, his heart sinking with pity for her. He saw the tension round her mouth, her pinched, white face. The world was full of people looking for missing relations.

"Yesterday?" He shook his head. "No, yesterday I was at sea, love. You should ask at the harbour master's office, over there." He pointed to the building at the edge of the wharves. "Maybe someone there can help you."

She nodded and retraced her steps to the brick building at the centre of harbour. She'd avoided it on her way in as she had seen it was guarded by German infantry. She kept her eyes down as she approached the front steps. At the top she was accosted by a soldier not much older than herself and very fair.

"Halt, miss!" he shouted at her in badly accented Polish.

She stopped obediently.

"What do you want?" he snapped at her smartly.

"Please, I need to see the harbour master."

"What's your business?"

Marguerite hesitated and he asked her again, louder this time. "What is your business, fraulein?"

"I'm looking for someone," she said.

This amused him. "Well, I'm 'someone'. Look what you found, little girlie." He called across to the guard on the opposite side of the large doors. "Hey, Franz, this kid's asking for 'someone'. You want to come and be 'someone' with her?"

Franz approached. He was older than his companion, his eyes more knowing. They ran their way over Marguerite's drab coat and the simple frock it covered. There was a moment when his eyes focused on where her small breasts were and then snaked over her waist and hips. She felt deeply uncomfortable and had to resist the urge to shield herself with her arms.

"Oh, I can be someone with her all right," purred Franz. He put his hand out and ran it down the front of her coat very deliberately, his hands cupping her breasts. Marguerite froze in horror. She didn't know how to respond. For a frightened moment she wondered if it would be impolite to turn and run, or if it would be more ladylike to simply ignore him and just carry on talking politely. His hand continued roaming down her slight frame to her hip, where it turned inland, reached the division of her thighs and stopped.

"What did you say you wanted?" he teased her. "Was it this?" and his hand shoved between her thighs and cupped her pubic bone. "I can give you what you want then, baby. Come to Daddy," he crooned at her.

Waking from her frozen horror, Marguerite yelped in shame and embarrassment, and jumped backwards, only to be caught by Franz's young companion. He held her by the elbows as Franz came nearer, this time shoving his body right up against hers. She was forced back against the blond soldier, whilst Franz ground his very clear erection against her hip.

"No, please no." She could hear herself sobbing, although she knew it to be futile. She could feel them feeding on her fear. The blond boy's breath was warm on her neck; she could feel his panting moving her hair. She twisted violently in his arms to free herself, but his hands were brutal, his thumbs digging deeply into her elbows. She was thin and light and no match for his fit, well-fed body.

Franz was unbuttoning his flies. She saw his erection burst

from the confines of his trousers. Slowly the blond boy behind her forced her to bend forward, shoving her face into Franz's groin. She could smell him, a pungent blend of stale urine and sexual arousal.

"Open your mouth, little girl," urged Franz. "Be a good girl for Daddy." Her face was rubbing on his erection now, and she felt herself gagging.

She shut her eyes and mindlessly kept up her plaintive begging. "Please no, please no, please ..." If she could have summoned the will to scream, she would have, but she was too afraid to open her mouth so wide. Her arms were twisted brutally up behind her back. She felt herself begin to topple, both physically and mentally. The realisation of just how vulnerable she was and how easily this could be done to her was something that would haunt her later.

She was released suddenly and stumbled forward, sagging for a moment in shock, then shakily straightening herself up. Slowly she opened her eyes to see her tormentors both standing to attention. Franz was hastily buttoning up his trousers and attempting to give a soldier's formal salute to an officer at the same time.

The man climbed the steps slowly. He was older than the other two. He had authority over them, of that she had no doubt. Whether this was good or bad for her, she had no idea.

The man approached. "What have we here?" he asked the blond boy. Marguerite noted that the boy had turned pale.

"This miss was trying to obtain entrance to the harbour master," reported the boy formally. "I have been trying to find out her reasons."

"Have you?" asked the man mildly. He turned to Franz. "And you?" His tone was courteous but there was no mistaking the steel beneath it.

"I was assisting with the questioning," declared Franz who was now standing to attention. His eyes were facing forward, his carriage erect.

Marguerite gazed downwards at that other part of Franz's person that had so recently been erect, and became aware that the officer's eyes had made the same journey.

"Now that both these soldiers have so assiduously interrogated you, fraulein," said the officer, "how may we be of assistance to you?"

She looked up at him. His eyes seemed kind, although there was a latent anger there. It didn't seem to be directed at her so she decided to trust her instincts.

"I am looking for my father, sir," she said falteringly. "He went out yesterday and never returned. And he would have, he should have ..." she stumbled on the words, aware of how difficult it might be to make a stranger aware of the urgency of the situation.

"Come with me, fraulein," he said. "We will go and see the harbour master together. I was just going there myself." He said something in swift German to the two soldiers which made them stiffen to attention and salute. Then he turned and escorted her inside.

She went with him into the building, and he led her down the dark corridor to a wooden door marked 'Harbour Master'. The man behind the desk was short, wide, with greying hair. He looked up as they entered and smiled slightly at the officer before standing and formally saluting him. His blue eyes were dramatic in a deeply tanned, lined face. He stared with curiosity at Marguerite.

"This young lady is looking for her father. She wondered if he had been down on the wharves yesterday and if anyone knows what happened to him," said the officer. "You know everything that happens in your domain. I thought you could help her."

The harbour master stiffened. He continued to look at Marguerite, but he addressed the officer rapidly. "It is in relation to this that I requested you to come here, sir." He looked significantly at Marguerite.

The officer hesitated. "Step outside, miss, if you will. Just stand by the door." He saw her reluctance. "I swear no one will hurt you. If you are approached, you may call for me, do you understand?"

Marguerite nodded. She shut the door behind her. She tried to hear what was being said, but the door was too solid. Eventually it was opened by the harbour master who gestured her back in.

"Sit down," ordered the officer. He was standing by the window with the light behind him. She couldn't see his expression. "Tell her," he instructed the harbour master.

"A man was down at the harbour yesterday morning. He approached several captains, trying to find passage out of Poland." He glanced at the officer, who stood unmoving. "This is illegal, you understand, miss? But sometimes, for enough money, a captain can be bought." He sighed. "News of such things travels fast. I don't know how it happened, but somehow the authorities heard of this man's requests." He ran a hand over his hair. "As the man left the docks, he was arrested by the military. They brought him here. Why, I don't know. They accused this man of being a spy."

Marguerite stared at him. "He isn't a spy," she said. "He's a tailor. Father could prove that."

"They said he was a spy," the harbour master reiterated, looking embarrassed. "He was wearing a homburg hat. They said that was proof. That he was an intelligence agent."

Marguerite made a little moan of despair; she put her hand to her mouth to stop it escaping. "Where did they take him?" she asked.

There was a moment's silence in the room.

The officer stirred from his position by the window. "They took him to the wall at the back of this building, and they shot him, fraulein. If this man was your father, I am very sorry."

Marguerite heard the words but they didn't register. "You mean he's here, in the building?" she asked. "Can I see him, is he all right?"

"Miss, he's dead. They shot him dead," said the harbour master. "I am so sorry for your loss."

"Where is he?" asked Marguerite. "Where is he? I must see him." She couldn't believe it. Father wasn't dead. Whoever this man was, he must be a stranger.

The officer bent and said something rapidly into the ear of the harbour master, who nodded.

"It is necessary, fraulein," began the officer, "for someone to identify the body. Do you have family, fraulein; an older brother, perhaps?"

Marguerite shook her head. "I must see him," she repeated pleadingly. "Please let me see him."

"It will not be pleasant," the harbour master began. "He was shot miss; it's not nice for you to see."

Marguerite felt her control weakening. A scream seemed to be building in her head. "I must see him!" she shouted. "It's not my father. *Please!*"

The officer walked forward and took her arm. "Come then."

They walked further down the corridor, through a door leading to steps which took them down to a basement. Marguerite could smell the briny tang of the sea in the cold, damp room.

On a trestle table rested a human-shaped form, covered with a tarpaulin.

They walked towards it. The officer stood behind Marguerite with his hands resting lightly on her shoulders while the harbour master walked forward towards the body on the trestle.

"Ready?" he asked her.

She nodded dumbly.

He folded back the tarpaulin to the corpse's waist. Beneath, a white sheet covered the body to chest level, giving the bizarre impression that the corpse was tucked into bed. After a moment's pause, Marguerite moved forward to look, afraid of being sick, afraid of what she might see. The naked body lay in front of her. She could see that the face on its far side had been blown away. Mercifully, the side towards her was intact. There was more damage in the chest area, judging from the stains on the sheet. The hair was dark and matted. The skin of the body, or what she could see of it amongst the damage, was a sallow yellow-brown. Nothing like her father, she thought, trying to meld his well-groomed appearance with the naked flesh in front of her. The corpse looked entirely alien.

She shook her head, dizzy with relief. "No, it's not him," she stated positively.

The harbour master nodded and re-covered the body.

"These were his possessions." The officer led Marguerite to a chair, on which were piled clothes. Marguerite stared at the hat which sat on top of the pile. She knew that hat. She picked it up then put it to one side on the floor.

"Look through them, please," commanded the officer.

Her hands were shaking.

Marguerite picked up and unfolded trousers. She put her hand in the pockets. Small change and a pocket comb. In her mind's eye she could see her father carefully parting his hair and combing it flat.

She turned to the jacket. Inside was a label. Two intertwined initials – CK – her father's signature on the garments he made. She had a moment's wild surmise that a stranger had bought a suit from her father. She glanced back at the body.

It can't be, it can't be, was repeating over and over in her head. The disfigured, yellow-skinned stranger on the trestle could not be Father. Not the warm man, with warm flesh who hugged her, protected her. The man who had always made her feel special.

As she turned out the jacket pockets, item after item was familiar. There was the silver cigarette lighter Mother had given him, engraved with his initials, a pocket book, worn and faded. There was a silver card case. She opened it.

Charles Komarov, read the card, *Tailor of distinction*. Marguerite gave a small wail of horror. She had been fighting the evidence, she didn't want to believe it, and she didn't want to accept the pain. Suddenly, quite without volition, her knees started to buckle.

The officer grabbed her as she slumped and sat her on the chair. Kindly but firmly he pushed forward on the back of her neck, forcing her down so her head hung between her knees. "Just stay there for a few moments, fraulein," he said. "Let the blood get back to your head. The shock has made you faint."

Marguerite sat there. It could have been minutes, it could have been hours. She shut her eyes. Bright stars of light flashed behind her lids. She gripped the card case tightly, as if it held all her father's lost identity and personality.

She heard a few movements.

In a moment the harbour master squatted beside her with a glass of water in his hand. "Have a sip, miss. You've had a terrible shock."

Marguerite sat up cautiously. The officer had moved and was standing beside the makeshift bier. He had uncovered the face again.

"He's yellow," said Marguerite plaintively. "Why is he yellow? He doesn't look like Father."

The officer turned. "It's just bruising in the tissues. It happens after trauma." He re-covered the head. "Is this the first time you've seen a dead person?"

"What?" Marguerite's brain wasn't working. "Oh, no, I saw my grandfather. But he didn't look like that." She felt a sob building. She tried to keep it in, but it refused to be confined. Suddenly she was crying, big gasping sobs, like a baby. She couldn't stop them, nor the shaking, as she clutched the card case to her.

A conversation was going on over her head.

"There was nothing authorised about this execution. This was murder."

"I know, but there isn't the faintest possibility of bringing the perpetrators to justice. Our forces are in disarray and retreat. This could have been done by almost any squad out on the beat yesterday looking for a little light relief."

"At least we can get it recorded properly with the poor man's name."

"The girl?" The officer seemed concerned. "I can get her home. But you'll need to deal with the family for a funeral. The troops and I will be gone this afternoon. It was only chance that I got your message this morning and had the time to spare." He sighed.

Marguerite's sobs were getting a little less hysterical. The officer touched her on her shoulder. "Come, fraulein. I will take you back to your family. My car is waiting outside."

The harbour master gathered the possessions together. He used Father's belt to tie them together into a rough bundle. "Here, miss. Do you know where you are staying?"

Marguerite looked at him. She had no idea at first, but then a name came to her. "Mrs Keppel's boarding house."

"Ah, I know it," said the harbour master. Directions were given to the officer who helped Marguerite to her feet and led her up the stairs. She turned at the top to look back and tried to say goodbye to her father. The idea didn't make any sense. She felt exhausted.

The officer brought her to his car. His driver put her in it and took her back up the road to the boarding house. The driver helped her out and handed her the bundle while the officer knocked on the door.

It seemed he must have explained the outline of events to Mrs Keppel, because although she couldn't remember getting there, the next thing Marguerite remembered was sitting in the kitchen, wrapped in blankets, watching Mother cry. At least she hadn't had to tell her the news, she thought.

Edith's grief was terrible and unrestrained. She was comforted and attended to by Mrs Keppel. If that comfort involved rather a lot of vodka, then the ladies grieved together late into the night.

Marguerite found she couldn't endure witnessing her mother's raw grief. She went to their room, climbed onto her bed, still wrapped in the blankets, turned her head to the wall and shut her eyes. Sometime later Katya climbed in beside her and curled into the pit of her stomach, a small, brave piece of comfort on that lonely night.

CHAPTER
FIFTEEN

To London, 1944.

DAYS BLURRED AND PASSED. THINGS GOT
done. Marguerite had no precise recollection of them.
The harbour master and his wife took control of the
arrangements. Their name was Srkowski, and while Mrs
Srkowski helped Edith and Marguerite lay the body out and
prepare the tea for after the funeral, the men organised the
formalities. Due ceremony was paid to the deceased and practical
help given to the family. The murder, pointless as it was, had
shocked the little harbour town. The seamen felt a responsibility
for a stranger murdered in their seaport, and pity for the family.
Marguerite's plight the day of the identification had shocked
even a community used to German brutality.

The Germans had finally pulled out of town that afternoon,
allowing a brief hiatus before the next army took up occupation.

The day after the funeral there was a knock on Mrs Keppel's
door. Two men stood there asking for admission. When they
entered the kitchen, Marguerite was able to recognise one of
them as her advisor from the docks. Apparently Mr Srkowski

had put out a discreet word that the survivors of the Komarov family had plans to travel, of the 'unorthodox' kind.

It seemed certain sailors from the port chanced their fishing fortunes on the open sea. Sometimes bad weather affected these ventures to such a degree that said sailors could end up in ports in foreign places simply to avoid the storms of the seas. It might also happen, that sometimes, and of course only in the interests of safety, these sailors might meet up with other vessels on the high seas. They might succour each other in times of need, as indeed was a sailor's duty to all in peril at sea. In short, if the Komarov family would like to join the ship for a fishing excursion, well, who could say where the fates could take them?

The two men stood, uneasily, in the Keppel kitchen. Having made their speech, it seemed to be the end of their social chitchat.

Mrs Keppel, Mother and Marguerite looked back at them. There was silence for a while. Marguerite looked round at the other women to see who would break it. When it seemed obvious that neither of the older women would take control of the situation, she spoke up.

"How much?" she asked bluntly.

As the boys had got together at the pub and passed the hat round to help the family, given that the breadwinner had been murdered … nothing at all. Anyway, if they wanted to travel, the offer was open.

Edith was still silent.

Marguerite spoke up again. "When do you plan to leave?"

"First thing tomorrow, just before first light. You would need to be at the docks at four-thirty. You get into the cabin, stay there, and it's a normal fishing trip for us. But you'll need to arrive in the dark, and we'll leave in the dark. If we cling to the coastline, we avoid any country's radar."

Marguerite turned to her mother. Now, surely, was the time for discussion and debate about their future? Neither woman had ventured into this territory yet, but it was clear it was only a matter of time before it became essential.

"What do we say, Mother?" she asked in quiet voice.

Edith spread her hands. "I don't know. If Charles were here

…" She tailed off and started crying helplessly. Mrs Keppel put her arm round her shoulders.

Marguerite looked at her. Pity warred with rage and resentment. She still half hated her mother for forcing her through the experiences of a couple of days ago, and she didn't want to be the one making the decisions now. There was only one adult left in the family. Mother had to make the choices for them.

Everyone in the room focused on Edith, waiting for her. But Edith, far from making any decision, was crying for the life she had lost. The minutes dragged on. Marguerite could see the men becoming restless. Not only did they not like being present in this haven of women, but they were practical men, with practical issues facing them. Either they had passengers on the morrow, or they didn't. She could see them working towards the phrases that would ensure their exit.

"We'll be there," she said firmly.

The whole room stared at her.

"What?" said Mrs Keppel. "I don't think, dear, that your mother is in any state to travel."

"We go, with these men, tomorrow," said Marguerite flatly. "I suggest an early night. We'd better be packed and ready to go."

A thought occurred to her. "I don't know how we're going to get our luggage down to the docks."

"That's all right," said Gregory. "The harbour master offered to pick you all up, if you want to go." Gregory's face creased in worry as he looked at Edith. "You do understand this is a secret matter, don't you?"

But Marguerite had no intention now of failing in this venture. "We understand perfectly and will be ready just after four for the harbour master. Please let him know we will be here, and we're very grateful for his help."

And so it was that the Komarovs, after a fond farewell was taken of Mrs Keppel, stood on the deck of the *Riga* in the early hours of the morning, heading out to sea.

Much to Marguerite's distress, the minute they were free of the protection of the harbour walls, the movement of the waves began to work on her stomach. Mother and Katya succumbed first, their nausea heightened by the unavoidable smell of fish throughout the boat.. As the swells became bigger, Marguerite felt her own insides churning. It did nothing for her spirits when Gregory popped his head around the door and assured her it was a wonderful day for sailing and conditions could get much worse.

He took one look at her face and laughed. "It truly is a good day." He smiled in sympathy. "It will just take you a while to find your sea legs."

Late that night the family were transferred from the *Riga* to another larger fishing vessel, this time operating out of Denmark. Marguerite soon realised this was a formal operation – a line of resistance operations that spread across Europe, as an underground railway, ferrying information and people. She said goodbye to Gregory and the crew of the *Riga*, wondering if she would ever be able to thank the men who were now returning to a country being reinvaded by Russia.

It took the family three months to make it to England and even longer to make it through the formalities of entry as refugees and finally settle in London.

By the time they had found lodgings and taken stock of their situation, certain things became evident.

Edith Komarov had relinquished her role as head of her family. While she was prepared to provide care for Katya, she was no longer capable of assisting Marguerite with the rather pressing problem of their finances. When Marguerite approached her to discuss such necessities as paying rent, buying food and purchasing clothing for the little family, Edith simply gave her a blank stare. When pressed, she burst into tears again. Marguerite noted sourly to herself that this was Mother's favourite way of avoiding unpleasantness. Her sympathy for her mother faded fast as she was forced to confront Edith's selfishness and idleness. While Charles had been there as her prop and hero, Edith had flowered. With him gone, she lost the will and energy to direct her own life. She had no drive to direct her children, but followed the strongest personality.

When they had sorted through Charles's effects, they had

discovered a little store of money in sterling currency. This sum allowed them to survive, if poorly, for the months of their travel but was fast running out. Charles's relations had helped them find lodgings, but after that their care and assistance had evaporated in the realities of life during a war.

England was poor, rationing in place, and its people xenophobic. Thanks to Grandfather Komarov, Marguerite's grasp of the language was fluent. Her accent, though, told against her. There was an unsaid suspicion the Komarovs could be Nazis. Marguerite went from one establishment to another seeking work. Her stitch craft was exemplary – Father had seen to that. She knew how to set a sleeve or tailor a shirt, but there were others also seeking work. Men were returning from the battle zones, and unemployment was high.

Marguerite returned home one evening to their lodgings, tired and disheartened. Her feet ached from walking the pavements, and the knowledge of failure clung to her like a wet shawl. She saw bags and a suitcase in the hall. Skirting round them, she entered the living room where she found a strange man being introduced to the residents as a lodger. She was included in the introductions to Mr Schwartz. A Jew, originally from Germany, he had managed to make his way to London and safety. He, too, was a tailor and was setting up shop with his cousin as a gentleman's tailor.

Marguerite, her head resting against the back of the stained old sofa she was sitting on, felt too weary to make yet another plea for employment that would be rejected. It was so unfair. In a better world someone would be looking after her.

"My daughter is a skilled seamstress, Mr Schwartz," said Mother. "She is looking for work. Have you a place in your establishment for her?"

Marguerite opened her eyes wide. It was unlike Mother to be so direct. Mr Schwartz looked at the girl slumped on the sofa. She didn't look very prepossessing; besides, he made it his business not to react to pleas like these.

Marguerite looked at him directly. "Mr Schwartz, I understand you will say no because there are no jobs and you wouldn't employ me anyway. Mother is right. I am very skilled, I learned from my father who, like you, was a tailor of the highest standard. I can show you suits we have upstairs that show the quality of workmanship our family prided itself on." Marguerite felt tears gathering. She must be run-down, she thought. She had learned over the last few months never to cry in public.

"If there is a position you could give me, I would be in your debt." She put her chin up and blinked her eyes fiercely so the tears didn't fall and give her away.

Mr Schwartz looked at her in silence. He understood pride and the pain of its loss. History hadn't been kind to him either. His mind sifted around for a while, chasing the elusive quality she represented. Gallantry: she was gallant, he thought. His shoulders sagged.

He sighed deeply and saw that she had seen the sigh and misread it. He watched her face turn to brittle ice and almost fell over himself to remedy the situation.

"Come with me tomorrow," he said. "I'll see if you are any use to me."

Marguerite blinked at him. She had expected rejection, and even this faint encouragement was more than she could comprehend. "Tomorrow? Oh, thank you so much." The smile that lit up her pale face was dazzling.

Mr Schwartz felt rewarded, if only in that minute, for what was clearly a silly offer on his part. Still, the girl could probably do something round the place and cost only pin money.

He smiled back at her. "Tomorrow," he echoed.

CHAPTER
SIXTEEN

London, 1944.

MARGUERITE FOLLOWED MR SCHWARTZ TO WORK the next morning. He introduced her to his partner, showed her round the rooms and set her to work in the sewing room. If his partner, Max Bloomfield, was distressed at her presence, he was kind enough not to show it.

She was put to work stitching shirts. Restrictive clothing rationing was in place and materials hard to get. It was impressed on her that quality and extreme care were critical for her place in the organisation. There was no tolerance for mistakes, because there were no spare resources for mistakes to be made on. She was very conscious that she had to earn her place, and at first barely spoke to either of her employers.

The quality of her work spoke for her. By the end of her first week, the partners knew they had struck gold. She was neat in her work, quick-fingered and tidy. She made cups of tea for the partners, ran errands as needed and shadowed Len Schwartz as he cut the precious materials into jackets and trousers. At the end of each day she swept the sewing room clean and saved any scraps of cloth or thread. There were strict government rules about styles for clothes to limit material use. No pleats, no creases, no turn-ups on trousers were allowed. Buttons were restricted.

"I am an artist," Max Bloomfield would moan. "How am I supposed to make well-fitting clothes with no cloth, eh?"

Marguerite smiled to herself. She was becoming fond of her employers.

Her work was fun but her family situation was less rosy. Katya was old enough to go to school, but Mother was resistant to parting with her 'baby'. Also there was the issue of where to send Katya to school. Her English was still broken, so she seemed very young for her six years of age. There were good schools, but they cost money. The state schools of the East End were, Mother declared in disgust, unfit to raise a puppy, let alone a cultured daughter of the Komarov family.

Marguerite blinked a little at their sudden pretention to culture, but she too had seen the slum schools as she walked past each day. She tried to imagine fragile Katya at one of these. She wondered what Father would have done but failed when she imagined him accepting a working class accent in his daughters.

It was a client who came to Bloomfield and Schwartz who provided the solution. He was on the board of a charity school just outside London and talking freely to Mr Schwartz when Marguerite overheard the conversation.

"We take charity children. There are so many from decent families who've been orphaned by this war and need a proper education and a place to grow up safely. But our numbers are down. Even though we're forty miles from London, there are people who feel we are too close to the centre of war operations for us to be safe. Ridiculous!" he harrumphed. "We even take refugees."

Mr Schwartz, busy measuring neck diameter, paused and looked at Marguerite pointedly. "I think my assistant here has a sister who needs a place at a decent educational establishment."

Marguerite was rapidly assessed by the client. "I'm Harrison," he said, presumably approving of what he saw. "Tell me about your sister. How old is she?"

"Six, sir," said Marguerite. "She hasn't been to school yet. We only arrived in London a few months ago, and she has been learning English with my mother. Do you have to be a complete orphan for your school ,sir? Father is dead, but we still have our mother."

"No," said Mr Harrison. "Not necessarily a 'complete orphan', as you call it. When the breadwinner is killed, then sometimes a child might just as well be an orphan."

"May I tell my mother about it, sir?" she asked.

"I'll be staying at the Devonshire Club tonight. If your mother is interested then get her to contact me there. If your sister is suitable, and your mother and I are in agreement, it may be that she could get a place at Reading. Here is my card," he said, handing it over.

Marguerite pocketed it, and the measuring and fitting continued.

After Mr Harrison left, Mr Schwartz looked at her seriously. "I don't usually let my workers interrupt clients. But for you, my little Marguerite, this could be the answer you and your mother look for. Your little sister has got to go to school. She can't hang around that boarding house forever, you know."

Mother, when consulted, said she couldn't bear to part with her daughter, and Katya flatly refused to go to boarding school, separated from her family. The ensuing discussion involved most of the inhabitants of the boarding house, because the Komarov family argument was too loud and emotional to be kept behind the closed door of their own room. Mother spent a lot of time in tears, accusing Marguerite of unnaturally trying to part her from her youngest child. Katya wailed in sympathy.

"But my dear Madam Komarov, you know very well that Katya must go to school," said Mr Schwartz, who belatedly joined the argument. "It is the law of this country. So the decision is quite simple. Will you send her to a day school close by in the East End which is rough and where the children urinate in the gutter? Or will you accept the opportunity to let your daughter learn the ways of a lady and get a decent education at a Christian school?"

He shook his finger at Edith.

"If I were your husband, madam, I would urge you to do the correct thing for your daughter, however hard the sacrifice you have to make." He stopped, but to Marguerite's amazement, far from resenting his intervention, Edith seemed to respond to it positively.

"Do you really think this would be the right thing?" she asked him.

"But of course, madam," he replied. "I believe you know this as well. Sometimes we have to be brave for our children so they can also grow up to be brave and strong."

So the decision was made. Katya was going to Reading orphanage. The weeks before were busy as mother and daughter organised sufficient clothes and uniform for the little girl. Marguerite sewed a lot of it in the evenings, making up the necessities for school life.

There were blouses, vests, knickers, skirts and hair ribbons. Mother sorted the items into piles while Marguerite climbed to the top of the wardrobe to bring down the suitcases. Some had been partially emptied of their contents when the family arrived in London, but the small size of their room meant that, with the exception of everyday clothes, the other cases and bags remained packed and had been stacked up there out of the way.

Marguerite had raided their contents for material to make up some of Katya's requirements. A couple of Father's shirts, pullovers and suits had provided the basic materials. It gave Marguerite a funny feeling to be cutting up her father's clothes, even in such a good cause. She didn't make eye contact with Mother, because she was pretty sure she was feeling the same way.

"What's in here?" she asked her mother when she came across the tin box her father had carried.

Mother looked up. "I don't know. That was your father's. Probably some family stuff he brought with him. Papers, I suppose. I think he once said he had it as a boy when he came from Russia with Grandpa Komarov."

"It's quite heavy." Marguerite tried to open it. "It's locked; do you have a key?"

Mother looked round vaguely from her work. "No, I suppose it's on a key ring somewhere. Don't bother about it now; just bring down a big enough case for all these things of Katya's."

Marguerite shoved the tin box back and brought down a battered suitcase. She checked its locks. "At least this one still closes properly, and we can always strap it shut to make sure it holds."

Marguerite and Edith travelled with Katya on the train. It was hard to leave the little girl behind when they said their goodbyes. As they parted, Mother became quite emotional, clutching her daughter to her breast and crying over her.

Marguerite was embarrassed. "Come on, Mother," she whispered, tugging at her sleeve. "It's only making things worse for Katya, and you're causing a scene."

Mother released Katya with a final hug and stood up. She looked round at the other families disparagingly. "That's because I have a warm Polish heart," she declared to Marguerite. "Not like these English, who are so cold. You're starting to turn English yourself, Marguerite. Cold, that's what you are," she scolded.

Marguerite was pleased to be on the train back to London. She reassured herself that Katya would now have friends and companions of her own age, and proper schooling. It helped ease the guilt she felt about her little sister's grief.

CHAPTER
SEVENTEEN

London, 1945.

WITH KATYA GONE, EDITH'S ROLE HAD to be revised. Without a clinging daughter in tow to define her days, she had no fixed purpose in life. She was listless, pining for Katya, a moody, pitiful woman, ready to tell anyone foolish enough to give her an ear just how hard her life was.

Marguerite was describing this to Mr Bloomfield. "She stops just short of wringing her hands," she exclaimed in exasperation. "There are other women out there who have lost husbands and sweethearts in the war, but they carry on without all this fuss."

Mr Bloomfield regarded her shrewdly. "Is it her you worry for, sweetheart, or is it for yourself, because she embarrasses you with all these scenes?"

"Both," said Marguerite shortly.

She was finding their situation claustrophobic. Their mutual care of Katya had allowed them to coexist peacefully enough, and there had been no financial alternative to the three of them sharing a room. With Katya gone, there was no intermediary, and the friction was getting worse each day. Edith wanted the respect due a parent, which Marguerite refused to grant her. She was the breadwinner and decision-maker for the family and wasn't going to concede her position to anyone.

"Don't you think you should get a job?" she asked her mother. "It would be good for you to get out of the boarding house each day. And we need the money."

Edith just sighed and went, as her daughter put it, 'all European'. She would put her hand to her heart and murmur, "You don't know how I suffer. You young ones, you can't feel the pain."

Marguerite saw this as amateur dramatics. Life was for the living. There was no place in it for the living dead.

She said as much to Mr Schwartz, expecting a laugh from him. Instead he turned to her in such real anger that for a moment she almost thought he was going to hit her.

"How dare you judge her pain? No, you don't share it, whatever you think. You feel your own pain, not hers. Yes, you bear yours with courage and dignity. You engage in life with appetite and energy, and you work towards your future." He carried on in a softer tone. "Your mother has none of those attributes. She lost her husband to death, and now her daughters, to life." He smiled sadly. "She is not a very brave woman, nor a very intelligent one. She is limited in all of her abilities, but she loved your father dearly, and now that is over. You have a future, *Liebchen*; she does not, and she knows it. That is what she is mourning."

Marguerite was abashed. She respected Mr Schwartz, recognising his kindness to her when she had needed it. It was in Marguerite's nature never to forget someone who was good to her. If she thought no more kindly of her mother, she was more circumspect about what she said in the future.

To her surprise, she came home two days later to be greeted with an announcement that Edith now had a job. How it occurred, Marguerite found hard to fathom, but it turned out an aristocratic Polish *emigré*, a countess no less, had needed a companion, and Edith had been chosen for the role. When Marguerite enquired as to just how this happy introduction between the two had occurred, Edith grew vague. Something to do with the women's refugee association, she muttered.

It did seem as if Mother had found the one position she could shine in. From what Marguerite could glean, most of her 'work' consisted of sharing the experience of being a refugee and the horrors involved with her employer. The countess had been lucky enough to be visiting England when the Germans had marched north into Poland, but had lost many of her family in the war.

Edith's position widened the gap developing between Marguerite and her mother. Daily conversations with the countess were returning Edith to her roots. She was walking Polish streets, talking the Polish language, discussing Polish politics.

Marguerite was adopting English ways where she could. She had trouble fathoming the class system that underpinned English life, but she had no doubt which end of that system she intended to be. Her spoken English had improved, and, with one exception, her accent was getting lighter. She had found Bloomfield and Schwartz's customers liked a European woman attending to their fashion needs. A European accent, it seemed, was a definite advantage in the clothing world, conveying a prewar world both glamorous and cosmopolitan. So at work Marguerite maintained her foreign accent as a selling point.

With both women working, their financial constraints eased for the first time since they had been in England.

Marguerite approached their landlady, Mrs Hogg, to book the right to take the next spare room that came up in the boarding house. This permission granted, Marguerite started on the process of softening up Mother.

"You know, Mother, if we had more space, we could unpack all your clothes," she began. "We've got summer coming up, and we could pick them over and make them up like new again. We just can't spread them out, cramped up as we are."

Edith nodded a wan agreement. New clothes would be nice, particularly as she would be accompanying the countess around now, and they often stopped at Lyons or some other corner house.

The next Sunday afternoon, her landlady informed her that

two rooms in the house were coming vacant in the next week. Mr Croft, the travelling salesman, was moving on, and old Mrs Jones, the boarding house's eldest resident, was being moved by her family back into the family home.

"You can have your pick, lovey," said Mrs Hogg.

Marguerite thought quickly. Mr Croft's was the larger room, but Mrs Jones' was on the south side of the house, with big windows that overlooked the small park next door. Light poured into her bedroom, and Marguerite made her decision before the choice got taken from her.

"I'll take Mrs Jones' please," she said. Then she braced herself to go and tell Mother.

Edith, encountered in the kitchen, was less resistant than Marguerite had feared. "That's nice, dear," she murmured vaguely, when Marguerite said she'd be moving her things out of their shared room. "Just remember to keep it tidy, and don't clutter it up like you have ours."

"And that," said Marguerite in amazement to her employers the next day, "was the only thing she said."

"Maybe she, too, is glad to have the extra privacy," suggested Mr Bloomfield. "And when your sister comes home in the holidays, there will be more room for all of you."

Marguerite shrugged. "Maybe, or maybe it's because I said I would sort out some summer clothes for her. Who knows with Mother?"

The next day, Marguerite stood politely with the rest as they waved Mrs Jones goodbye and then went to take possession of her own space. She had already told Mrs Hogg she was happy to do all the cleaning of the room, and it was with a happy heart that she polished and hoovered the little room, and made up the bed.

Her kingdom now consisted of a bed, a dressing table with a big round mirror, and a wardrobe in the corner. She transferred her possessions across from Edith's room and arranged them carefully. It was amazing how proprietorial she felt about her space and her few belongings, now she could legitimately call them her own, rather than an extension of her Mother's.

Edith, at first inclined to be indignant as her things were ransacked to furnish Marguerite's room, suddenly realised this was a heaven-sent opportunity to clear out clutter and began to enter into the spirit of sharing, as she now called it. Edith got sniffy when Marguerite declined to take possession of all the suitcases on the grounds that they wouldn't fit in the room. Compromise was reached when Marguerite took the old tin box, which she set up as a bedside table, and a couple of smaller suitcases that could fit on top of the small wardrobe.

"We really must find the key to this one day," said Marguerite as she covered it over with a cloth to make a proper table of it and arranged her current book and a tumbler of water on it.

Later that night she lay in her own bed, in her own room, looking at the different shadows and shapes in the muted darkness. The blackout rules had recently been downgraded to dim-out rules, and some house lights still made their way under her bedroom door, allowing the silhouettes of the furniture to fall into deeper shadow. It was the first time she had slept alone in a room since her childhood in Poland. Then she had been afraid of ghosts in the corner and ghoulies under the bed. She smiled at the memory.

There was a feeling of optimism in the air. The war was moving towards its closing days – everyone could feel it – and though the reports of fighting were in some cases worse than ever, there was renewed hope that the men would return from the war soon and life would return to normal.

CHAPTER EIGHTEEN

London, 1945.

EDITH WENT DOWN WITH THE FLU, and Marguerite, enormously grateful not to be sharing a room, dutifully brought her hot cups of tea and changed the sheets. More than half the other residents took to their beds with the infection.

Marguerite was at a loose end one Sunday afternoon when there came a knock on the front door. Mrs Hogg didn't answer it so Marguerite got up and opened the door.

Facing her was a young woman not much older than herself. Her red hair was in a short bob and flamed like a bright halo round her vital and animated little face. Even at first meeting, it was hard to miss the energy that poured from her.

"I saw in the window that you have a room to let?" enquired the stranger. "I'm Peggy," she said. "Is it still available?" She spoke with a soft Scots accent.

Marguerite opened the door wider and let her in. "If you'd just come through," she said, "I'll go and get the landlady for you."

Mrs Hogg was duly fetched. "What can I do for you, miss?" she said, inspecting the girl in front of her. Something about the newcomer fascinated Marguerite so she stayed, although good manners should have made her discreetly withdraw.

"I'm Peggy Darling," replied the young woman. "Is your room still free? I need a room for the next few months. I've got references," she said helpfully.

"What are you doing in London?" asked Mrs Hogg.

"I'm in the theatre. I'm in the review at the Odeon," said Peggy proudly. "It's expected to run for months, and I need somewhere to stay."

"On the stage," repeated Mrs Hogg with a sniff. "Let's look at your references then." Whatever she saw in them must have reassured her, because she became slightly more conciliatory. "It's two weeks rent in advance, and then you pay weekly," she said. "If you default, you're out, right away."

Peggy nodded. "That is fine," she said.

"I know theatre folk," said Mrs Hogg gloomily. "The whole lot of you are like gypsies, rich one minute, poor the next." She paused for thought. "All right, I'll show you the room, and you can decide if you want it."

She took Peggy to the room, and indicated the various facilities of the house. Peggy agreed it was satisfactory and that she would take it straight away, if that was all right, so she could move in that evening, it being her night off.

Mrs Hogg sighed but agreed. The agreement was signed, cash changed hands and Mrs Hogg left Peggy to move her belongings in at her convenience.

Marguerite offered to help, but it turned out Peggy's sole possessions were in the carpet bag she was carrying. "I have to travel light," she explained. "I spend all my time in digs, so I can't carry too much round with me."

She was busy unpacking a large box of cosmetics from the bag as she spoke. "The most important things really are my 'audition' costume, my dancing shoes and my makeup, so I always lug them about with me. The rest of the time I spend either in rehearsal rags or on stage, in costume, so I don't need that much." She shoved some underwear in a drawer, a nightie under her pillow and smiled in satisfaction.

"That's it. I'm now at home again." She looked at Marguerite. "What about you. What do you do?"

"I work for some tailors," replied Marguerite. "I'm a dressmaker really, but I help with the tailoring. One day I want to sew high-fashion clothes, but at the moment I'm happy where I am."

"Are you really a dressmaker?" asked Peggy in delight. "That's wonderful. We always need things fixed or altered, so maybe I can get you some work, that is, if you want it?"

Marguerite agreed that yes, she probably would. She was fascinated by this bright, exciting girl who seemed so poised and independent.

Over the course of that evening Peggy told Marguerite her story. She was a dominee's daughter from Scotland, 'the Border Country' as she described it, who had been drawn to the theatre. Against her family's wishes she had started on the stage in local pantomime but soon decided to try for fame and fortune further south. She had now been in London a year, surviving at first from hand to mouth, with the occasional walk-on part, or a chorus line turn for a few weeks. Her best break had been with a travelling company that toured Shakespeare to schools in the Counties.

"I got all the ingénue parts, you know – Ophelia, Juliet," she said.

Marguerite wasn't familiar with Shakespeare, but she nodded.

"It's been hard work, but fun, said Peggy. "My constant fear is I'll fail and have to return, tail between my legs, to the manse in Scotland."

A couple of days ago her luck had changed, and she had won a permanent place on the cast of the revue at the Odeon.

"I have to dance and sing, and I've got a small solo part, so it's really exciting," she confided to Marguerite. "I feel I'm on my way now. If I can make friends and contacts through this role, then things are going to be on the up and up."

She seemed to find Marguerite's story every bit as exotic and fascinating as Marguerite found hers. She exclaimed with horror when Marguerite talked about her father's death.

"That is so terrible," she exclaimed. "You poor darling, and then after all that, you make it to dear old England in the middle of a war. What an adventure for you all."

By the end of the evening, Marguerite felt that she and Peggy were friends. It felt good to have someone to talk 'girl talk' to and someone whom she could admire.

Peggy's work hours meant she was a nocturnal creature. She was never home before two o'clock in the morning, so the two girls' lives rarely coincided. Still, Peggy had Sunday and Monday off, which meant they could at least spend Sunday afternoon together.

Marguerite came home from Bloomfield and Schwartz's to find the house in an uproar. She traced the hubbub to the kitchen where she found her mother, in floods of tears, being consoled by Mrs Hogg, whilst the other residents gathered round, forcefully expressing various opinions. Marguerite pushed through the huddle of people to get to her mother, quite frantic with worry.

"Thank heavens you're here," exclaimed Mrs Hogg. "She's been hysterical. I can't work out what's wrong. She doesn't seem to be hurt."

"Mother, what happened? Have you heard from Katya? Mother, what's the problem?" she asked, kneeling beside her. Her worst fear was that Katya had had some terrible accident. The guilt of sending her to school would then haunt her forever. "Mother, what's wrong?" she repeated.

Edith threw her arms around her daughter. "The countess has gone," she sobbed. "I'm fired, and maybe she wasn't a countess anyway." She was almost incoherent with emotion.

"Sorry," said Marguerite. "I mean, I beg your pardon. What do you mean, the countess has gone? Gone where?"

Between sobs, the story emerged. Edith had returned to work after her recovery from the flu, to find the countess had vacated her apartment, with no notification left for her companion. None of the neighbours seemed to know where she had gone, or indeed anything very much about her at all.

"But you telephoned her when you were sick, didn't you, Mother?" queried Marguerite, furrowing her brow over the problem. "What did she say then?"

"She seemed fine. Genuinely sympathetic to me," sobbed Edith. "She told me to take off as much time as I needed as she didn't want to be infected by me."

"Well, maybe she's gone away for a few days," said Marguerite. "Just because she wasn't there doesn't mean anything. She may not have expected you back so quickly. That doesn't mean you are fired."

It turned out, though, that Edith had checked the apartment and it was empty. There were no furnishings, no clothes, paintings and no forwarding address that Edith had been able to discover.

"When you met her and took the position who introduced you?" asked Marguerite. "Maybe they'll know where to find her."

But, as Edith tried to explain, it seemed the situation was even more mysterious.

There had been no intermediary. Nor had Edith found this placement through the good offices of an employment agency or a refugee channel, as Marguerite had assumed.

The countess had introduced herself to Edith directly. They had met by chance at a tea house, where the countess had commented on Edith's accent and fallen into conversation with her, as a fellow Pole. The job offer had flowed from there.

"So," said Marguerite slowly, "you accepted a job with this woman, knowing nothing about her at all."

"She looked very respectable," wailed Edith. "She always dressed beautifully, and we went to nice places for tea when we went out."

Mrs Hogg sniffed. "She sounds like a con artist to me. What did she want from you?"

"Yes," cut in Marguerite. "Did you give her anything? Did she ask you for anything, or make you do anything?"

"We just talked," said Edith. "She wanted to know what had happened to us in the war, that sort of thing. She was interested in our family history, so I told her a few stories, that's all. But she didn't want anything from me, or try to sell me anything. I'm not stupid," she said indignantly. "I just thought she was lonely and wanted to speak to someone from the old country. And now I've lost my job." A fresh burst of sobbing ensued.

"Why would she be interested in our family history?" wondered Marguerite aloud. "Did you ask her why she was interested?"

"Well, no," said Edith. "She was interested in how your father had been a refugee when he arrived in Poland, and she was interested in the stories about old Grandfather Komarov. It amused her he was a saddle-maker to the old Tsar."

"Did you find out anything about her?" asked Mrs Hogg.

"She said she had family in Poland, and she certainly knew the place, because we could talk about streets and places we both knew. I thought she was bored and just liked my stories. She wondered why Grandfather Komarov had stopped his travels with Charles in Poland rather than carrying on further to the West. She seemed genuinely interested in me."

"Grandfather always said they settled in Poland because Grandmother was ill and they couldn't travel further," said Marguerite. "So I don't see how that could be of any use to a con artist." She looked up at Mrs Hogg. "What do you think?"

Mrs Hogg shrugged her shoulders. "I don't know, lovey, but something smells fishy."

Edith blew her nose.

"You'll find another job," Marguerite assured her. "Next time go through an agency. At least you'll know the client has been screened in some way." She was puzzling over the affair. "I still can't see why she did what she did, though. Was she committing a crime against someone else, do you think?"

But Edith was adamant. Her role was to be a companion. She had met no one else in the countess's company, and their main interaction had involved what Edith thought of as gossip.

"It's quite obvious you told your countess a lot more about our affairs than she told you about hers," said Marguerite tartly. "Not that I can see anything very interesting about our affairs anyway. But maybe you need to be more careful in future, Mother."

"I'll never trust anyone again," declared Edith.

"You'll feel better once you've got another job," said

Marguerite. "Not everyone is as dodgy as your countess, Mother. Just go out tomorrow and start looking for something else." Marguerite was already starting to calculate the difference to their lives that Mother's loss of income could mean. The sooner Edith found another position, the better.

"That's right, dear," said Mrs Hogg. "Always get straight back on the horse when you've had a fall."

CHAPTER NINETEEN

London, 1945.

MARGUERITE WATCHED PEGGY PUT ON 'HER FACE' from the big makeup kit. She had never tried cosmetics, but they fascinated her.

Peggy, checking her face out in the mirror, noticed Marguerite's fascination. "Do you want to try some?" she asked.

"Oh no, no I couldn't," said Marguerite hastily, her mind conjuring up Edith's reaction to her becoming a 'painted lady'.

"Don't be silly. It's all part of growing up," said Peggy confidently. She looked carefully at Marguerite's face. "You know, I think we could make you look pretty stunning if we tried."

Marguerite blushed a little at her words but made no resistance as Peggy approached her.

"Don't worry," Peggy assured her. "I'm very good at this. First of all, let's get rid of these. Very demure, I'm sure, but two plaits and a centre parting aren't doing a lot for you, you know."

Marguerite loosened her hair and waited while Peggy brushed it out and back off her face.

Peggy was humming to herself all the time, shifting Marguerite's hair back, up and to the side. "You could have it cut, you know," she said at last.

"But I like long hair," wailed Marguerite.

"OK," said Peggy, recognising defeat. "But having it parted in the middle isn't suiting the shape of your face." She positioned Marguerite in front of the mirror. "Look, you've got quite a round face. It's cute and it's pretty, but you've got to help it out a bit. Brushed back is good, or you could go for the Veronica Lake look. See?" She lifted Marguerite's heavy hair to the side and started pinning it into waves.

"Actually," she announced after a while, "you've got really nice hair. It's lush and beautifully shiny," she said. "It would look great under stage lights."

Marguerite blushed. Personal compliments weren't something she was used to.

After a bit of fiddling, Peggy stood back and looked at her. "You know, you look pretty stunning. Let's just put a tiny bit of makeup on to finish it off." Marguerite drew back in alarm. "Don't worry," said Peggy grinning. "I've got little sisters too. All you need is just a dash of eye shadow to deepen your eyes, and a smudge of mascara. You won't even know it's there, you'll just look amazing." Peggy's slim fingers moved lightly over Marguerite's face. "There, now look at yourself," she commanded.

Marguerite looked in the mirror. The girl staring back was definitely her but with little trace of the refugee schoolgirl left. The woman in the mirror was young and fresh, well groomed, unaffected and pretty. Her eyes 'popped', her skin was more even and her hair balanced the shape of her face. She searched for the words and failed. "I look ..."

"See," said Peggy, "you look amazing, like I told you. You also look classy. Not that you are overstated or anything, but you look pretty swish." She scrutinised her friend. "I think you'd even pass muster at the old manse, and that's not easy, let me tell you."

Marguerite continued staring at herself in the mirror. Would she be brave enough to face her mother looking like this?

As if she read her thoughts, Peggy said, "Come on, let's go downstairs and get some tea, then we can go out for a walk and give your new style an airing."

Mrs Hogg was in the kitchen, presiding over the teapot. She looked up as the girls walked in, and her eyes widened when she saw Marguerite. "Goodness me!" she exclaimed. "You do look lovely. What a pretty young lady you make."

Marguerite blushed but was secretly relieved and delighted. "Peggy suggested I try something new."

"Well you look very nice," said Mrs Hogg firmly. "Quite grown-up."

The other residents all endorsed Mrs Hogg's approval, each one raising Marguerite's self-confidence.

The only dispiriting comment came, perhaps not surprisingly, from Edith. "My, oh my," she said thoughtfully, surveying her daughter.

"Do you like it, Mother?" asked Marguerite shyly.

As it happened, Edith was feeling rather vulnerable. The affair of her bogus job with the countess had humiliated her, and she knew she was on the back foot when it came to authority over her daughter.

"Well," said Edith at last. "It's certainly changed the way you look. Just remember, though, fine feathers don't make a fine bird. It's what is inside that counts."

"At least she didn't say no and try and stop you," said Peggy as they were walking down the road towards Hyde Park.

Marguerite, who felt quite buoyant, laughed. "By Mother's standards, that was almost an endorsement. You must have got it right for her not to criticise me. You're so lucky," said Marguerite, responding to both the beauty of the day and her own enhanced appearance. "It must be so glamorous to always dress up and act."

"That shows you've never been involved in theatre. There's precious little glamour in it. Just long nights, too much makeup all the time so your skin gets ruined, and hard, physical work." She saw Marguerite's crestfallen face and laughed.

"That's the reality, but not one of us in the business really sees it. We're all just like you, a little bit in love with the glamour." She gave a little shiver. "The shadow of that manse is never far from me you know. I dread the thought of going home as the prodigal daughter if I fail."

"You've made it this far, and that took more courage than most people ever have." Marguerite thought deeply before adding, "It seems to me that many people just give up too quickly. Those who hang on, regardless of anything else, seem to get where they want to be in the end. You'll be a star one day."

CHAPTER
TWENTY

London, 1945.

IT DIDN'T TAKE LONG BEFORE MARGUERITE'S obvious fascination with the theatre led to Peggy offering her a visit backstage. "I think I can sneak you into the back of the theatre. Joe, on the door, is a mate of mine, so he'll look the other way while I get you in. Once you're there, just sit quietly and hope no one notices you."

As she had predicted, Joe let them both in without a quibble. "Hello, Miss Darling. Good afternoon, miss," he added to Marguerite.

"You're in charge of her," he said to Peggy. "Just keep her out of sight, all right? I don't want to have my job on the line for you."

"You're a real sweetie, Joe. Thank you so much." Peggy blew him a kiss as they entered the stage door.

Inside it was dingy. A corridor with painted brick walls led deeper into the theatre, with steps at one end. The lighting was dim, unflattering, and the wooden floors seemed dusty.

"It's not glamorous at all," Marguerite said to Peggy in

surprise.

"Shh! No, the glamour is all for the punters who watch the show. Backstage is the working area, and that's not glamorous at all."

She led Marguerite up the stairs and through the door at the end of the corridor and they were in a different world. The seats that ran round the circle were rich red velvet; the baroque decorations on the wall glowed gilt and ivory.

"It looks like a palace," she whispered to Peggy. She got a nod in reply.

"Here's where I'm going to leave you," said Peggy in a low voice. "You can watch the rehearsal from here, but make sure you don't make a noise. I'll come and get you at the end of practice."

Marguerite settled down. She could see over the edge of the circle to the stalls far below. At either side of the stage were individual boxes, framed with coloured curtains that matched the stage. It seemed like a romantic dream to sit in one of those, sipping champagne and watching the show. Marguerite made a vow that one day she would be cultured and refined and sit there with her friends.

The cast came on stage. Marguerite picked out Peggy who had changed from her street clothes into a brief, belted tunic with slits up the side that showed off her long legs. Marguerite wondered what Mother would make of the skimpy costume, or indeed what Peggy's parents would think if they knew. All the dancers wore variations of this basic outfit which was obviously easy to dance in. Shoes were flat pumps. After some warm-up exercises they were on to the actual show moves.

In spite of Peggy telling her about hard work behind putting on a show, Marguerite had still imagined an ethereal process, where performers glided effortlessly around the stage, and if they sang or spoke, it was naturally perfect.

Instead, she could hear the heavy thump of the dancers' feet as they leapt around the stage. The person she supposed was the director kept shouting orders, making them start movements over again. He never seemed satisfied. Marguerite could clearly see the sweat on the girls' faces, soaking into the tunics between their breasts as they danced. The work was punishing, yet every girl had a smile on her face. Even those chastised by the director for some error never faltered in their happy smiles as they danced through sore feet, tired legs and sweaty bodies.

Peggy had made laughing referrals to 'the show must go on', but Marguerite had never truly appreciated how hard that could be to achieve, nor how dedicated the artist had to be.

At last the girls were released, and it was the turn of the male dancers. Again, nothing they did seemed to please the director, and he shouted and abused them as they worked through their tasks. If the girls had portrayed grace and delicacy with their movements, the men seemed so astoundingly strong, male and physical.

After a short break, the act was run from beginning to end, combining singers, dancers and spoken parts. It was a simple enough comedy of 'boy meets girl, meets obstruction, overcomes all obstacles and wins girl'. What Marguerite saw was a magical world of love and loss, hope and despair, beauty and ugliness. In short, Marguerite had fallen deeply under the spell of theatre. When, at the end, the lovers were reunited, she couldn't help herself becoming tearful with the sheer beauty of the moment.

She was drying her eyes during the curtain call and had lowered her handkerchief to watch the final curtseys when, resting as it did on the rail of the circle, it slipped and fluttered down into the stalls below.

It was possible that no one would have noticed the fluttering object, but Marguerite, in terror that she had betrayed her position, lurched forward to follow its progress downwards. Her white face, ghostly in the gloom of the theatre, was seen from the stage by Maureen Sanders, the leading lady.

Maureen gasped, gave a little half scream and pointed directly at her. "It's the theatre ghost," she declared, before clasping her hand over her mouth in exaggerated horror.

Everyone turned and gazed up at Marguerite. The director gave Maureen an irritated look. "It's not the theatre ghost, for heaven's sake, it's an interloper." He shouted into the wings,

"Fred, Mike, go up and get that person down here immediately."

"Yes, Mr Martin," they chorused.

Marguerite stood up in terror, looking for a way to escape. By the time she was working her way down the stairs in the dim light, Fred and Mike had caught up with her.

"What have we got here?" asked Fred, grabbing at her arm.

Mike gave her a lazy look over. "Well, what a naughty girl you are," he remarked cheerfully. Between them they escorted a terrified Marguerite into the theatre and forced her down the aisle to the foot of the stage. She stood there while the director glared down at her from the stage above.

"What's your name?" he asked.

"Marguerite," she whispered.

"What?" he commanded. "Speak up, girl. What's your name?"

"Marguerite, sir," she replied, a little louder this time.

"How did you get in here? Who helped you get in? By God, I'll have them fired for this. Who helped you?"

Marguerite was aware of Peggy's agonised eyes on her. There was no possibility that she could betray her friend, or Joe's part in her predicament.

"No one helped me," she replied. "I picked a moment when the doorman's back was turned and slipped in," she said in an anguished tone. "I didn't mean any harm."

"Harm, harm?" bellowed the incensed man above her. "What do you mean you 'didn't mean any harm'? Each person here makes their living selling tickets to the public. What made you think you could get in without paying. It's theft, that's what it is."

"I'm sorry," stammered Marguerite, dying of embarrassment. "I didn't think of it like that. I just wanted to see the theatre. I'd never seen it before."

"I'll call the constable," shouted the director. "He can take you and charge you under the law for trespass and anything else they can throw at you."

"I'm sorry," said Marguerite again. She didn't know what else to say.

"Sorry just isn't good enough," declared the man.

He looked the wretched girl in front of him over and knew his bullying was mostly bluster. He wasn't hard-hearted enough to send her off to the local police station, much though she might deserve it. "What are you going to do to make up for your trespass, is what I want to know."

Marguerite blinked at him. "I beg your pardon, sir?"

"Well, I don't imagine for a moment you have enough money to pay for a ticket, so how are you going to pay off your debt to the cast of this show? What do you do? Have you any skills?" Really, he thought, the girl looked quite retarded with her mouth half open, just gawping at him.

"Er, I'm a seamstress, sir. I work for tailors, but I'm also a dressmaker." She didn't know what he was asking really. "I sew," she added helpfully.

The director continued to gaze down at her, but his interest had quickened. "You sew? Can you sew dresses and fit them properly?"

Marguerite started to nod, and he interrupted her.

"No, no, I mean can you do it properly, professionally?"

Marguerite nodded. "Yes, sir. I'm good at it," she added simply, without false modesty.

The director snorted with amusement, and a titter ran round the assembled cast. "So you're good, are you?" He made his mind up. "All right, stay there and I'll come down and talk to you. The rest of you can relax. We've done enough for this afternoon."

CHAPTER
TWENTY ONE

London, 1945.

CHRISTOPHER MARTIN, THE DIRECTOR, VAULTED DOWN from the stage and walked round the orchestra pit towards Marguerite. He was tall and seemed very young, as if he had barely finished growing, with a boy's fineness to his wrists and a slender throat with a pronounced Adam's apple. Later Marguerite learned he had been in France but had been invalided out a year earlier after getting typhus at the front. He had applied to return, but his theatrical ability had seen him assigned to organising theatre to amuse the troops on leave in London.

Marguerite didn't make the mistake of assuming his youth made him less dangerous. She dropped her eyes as he approached, watching him from under her lashes, wondering whether she could yet run.

It appeared not. It was quite obvious he had a long reach. He had to be a good six foot three, she thought.

"Follow me," he said, after a brief scrutiny of her face. He led her down a flight of stairs and opened the door into a large room filled with row upon row of clothing. It took Marguerite a few minutes to get a sense of the logic behind the arrangement of the garments. Then she realised there were signs everywhere indicating such delights as Music Hall, Edwardian, Elizabethan, Nun's costumes, The Immortal Hour.

She gasped with pleasure. "Oh," she breathed.

It was like a little girl's dressing-up box, only on an adult scale, and presumably available for the actors in the shows. Fabrics Marguerite had never even imagined glowed with their silky sheen in the soft light of the room. There was sparkle and glitter on costumes that were impractical, if not actually indecent for street wear but looked wonderful here. In all the deprived years of Marguerite's childhood, she had never seen a treasure trove like this.

She forgot the menace Christopher represented and turned to him with her face alive with pleasure. "Oh, it's just lovely, sir. Aren't they all lovely?" She touched a couple of the dresses. The net of one was firm and a little rough against her fingers. The other was the softest silk and slipped like water through her hand. She gave a great sigh of pleasure.

Christopher looked around. "What you see here was saved during the Blitz. Our wardrobe mistress, Miss Eggers, made sure they were stored in the deepest cellars under the theatre until she was sure the bombings were over. Since then, she's managed to keep them together and intact, despite various war-effort officials wanting the materials for rationing."

He gave a quiet laugh. "Mind you, I don't envy the poor bureaucrat who tried to take one of these from Sally Eggers. She'd have him in pieces before we could save him."

He smiled for a moment absentmindedly then returned to the present and the hapless Marguerite. "Your punishment for this afternoon's little jaunt is to help us out while Miss Eggers is away. I just hope you are as handy with a needle as you claim to be."

"What sort of things do you want me to do?" She couldn't imagine what she should do to all these treasured costumes.

Christopher pointed at a large hamper of clothes. "That's

the mending. I understand there is quite a lot of darning and sewing on of buttons and such to be done. Oh, and Miss Sanders needs to be refitted for a couple of her costumes. It seems they are too tight for her. Obviously wardrobe department got the measurements wrong." The way his eyebrows quirked made it quite obvious to Marguerite that the fault wasn't in the wardrobe department at all but related to Miss Sanders' eating habits.

She choked down a private laugh. So the director had a sense of humour, did he? She took a second look at the hamper and assessed the work involved.

"I can start on the mending straight away sir, but I won't finish all that this afternoon. I work during the day. I could come by after work tomorrow evening, if the theatre is open, and finish off what I can't do today, if that would be all right?"

At least someone was committed to their work, which was more than he could say for half his cast, thought Christopher. Then he reproached himself. His cast were wonderful. He just didn't need prima donnas to complicate things.

As if on cue, there was a slight cough at the doorway, and Maureen Sanders appeared, framed. Christopher had no doubt at all that she had been listening to hear if there was anything interesting being said, before she made her presence known.

"Am I intruding?" she asked sweetly. "After all, Christopher, you're down here alone with this young woman. I wouldn't want to interrupt any plans you might have, dear." She walked over to them.

Maureen Sanders was a particularly beautiful woman. Her blonde hair framed an oval face with a peaches-and-cream complexion. Marguerite had admired her on stage, but up close Maureen was stunning. Marguerite had never seen anyone walk in that deliberately sinuous way before, hips thrust forward, the line of slender thigh apparent under the skirt.

"Don't be fatuous, Maureen," snapped Christopher. "Keep your nasty insinuations to yourself. We've been discussing getting your costume refitted for you."

"Oh good," said Maureen. She smiled warmly at Marguerite, switching her charm on. "Can you start on that right away, darling? I need it for the next performance. I cannot be expected to perform when the bodice is so tight I can't breathe properly." She sighed dramatically at Christopher. "Really, I can't work if the tools I use aren't up to par." She smiled at Marguerite. "Yes?"

"Um, yes, miss. If you would like to put the costume on, I will see what I can do about fixing it for you," said Marguerite, well into developing a crush on Maureen.

While Maureen disappeared behind a screen to change, Marguerite rummaged around in the drawers that lined the walls. She soon found the basic tools of her trade: shears, marking chalk, needles, threads and thimbles. Christopher sat on a chair and watched her with amusement. It seemed his 'punishment' wasn't as punitive as he had envisaged. The little seamstress was actually enjoying herself, and she seemed efficient.

By the time Maureen returned, Marguerite was ready for her. Christopher left them as Marguerite started work, telling her to report to him before she left the theatre.

The bodice in question was undoubtedly too tight for Miss Sanders' curvy figure. Initially Marguerite tried to zip Maureen in, but the seams were straining in a dangerous fashion. Whoever had made the garment had left plenty of material in the seams, so adjusting it to fit was simply a matter of unpicking the flat-felled seams and resizing. By the time Maureen had become bored with the operation, Marguerite had the main side seams unpicked and was able to pin a rough fit on her. She promised to have the bodice ready for a final fitting by the time she left the theatre and felt certain she could finish the task by the next evening.

Then she was alone. Resizing the bodice was relatively simple. She basted the seams and put it aside, turning to the mending basket. As Christopher had said, it was mainly missing buttons, torn lace or hose that needed darning. She'd noticed today, in rehearsal, that the dancers stitched their stockings to their drawers to give them a form of stretchy hose. Several of these needed mending.

"There you are!" exclaimed Peggy. "I've been looking

everywhere for you. Are you all right?"

Marguerite jumped. She hadn't heard her friend come in. She smiled at her. "Yes, I'm fine. I've been asked to fix these things up. I didn't know there were all these costumes backstage. Aren't they all wonderful?"

Peggy looked round her. "Yes, some of them are lovely. Look," she paused awkwardly, "thanks for not dropping me in it with the director. Did he give you an awful time?"

"No," said Marguerite, in slight surprise. "I mean, he was cross at the time, but I think he's OK. He just needed someone to fix these up. Your wardrobe lady is away. I don't mind at all, it's fun for me to work on these fabrics. You can't get anything like these in ordinary tailoring, with fabric rationed. I think it's rather a privilege to be able to see all this stuff."

Peggy grinned at her. "You know you're an odd one, don't you? Anyway, thanks for not snitching on me. I bet Joe was sweating as well. Have you finished? Because the theatre will be closing in a few minutes, and we need to get home."

Marguerite started tidying up. "I've said I can come back after work tomorrow evening to finish off. I can meet you here then as well." She piled the folded clothes up neatly, separating the finished work from the pile still in the basket. "Do you know where these go? They've all been fixed up."

"I'll take them up to the dressing rooms," said Peggy. "We'll drop them off as we go past."

On the way out Marguerite remembered to find the director. She approached him shyly. "I've finished for now, sir, but I'll be back tomorrow if that's all right, to finish the work off."

He smiled down at her. "Well, I hope you've learned your lesson not to stow away at the back of a theatre, although it looks as if it has been a fortunate bit of serendipity for us. I'll see you tomorrow night, and if everyone is happy with your work so far, maybe we can see if you have any more spare time to come and help us." He held out his hand to her, and shook hers. "It's been a pleasure meeting you, Miss Marguerite. Until tomorrow then."

Marguerite's usefulness to the company was such that soon it was tacitly accepted she was part of the theatre.

Sally Eggers, newly returned from Cardiff, viewed her with suspicion when they were introduced, but Marguerite, careful to defer to her in everything, was willing to do the more mundane mending jobs. After a couple of weeks, Sally was able to concede that Marguerite might just be a 'treasure', and Marguerite became part of the theatre family. To her surprise, she found performers were a cheerful and friendly bunch who made her feel at home. Maureen Sanders was the only prima donna of the troupe, tolerated by the others because they recognised her star power.

Having realised that Marguerite was useful, Maureen always treated her with courtesy, so Marguerite retained her admiration for her. If Maureen needed mending done, or seams taken in or out, she called on Marguerite to look after it. There was the occasional private commission from Maureen as well, and although Marguerite was shy about charging, the additional income helped, and she began to be able to save some money.

Privy to the most personal details of her measurements, Marguerite also became privy to the personal details of Maureen's life. While she pinned and measured during fittings, the star would chatter about her life – chiefly about the men in her life. Marguerite, shocked by some of the revelations, learned to be extremely discreet.

It was good to be part of a group. Many of the chorus girls were barely older than she was, and she learned a great deal from listening to their gossip. Edith would have been morally outraged if she'd heard even a fraction of the frank conversations that occurred in the dressing rooms, but Marguerite wasn't about to disclose to her mother that her store of worldly and sexual knowledge was increasing on a weekly basis, even if it was only theoretical.

The cast fascinated her with their extroverted ways, dedication and talent. She was intrigued by the complex mix of personalities. They seemed so confident in themselves, projecting across the stage lights to the audience, full of élan, energy and charm. Then backstage they could be nervous, self-deprecating and highly strung.

Stage-struck as she was, Marguerite had no wish to be on stage herself, but she enjoyed being part of the theatre.

Her life was now so busy that the year flew past. Katya, released from school for the holidays, came home to visit. The breach between the sisters remained. Marguerite had missed her little sister and offered to take her to the theatre and introduce her to the company, but Katya just shook her head when the outing was suggested.

Katya remained resentful and surly, and Marguerite, busy with her own affairs, shrugged her shoulders and hoped her sister would grow out of it. Time would, Marguerite assumed, heal the rift, and in the meantime she was happy exploring the boundaries of her own life.

CHAPTER
TWENTY TWO

Moscow, Present Day.

PYOTR KAROLAN HATED FUNDING APPLICATIONS. THE torment of trying to convince his peers that his work was worth supporting made him quail. They sat looking down on him from the tiered seats in the university theatre. He ducked his head and consulted his clipboard again. The list was so familiar he could have recited it backwards: Necessaire Egg – 1889 (missing), Cherub with Chariot Egg – 1888 (missing), Alexander III Portraits Egg – 1896 (missing) … the list went on.

In front of him Nikolai cleared his throat. "Have you made any progress in your search? We look forward to hearing the details."

Pyotr replied to Nikolai. Perhaps if he addressed the man personally he would make a better impression, and it meant he didn't have to see everyone else staring at him.

"I've been back through as many relevant documents as I can. The early days of the revolution were a time of looting and pillaging of the imperial palaces. Lenin made an attempt to preserve our heritage, and most of the Fabergé Imperial Eggs, along with gold, silver, jewels, artworks and icons were packed in crates, inventoried and taken to the Kremlin Armoury. There they stayed, lost in a dusty passage for years. They were rediscovered in the late 1920s, and many were sold to foreign interests to finance Stalin's political interests of the time.

"We know many treasures were lost in the days between the arrest of the last Tsar and Lenin transferring them to the armoury. At the time, suspicion centred on a General Mirov. One of the earliest records I have been able to find is a statement from a police informant, one Sergei Petrovich. He testified that Mirov was in possession of 'something extremely valuable' following the arrest of the Tsar, and that the source of this treasure was the Tsar himself. It was Petrovich's opinion, unsubstantiated I might add, that this valuable package was given to a trader who subsequently fled to the West. The trader's name was Kyril Komarov."

Pyotr paused in his presentation. "Unfortunately, General Mirov was executed within two weeks of the events Petrovich describes, so there is no first-person testimony from him in this matter. Certainly, nothing 'extremely valuable or significant' was found in his effects." He turned pages on his clipboard.

"I have researched the Komarovs. They were a reputable and prosperous middle-class family, resident in Moscow. There were two brothers – Kyril and the younger one, Ilya – both involved in the family firm. Their factory specialised in making harnesses for sleighs, both tandem and the troika, and other equestrian products. Presumably, realising they were unsafe in revolutionary Russia, they closed down their factory and fled."

Pyotr surveyed the room. "At that time, gentlemen and ladies, the new state had very little interest in the decadent baubles of the previous regime. It is only more recently that the importance of our shared heritage has been recognised in government circles. If the Komarovs were involved in the story of the Imperial Eggs, they left Russia long before authorities became concerned with the matter."

A hand was raised in the group listening to him.

Alexei Nikolevich spoke. "What do we know of this General Mirov? Why do you assume he had the eggs in the first place?"

"Mirov was a famous soldier, decorated for his valour in the First World War. It is almost certain his loyalties were Tsarist. He had free access to the court and to the Tsar and his family," Pyotr replied. "Remember this is based on probabilities. At the time there was serious political unrest. The Tsar and his family must have realised their position was threatened, because there had been talk of abdication for weeks. When the family were finally murdered some months later, one of the complicating issues of that massacre was that it took them, the girls in particular, a long time to die. They were protected from the bullets and bayonets by the diamonds and other precious stones sewn into hidden places in their clothing. In other words, the family may not have known the full horror of the fate that awaited them, but they certainly made a determined effort to save what they could of their fortune and effects."

Pyotr paused, rubbing the back of his neck. "I believe Mirov was part of that planning. He seems to me a logical caretaker for a treasure of this sort. Petrovich's testimony substantiates that there was 'something significant entrusted to him'." He grinned at the room ruefully.

"Fellow colleagues, this may sound like a tenuous lead to you, but it is a lead. It is also the only lead we have. I would have had mixed success in tracing the Komarovs once they left Russia, but a previous researcher based at the Kremlin Armoury took it upon himself to follow the clue left by Sergei Petrovich. This researcher, whom I know only by his initials, EZ, worked around the time of the Second World War. He found that the elder brother, Kyril, had moved west with his wife and son, and stopped his travels in Poland. Why the family didn't carry on through to England or America, we don't know. They settled in Warsaw for a generation and became tailors. The son grew to adulthood, married and had two daughters whose births were registered in Warsaw. It seems the family survived the German occupation. However, by the time Russia annexed Poland, under the redesign of Europe at the end of the war, the family had already left, this time moving to England."

Pyotr surveyed the room. "Here, it seems, our earlier researcher got lucky. EZ had a contact, probably a family member, who happened to be in London. I can only speculate that this woman was one of our Soviet agents there undercover at the time. She came across the name Komarov registered with the Polish Government in exile in London. Further, she recognised the name."

Pyotr smiled at the people round the table. "I like to think that our researcher had bored his family for years with speculations about the Komarovs. Anyway, the woman recognised the name and made contact with the family. She employed Edith, the wife of Kyril Komarov's son Charles, and the mother of the two girls. Edith's husband had died at some point in their flight from Europe, so only she and the two girls had arrived in England. The woman writes that ..." Pyotr turned another page or two on his clipboard, "... and I quote ...

"'She is a silly, helpless and self-centred woman, still deeply in mourning for her husband, whom she claims was executed as a spy when the family fled Poland. It seems evident that he was pater familias in every sense of the word, and I would think it most unlikely that any man of sense would confide a family secret to this woman. It would be like confiding in a leaky sieve. If any family knowledge exists regarding the treasure you seek, the only likely repository would be the elder daughter, Marguerite. It appears she has now adopted the role of head of the family, and, if she were close to her father, it may be that he confided in her. I was unable to pursue this further for you as circumstances unrelated to this matter compromised my security and I had to depart London rapidly. I hope this bit of gossip helps feed your research, sweet cousin. I look forward to ...'."

Pyotr looked up. "I like to speculate on who EZ was. I have looked up curators and museum researchers of the appropriate period, but I have found no one with those initials. Of course, I don't know whether EZ was an academic researcher, secret police or even doing this for family reasons. He left no clue as to his identity, and equally, he could be a woman, I don't know.

Even the snippet of the letter I have just read to you is only that: one page from what was obviously a longer letter. So there is no clue at all. Each bit of research is meticulously documented and annotated but with no reference to the author."

"Has any further research been done with the Komarov family?" asked Elizabeth Markova. "Was this daughter ever interviewed?"

Pyotr shook his head. "Not to my knowledge. The Cold War years intervened shortly after the Second World War, and access to the West became very difficult. Also there were successive changes in personnel, state policies and academic interest, so I don't believe the research went any further at that time. I only discovered the file by chance in a batch of old files in the basement when I was researching another matter.

"I have also tried to research the younger Komarov brother, Ilya, and where, or if, he left Russia in 1917. There was of course quite a large movement of population at that time, as White Russians fled the Bolsheviks. I researched two sites in particular – Odessa and Vladivostok. It seemed to me probable, as he had separated from his brother when they left Moscow, that his likely route would have been to the Far East, or south through the Black Sea. My personal preference is for the Far Eastern option. We know many Russians moved in that direction, and a large number entered China, eventually settling in Shanghai. So far, I have been unable to trace any exit documentation at either site, but of course, that is not conclusive. The times were unsettled, records may have been destroyed, or some calamity may have occurred and he may not have survived the journey.

"I have also done some further research on the London branch of the family. The daughter referred to in the letter married in 1955 into a family that founded a large retail company well known in Britain. She has become a wealthy woman. I think there may have been a child of the marriage, but I am unable to confirm that at this time."

"Surely this woman must know if she possesses an Imperial Egg?" asked Alexei. "What makes you think she doesn't, or that it might still be hidden?"

"Simply that there has never been any publicity to suggest otherwise. I remind my colleagues it was only last year that one of these eggs was rediscovered on a shelf in an obscure museum. Its curators thought it was a lamp fitting."

"So what is your proposal?" enquired Nikolai.

Pyotr gathered his thoughts and spoke formally. "My proposal, director, and my request of this committee, is that I be allowed to join our delegation to the international archaeological forum to be held soon in London. This forum, as you know, is specific to artworks and treasures lost during war and international policies regarding their repatriation. Further, I request approval to approach the daughter, Marguerite, now an elderly woman, and research any family history or stories pertaining to the matter of the Fabergé Imperial Easter Eggs."

"What makes you think she is still alive?" asked Alexei. "She would be fairly old by now; she could be dead."

Pyotr grinned. "Thanks to the wonderful Internet, I can confirm that she is still alive. She has recently been widowed, and as far as I am aware, has no surviving offspring. She may be delighted to confide the whereabouts of our treasures to a cultural representative of our country."

Nikolai snorted again beside him. "You may have overestimated the effect of your charms on the fairer sex," he growled.

Pyotr saw Elizabeth Markova glance at him sympathetically. One of the positive spins, if his proposal was accepted, was that the lovely Elizabeth already had a confirmed place on the delegation. Her interest was purely in treasures looted from the Ukraine during the Second World War, but she would be a great companion if they both found themselves in London.

He smiled back at her.

He was sent from the room whilst the committee debated his request. Pyotr knew money was tight. He hoped his research was populist enough to have captured the imagination of those on the committee who held the purse strings, otherwise it would be back to his day job.

He paced around the corridor for an hour before the door

reopened and he was ushered back in to hear his fate.

Nikolai stood to greet him. "Pyotr Karolan, the committee has considered your request, and the decision has been reached that you may make up part of our delegation to London."

Pyotr never heard the rest of Nikolai's speech, he was so excited. He was going to London, he would complete his research, and he would spend time with Elizabeth. If he were successful in his investigations, he might even win her admiration and approval.

He stammered his thanks to his colleagues and sat down, a smile stretching from one side of his face to the other.

Nikolai looked at him and snorted yet again. "Don't ever play poker, son," he remarked.

Pyotr just grinned back at him.

CHAPTER
TWENTY THREE

London, Present Day.

PURDIE STOOD IN THE ARRIVAL HALL at Heathrow and stared around. The queue moved, and she shuffled forward. Just ahead of her was an Indian family. The mother carried a small, sleeping infant in her arms, while the father sought to amuse two little girls who were tired and fretful. Purdie sympathised with them. She was starting to realise the enormity of what she had done. She had rushed into this trip with no real forethought or planning, a situation very much at odds with her usual policy. She only hoped her grandmother did intend to meet her from this flight.

She remembered her phone and dragged it out of her bag. There was a sign on the wall warning people to keep their cellphones off, which was largely ignored. Most passengers already had their phones to their ears or were busy texting. She had just switched hers on and was checking for messages when there was a tap on her arm.

"You can't use your phone here, miss," said the official.

Purdie started to protest. "Everyone else is ..."

But the man was firm. "Put it away please, miss."

Purdie scowled but complied, turning it off and shoving it into the hip pocket of her jeans. She would have to check it later.

By the time she was processed, stamped and released from customs and immigration a good hour and a half later, her needs had shrunk to a cup of coffee and somewhere to put her feet up. She walked down the aisle into the terminal and looked round her. There were crowds of people waving placards with names chalked on them, and suddenly she spotted 'Purdie Davis' in large white letters and relief surged through her. The man beneath the sign looked at her when she approached him. "Miss Davis?" he asked. He was Asiatic, but the moment he opened his mouth, there was no doubt at all in Purdie's mind that he was from Australia.

She nodded, grateful that someone was waiting for her.

"If you would come this way, I have a car here for you. Are those your bags? I'll grab them. Did you have a good trip over?"

And as easily as that she was escorted from the airport terminal, her luggage carried across to the car, and they were on their way. Purdie felt like a celebrity.

She settled herself into the back seat.

"Where are you from?" she asked her driver.

He grinned at her. "Sydney, but now I live in the UK."

Purdie smiled. "Yes, I thought you must be."

"Did the accent give it away?" he laughed. "I don't imagine I'll ever lose it, not even working here now."

Purdie nodded, leaned back and allowed herself to relax. They drove in silence past industrial sprawl and rows of brick housing until they entered Central London itself.

She perked up. The skyline was familiar from so many different TV programmes, and seeing her interest, the driver pointed out a few sights. She spotted the Eye in the distance, framed between a couple of high rises, and her excitement rose. She could still hear her mother saying there was no city in the world as wonderful as London. Her adoptive mother, she reminded herself. Relationships might get complicated over the next few weeks, and she hoped her grandmother would understand her need to accept two lots of heritage.

Purdie was surprised when the car eventually pulled up outside a modern apartment block. She had imagined her grandmother living in an older, more traditional home than this stylish glass and concrete building. The driver came round and opened the door for her.

"If you'll follow me," he murmured, "I'll bring your bags up in a second."

They approached the front door, which was opened by a uniformed porter.

"Miss Davis, for flat 17."

The porter nodded and escorted Purdie to the lifts while the driver returned to the vehicle to get the cases.

"I'll take you up, miss," said the porter.

The lift doors opened into a hallway, and she was ushered across the marble floor to large, highly lacquered double doors. As they opened she was bowed into the apartment by the porter.

The apartment was darkly beautiful. Natural light was kept to a minimum by deeply shaded drapes on the windows, and discreet lighting shone down in alcoves onto highly decorated walls. The formal seating was covered in scarlet silk, and the chairs and sofas surrounded a deeply piled rug. A heavy black dresser covered most of one wall; a large oriental landscape painting hung on another. In a corner of the room a marble staircase led to an upper floor. The impression was of exotic opulence.

This was not what Purdie had expected. She turned to speak to the man who had ushered her in, but he had closed the doors behind her and no one was there.

She stood, convinced this couldn't be her grandmother's home, but not knowing whether to go or stay.

She decided to leave, and as she turned towards the double doors, a door she hadn't noticed on the far side of the dresser opened and a man stepped through. He was young, slim, dressed formally in a business suit, and another Asiatic.

"Good afternoon, Miss Davis," he said, approaching her. "Please take a seat and make yourself comfortable. May I ring for tea, or is there something else you would prefer?"

"No thank you," replied Purdie, slightly startled by the use of her name. "I don't think I am supposed to be here. I'll just leave."

"But of course you are supposed to be here, Miss Davis; you were brought here directly by our driver. Please be seated. Our chairman is looking forward to meeting you."

Purdie was starting to feel very nervous. "I don't know your chairman, and I don't want to meet him. I must ask you to let me leave. Oh, and I need my luggage please."

The man smiled at her. "I assure you our chairman wants to meet you very much. Please don't worry about your luggage, it is being looked after."

"No, I wish to leave, now," said Purdie firmly. She couldn't actually believe she was in this ridiculous situation, and she felt very uncomfortable. Random thoughts of white slavery crossed her mind. How could she have been so stupid as not to have checked out the driver before she climbed into the car with him? Peter Harris's text and the bizarre sequence of events back in Wellington should have put her on guard, but she had been tired and unsettled. It had been easy to leap to the assumption the car had legitimately come from her grandmother. She had been beguiled by the Australian accent and the spurious surge of antipodean kinship it had engendered.

The man said nothing, just smiled politely and gestured towards the chairs. Ridiculous as it was, it felt like a gross breach of good manners to turn and head purposefully for the doors. Purdie firmly pushed that thought aside and marched straight across the floor, trying to control her panic. She grabbed the handles and pulled, but the doors didn't move. She tried pushing, then tried each one individually. She stood there looking at them for some time.

The man behind her still said nothing.

Eventually she turned and faced him. "Why won't the doors open? I wish to leave."

"The chairman wishes to meet you," the man reiterated. "He will be free to see you shortly. Please do sit down and make yourself comfortable. Tea can be very soothing," he offered again. He sounded such a courteous and considerate host. It was a bizarre performance when he was imprisoning her against her will.

Purdie stared at him. As there didn't seem to be any other option, she walked forward and took her place on a chair. If this was a white slaving operation, she had read enough potboilers to know accepting food or drink could be exceedingly dangerous. The possibility of drugs worried her. She was going to have to be very careful and look out for danger from now on.

She just hoped she could get herself out of this mess. It wasn't very reassuring to realise she was in a town she didn't know, and no one knew where she was. If she read about this happening to someone else in a newspaper article, she would be scathing in her remarks about their silliness.

She thought about her phone in her pocket. She might be able to contact the police. Was it 111 in this country, she wondered, or did they use 999? It occurred to her this was the sort of research that should be done by travellers before they left home. Maybe she could write a travel book after this, pointing out these useful tips!

The man's quiet calm was unsettling. He made no attempt to start a conversation with her. His offer of refreshment seemed to have exhausted his small talk, and Purdie didn't know whether to win him over by chatting or to remain silent. They sat together as the afternoon passed.

Purdie made a conscious effort to study the room in case she could gather any information. She saw that the only ways of escape were the doors she had entered by (locked); the door the man had entered by (he was sitting between it and her); and the staircase leading upstairs (unknown territory which might have to be reconnoitred later). She reminded herself they were on the seventeenth floor of the high rise, so abseiling out of a window wasn't going to be possible, even assuming the windows opened and the curtains could be torn up while her companion watched without interfering.

Really, she thought with irritation, after all the spy books she'd read, she should be able to find some viable ideas for escape. She'd watched Tom Cruise, Angelina Jolie and Harrison Ford escape from enough situations on screen. As her mother had said to her long ago, 'you can't believe everything you see on the screen. Real people don't behave like that'. Mind you, her mother had been talking about morality, not *Escape 101*.

She found that sitting quietly had refreshed her. If it hadn't been for her silent companion, she would have kicked her shoes off and curled up on the seat.

She glanced at her watch; it was now two-thirty. She wondered how long she was going to be kept here, and who the 'chairman' was. She couldn't for the life of her imagine what possible connection there could be between herself and the Chinese.

It was another half hour before an electronic beep sounded from her companion's pocket. She watched him draw out his phone and check it. He must have been summoned, because he rose to his feet.

"The chairman will see you now," he announced, with all the air of doing her a favour.

CHAPTER
TWENTY FOUR

London, Present Day.

THE MAN – SHE CHRISTENED HIM MR Zen in tribute to the silent vigil they'd shared – courteously indicated that she should follow him up the stairs. Instantly her calm deserted her. She felt her heart begin to pound, but she followed.

They climbed the marble staircase and emerged onto a landing with several closed doors. Her companion knocked on one, opened it and had a brief exchange with someone inside. A moment later the door was thrown wide open, and she was escorted into a large room. Several people were there already, one of them being the man who had brought her from the airport. She glared at him.

A group were standing around a very elderly gentleman who was sitting; those flanking him were considerably younger. The men wore suits and ties, and the women were wearing office-formal clothing. For all the world it looked as if she had stumbled into a company meeting.

A young woman rose as she entered and welcomed her into

the room, indicating a chair for her. She seated herself nervously. What could possibly connect her to this roomful of people?

"Miss Davis." A man stood and addressed her formally. Purdie looked at him, thinking he was probably in his 60s, as she gave him her attention. "Thank you for your time today. I apologise for interrupting your schedule, but we needed to meet with you. I am Yuan Li, and these are members of my family."

Purdie nodded, wondering where this was leading and whether kidnapping her was really covered by the phrase 'interrupting your schedule'. She was aware of the elderly gentleman scrutinising her carefully, and shifted a little, uneasy under his watchful eye.

"We hope you have enjoyed the items we delivered to you in New Zealand?" Yuan Li continued.

"Yes, but why …?" At least one mystery was about to be cleared up, it seemed.

The man smiled slightly. "Those items were in the nature of a duty owed between my family and yours."

Purdie stared at him blankly. She couldn't imagine a situation in which her adoptive parents were owed a debt by a Chinese family, so this must involve her birth family. She wondered again what she was getting herself into.

"Miss Davis, does the name Komarov mean anything to you?" Yuan Li asked.

She shook her head. Surely Komarov wasn't an Asian name?

The old man suddenly spoke in Chinese. Yuan Li turned to him and listened, then nodded his head.

"My father says you should now be told the story of your ancestor," he said. Purdie waited. "I believe you don't know your family yet?"

"Er, no, not my birth family," said Purdie reluctantly. She didn't want to give information away when she didn't know how it would be used.

There was a short break while the standing audience made their way to seats at the back of the room.

Yuan Li continued. "Last century there was a revolution in Russia, a land with which China shares a long border. At the time of the upheavals, many White Russians – that is, those not Bolshevik in their sympathies – fled and came eventually to Shanghai. It was a very cosmopolitan city, and many refugees made their homes there." He paused for breath.

"At the time, my great grandfather, Chi, was an extremely poor man eking out his living as a coolie and a cleaner. He was clever and ambitious, but destiny had given him a hard road to walk.

"One day, in the night club where he cleaned and swept floors, he became aware of one of these Russians at the gaming tables playing mah-jong. Chinese love to gamble, and the young Russian was playing with some serious players.

"In such situations, it is usual to let the inexperienced player win a couple of hands, to suck them into the game. When asked, the young man elected to continue playing; lady luck, he declared, was on his side that night. Liquor of course was easily available, and he was drinking heavily. My great-grandfather was amused at the ease with which the other players were setting him up, and stayed to see the fun.

"Sure enough, a few hands later, the Russian began to lose. Not much at first, but then steadily. After a few rounds he had lost his earlier winnings. The drink was still flowing freely, and the men waited to see what the foreigner would do. Did he have more money or valuables to stake, or was he already drained dry, in which case they could move on to another target.

"One of the women at the night club had been primed to interrupt at this point. Under the guise of seducing the stranger, she was able to frisk him, and reported that there seemed to be hidden pockets in his clothing. This hostess was Russian born, so her loyalties may have been divided, and she may have warned him of the other players' intent. Or maybe the young man himself was quite aware of his situation, because unaccountably, his luck began to change again for the better.

"Over the next hour, the man won back both his own money and that of the other players. Eventually he cleared the table. When he stood to leave, he was a much richer man. He also appeared to be seriously inebriated. The players let him go.

They had already sent others out to intercept him and knew he wouldn't get far. He looked an easy prey for their thugs.

"My great-grandfather lost interest in the game at this stage and left the club to go home for the night. It happened that he reached the spot where the stranger was being mugged in time to see the fight he put up. This was no inexperienced young man but a seasoned fighter who was withstanding the attack of three other men. His valour impressed my great-grandfather to such a degree that he was drawn to assist him. Just as he thought to join the fight, though, one of the thugs managed to get past the Russian's guard and stab him. The Russian fell to the ground. At this point my great-grandfather did something that would change our family's history. Instead of retreating carefully, he rushed to the aid of the stranger and stood over him protecting his body from further attack. I suppose my ancestor had street-fighting skills, because his demeanour discouraged the attackers.

"They had been badly mauled in the fight. I believe at least one had a broken limb, and there was other serious damage. Seeing a fresh and determined protagonist join the fight, they retreated and left my great-grandfather with the Russian.

"At first Chi thought the foreigner was dead, for at some point he had fainted. My great-grandfather examined him and brought him round. There was a deep puncture wound to his chest, and it seemed likely the Russian would not survive. My great-grandfather took him home, however, and arranged for a doctor to look at him."

Here Yuan Li stopped his story. Purdie, who in spite of her nervousness had been following the tale intently, came back to reality with a shock.

Yuan Li smiled at her. "In your culture, Miss Davis, I believe that if you save someone's life, the victim is grateful and feels indebted to their saviour. In ours, there is a different perception of the situation. If you interfere in another person's fate by, for example, saving their life, then you have taken responsibility for the results of that action. In other words, my great-grandfather had, by his impulsive behaviour, taken on responsibility for this stranger's life. It is serious to interfere in someone's fate, and not to be taken lightly." He resumed his tale.

"As I have said, my great-grandfather's situation was one of extreme poverty, and the folly of his action cannot be sufficiently stressed. But he had taken on this responsibility, and he was not one to back away from his actions.

"Fortunately, in this case, his kindness was rewarded. For though the stranger hovered between life and death, he was stronger than he looked, and the flesh wound healed cleanly, but his lung had been punctured, and this was more of a problem.

"Right from the beginning, the foreigner made a difference to our family. He gave his winnings from that night to buy food, medicine and eventually better lodgings for Chi and his wife. If my ancestor felt bonded to Komarov by ties of fate, the stranger himself seemed to recognise he was beholden to his rescuer and sought to pay back that debt in the only way he could, by sharing his wealth with them. And Komarov had more wealth than Chi had realised, for sewn into his garments, as the hostess at the nightclub had discovered, were gems of the highest quality. Unimaginable treasure for Chi and his family. And when Komarov's possessions were recovered there were other beautiful items – an icon, a jewelled egg and other small treasures."

Purdie started at those words and Yuan smiled. "I see you recognise the items. Well, they were his."

He carried on. "Who knows what might have happened next if he had lived, but fate is not always kind, and death cannot be tricked. Komarov gradually recovered strength and eventually was able to go out and about. He was still weak, but his health was returning. Although he was Russian, he was not that distinctive in Shanghai because, as I have said, there were many refugees there. Such a figure would ordinarily have gone unnoticed, but the men at the nightclub had not forgotten him, or their losses from that night. Worse, they were members of a gang, and it was not their policy to let a victim escape.

"Eventually they caught up with Komarov. Chi never knew the details of his capture, but Komarov disappeared and my great-grandfather could find no news of his fate for seven long days although he searched frantically. He found him, or what was left of him, on a city midden. He had been brutally tortured – cut, burned and beaten. Several fingers had been cut off, one of his ears had been cut away and he had been blinded with hot irons. Chi once again brought him home and called the healer. It was evident this time he was not going to survive his ordeal.

"Komarov told my great-grandfather that he would have said anything to his captors to stop the pain. Such treatment took a man well beyond willpower or courage to a broken place where his soul shrivelled and cringed like a whipped puppy. These thugs had extracted information from Komarov that must have exceeded their wildest dreams. On his deathbed, he confided these things to Chi.

"He told of two brothers, fleeing Russia. One went to the East, and one, with a wife and child, to the West. The night before they fled, they had been entrusted with Russian imperial treasures, namely Fabergé Easter eggs. The older brother had taken the eggs for safekeeping, presumably to the West, but shared the reward for his efforts – jewels and gold – with his younger brother who came east.

"You may know, Miss Davis, that the Fabergé Imperial Eggs were fabulous constructions made on an annual basis for the Tsar's family. The Romanovs were wealthy as rulers of Russia, but the eggs' value as art objects far outweighs the value of the materials used to create them. They would be worth a fortune nowadays. As far as the world knows, these eggs disappeared without a trace, but it seems your ancestor was made the custodian of this treasure.

"Komarov bequeathed his possessions, which included the gold and jewels, to Chi and the family that had helped him. But he left a legacy to his own family as a remembrance of him, and as proof of his fate. These were an icon, a locket and an egg, but not, it must be said, an Imperial Egg. Chi was to return these to the other brother in the West, or his heirs, when it was possible to do so. It was a sacred trust, and Chi recognised it as such, accepted it and passed it on to his successors. Ilya Komarov passed to his God in peace and will always be honoured in our family.

"Chi bundled up his family and their possessions and left Shanghai immediately, before the Triads could catch up with him. The inheritance from Komarov provided the family with funds to reach Hong Kong, and there Chi settled. He changed his name, changed his appearance, and began his transformation into an entrepreneur.

"Our family has prospered since. The capital that Komarov left to Chi allowed him to invest and build. His latent intelligence and ability had only needed that initial capital to allow him to build his empire, and every member of his family, including the people in this room, owe their fortune and prosperity to Komarov's legacy. Of course, carrying out the rest of the bequest, finding Komarov's brother or his heirs, was not a simple thing to do. There have been world wars, communism has been and gone, and there have been massive movements of peoples across the globe. It took many years of searching, but our family were committed to their quest. Now, in you, we are confident that we have found the last heir of Komarov's line. Ilya Komarov's elder brother, Kyril, went west with his wife and son. Eventually there was a granddaughter who still lives, Marguerite, who married Eugene Dunning. I believe she is your grandmother, and that she has invited you to stay with her?"

Purdie gaped at him. She'd never imagined the sheer exotic scale of her heritage. It was a long way from being heir to a line of shopkeepers. She nodded her head in answer to his query. "Yes, and thank you so much for telling me the story, and bringing me those items," she said warmly. "It's a wonderful tale, and I'm glad Chi benefited from his generosity."

A thought occurred to her. "But I don't understand. How did you know how to find me?" Even as she asked, the answer became obvious to her. "You are the people that bugged my flat, aren't you?" she exclaimed. "Were you watching me in New Zealand?"

Yuan inclined his head.

"We have had to do a great deal of research to ensure you are the correct person to hear this story. We have had investigators working here in England and, once we were aware of your existence, in New Zealand."

Purdie was indignant. "That's all very fine, but what about my privacy? You invaded our flat, which I am pretty sure is criminal. And then you intercepted me at the airport and brought me here, which is tantamount to kidnap. How did you know my flight, anyway? Did you intercept the airline tickets from my grandmother? You've been spying on me, and maybe my grandmother as well."

Yuan shrugged. "I believe the English have a saying that to make an omelette you have to crack some eggs. How else were we to confirm your identity?"

He would say no more, and after a brief internal struggle, Purdie allowed the matter to lapse. After all, she thought with a shrug, she was safe now. And what a heritage to have! Just wait until she told Nick, Sophie and Katy. Her thumb itched to text them then and there, but good manners made her refrain. "Well, I suppose in spite of your methods I must thank you. It's been lovely to meet you all and hear your story," she said cheerfully. It seemed as if her whole life was turning into a fairy tale.

The old gentleman spoke sharply again. Yuan Li bowed slightly to him and turned to her. "My father asks one thing more," he said.

Purdie looked at him enquiringly.

"Where then are the Fabergé Imperial Eggs?" he asked.

Purdie gave a little gasp of surprise. "Pardon? Oh, I don't know anything about the eggs. The only one I know about is the one you gave me. How would I know anything more? You were the ones who told me the story, remember?"

"This was our assumption," said Yuan Li. "It means the person with this information is likely to be your grandmother. It would not be unreasonable to assume that, in the same way our family kept alive the story of Komarov, your grandmother's family kept alive the knowledge of these eggs."

Purdie shrugged.

Yuan Li smiled slightly. "Our family would like to obtain this treasure, Miss Davis. Indeed, the purpose of meeting with you today is to make progress towards this goal."

"I don't imagine she is going to hand family heirlooms over to you, just because you ask," said Purdie tartly. Just when she had let her guard down and thought they might have been doing her a favour, it turned out they wanted her family's secrets. So much for repaying their obligation to her ancestor!

"Well, no. We don't think she'd just hand them over either," said Yuan Li apologetically. "But we know she very much wants to have her granddaughter. We believe she may be induced to part with her secrets in exchange for you."

Purdie felt herself freeze. She had thought she would be free to go after they told their story. Instead she was to be used as leverage.

"As I haven't even met the woman," she said, "I really don't see that she is going to pay some sort of ransom for me, if that's what you have in mind. I shouldn't think an appeal to her sentimentality is likely to work."

The old man spoke again. Yuan Li nodded to him and addressed her. "Miss Davis, while no doubt you are precious in your own right to your grandmother, there is another pressing reason for her to want to recover you. At the moment, following the death of her husband, she is in a fight for control of her company. This hinges on there being a direct descendant of hers to put on the board. With no direct heir, the company passes to her stepson, a person we know she detests, and who despises her in equal measure. You are, therefore, significant. We believe these two pressures may indeed be sufficient to persuade her to part with any information she may have, or even with the eggs themselves, should she be in possession of them."

He smiled at her, with a grim expression.

Oh, shit! thought Purdie. Yuan Li's presentation sounded very convincing to her. She tried to think of a way out of the mess but couldn't.

"Surely you wouldn't treat a descendant of Komarov badly?" she said. "Not after all you have told me of your family's obligation to him." Even to her ears it sounded like a fairly desperate ploy, but to her surprise, Yuan Li appeared to take it seriously.

"We have considered this," he assured her, "and have concluded that you are not a direct descendant of Ilya Komarov himself, but only a member of his extended clan. Moreover, we have discharged our obligations to you and returned those possessions to his family, as he requested. You will, of course, be treated as an honoured guest during your visit with us. It will not take long before your grandmother realises the necessity of dealing with us. So for a short period we will make sure you enjoy your stay."

"But you can't just hold me," she protested, really alarmed now. "It's illegal. You must realise that! There would be shocking repercussions if you kidnap a New Zealand citizen."

Yuan Li made no reply. He inclined his head slightly to her, and she understood that the meeting had finished.

She was still saying "But …" when Mr Zen came up beside her.

"Please come, Miss Davis," he urged. "I will show you to your room."

Just like a well-trained hotel concierge, thought Purdie furiously.

"I am not your guest. You are holding me against my will. I urge you to rethink this," she said to the room at large, Yuan Li having made it quite clear their conversation was over. "I have done nothing to you, and it's highly unlikely that my grandmother will be interested in a deal, you must see that," she said urgently.

"This way please, miss," said Mr Zen and, regardless of her protests, she was escorted politely but firmly out of the room.

CHAPTER TWENTY FIVE

London, Present Day.

"WHERE IS SHE?" MARGUERITE BURST INTO Clive's office. "What have you done with her, you bastard?"

When Max returned from the airport without Purdie, reporting her as a no-show, Marguerite had taken immediate steps to trace her. The airline was largely unhelpful but able to confirm her granddaughter had arrived on her intended flight. Customs and airport security also confirmed that Purdie had passed through their hands. It was once she had entered the public concourse that she'd disappeared.

One advantage of Marguerite's wealth, position and contacts was her ability to make people listen, and achieve results. She pulled strings with the airport authorities, and they searched security camera footage for signs of the girl. It didn't take long for it to be obvious she had been intercepted before Max arrived to pick her up. Marguerite's immediate thought was that Clive had stolen her, as a move in the game between them, and rushed over to deal with the situation face to face.

"How lovely to see you, Marguerite," drawled Clive, laying

down the papers he was studying. "Please take a seat, you seem agitated. May I get you some tea?"

His large office had a fine view overlooking the river. For a man as independently wealthy as Clive, the room was surprisingly spartan and impersonal. Most of the furniture was from IKEA. The art was standard business décor prints enlivened only by a large mirror which hung on one length of wall, reflecting light. Nothing about the room gave you an impression of the man who worked there. Apart from the multimillion-pound views of the Thames, of course.

"What have you done with her?" asked Marguerite, again ignoring the view. She sat down and glared at her stepson. "If you've done anything to her, I'll hang your balls out to dry, I swear."

"Dear me," said Clive, even more unctuously. "What fun to see you in such a taking. I have, of course, no idea at all what you are talking about, but it does my heart good to see you so passionate. Who would have thought it of you after all these years?"

Marguerite gritted her teeth to control her outburst and took a deep breath. "I am talking about my granddaughter, Purdie. What have you done with her?"

"Ha!" exclaimed Clive. "Are you telling me your star has done a runner?" He grinned at Marguerite wolfishly. "It's so hard to get good hired help, isn't it? Maybe you didn't pay the little imposter enough."

"She's not an imposter, Clive. I told you that at the last meeting we had. Purdie's my granddaughter, Tamara's child, and you'd better believe it. Are you saying you haven't kidnapped her?"

"Most certainly not; I'm wounded that you could even think it," grinned Clive. "Mind you, I'm surprised I *didn't* think of it. We could have had her DNA tested, you know, and put this whole matter behind us." He stood up suddenly, reminding Marguerite of how powerfully built a man he was. Even sitting, he loomed large behind his desk. Standing in front of her he seemed monstrous.

"Marguerite, my evil stepmother, you know as well as I that

Tamara never had a child. If she had been pregnant, believe me, I would have known. Why don't you stop this sham now, before I call you on it and you get dragged through all the papers? I know you want Dunnings for yourself, but please let's have a little dignity about how you go about it."

Marguerite studied him. "What makes you think you'd have known if Tamara had a child?" she asked steadily. "I can think of no reason why it should have been your business. Unless you are telling me that it was?" Marguerite let the question hang. "She would hardly be likely to tell you herself, now would she? And I certainly wouldn't tell you."

Clive gave a short little laugh and turned away. "You silly cow," he said. "My inheritance rested on the breeding capabilities of that spoiled little slut. If she'd been pregnant, that child could inherit Dunnings, remember? Or if Tamara was childless, the company would come to me. Of course it was my business, and I made it my business to know. From the time she started menstruating, I watched her. Believe me; she took some watching as well. For a while there she was the bicycle of Belgravia with her partying habits. Remember the stories in the press? So yes, Marguerite, I would have known. If you are going to claim some last-minute bastard as hers, forget it. There wasn't enough time for her to get pregnant."

Marguerite kept her face impassive, but anger showed around her eyes at his abuse of her daughter. She focused on the area between his shoulder blades, imagining the satisfaction of sticking a long stiletto there. *One day*, she thought, *I will fix you for good.* She'd nursed her hatred of this man for so long she could feel herself choke on it. Worse, for Eugene's sake, she had concealed so much.

I'll get you yet, you bastard, she thought. *When I've finished with you, you'll be a castrated pariah and no one will touch you.*

Clive turned back to her and said bitterly, "Whatever game you think you're playing, Marguerite, you'd better be grateful that trollop is no longer around to make a laughing stock of you and the company. And please don't offend my intelligence by putting an imposter in. I can disprove any claim you make far too easily." He sighed wearily. "Give it away, Marguerite. You've had your day. Let it lie now and accept the future lies with me. You can have a nice retirement." He smiled at her evilly. "I'll even approve your superannuation cheques if you behave."

Marguerite stood up. Beside Clive she seemed tiny and frail. "Right, Clive, have it your way if that is your stand. The girl is Tamara's, whether you want to accept it or not, but we can deal with that later. If you say you haven't taken her, then I don't know who has, but she's certainly been spirited away. I have the police searching for her. I say again, if you've harmed her, or are holding her, I'll make mincemeat of you." She pushed her handbag up her arm, steadied herself and marched to the door. "Consider yourself warned," she muttered.

Clive watched her leave. "Interesting and yet more interesting." He picked up the phone to his secretary. "Get Parsons in here please, Genevieve."

The man could prove his loyalty by taking some time off for research purposes. Marguerite's claim was fraudulent, but her continued assertion meant he would have to check it out. If Tamara Dunning had a child before she died, there must be a birth registered somewhere. Nathan Parsons could do some digging.

Marguerite was breathing deeply when she entered her dead husband's office. Clive always affected her badly, she thought. Spending too much time in his proximity could raise blood pressure to levels likely to be dangerous at her age.

The fight for supremacy meant Eugene's office remained officially unclaimed. She still held the key, of course, and no doubt Clive himself could get access if he wanted, but for now it was unoccupied and empty.

There was a framed painting of Eugene on the wall. A formal portrait, commissioned to demonstrate his position in Dunnings, and had always seemed a bit stuffy to her. More poignant was the small framed photo, still on his desk, showing the two of them on their wedding day.

She smiled, a little grimly. What constituted a good marriage?

It was only a few months ago they had celebrated their diamond anniversary. Toasts had been drunk, fireworks let off, beautiful dresses worn, and all the right people had turned up to celebrate the success of the Dunning family.

Dear God, how she missed him. Missed his presence in her life, missed the habits that had formed the ebb and flow of their days together.

She racked her brain to find a reason for Purdie's abduction, and failed. Who would so deliberately cause harm to her and her kin? Offhand, she could think of no one, but she sifted through the years of her life, searching for a clue. She wondered what Eugene would have done in this situation and gazed thoughtfully at his picture, longing for wisdom.

CHAPTER
TWENTY SIX

London, 1954.

MARGUERITE'S INVOLVEMENT WITH THE ODEON EVENTUALLY led to private dressmaking jobs, first for Maureen Sanders, then for the stars who, show after show, followed her.

Marguerite combined simplicity of line with an ability to make the most homely figure look graceful and elegant. Her natural talents, honed by the disciplines she had learned at Schwartz and Bloomfield, flowered in a more theatrical atmosphere. Those who knew about Marguerite kept her as their well-guarded secret to be shared with only their closest and most devoted friends. Naturally her reputation grew rapidly.

By 1951, Marguerite was confident enough of her combined earnings to put a deposit on a house in a quiet street in Kensington and move into it with her mother. She leased out the upper two floors and kept the rooms on the ground floor and basement for their own use.

This provided her with a relatively spacious front room that Marguerite christened the salon, and a smaller back room that served as her workroom. When Marguerite had private dressmaking commissions she used the front room for her clients, for fittings and consultations. Downstairs, in the basement proper, was a separate room that Marguerite offered Edith.

She herself slept in the workroom in a pull-out bed that folded up against the wall during the day. Edith's room, though of reasonable size, was gloomy and subterranean, with only a small window high up for light and air. This looked out at pavement level to the street which, Edith snorted, gave her a wonderful view of people's feet as they walked by.

As far as Marguerite was concerned, the street address, though modest, made up for any inconvenience she and Edith might suffer. When Katya came home from school and shared Edith's basement bedroom she was loud in her criticisms, but Marguerite overrode her.

The place was perfect for 'Madame Komarov, Couturier'. A small, discreet brass plaque to this effect was screwed onto the outside wall. Marguerite would have died rather than admit it, but the sight of it brought a thrill of pride to her every time she passed.

Katya had never forgiven Marguerite for sending her to school and now, fully into the torments of her adolescent years, enjoyed portraying herself as a martyr. Marguerite, having never had time to be an adolescent, or a 'teenager' as the Americans now called them, impatiently dismissed Katya's woes as self-dramatisation.

"Heavens," she said, "I spend my nights at the theatre; I don't need to have dramatics during the day as well."

The memory of a time when they had liked each other was so long behind them it was hard for either sister to remember.

Marguerite was rather worried about another set of dramatics going on. Peggy had, for the last two months, been seeing a married man. She had known he was married from the beginning of the relationship, a fact that had shocked Marguerite. It was one thing for a flash Johnny to put one over, forgetting to mention the wife and children back home. It was quite another for a nice girl to deliberately entangle herself in an adulterous union.

Marguerite had expressed this opinion with considerable frankness, but Peggy chose to ignore her. Instead she said Peter made her laugh, and seemed quite unrepentant.

Marguerite suspected Peter's appeal lay in his involvement with the new film companies forming in England. Peggy was as ambitious as ever. They had met at an audition at the studio where Peter was a co-director on the project. Marguerite hated the thought her friend might have succumbed to temptation purely to get a part in a film, but the suspicion remained.

Marguerite had her own reasons for disliking Peter Humphries, some of which stemmed from the snobbishness inherited from Edith. This both amused and appalled her; but she would, she reflected, under any circumstances, have disliked and mistrusted Mr Humphries.

She conceded he was a good-looking man, but he was, she thought, 'too much': too much Brylcreem in his perfectly parted hair; too broad a smile; too dapper in his clothing to be a gentleman, and too smooth and polished in his address.

He had also once made a too-suggestive remark to Marguerite which she had speedily repulsed. Since then he had treated her with disdain. Consequently, on the one occasion Peggy had tried to arrange a 'double date' with Marguerite and her current beau, Peter Humphries had made it obvious that it was 'too much' trouble to be courteous to a little refugee seamstress and her friend.

Marguerite was certain Peggy's infatuation would end in tears, but in the meantime, she was there to provide support and solace as the relationship ran its course. For all the bohemian glamour and exotic appeal of the stage, the Lord Chamberlain's Office held the power to shut down a performance on moral grounds, and sensible theatre managers complied with directives, even if their artistic directors tried to push the boundaries. An actress having an illicit liaison with a married man would have caused all sorts of problems. Long gone were the freewheeling war years when a blind eye was turned on the actions of young lovers who might be parted forever after the next tour of duty.

Marguerite's role was to provide cover for Peggy after the

shows and deflect those who wanted to speak to her personally, thus her presence the night Eugene Dunning chose to attend the theatre and visit its star.

He had come backstage wearing evening dress and carrying a bunch of flowers, eager to meet Peggy, by now the star of her own show. He was ushered into her dressing room, only to find Marguerite perched on a stool mending the hem on a costume. Peggy was long gone, leaving a trail of cotton wool and cold cream in her wake, and her best friend Marguerite to cover for her in the event of visitors.

"Oh," he exclaimed when he saw Marguerite. "I'm sorry; I was here to visit Miss Darling. They told me she was here." He tried to peer over her shoulder into the room, in the hope of spotting Peggy.

Marguerite looked at him. Tall, dark and handsome, she thought. Every woman's clichéd desire rolled into one personable man. She judged him to be in his late twenties, somewhat older than herself, and utterly dishy, dressed as he was in evening clothes.

"I'm so sorry," she said politely. "I am sure Miss Darling would have enjoyed meeting you, but I am afraid she had an urgent appointment and had to leave early this evening." Marguerite smiled at him. "If you have a card I can give it to her."

He hesitated. "Yes, thank you, it would be very kind of you." He rifled through his pockets. Apparently he hadn't foreseen the need for a card, as he was having a hard job finding one and was getting a little flustered. His search wasn't helped by the fact he was still clutching the flowers.

She took pity on him. "Are those flowers for Miss Darling? Would you like me to pop them in water?"

He handed them over gratefully. "Thank you."

He finally found a card. She read it with more attention than she would normally have paid to an admirer of Peggy's. 'Eugene Dunning' was boldly engraved on the card with a London telephone number beneath. There was no further information. She put the flowers in a vase and tucked the card into the flowers in a place where Peggy could see it. "There you go," she said cheerfully. "Miss Darling will see them tomorrow."

"Are you a friend of hers?" he asked.

Well, that was an improvement on other stage-door Johnnies, she thought to herself. Most assumed she was a servant and treated her accordingly.

"Yes."

"Look, I don't want to be forward," he said impulsively, "but I was going to invite Miss Darling out, and as she's not here, well, I wondered if you would like to join me. I've got a table booked." He looked at her appealingly. "Please, it seems a waste of a good evening." His smile, she noticed, was particularly charming.

She had no particular reason not to go out. Her work was up to date. Katya and Edith were back at home and likely to be in bed already. A handsome stranger who wanted to wine and dine her was an appealing alternative. She had few illusions about his intent. She'd be pumped for information about Peggy, but she could be discreet and still enjoy an evening out at his expense.

She smiled at him. "I'm game," she said. "Why not?"

He grinned back at her. He wouldn't tell her, but every thought she had was reflected on her mobile little face. "To an evening of mutual enjoyment then," he declared. "Do you have a coat?"

Marguerite fetched her wrap and shut the dressing room door.

"Let's go," said Eugene.

He escorted her to the restaurant where, indeed, a table for two was waiting. It was only as she was seated that he suddenly said, "I've displayed some very poor manners. I'm so sorry, I haven't introduced myself. My name is Dunning, Eugene Dunning." He smiled at her. "May I know your name? It's inexcusable of course that I haven't already asked you for it."

Marguerite grinned at him. It wasn't like her to be impulsive and going out with a complete stranger ranked high on the list of things Edith would most certainly counsel her against. "I did wonder if we would ever be formally introduced," she said. "I'm Marguerite, Marguerite Komarov."

"Ah, that explains that lovely accent you've got," he said. "It's so exotic; it makes you sound mysterious, like Marlene Dietrich.

Where are you from originally? That accent never came from the Home Counties."

His smile was particularly vivid. It had a slightly wolfish quality that offset the otherwise elegant cast of his face and made his bright blue eyes light up dangerously. Altogether a very handsome man, Marguerite thought. It was a pity his interest was in Peggy.

She smiled. "Well, it's a long story, but I'll tell you after you tell me about yourself." She picked him as being a few years older than herself, but apart from a posh accent, there was nothing else about him she found easy to identify. Marguerite considered that accent. 'Queen's English', she thought, that's what he spoke. Or, as Len Schwartz would have put it, 'Eugene talked like a toff'.

"My story's not that interesting," began Eugene, fiddling with the cutlery. "Born in Bristol, minor public school and then the army. Got shipped out to the Mediterranean and had a spot of bad luck when we were captured. I spent the last eighteen months of the war in a prisoner-of-war camp in Germany. After liberation I came back and started helping in the family shop. We've got an emporium type of place my father started back in the twenties. I've got plans to expand, though, and open branches of the store throughout England. We opened one in Cardiff a couple of years ago. That's why I'm in London now. I've been looking at suitable sites for us to open here."

Marguerite watched his face light up with enthusiasm as he spoke of his work. She recognised his hunger and drive. "I know how you feel," she said. "I've just started operating on my own, and watching your own business expand is thrilling. It's like having your own doll's house to play with and being able to move the bits round as you like. You can make it into something that suits you."

"Exactly," said Eugene enthusiastically. "It's the sense of building something I enjoy. Putting it all together and making it happen. My father was prepared to take things so far, but now I want to turn our small family store into a big, countrywide business." He gave a little laugh. "As you see, I could talk all day about it. What is your business?"

The food arrived, but neither paid it much attention. When Eugene learned that Marguerite was a dressmaker – 'couturier', as she liked to describe herself – he was thoughtful.

"I want fashion clothing in our shops. People are tired of restrictions and rationing. We need stylish, affordable, ready-to-wear clothing for the young generation, who want to dress well and celebrate that they are young and alive. They had too much grey misery growing up; now they want everything to be new, exciting and fresh."

Marguerite nodded. "I can understand that. The women that come to me want high-fashion garments. But they can afford to spend more money on clothing than most. If there was a really good ready-to-wear option, I think you could do very well, as long as the clothes are both stylish and good value. If you are opening stores across the country, it would be very exciting."

They grinned at each other in a moment of perfect understanding. Marguerite dropped her eyes in sudden embarrassment. It was, after all, no business of hers what Eugene did with his company, but for a moment she'd been caught up in someone else's dream, and it was magical. She'd envied theatre folk their passion for the stage but had never managed to explain to anyone how she felt about her own ambitions. Eugene was different. For a second it had felt like he understood her.

She pushed her food round the plate, concentrating on a solitary mushroom.

"Why don't you come with me tomorrow and look at the site I am thinking of using in London?" Eugene sounded suddenly uncertain, and she glanced up at him. "Look, I don't usually talk like this with people, not girls on dates, anyway," he said apologetically. "I know I may be boring you."

She gave a sudden shake of her head. "No, I'm interested," she assured him.

"Really?" He gave her his dazzling smile again. "Will you come with me tomorrow then?"

Marguerite nodded. "I'd love to, if I'm not in the way."

They smiled at each other. "I think I'm very glad that Miss Darling went out early tonight," he said cryptically before plunging back into explaining his plans for Dunnings.

CHAPTER
TWENTY SEVEN

London, 1954.

SHE LET HERSELF INTO THE HOUSE and settled into the privacy of her bed. It was effortless to talk with him, she thought. She'd had a few boyfriends previously but they'd seemed so young and unformed, with no plans for their careers and life. It had been difficult to find something to talk about, and they'd been uncomfortable with her focus and drive. Boys, she thought. That was the difference. The boyfriends had been boys, not men. Eugene was most certainly a man – very certain of his direction and comfortable in his own skin. It was restful to be with someone so strong and certain about what they wanted.

She wondered what life had been like in that German prisoner-of-war camp. The knowledge that he'd experienced hardship made her more comfortable about eventually telling him her own story.

Eugene's feral smile and bright blue eyes were the last things she thought of as she drifted off to sleep.

Her mood persisted into the next morning. The blue sky and

early morning sun that filled the little courtyard garden with bright light and sharply defined shadows seemed a personal present from nature to match her mood and fill her with optimism.

"Good morning!" she greeted Katya and Edith. "Isn't it a great day to be alive?"

Katya stared at her. "What's got you in a good mood?" she asked. "It's not like you to be pleasant to anyone at this time of the morning."

Marguerite shrugged. "It's just a beautiful day."

Katya sniffed. "Well, it's still not like you." She looked at Marguerite. "Have you got a boyfriend or something?" Marguerite chose to ignore this, but Katya grinned. "I think you've got a boyfriend." When she still got no response Katya decided she was right. "You've got a boyfriend, you've got a boyfriend," she chanted. "Mother, Marguerite's got a boyfriend."

Edith looked up from her tea and toast and stared at Marguerite. "Have you, dear?" she asked in surprise.

Marguerite felt herself getting flustered. "No, I haven't," she replied, shortly. "Don't be silly, Katya."

"Well, I do wish you would find yourself a nice young man," said Edith wistfully. "You're wasting your youth away, Marguerite. You won't stay young forever, and girls only have a few years in which to establish themselves. There are younger ones coming along all the time, and your looks won't last. Since the war, there are more young women around than young men, so if you don't find one soon, all the good ones will be taken."

Marguerite sighed.

"Thank you for your comments, Mother," she said sarcastically. "I'll be sure to get out there and trap myself a man before I end up looking like a crone."

Katya refused to be deflected. "I think you have got a boyfriend. What's he like? Is he handsome, is he rich?"

Marguerite gave an inelegant snort. "I haven't got a boyfriend," she repeated, "and if I did, I surely wouldn't tell either of you. You really are such a child, Katya," and with that she stalked back to the workroom to tidy up and start her working day.

She resented Edith's comments. She was concerned enough

about her single status and the passing years. She had a brief vision of walking down the aisle beside Eugene, realised what she was doing and deliberately changed that train of thought. Things were different in theatrical circles where her friends formed relationships that didn't necessarily end in wedlock.

Eugene was a nice man, and it had been a pleasant encounter, but there was no reason to assume there was anything more significant about the evening. No reason he would invite her out again or even take her to see the shop he'd mentioned. After all, many promises and assurances made at night evaporated in the morning light. Still, she waited in earshot of the telephone.

It rang at 9.30, and Marguerite leapt to answer it, only to hear her 10 o'clock client cancelling the appointment and unable to commit to another time. Convinced by now her day was going to turn out badly, Marguerite stitched a seam grimly. Her mood wasn't improved either when she pricked a needle into the quick of her nail. The small but pungent pain caused her to swear fluently.

Katya looked at her. "I hope I can swear like that when I grow as old as you," she said sweetly.

Marguerite glared at her and carried on stitching. Katya laughed.

When the phone call came, though, it was all Marguerite could have hoped for.

"Lunch, then a tour of the premises, perhaps? Maybe dinner?"

Marguerite agreed to it all with the proviso that she was needed at the theatre until after the performance, so it would be a late supper.

She put the phone down, unaware of the small smile on her face. Katya watched her, saying nothing, but storing up valuable information to share with Edith. Marguerite could deny it all she liked, thought Katya, but something was going on, and she was certain it had been a male voice at the other end of the phone.

The reality of the phone call threw Marguerite into a panic. Last night had been an impromptu bit of fun that had turned out spectacularly well. Today, in bright daylight, she wondered if the magic would hold. Maybe Eugene would see her clearly and be disappointed. He had, after all, originally hoped to squire the glamorous Peggy to dinner, not her dresser.

By the time she met Eugene her native shyness and nervousness had driven her to tongue-tied tension.

After a couple of conversational gambits had failed to summon up the spontaneous girl of the night before, Eugene looked at her thoughtfully. "Have I offended you in some way?" he asked quietly. "You seem a little tense with me, and last night I thought we forged the beginnings of a friendship?"

Marguerite rubbed the back of her neck, a habit she had when nervous. "I suppose I'm afraid that by daylight you might think I look like a vegetable."

In her shyness the Polish accent was suddenly strong. Eugene looked at her in puzzlement for a moment trying to work out what she was saying. Then he laughed. "A pumpkin," he said. "You thought I might think you had turned into a pumpkin? I might just as well wonder if you thought I had turned into a rat in daylight. No, you are most certainly not a pumpkin, or any other sort of vegetable. You look as wonderful today as you did last night. I just hope I don't disappoint by daylight myself. Please let me know if I have turned into a rat."

Marguerite gave a small grin. "No, I don't think you're a rat at all. Prince Charming maybe …" she trailed off, embarrassed by what she had said.

"No," said Eugene, "I'm no Prince Charming. I've never understood the sort of man who chases after a girl silly enough to wear glass slippers. Think of the expense of replacing them all the time."

They looked at each other a moment, both smiled, and the ice was broken.

Although their experiences had been very different, the war years had scarred both of them. He told her of the prison camp, the hunger, the hard physical work in the quarry, and the frustration and hopelessness of wasting his youth in that prison. She told him about her father's death.

He took her to see the premises in Oxford Street. Marguerite was impressed. Even battered and smashed up in the war years,

Oxford Street had been a name to conjure with. Now it was growing and glowing with optimism. If Eugene was planning on setting up here, then he'd set his sights high. They walked through the empty space, Eugene occasionally stopping to ask the agent a question, but saying little. Marguerite followed, wondering at the sheer scale of the operation he was planning. She liked his attitude, confident, but not flashy.

She wondered what he was imagining as he walked through the empty spaces. Did he already see the completed store clearly before him? She tried to envisage racks of clothes, rows of shoes and bags, cosmetics and other luxury goods. He surely had to be targeting the upper end of the market if he was setting up shop in Oxford Street. She wondered what it must feel like to be taking this step, how much money and time he was investing. How much cash did he have to invest? She had no doubt at all that he had the required energy.

They were both subdued when they parted from the agent, and walked in silence. She was happy enough to walk through the early summer sunshine and let him work his way through his thoughts. Finally he raised his head and looked at her. He gave a grin. "Quite a venture, don't you think?"

Marguerite gave a cautious nod.

His smile widened. "Scared?" he asked. "Imagine your clothes there, all hung up, ready to model and show. Imagine the clients you want coming in to buy."

Marguerite nodded again. She could imagine this easily, almost touching the racks of pretty summer dresses displayed to entice women to stop and touch. What did he mean by his question anyway? It was the second time he had referred to her being part of his venture.

They stopped at the bus stop for her ride back to Kensington. She hesitated, not sure of the correct form or how she was to convey her pleasure in his company without appearing forward. Somewhat abruptly she thrust her hand out to him.

"Thank you so much for lunch," she said formally. "I thought the premises looked very interesting." She winced at the banality but seemed incapable of being light, witty and sophisticated.

Eugene took her hand and held it for a moment. "I too enjoyed lunch, and I'm particularly looking forward to seeing you again this evening. I'll meet you where I met you last night." His eyes were laughing at her. "Although this time I'll be seeking a different lady."

Marguerite smiled back at him. "Until tonight then," she said. Her bus was pulling up at the pavement and she started to pull her arm back. Instead of releasing her hand, or shaking it, as she'd expected, he turned it so her palm faced up. He bent swiftly and planted a soft kiss on her wrist, just above where her lace glove finished. Startled, Marguerite gave a soft intake of breath.

Eugene released her, smiled and stepped back to allow her to climb onto the bus. He waved as it pulled away. Marguerite barely made it to a vacant seat before her legs gave way under her, and the conductor had to ask her for her fare three times before she recovered herself sufficiently to reply and pay for her ticket.

The soft kiss burned itself into her skin. Absently she turned her wrist up and gazed at it. It was completely unmarked and unchanged, yet Marguerite could still feel the touch of his lips on the soft skin. She gave a slight shiver.

CHAPTER
TWENTY EIGHT

London, 1954.

MARGUERITE HAD INTENDED TO TELL PEGGY everything. She arrived at the theatre a little early with that purpose in mind. Unfortunately, 'Too much' was already seated in Peggy's dressing room, so she was effectively silenced as she laid out Peggy's costumes and makeup quietly, hoping Peter would be gone soon.

She was amused as she watched him observing himself in the well-lit makeup mirrors. Even as he chatted to Peggy he was checking the set of his hair, combing it with his fingers so it fell a little more stylishly over his brow, creasing his collar so it set more crisply, and straightening his tie.

His eyes met hers in the mirror and, correctly interpreting her amused contempt, he turned towards Peggy, made a couple of half-hearted farewell remarks, rose and left the room.

"He really is a bit of a nancy boy," remarked Marguerite. "He's as vain as a girl. If you spent half the time he does admiring yourself in the glass, you'd never get yourself on stage."

Peggy sniffed. "Well, he's a good-looking man," she said,

"and there's nothing wrong with looking after your appearance."

Marguerite handed her a pair of stockings. "He needs someone like my mother to tell him that vanity is a sin, and that a person's worth isn't found in a mirror," she said tartly.

Peggy looked at her in surprise. "What's got into you? Did you get out of bed on the wrong side this morning?"

If ever there was a cue for her to 'spill the beans' Peggy had provided Marguerite with the perfect moment, but she found she didn't know where to begin. Instead she just smiled, shook her head and said, "I suppose with Peter being in the film business, appearance is important to him."

The interval came and went. Marguerite knew better than to interrupt Peggy when she was in role. Peggy became totally focused on her performance, and light chatter went by the board.

When Marguerite went down to the backstage kitchen to get a cup of tea, still without telling Peggy about Eugene, she admitted ruefully that Katya could have handled the situation better.

Peggy came off-stage elated with the applause. She was always the same; tense and highly strung before a performance, glowing and incandescent during it, elated at the end. Then over the next couple of hours the energy she expended caught up with her, and Peggy reverted to a tired child in need of supper, alcohol and men.

She emerged from behind the screen having dumped her costume, and Marguerite wrapped her up in her robe and sat her down at the dressing table.

She tended to her friend, setting out the cotton wool and cold cream, helping her brush her hair out and picking up discarded costumes for cleaning and pressing. She found herself nervously listening to any sound from outside the dressing room. She could hear the odd snatch of conversation as people walked past.

She was all fingers and thumbs, although she told herself firmly that she was not at all agitated and could carry out her duties perfectly well.

After she had dropped the hairbrush twice she looked up to see Peggy looking at her.

"Are you all right?" Peggy asked. "It's not like you to be so butter-fingered."

Marguerite had just opened her mouth to reply when there was a knock on the door. Marguerite promptly dropped the brush again. She swore violently, picked it up a second time and dashed it onto the dressing table.

"Tell whoever it is I'm not ready ..." started Peggy, but Marguerite gave her a small, apologetic grimace and went to open the door.

Eugene was standing there with another bunch of flowers. "Good evening," he said. "Tonight I've brought flowers for the right girl." He gave her a big grin.

Marguerite grinned back. "Please come in," she said.

She turned to Peggy, who was staring at her, wide eyed. "Um, Peggy," she started, "please may I introduce Eugene Dunning?"

Peggy smiled graciously at Eugene. "I'm charmed," she said, inclining her head. She beckoned him in to the dressing room and looked him over. "I'm very pleased to meet you," she said. Her manner was flirtatious and amused.

Marguerite felt like murdering her.

"The honour is all mine," Eugene said. "May I say how wonderful you were on stage tonight?"

Peggy smiled a little complacently. "Thank you. What may I do for you, Mr Dunning?"

"I've come to steal your dresser away when she's finished her work," Eugene added. "Am I in the way? I can sit quietly in the corner until you have both finished."

Peggy turned to Marguerite. "Oh, we won't be very long," she assured Eugene. Her eyebrows were raised as she looked at Marguerite. "Have you known Marguerite long?"

Marguerite's eyes met Eugene's in the mirror. His were laughing at her. "Oh, about twenty-four hours," he replied breezily.

Peggy gasped. "Well, that's not long at all. Please sit, Mr Dunning. The sooner Marguerite returns me to normal, the sooner I can let her free."

"We met yesterday when Eugene came up to see you and you weren't here, you remember?" rushed out Marguerite, returning to her duties.

Peggy grabbed the hairbrush in exasperation.

"Was this something you forgot to mention?"

Marguerite blushed and whispered back. "I couldn't find the words, or the time."

"Tomorrow," said Peggy firmly. "All the gossip."

"Tomorrow," Marguerite agreed.

Eugene discreetly buried himself in a magazine and pretended not to hear.

CHAPTER
TWENTY NINE

London, 1955.

MARGUERITE SCOWLED AT HER FRIEND IN mock confusion.

"For years I've pottered on, never really worrying about all the lovey-dovey stuff and now I can't get enough of it. I constantly think about him. I want his smell, his touch, everything."

Peggy laughed. "That's what being in love is like. Enjoy it while it lasts. In the meantime can you pour another cup of tea?"

Marguerite reached for the teapot, looking shocked. "I can't imagine it not lasting. I think this is the real thing."

Peggy smiled. "I hope it is, for you both," she said, accepting the cup. She looked sideways at Marguerite. "How far have you gone with him?"

Marguerite flushed. "Not very," she confessed. "Just kisses, hand-holding and so on."

Marguerite was certain that, in her situation, Peggy would already have become Eugene's lover although he had never once suggested this. She was prepared to go all the way with him, but she was too shy to bring the subject up herself. She didn't feel comfortable telling her friend about an odd scene that had played out the other night.

That evening, they had stood in the porch to say goodnight. Emboldened by two glasses of wine and the warmth of the summer evening, Marguerite had tried to encourage Eugene to take liberties with her. She had run her hands down to the front of his trousers and felt the hard mass beneath. She had slowly started to rub and stroke the promising growth and heard him take a quick, shaky breath, which encouraged her. She was feeling rather shaky herself. But instead of allowing the situation to develop, Eugene grabbed her by the shoulders and pushed her back.

"No," he murmured as he stepped away from her. He was drawing deep, ragged breaths, as if he had been running.

Marguerite turned away, not wanting him to see her sudden tears. She felt mortified, like a stupid child. The sense of rejection was overwhelming. Obviously she was doing it wrong, or he didn't feel the same as she did. If the ground had swallowed her up, or a bus run her down, she would have been endlessly grateful. As neither of these catastrophes seemed imminent, she wanted to get behind her front door as soon as possible.

After a moment Eugene stirred. He reached out to her and pulled her into his arms. Marguerite moved stiffly, rigid with pain and embarrassment. Eugene held her like a small child, cuddled into his shoulder. He rubbed her back gently. "Shh," he said.

Marguerite dropped her head in shame, just wanting to go home.

Eugene put a finger under her chin and lifted her face to him. "Marguerite, this ..." He faltered, then started again. "I don't want you as a lover, Marguerite. It's not the way I feel about you."

Marguerite's humiliation was now complete. Helplessly she started to cry.

"Shh," he said again. He fumbled in a pocket and drew out a handkerchief. He dabbed at her face. It was a nice thought, she supposed, but a bit ineffectual. Eventually she grabbed the cloth and wiped her eyes herself.

He pulled her back against his shoulder again. She turned her face away so she didn't have to look at him.

"You must know the saying 'if you bed them, you can't wed them'?" he said softly. "I think of you as someone who might one day consent to be my wife, Marguerite. I don't want an affair. I want us to do things properly. I want you to go to the altar on our wedding day with no one questioning your morals and virtue." He laughed. "Look at what I want for the store; everything is going to be about quality. I feel that way about you too: a woman of quality. I don't want a good-time girl. I want a forever girl."

Marguerite turned her head and stared up at him, not knowing what to say, or even what to think. "Ohh," she breathed. Her eyes were round and enormous in her face, her mouth a perfect 'O' of surprise.

Gently Eugene eased her away from him. "We are going to wait, Marguerite, my darling. We are going to do the right thing, and our time will be all the sweeter for the waiting." He smiled at her with warmth that melted the pain away. "OK?"

As she lay in bed, Marguerite considered what Eugene had said. She wasn't used to doing what someone else told her. She was used to thinking of herself as a war refugee and outside constraints which might otherwise shackle a girl of her class. She supposed it boded well for the security of marriage that Eugene was deeply against premarital activity. Even so, as she tossed and turned that night, she couldn't help wonder whether Eugene loved respectability more than he loved her, and what he would think about the fantasies that invaded her mind.

The months flew by as Eugene and Marguerite grappled with the formation of the store. At first Marguerite felt like an imposter, crowding in on Eugene's work, but once the process of stocking the store was under way, her flair for design came into its own. Without her realising it, the years spent at the theatre had developed her eye for the dramatic and exciting. Displays of merchandise, boring and stagnant in someone else's hands, became creative masterpieces when Marguerite was involved.

She used colour and texture in ways that were closer to the theatre than to commerce, but the results were eye-catching and compelling.

Dunning's slogan, *Fine Quality: Fair Prices*, was an instant winner, particularly with young women who embraced the ready-to-wear market. Older clients, used to having a dressmaker, were harder to entice, but Marguerite had faith that where their daughters went, more mature women would follow. She began to feel a proprietorial interest in the store.

Eugene had made it clear that decisions about what clothing and accessories to stock were her responsibility. Accustomed to working on a small scale with individual clients, Marguerite now had to find factories and designers who would work with her concepts and deliver the final product. It was a big leap for the girl from Schwartz and Bloomfield, but Marguerite rose to the challenge.

Autumn was fading, and winter setting in. Marguerite hated the early darkness, the fog, smog and murkiness of London. She felt the weather wearing away at her optimism. Katya managed to stir her up at every opportunity, slyly making digs at her continued spinster state. Eugene hadn't raised the matter again. Marguerite knew he was totally focused on the store, but in her heart she resented playing second fiddle to a shop.

Consequently she was slightly offhand when he invited her to visit his parents. She had met them before and was aware of their opinion that their son could do much better than a scrubby, middle European refugee.

Edith, of course, held the opposing view that no grocer's son was good enough for a Komarov. Marguerite pointed out that, to the best of her knowledge, the Komarovs had always been in trade. She remembered Grandpa's stories about the factory in Moscow. Her own father had been a tailor, and she herself earned her income through her needle. Edith just sniffed.

They caught the train and managed to find an empty carriage. Eugene seemed quiet and preoccupied, and Marguerite gazed out the window at the ubiquitous murk. Usually she enjoyed travelling by train, relishing the ability to see people's backyards and houses as they rode along. This evening there was little to look at. It was dark and gloomy enough outside for her only clear view to be a reflection of the carriage in the glass. She studied Eugene for a while without him realising she was examining his reflection. He looked good in the subdued light. Suddenly he looked up and caught her gazing at him. He grinned and reached out to pull her towards him.

"I have a serious issue to raise with you," he said.

Marguerite thought guiltily of the overrun of costs in her design of the millinery department. "Yes, I know it cost more than I anticipated, but I'm sure we'll recoup it once people start buying," she said optimistically.

Eugene stared at her blankly. "I beg your pardon?"

It was Marguerite's turn to be confused. "Weren't you talking about the haberdashery display?" she asked.

Eugene gave a little choking sound. "No, I'm not. Marguerite, my darling, I am trying to ask you to marry me and obviously making a mess of it." He slid off the seat onto the floor and knelt on one knee. "Miss Komarov, would you do me the honour of being my wife?"

Marguerite stared at him and then started laughing. The situation was just too absurd, particularly after what she had been thinking. Eugene looked hurt, which set Marguerite off again.

"I thought you wanted to discuss budgets. Oh, Eugene," she said. The moment, so long anticipated, was here. Her answer would mean changing everything, and suddenly she was a lot less certain than she had thought she'd be. It was a form of stage fright, she supposed.

Eugene kept his gaze fixed on her, but there was now a twinkle in his eye. "I don't go down on one knee to discuss budgets, not even for our store." He winced a little. "I don't mean to press you for an answer, but this floor is devilishly uncomfortable, not to mention the fact that my trousers are almost certainly getting dirt on them."

Marguerite giggled. She looked at him and saw again the man

who had so attracted her the first time they met: the slightly feral face, the enthusiasm, drive, honour and responsibility that were all part of him. She read in his face a slight self-doubt which was foreign. Apparently Eugene wasn't as certain of the outcome as he appeared. She smiled to herself.

"I, Marguerite Komarov," she said seriously, "do gladly accept your offer. If you're certain," she added nervously.

He jumped up off his knees and, sitting beside her on the seat, pulled her into a tight embrace. "Oh yes, my darling, I have never been more certain of anything in my life. We make an amazing team, and, on top of everything else, I love you so much it's driving me crazy. I'm sure some American crooner would have the words for it, but all I can do is this … and this … and this," punctuating each pause with a kiss.

"And I love you too," said Marguerite, when she got her breath back.

He pulled a jewellery box from his pocket. The ring was set with three diamonds. "It's a London Bridge setting," he explained. "I thought, as our shared future is so tied up with London, you might like the thought."

Marguerite gazed at it in delight. "Put it on," she begged. "Please."

Eugene held her left hand and gently slid the ring over her knuckle. "With this ring I thee pledge," he said formally, "and if I'm not prepared to quite worship you with my body before we get a wedding band on this finger, I hope you will see this as a foretaste of what's to come," and he kissed her thoroughly.

CHAPTER
THIRTY

London, 1955.

S HE WORE A LIGHT CREAM SUIT, with a hat and
short veil. Katya and Peggy were her attendants, and Mr
Schwartz gave her away. There were only a few guests, but
they were all dear to Marguerite. A few friends from the theatre
had come to wish her well, which added glamour and touched
her. Otherwise, as she said later to Eugene, "It was a day just to
please ourselves."

While Marguerite loved the store and her work, there were
times when she felt too much in the public eye. She wanted
Eugene to herself for once. Even so, an official photographer
had been there to capture this bit of Dunnings history, and a
journalist had been sent along to report on the day. Eugene
regarded these things as necessary to build Dunnings' profile.
He was superb at making contacts and generating publicity for
the company.

It had been a simple Church of England ceremony, this
last having caused heated debate in the Komarov household.
Edith maintained that Charles would have wanted his daughter

married in a Russian Orthodox Church, which gave Marguerite a twinge of guilt. When consulted, Eugene said he had no particular preference, but Marguerite, conscious of his family's reservations about her background, wanted to be as English as possible for the occasion.

True to Eugene's word, she had gone to the altar a virgin.

"Fully entitled to wear white," was the acid comment she made to Peggy as she was getting dressed for the occasion. Inadvertently, she made this statement within Edith's hearing.

"I should hope so," said Edith roundly. "How do you expect a man to respect you if you don't respect yourself?"

Marguerite shared a look with Peggy in the mirror, and Peggy rolled her eyes. "Oh well," she murmured, "I suppose I'll have to skip the respect and just concentrate on their bank balance."

Edith was shocked. She wouldn't say anything that marred Marguerite's wedding, but she made a point of avoiding Peggy for the rest of the day.

They spent their honeymoon in a waterfront hotel in Brighton. Both Eugene and Marguerite agreed they couldn't afford to be away from the store for too long.

After her long wait, and eagerness to divest herself of her virginity, Marguerite took to the marital bed with enthusiasm. After some initial discomfort, she found the process to be pleasant, and often a good deal more than just pleasant. She liked the intimacy, and the way her mood improved after the act. She enjoyed pleasing Eugene, and it seemed he was very pleased with his bride. Her initial shyness faded as she learned her power to please or tease him.

She became more aware of herself, and it affected her approach as to how she presented herself. She began to appreciate what Peggy, who'd had experience in these matters, had been trying to say and share with her.

"If you don't know that you don't know something, then it's hard to imagine what that something is," she said to her friend.

Peggy giggled. "Hm, that's a little muddled, but I take your point."

Back in London, Eugene had set them up in a new apartment

in South Kensington. Marguerite felt like a true bride, living with her husband and not with her mother and sister.

She kept the old house for their use but also as a work studio for herself. The new apartment was charming, stylish, modern and small. There was nowhere to set up her sewing machine.

Katya had left school and was working. Her salary, combined with Edith's, meant they were in a position to pay Marguerite rent, making a large contribution to the mortgage. Keeping the old place seemed a good investment for the future.

The couple settled into married life. There were a few awkward moments when Marguerite, used to pleasing herself, forgot to include Eugene in her plans. Then he did things she regarded as entirely alien. Used to living with women, she found male personal habits to be extraordinary. "Do they really have to pass wind and find it funny?" she asked Edith.

Edith laughed. "That's just men, my dear."

Her mother had avoided any discussion of the marital bed prior to the wedding but now felt free to give advice about pleasing and keeping a husband. "You have to remember all the time that you are partners," she cautioned her daughter. "Where he goes, you go. No long separations, whether it's convenient for you or not. Make sure he is part of your life, and you are part of his."

Edith made it clear she was looking forward to grandchildren, and as time passed she began to make marked comments. "I want to see my grandchildren before I die," she would say plaintively.

Marguerite was amused, but as month after month went by with no sign of pregnancy, she began to wonder if there was a problem. It wasn't until they had been married for two years that Marguerite knew for certain she was pregnant. She kept the news to herself for two weeks before she told Eugene, just to be certain. His excitement and enthusiasm was everything she could have hoped for.

The miscarriage, two months later, was devastating. Marguerite had been bending over, pinning a pattern out. As she straightened up she'd felt the sudden pain grab her, and gasped. She was rushed to hospital, but it was too late.

Her grief and guilt overwhelmed her. Nothing Eugene said

could convince her it hadn't been her fault.

"I feel like Catherine of Aragon, or Anne Boleyn," she said sadly to Edith. "Eugene never complains, but I feel I'm not keeping my part of the bargain in providing an heir. Maybe he will chop off my head one day." It was a sad little jest, and Edith patted her on the hand.

"If God wills it, then it will happen, and you will have a child. If God decides otherwise, then who are you to know better?"

"Bloody God should have better things to do with his time than interfere in my life," replied Marguerite harshly.

Her involvement with the store was changing. If she saw something about a display or range of clothing that displeased her, she would intervene; otherwise she left the staff to manage on their own. Her interest was now centred on helping Eugene expand the business.

Other branches of Dunnings opened, and Marguerite attended these ceremonies and was photographed accordingly. She was becoming a glamorous figure in London society, while Eugene was regarded as an important up-and-coming entrepreneur. Their photos appeared in the social pages of the press on a regular basis, and they learned to accept the intrusion as a necessary evil.

Their social life became a round of cocktail parties with other celebrities. Marguerite sometimes found herself yearning for the days when she, Peggy and the cast used to party backstage, at the wrap of a show, on fish and chips.

CHAPTER
THIRTY ONE

London, 1966.

LIFE, THOUGHT MARGUERITE, WAS VERY NEARLY perfect if you ignored the lack of a child. They moved from their apartment into a house in Mayfair. The old house in South Kensington was sold. Katya now worked in a banking office and was doing well. She and Edith moved into an apartment.

For the first time in their married life Marguerite and Eugene took on domestic staff. They decided they needed a cook, or at least a part-time kitchen worker.

Then Max entered their lives. A friend mentioned that his cousin's son, from New Zealand, was looking for work. Did Eugene know of anything? Max was offered a job as general assistant, which came to include butler, valet and social secretary. His responsibility was to make the Dunnings' life comfortable, and he achieved this with a maturity beyond his years and experience.

"He truly is magnificent," said Eugene with a great deal of respect. "It's just as well he's from New Zealand. He doesn't seem to know anything about appropriate limits to his role. No English servant would be content to have such a wide-ranging brief, or be intelligent enough to keep everything going smoothly."

On the night of the Harcourt's charity dinner and auction Marguerite was wearing a strapless, long silk gown. The boned bodice clung from breast to waist before flaring into a full skirt. Dior might be dead, but his influence on fashion was still felt. The shape accentuated Marguerite's slender, hour-glass figure. She was particularly pleased with the material, an abstract pattern of deep green, silver and black, which draped beautifully. She had put her hair up in a simple chignon and gave a little spin in front of the cheval glass to admire herself.

Eugene, struggling with his gold cufflinks, looked up and smiled. "You look very special tonight."

Marguerite went to help him with his tie. "Why, thank you, my husband." He bent his head and kissed her.

"Don't," she squealed. "Do you know how long it's taken me to get my hair and makeup right?"

He laughed at her. "Trust me, my darling. Every man in the room is going to want to do that to you tonight, Lizzie Arden or no Lizzie Arden."

She giggled at him. "Well, if we are still sober when we get home, you can muss me up then." She wrapped her fur stole around her shoulders.

The occasion was in support of the Save the Children Fund. Invitations had been issued to entertainment and business elite. The cream of society would be there, ensuring most guests already knew each other. If there were unknowns, they would be new artists or business people, and such functions were a way of launching them into the mainstream.

Eugene and Marguerite split up, the better to work the room. Marguerite saw Eugene in the distance, shaking hands with the men and charming the women. She smiled tolerantly as she watched a young actress give him the glad eye.

Peggy was at the same dinner, in the company of her present flame, a French art house film director. She looked very beautiful and sultry. The red hair had morphed into a strawberry blonde, but the slender figure and long legs were the same as ever. Peggy, now one of the established stars of British film and theatre, had a constant following of young actors and actresses seeking her attention. Marguerite hoped the French director was looking after her well, otherwise his future would be short and sweet.

The two women smiled at each other across the room, but their duties meant neither could cross to the other.

Marguerite exchanged 'mwah' kisses with a number of ladies and was introduced to others. It was a perfect place to pick up gossip. Some of the artists, whose works were for sale, were also present, looking hopelessly ill at ease. They were dressed appropriately but most looked as if they'd be happier in a duffle coat and denim jeans. Marguerite was introduced to one such young man in an ill-fitting suit. She assumed he'd hired it for the occasion, or else borrowed it from an older brother or his father. His bow tie was clearly ready-tied.

She barely heard his name through the din, but established that it was David. He looked so out of place as to almost be a caricature. "The artist as a young man," a friend murmured scathingly from behind her.

"You are one of the artists?" she enquired politely. "Is your painting one of those on display?"

He mumbled that this was so, and when pressed, pointed to one on the right-hand wall.

Oh dear, thought Marguerite. If she'd been asked to pick which painting was least saleable, this would have been it. It was a mass of orange and pink blotches and swirls, with an occasional khaki stripe within the mix. Marguerite considered the whole thing to be rubbish.

Tactfully she enquired, "What is the name of your work?" Experience had taught her this question usually launched an artist into a full description of the piece and relieved her of the burden of conversation.

"Rubbish," he said.

"I beg your pardon," said Marguerite, startled. "I didn't catch that. Did you say 'rubbish'?" She wondered if she had voiced her earlier thoughts, and the fear that he might be hurt gripped her with embarrassment.

"It's called 'Rubbish', and it is rubbish," said the young man belligerently. "I threw it onto canvas as a protest against society's endorsement of pretty art. Fools that they were, they went and selected it for this auction."

"Don't you support Save the Children Fund?" asked Marguerite, amused by his passion.

"I don't care about the fund," he said. "I hate this whole hypocritical 'appreciation of the arts' nonsense. Not one person in this room really knows anything about art, or even cares about art. They are here to be seen and to bolster each other's egos. It's all about money and nothing about charity or art. It's all just a sham."

Marguerite regarded him sceptically. "Forgive me for mentioning this, but these are probably the people whose taxes funded your education. If good things come out of such associations, is it right to be so critical? I doubt if those who receive funds from Save the Children are really going to care if the donors knew a Monet from a ..." She groped for a name. "... from a Manet," she finished triumphantly. As Marguerite was most certainly one of those who knew nothing about art, she was pleased she'd managed to finish her argument succinctly.

He turned and stared at her. "What's it to me what the pampered wife of a plutocrat thinks? You're well kept by your capitalist husband; you don't have to work, you don't have to care, feel or try to express something of yourself in art. You don't have to turn up in places like this, like a trained zoo chimpanzee, just to make ends meet."

It had been a long time since anyone had tried to challenge Marguerite, and his nerve took her breath away. Who was he to judge her life? She did know what it was like to be young and struggle, to hunger for self-expression, notice and approval. The line between the refugee and the society lady wasn't so far that the boundaries couldn't blur!

"Well, it just shows you know nothing about me then, doesn't it," she replied indignantly. "I've never heard a stupider line of argument. You've taken a general argument about art appreciation and tried to make it personal, about me and my life. Well, as an argument it won't wash. If you consider your own work rubbish, then no doubt it is. If anyone should know, it would be its creator, don't you think?" and she turned angrily and walked away.

Across the room she saw Peggy watching her progress with raised eyebrows. She would have to catch up with her friend and have a chat. It had been years since Marguerite had felt so challenged and defensive about her life. Who the hell was this boy to judge her and the way she chose to live? She took a deep breath, fixed her most pleasant smile on her face and moved on to another group.

Later that evening, after the meal, the auction began. The auctioneer presented each painting to the audience. His experience in working a crowd was evident.

"He could extract cash from a corpse, so he could," mumbled Henry Brown, another guest at their table. Henry, in spite of his name, was from Ireland, and his soft accent amused Marguerite. "I can't compete with the rest of these chaps. My pockets aren't deep enough," he complained.

Just then the Rubbish painting was brought to the block.

"I imagine you could afford this one," said Marguerite.

"What is it?" asked Henry. He had taken a cocktail or two too many before dinner, and his gaze was blurred as he viewed the work.

"It's called 'Rubbish'," she informed him.

"It looks like it and all," he said. Suddenly he looked at her and smiled. "I'll bid for it, and if I win, I'll give it to you," he exclaimed and put his hand up.

Marguerite tried to tell him that no, she didn't want the painting, but she could tell she wasn't winning.

The auctioneer did a good job of explaining the work as part of the movement amongst young British artists to explore the medium and try to express themselves outside the restrictive boundaries of form, line and colour. The audience listened but remained unimpressed. Henry's bid was the only one on the table. The auctioneer brought his gavel down, and the lot was sold to 'Mr Henry Brown, Table 23'.

There was polite clapping throughout the room before the bidding moved to the next work.

"There you are," said Henry exultantly. "I managed to buy a painting for charity, and I gift it as a present to you, my sweet Marguerite."

Eugene's eyebrows were slightly raised. Marguerite could tell from the quirk of his mouth that he'd correctly identified her feelings about the painting and was amused.

Henry was insistent the painting was hers. Marguerite tried every tactic she could think of to make him change his mind, but Henry, with the determination of the slightly drunk, wasn't to be swayed.

"I bought it for a beautiful lady," he said. "It's the quickest way I know to turn rubbish into beauty." As this was a direct dig at those who had criticised his burgeoning business in waste disposal, Marguerite felt she couldn't be brutal in her rejection. She turned to Eugene for support, but he was enjoying himself too much to intervene.

"It will look lovely hung up on your wall," he purred. "Do you think the bedroom, or were you more inclined to put it in the studio?"

Marguerite let her eyes show him what she thought of that. Eugene remained unrepentant. "I'll organise for it to be delivered, shall I, darling?" he said as he left the table.

Furious with her husband, Marguerite was left fuming. Henry, in a happy fog of alcohol, had gone off to deal with the auctioneer.

She was suddenly joined by David, the artist, who appeared out of the crowd and sat beside her at the otherwise empty table.

"You bought it," he said.

"No," said Marguerite sourly, "I didn't buy it. A friend bought it, then gave it to me."

She was rewarded by the most spontaneous smile she thought she had ever seen on a human face.

"I hope you enjoy it very much," the artist enthused. "I thought it was too avant-garde for the group tonight and was afraid it wouldn't sell." He looked sheepish. "I risked being evicted if I couldn't come up with the money tonight." A sudden thought occurred to him. He turned to look at her, and said, with great determination, like a schoolboy reciting lines, "I am sorry, I was out of line earlier. You were right; I don't know you, and I didn't have any right to say what I did."

Marguerite gazed at him dispassionately. By the end of this little speech he was quite red in the face. She realised he was very young. Twenty-five at most, she supposed. Usually this would have moved her to mercy. Instead, furious with having ended up with a painting she didn't want, she was in no mood to be nice.

"As you said, Rubbish by name and rubbish by nature," she said. "I was given the painting as a present by a drunken society nob who, as you already remarked, knew nothing about art. No doubt he is already settling the debt, so you won't be out of pocket."

"If you call round tomorrow," she said, "I will arrange for you to take possession of it again. Maybe you can find someone else to buy it, this time into a permanent home. You could try tonight's purchaser, his business is based on rubbish collection."

She got up and turned away before she had to see the chagrin on the boy's face, or deal with his distress. Really, she had enough to do without this sort of drama.

CHAPTER
THIRTY TWO

London, 1966.

"WHAT DO YOU THINK OF IT, Max?" asked Marguerite, once he had removed the brown paper and string from the painting.

It was propped up on the sofa in the drawing room, and soft morning light fell on it from the window.

They stared at it for some minutes. In the kinder light, the painting looked less abrasive than the night before, but her eyes still struggled to see any meaning or point to the swirls of colour in front of her.

Max was silent for a while then moved across the room to see it from a different angle. "It's a very dramatic piece," he said. "Very strong."

He moved up close to the work and stared at the brushstrokes. "It's been well executed. It's not your usual taste, of course, but I have to say, I like it. I think it's an exciting work."

"You do?" asked Marguerite, surprised.

"Yes," said Max. "Abstract art has been around for fifty years or so, so while it's not exactly ground-breaking in itself, what the artist has done with the painting is interesting."

"Yes, but what does it mean? What is it supposed to show?"

"There's an argument that says abstract art, by definition, isn't supposed to show recognisable subject matter, and that by banishing obvious realities you can create new ones." Max smiled at Marguerite.

"That sounds a bit pedantic, I know. I think you just have to enjoy it on its own merits. If you study it, eventually you'll probably find recognisable form in it yourself."

Marguerite glared at him. "I didn't realise you were an art critic along with all your other skills."

Max smiled sheepishly. "I did a couple of papers on art at university. It interested me, particularly modern art. I don't have any talent myself, but I can certainly enjoy the work of someone who has."

Marguerite lit a cigarette and gazed at the painting once again. Her work with textiles and patterns had given her an appreciation of form and texture. Perhaps she should approach this work as if she were judging a length of material. Viewed like that, it sort of made sense. Interesting that Max had admired it. Maybe she was becoming too old and narrow-minded in her tastes. In which case, so was Eugene, something they might need to consider in terms of the store.

It was early afternoon when there was a knock on the door, and Max admitted David Mallet.

Marguerite hadn't been sure he'd be brave enough to come. Max showed him in.

"Hello, er, I came about the painting," said David.

Marguerite waved him to a seat. "Please, sit down," she said.

He seemed a different man. Casually dressed in corduroy trousers with an open neck shirt, he looked more relaxed and a good deal more attractive, she noted approvingly. He occupied his clothes in their own right, not, as last night, like a shabby costume in a play.

"I wasn't sure you would come," she said.

"You made it obvious you didn't want the work. I'd be a fool to throw it away," he said curtly. Even his voice was more authoritative. He wasn't quite as young as she had previously thought. He had looked youthful because of his gaucheness, but now she placed him in his mid to late twenties.

"It seems the situation has reversed, and I now owe you an apology for last night," said Marguerite. "I was angry, and I felt manipulated. I hope you will forgive my ungraciousness."

David looked at her.

He hadn't expected that, thought Marguerite with satisfaction.

"I thought you made your viewpoint perfectly clear, and I don't require your graciousness. I've come to take the painting, if the offer is still open."

So much for her apology, thought Marguerite. This was a very direct young man. "I hope you will accept my apology, because it is sincerely meant," she said. "Unfortunately, I've had a change of heart about the painting, and I want to keep it. I'm sorry I misled you last night."

"Why?" he asked.

"Why? Well," started Marguerite, feeling more than a little flustered. "I've seen it in a new light this morning and feel differently about it."

David's eyes narrowed. "I ask again, why? People don't change their tastes overnight. Has someone told you it might be valuable, or of use to you?"

"No, no, nothing like that."

"That's the reason, though, isn't it," he challenged. "You've suddenly realised it might not be the rubbish you thought, and maybe it can be another asset for you to stick on your wall or in your bank." He stood up and paced the room. Marguerite looked at his progress around the furniture with concern.

"God," he said, "people like you disgust me. Collectors! At least your reaction last night was authentic. Today you're like a merchant banker. I think I'll take it with me anyway. Why waste it on someone like you?"

Marguerite was appalled. "It's mine, whether you like it or not. And I now choose to keep it. It was a fair sale, Mr Mallet, and if I misled you last night, I've already apologised. I'm not about to do so again." She had rarely felt so angry. She had tried to be gracious, but he'd just brushed her off.

They glared at each other, both refusing to back down.

Max entered with the tea service. He took in the situation without a quiver of his face. "Tea, madam?" he said, at his most formal. "Would you like to pour, or shall I?"

Marguerite steadied herself. "Would you pour for us, Max?" she asked. "Perhaps Mr Mallet would like something stronger as well?"

David returned to his seat. "I'm fine, thank you."

Max brought a cup over to the table beside him. "How do you prefer your tea, sir? With cream and sugar?"

David opened his mouth to refuse but was overcome by Max's urbane courtesy. "Oh, all right, yes thanks," he said.

"Would you also care for a drink, sir. A scotch, or perhaps a cocktail?"

"No, I ... oh, a whisky please." He glared across the room at Marguerite who had taken advantage of the interchange to regain her poise.

"I should let you know that I don't usually drink liquor in the middle of the day. You've turned me into a drinking man."

Marguerite's lips twitched. "That's not usually the effect I have on men."

"I pity your poor husband," said David, but his tone was less belligerent.

They drank their tea in silence as the tension eased.

After a while Marguerite said, "You asked what changed my mind. Actually Max explained something about what I was looking at. I don't know if his exposition is what you had in mind, but I was able to see that I shouldn't look at your work like I do a photograph. So I thought about it in terms I use when I choose textiles for my designs. It made more sense."

"So what do you look for when you look at fabric?"

"Colour, texture, pattern, flow, line; all sorts of things. There are no firm rules for designing a gown, just that everything has to work together." Marguerite looked at the painting again. "It occurred to me that in your painting everything was perhaps working together. And," she added, "just because someone comes from a culture that values a grass skirt and is unused to gowns, that doesn't mean the gown is wrong, nor the grass skirt. It's just an education of taste."

David gave what sounded suspiciously like a snort. "Are you trying to tell me that my work is a grass skirt?"

"It could be the French gown," countered Marguerite. "Either way, it can stand on its own."

They looked at each other. "We do seem to spend a lot of time saying we're sorry to each other," he said. "But I am sorry, I was rude. When you create something, you feel so personal about it, it is hard to let go. I suppose it's like having a child, not that I have one."

Marguerite winced. "Well, speaking as someone who also doesn't have a child, I would imagine you are right. Shall we agree to declare a draw and start again without hostilities?"

He smiled back at her cautiously.

"How did you start painting?" asked Marguerite.

Working-class born, he had grown up in a world utterly deprived of art. Poor, driven by ambition, he had won a scholarship and struggled through ever since. Marguerite smiled to herself. It didn't sound so different to her own start, give or take the war, she supposed. David proved an entertaining visitor.

As he left he said, "If you are going to be interested in modern art, you should go to the Tate Gallery. That way you'll get a real overview."

"I suppose I should, although I'm not sure I'd know enough to know what I was looking at yet."

"Why don't you come with me?" he asked. "I always love going there, and I could explain some of the art that's important to me. I'm not a qualified guide," he said hastily, "but I do know something about art."

Marguerite thought for a moment. "I would like that. Thank you. When would you be free to go?"

They agreed on a time, and she showed him to the door.

Marguerite hadn't felt so energised by someone in years. She looked forward to the gallery trip.

CHAPTER
THIRTY THREE

London, 1964.

WHEN MARGUERITE TOLD EUGENE ABOUT THE encounter he was amused. "So our Max is an art connoisseur, you now understand abstract art and our fire-eater artist wants to educate you? Not bad for a day's work."

"Everything needs change to keep it healthy. Maybe we've become complacent," he said when she expressed her concern Dunnings might have become stale. "Do you think you can research this yourself? Your young artist might have some useful ideas."

Marguerite nodded. "I can't help thinking that the way David was dressed today was a uniform for young people. Every era has its own style. I wonder what the female equivalent is? It's not the clothes we've been promoting recently, that's for certain."

"Look into it," her husband advised her. "Dunnings never got to where it is today by ignoring current trends and tastes." He gave her a hasty kiss before adjourning to his club.

Marguerite shrugged lightly and rolled her eyes. They had been married too long and too comfortably for her to object to him being out for the evening. She settled down with the *Tatler* but found herself looking at the painting repeatedly. She hadn't yet decided where to hang it.

The visit to the Tate was successful. David was an informed, if irreverent guide. His comments about some of the paintings and the artists involved, particularly the more modern, were pungent and scandalous.

It was followed a week later by a visit to the British Museum, later still to the National Gallery, and to various avant-garde art galleries.

Marguerite began to shed her formality. Dining at cafés was replaced by casual meals, picnics in a park or a baked potato from a roadside stall. She felt a girl again.

She met him one afternoon for a gallery visit. She had dressed in a smart but casual shirt and trousers, abandoning her usual formal daytime suits. Her hair was out of its restrictive chignon.

David's eyes lit up when he saw her. "Hey, you look great," he said. "Informality suits you."

She began to lose weight and was particularly pleased the day she found that a favourite belt, unaccountably too tight in recent years, suddenly fitted round her newly slender waist.

She tried to study the fashion choices of younger women. Girls wore skirts and little jumpers, or shirts and slacks. Formality was declining, and anything restrictive in clothing or manners was being rejected.

Perms and home-based perm kits, meant women could maintain their hairstyles themselves. Most young women went to bed at least once a week with curlers in their hair.

Marguerite found herself startled by the self-confidence of the young, and by their sense of self-importance.

"Was I like this?" she asked herself.

The world of a younger generation was suddenly open to her, where previously she had been blind. It was not unlike the way David was teaching her to appreciate modern art.

They were sitting at an outside table in Regent's Park, both drinking a coffee. Marguerite watched people walking by while David watched her.

"Penny for your thoughts," he said.

She focused on him. "Why?" she asked.

"You've been in a dream for most of the morning. I want to know what you're thinking."

She looked sheepish. "I've been thinking that maybe I'd stopped looking at what was going on around me." She smiled. "You've been good for me," she confessed. "It's important to learn new things."

He returned her gaze. "Do you know that you're quite a different person now to the woman I met that first night? Here you are, fun and friendly. At first ..." He tailed off.

"Yes?" she teased him.

"Well, I don't know really. You were more formal, restricted, buttoned up. You are such a lovely, natural person. And I would never have picked it that first night. I thought you were a right cow." He smiled to soften the criticism.

"And I thought you were gauche and defensive," Marguerite replied. "So neither of us are good at making that all-important first impression?"

"It's not that," said David. "I am, actually, both gauche and defensive. I was brought up that way. My background is working class, and in England that matters. You really don't understand our class system, do you?"

Marguerite smiled. "You know my history now. I've never been quite certain where I fit in to English society, so I've made my own rules." She laughed. "Eugene supplies my respectability. We're nouveau riche, but frankly it's better than being nouveau poor. No, I don't know what it's like to be 'working class' but I know how to work hard. I'd have thought that being poor and then achieving success was a good thing."

"In England, that's not a given. I don't think you ever really were a 'right cow'," said David. "I think I was too quick to judge. I was frightened, so I made everyone my enemy. You've made me see how foolish I was. Because you're an outsider, you've also made me see other things more clearly."

They smiled at each other.

Eugene was interested in Marguerite's observations about change, but he left it to her to define their look and signature style. Any contribution she made to increasing revenue could be critical. Dunnings was losing ground in the marketplace, and most of his thoughts centred round Profit and Loss. Marguerite's involvement had never extended to the financial side of the business, so he didn't raise his concerns with her.

She kept him up to date with her projects but was less than frank about the degree to which David was influencing her life.

If you had asked either of them if such behaviour was deceitful, they would each have been genuinely startled. They had different areas of responsibility, that was all, and neither saw it in any way a detraction from their marriage.

"He's very pretty," said Peggy. "You might want to watch yourself."

She and Peggy had met for a cup of coffee. Marguerite flushed slightly as she stirred the sugar in.

"Oh, nonsense," said Marguerite. "He's just a friend. You know, young, gauche." She had told her friend the full story of the original meeting.

"Well, my dear," drawled Peggy, "if you can't see that he is the sexiest thing around, then you need your eyes tested. He has a 'lean and hungry look', if ever I've seen one."

Marguerite considered this. David was tall, slim, with slender hips and what Peggy referred to as a 'nice bum'. He had a lovely laugh when he relaxed, and a face marked by high cheekbones and olive skin. His dark hair was usually too long, and dishevelled. Marguerite imagined him as a romantic painter: Dante Gabriel Rossetti or some such, in a white, loose-sleeved shirt and tight trousers. It might not be conventional matinee idol perfection, but he was a very attractive man. She decided not to pursue this line of thought. Enough, she thought, that she was ten years older than him.

Marguerite and David had been to most of the museums and art galleries, so now their roles reversed. She used Peggy to get them into film studios so David could see what went on in the movie industry. He liked it immediately. His eye for artistic design, for colour, form and structure drew him into this medium. She could see how he glowed when other professionals recognised his talent. He was offered work, small stuff at first, designs of sets in B-grade films, and when completed, his name was on the credits.

"It seems I could have a new career ahead of me," he enthused. "Film is such a fluid medium, you can create so much with it."

Marguerite was pleased to see him so happy.

When she said goodbye to him that evening he stood with his back to her for a moment. Then, suddenly and without warning, he turned, grabbed her shoulders, bent his head and kissed her on the lips. Marguerite was so surprised she didn't resist. Then he pulled back, made what she assumed was a muttered apology and disappeared down the street.

Shaken, Marguerite climbed into the cab. She had no idea what to think. She hadn't allowed herself to think her relationship with David was anything other than friendship. The sense that he might care for her, though shocking, was a powerful aphrodisiac. Now she had to reassess her involvement with him.

She had never considered being unfaithful to Eugene, and she intended to make it clear at their next meeting, politely of course, that David's actions were inappropriate. She had no intention of making him her lover.

As it happened, David pre-empted her, phoning the next morning to apologise. "I shouldn't have done that," he mumbled down the phone. "I got carried away, I'm very sorry."

Marguerite was caught unprepared.

"Oh no, please don't worry. I'm sure it was just one of those things, and it won't happen again."

There was a significant pause before he continued. "The thing is, Marguerite, although I didn't mean to grab you like that, I admire you enormously and have wanted to kiss you for a long time. I'm sorry. I realise you might think it inappropriate, but I can't deny my feelings for you."

Marguerite sat still, with the phone held against her ear. The painting which had started their relationship was hanging across the room from her. She gazed at it. Whatever she had expected to hear, it wasn't this. Her pulse was beating fast.

"Marguerite, Marguerite, are you still there? Please tell me I haven't offended you."

"No," she said honestly. "How could anyone be offended by that? It's a compliment and very flattering. It's just, I'm married." What an inane thing to say, she thought.

"Yes, I know. That's why I phoned to say I was sorry. I don't want to distress you in any way. I don't want our friendship to end because of this."

"Our friendship is important to me as well. I'd hate to lose it."

She could hear the smile in his voice as he said, "In that case, as a friend, can I invite you to the opening of Matt Tremayne's new exhibition? Tomorrow afternoon. The exhibition opens tomorrow evening, but he is inviting friends over for a pre-exhibit show at lunchtime. Will you come?"

Marguerite sagged with relief. "Tomorrow afternoon it is," she agreed.

She opened her eyes to find that Max had entered the room with the morning post. "Oh, Max, I didn't see you. Anything in that lot for me?" Had he overheard her conversation? How did women manage having affairs? It must be difficult to keep things secret, particularly if you had staff who knew you and your routines as well as Max did. She must ask Peggy.

CHAPTER
THIRTY FOUR

London, 1966.

S HE MET DAVID AT THE GALLERY, vowing to put the past 24 hours behind her and treat him exactly as she always had. All things considered, she did quite a good job of it. She bantered with him as they took in the exhibition. He rolled his eyes at her over one particularly complicated piece, which of course made her exclaim over its style and execution.

The fault was not David's. He was behaving impeccably. The fault was hers. Suddenly she was aware of every move he made beside her; she watched his hands as they turned the pages of the catalogue. Had she ever noticed before just how shapely his hands were? His fingers were long and well shaped, and there was real strength and grace in them. Working hands, she thought. The hands a musician, a surgeon or, of course, a painter might have. Hands that might wander skilfully across flesh.

She was even aware of his light, natural scent as he stood at her shoulder quietly reading to her from the catalogue. Marguerite took a step backwards. She loved her husband and had no intention of being adulterous, she reminded herself. A little self-discipline could contain this problem.

Then she looked up and saw David looking at her. Without shifting his gaze he asked, "Have you seen enough here? Shall we go?"

He led her out of the exhibition. They waited in silence for a cab. "Would you care for a cup of tea, or perhaps coffee?"

Marguerite agreed to a cup of tea. Most English issues were settled by cups of tea. The way she felt at the moment, she didn't dare go home. Feeling like a firework ready to go off and sure it showed on her face, Marguerite knew it would be impossible to face Eugene and Max right now.

They gave up waiting for a cab. There was a café a block down the street. David ordered for them, and they sat at a table far enough from other diners so they could talk.

"This has to stop," said Marguerite, rather desperately. "I can't see you after today."

"Why not?" he asked.

Marguerite shut her eyes. The only way to protect herself from him was to shut him out of her consciousness. "It's just too hard."

"What do you mean, too hard?" he queried. "I thought the issue was that I cared for you. Are you admitting now that you care for me too, that this is as hard for you?"

"Oh God," exclaimed Marguerite in embarrassment. "I didn't mean to, but once you kissed me, I started … Well, you know." She didn't like to add that it seemed her body was doing the thinking. Her brain was giving her a completely different set of instructions, but Marguerite knew it wasn't her brain she was listening to.

"No," said David. "As it happens, I don't know. I've been going through hell thinking I forced myself on an unwilling woman. But now I find you're not immune? Shit. I thought you were the snow queen. That I defiled you even by thinking about you the way I do. But if you want me too, then that's quite a different story." He looked at her closely. "You do want me, don't you?"

Marguerite shook her head. "You know I *can't*. I'm married," she cried.

"That's not what your eyes say. Do you know that your pupils are enlarged?"

Marguerite stared at him.

"I once read that if a woman's eyes, or rather, if her pupils expand, it's a fairly strong signal that you are seducing her and she is responding." David was more confident now. He leant forward, "Then there's a rapid rate of breathing ..." He seemed to be counting before saying, "I think we can tick that one off."

"A rapid pulse rate?" He reached out and touched her wrist. A bolt of electricity went through her skin.

"I'm a wife, I swore a vow before an altar," she said, desperate to stop the sensations running through her.

This was different to how she had felt with Eugene in the early days. Was it the lure of the forbidden that made it so compelling? She had never felt so alive, so aware of her breasts' sensitivity, so aware of how soft her hair felt against her face, how her pulse leapt. When Eugene courted her, she'd been a virgin, and her body, its needs and responses had been a foreign country. Now, educated in the ways of sexual pleasure, her reactions were intense and unruly.

David's clasp on her wrist was making her gasp, as if she couldn't get sufficient oxygen into her lungs.

She opened her eyes to look at him. He grimaced, as if in pain. "My lady," he inclined his head to her, and half smiled. "I suspect we are both suffering from the same little problem."

"I'm too old for you," said Marguerite. She was on her last line of defence.

He treated that with the contempt it deserved. *"Had we but world enough, and time, this coyness, lady, were no crime,"* he quoted in a low voice. He was still holding her wrist, and now his thumb was making assured, knowledgeable circles on the inner part of it.

"Sorry, but I don't know what you mean."

"It's a poem. *'To His Coy Mistress'*. It's about not wasting time." He smiled. "The only decent teacher we had in the fifth form was the English master. He taught me to appreciate poetry. We'll all be dead and buried soon enough. Why waste this glorious thing that God has given us? Some people search a lifetime for moments like this." His thumb was still tracing the same, soft, circular pattern on her skin.

They had given up any pretence of drinking tea. She gave a low moan as she watched his fingers move, so slowly and seductively. She felt she was melting.

"Come home with me," he suggested. "Or if that feels too much like slumming for you, name somewhere else. We can't abandon this, it would be a crime."

Marguerite remained silent, the enormity of her projected betrayal appalling her. Finally, in desperation, she looked at her watch. It was already three-thirty.

"I have to be back. I told Max I would be back by four. There isn't enough time today for anything." She gave a shaky smile. "Not even time for a sensible decision."

She had come so close to the precipice, and now she had time to step back, at least for today. There was even a sense that delaying gratification might make it sweeter.

"I can't bear to become an unfaithful wife, and I can't bear not to see you."

"I promise you will see me, and soon," he reassured her. "Go now, we don't want to hurry things when we finally get together, but I won't let you go. This does not end today."

When she got home she hadn't been missed. Max was inventorying the wine cellar, and Eugene was in for dinner that evening, something uncommon these days. He had become increasingly a part of London's business world. Dunnings had consolidated its place and permanence on the London shopping scene, and he was often called upon as a charismatic speaker at charity events, or as a mentor to small business groups.

At dinner they discussed the exhibition Marguerite had attended. "Oh yes, were you photographed?" he asked casually.

"Not today," she said. "It was informal, just Matt's closest friends at a preview."

She had become a well-known member of the art world over the past year. It was usual for her photo to be taken by one of the gossip magazines as she arrived or left these functions. It had been noted David was her frequent companion, but as neither Marguerite nor Eugene seemed to consider this an issue, any gossip had been cut off before it began.

She wondered how Eugene viewed her relationship with David. She'd never questioned him about it, having never felt the need. She suddenly wondered if he had ever had an affair. It was possible, given the number of evenings he was late home. She had no reason to think he would be unfaithful, but then until a few days ago she would have said the same of herself. What a slippery slope it was. You thought you were in control of your life, and then it suddenly slips away.

Was it possible to love two people? She owed Eugene so much. It seemed inconceivable to her that she would ever do anything to jeopardise her marriage.

It took something less than two weeks.

During this time Marguerite affirmed that she didn't intend to be an adulterous wife. She loved Eugene, and that was that. As long as she didn't have to see David, she was safe. She ensured her diary was filled with social functions and duties and had Max screen her telephone calls. She simply said she was too busy. She was in the middle of creating a couple of gowns for Peggy, so her time really was occupied. If she worked hard at it, she could forget David for, oh, at least minutes at a time.

She came to believe it was a grown-up version of a schoolgirl 'crush' and would pass as long as she did nothing about it.

Her intentions were impeccable, so it was unfortunate, but perhaps inevitable, that the one phone call she answered was David's. It was mid-morning, and apart from Cook in the kitchen, Marguerite was alone in the house.

As soon as Marguerite heard David's voice she knew she was in trouble.

"You've been avoiding me," he accused. "I've tried several times to phone you, but I've always been put off by that factotum chap you have."

Marguerite was too honest to deny it. "I can't do it, David," she said. "I've thought about it so hard, and I can't bring this sort of pain to Eugene. I love him. It's not as simple as some situations. If he was a wife-beating, abusive man, then perhaps I would be justified in having an affair, but he's never treated me with anything but kindness. I owe him better."

There was a pause, then David said, "So you don't want to sleep with me because it would cause your husband pain, and he doesn't deserve it. But what about me? I've been in agony these past few months and never said a word to you. I can't give you the fortune your husband can, but I love you as truly as any man can love a woman. How much pain are you prepared to cause me?"

Marguerite gave a little sob. "I don't want anyone to suffer pain. I wish I'd never become aware of how you feel. I was naive, but I never knew. I didn't go out of my way to tempt or seduce you."

"By your very person you couldn't help but seduce me, knowingly or not," he replied. "I say again, how much pain do you want to cause me? I've never felt anything as explosive as this. You make me view everything differently, as if I'm alive for the first time. Do you want to kill that?"

"No," whispered Marguerite. "I don't want to hurt anyone."

"Then you have a problem," said David. "You either hurt your husband, who after all may never find out, or you hurt me, and I will suffer terribly. It seems to me you need to choose, honestly and truly, what you want. If you can't please everyone, then you'd better choose what you want. There's no other way for you to choose, is there?"

Marguerite was silent.

"Is there?" he repeated. "So what is it you truly want?"

Marguerite tried to decide what she wanted. She groaned in pain and confusion.

David's voice came again, insistent, merciless. "What do you really want, Marguerite? Don't tell me you don't want me. You've gone off like a Catherine wheel every time I touch you. You know you want me, that you want to try it."

And of course, Marguerite knew he was right.

He spoke again. "I will be at that same café tomorrow morning at eleven. Come and see me then. We can talk it through. We are old friends, after all." She heard the smile in his voice. "I didn't think we would be having a conversation like this when we first met."

"All right, tomorrow then, but the answer is still no."

The next day the answer was still going to be "no". It was pure coincidence that Marguerite chose that morning to put on lace lingerie. A woman in her situation could well wear this kind of underwear any day of the week. The only reason she didn't was that it was inconvenient to hook herself into such a corset without assistance. It did do wonders for her figure of course. In just her underwear she looked amazing, and the fit of her garments on top was pretty impressive. Her breasts high and pointed, her waist wrenched into slenderness before flaring to her hips. She felt pleasingly decadent.

"Walk with me," David commanded after a quick cup of tea. They wandered across the park. An elderly man was throwing bread for ducks. Nannies promenaded with their charges. Marguerite and David made an unexceptionable couple. In the end there was little discussion. David took her acceptance as a forgone conclusion, and his confidence carried her with him. They were silent as the taxi took them to his flat.

She was shy undressing in front of him, she was so much older, but he undid the hooks and eyes, and took his time unwrapping her. "You are so beautiful," he breathed against her shoulder. He made her stand in front of the full-length mirror, clasped in his embrace.

"Look at yourself," he urged. She watched as his hands ran over her body and down her rib cage. When they caressed her breasts and gently pinched her nipples she groaned, her body writhing in response to the slight pain. She felt her knees weakening and parting.

He laughed, his right hand moving lower to her cleft. He slipped his fingers into her and began to stroke. She moaned as she writhed against him.

He stood behind her, his head inclined into her neck as he

did so. "I want to paint this," he groaned. "This is Héloïse and Abelard, Tristan and Isolde." His lips were wandering up her neck.

"I don't think either of those stories had a happy ending," she gasped. He groaned into her hair.

David was taller and more slender than Eugene, with long planes of elegant muscles. His youth was apparent, although there was nothing weak or immature in his body. She thought his more personal equipment was rather smaller than her husband's, a discovery which surprised her. She had assumed all men looked the same down there, but clearly she was wrong.

His bed was narrow and his studio plain, but Marguerite was in no mood to be fussy. She lay down with him and tried to blot out anything else.

It might have been her mindset, or perhaps her lack of sexual proficiency, but the act, though pleasurable, was not overwhelming. It wasn't the life-affirming, desperately passionate event she had been anticipating.

David was tense as well. He climaxed too early for her, and she put this down to the stress of the last few weeks. Years of married life had trained her to be tactful in such matters. Her conscience, which she had managed to blot out for the last hour, was back whispering in her ear.

An hour or two later they coupled again. This time they were technically more proficient but although he was a considerate, gentle and skilled lover, Marguerite felt more and more that her place was not in David's bed.

Afterwards he helped her dress. "Do you need me to order a cab?"

"Thank you." A quick check of her watch and she realised it was barely half past two. A small amount of time for such a defining experience. They kissed each other goodbye.

"I'll call," he promised.

She smiled. "I count upon it."

The cab felt solitary and safe as she made her way home.

CHAPTER
THIRTY FIVE

London, 1966.

THE HOUSE WAS QUIET AS SHE let herself in the front door. Max must be out. She climbed the stairs to the master bedroom. In front of the cheval mirror she stood and looked at herself. Her hair wasn't as groomed as usual, but beyond that there was nothing to give away what had occurred. Why did she feel so confused? Shouldn't she feel fulfilled? She'd taken a lover, one a decade younger than herself. Surely a milestone in any woman's life?

She unbuttoned her dress and slipped out of it. She could hardly wait to have a hot bath and wash all trace of the day away. Her underwear was going to be a struggle to get out of by herself, but she turned and twisted trying to get to the hooks.

Out of the corner of her eye she caught a movement. She spun round and saw Eugene sitting in the large wing-backed chair, watching her. She gave a little shriek. "What are you doing? You gave me a terrible fright; I didn't know who it was. I thought you were a burglar or something." She looked at his face and realised that he knew. Never mind that was impossible, she was suddenly and absolutely certain he knew.

"I might ask you the same," he said. "What are you doing, in the middle of the day, dressed to the nines in your best underwear? Have you been to some function?"

"I was just about to take a bath." Maybe she could bluff. He couldn't really know what had just happened.

"I'm sure you need a bath." There was freezing scorn in his voice as he agreed. "But you'll just have to wait. We are going to have a little chat, you and I, about your responsibilities as a wife."

Marguerite gaped at him. She understood what the term 'caught in the spotlight' meant now. She couldn't move, couldn't even reach for a robe to cover herself. She opened her mouth to speak, but he cut her off.

"I know all about your little escapade this morning," he said coldly, "so please don't put us through a silly set of lies and denials. I am here to tell you that I will not tolerate an adulterous wife and to teach you to respect your husband."

He stood up, and Marguerite saw he had a riding crop in his hand. She was too scared to speak. Where had he got such a thing from?

She started backing away from her husband, but he was too quick for her. He grabbed her by her left arm and spun her violently. As he released her she was flung face down onto the bed. She scrambled up, desperate to get away, but before she could get a leg up under her to flee, Eugene was on top of her. He put a knee into the middle of her back to hold her in position, twisted one of her arms to hold her there then slashed the crop down hard onto her bottom.

Marguerite screamed. She had never felt anything so painful, nor had she ever been so terrified. She struggled with all her might, but she was no match for her husband's strength. She realised he could beat her half to death if he wanted; she was powerless to stop him.

Without saying anything, he slashed the crop down again and again.

Marguerite screamed with each blow, her words a confused

tangle of, "I'm sorry, please stop, I'm sorry."

Eugene flung the crop away. It thudded on the wardrobe door as it fell. After a few minutes he removed his grip on her arm and stood back from the bed. Marguerite lay immobile, howling into the mattress.

After a few minutes of this Eugene said impatiently, "Stop being a baby. You've only had six strokes, for God's sake. Any boy at school would get the same for failing to hand in his homework. You're not dead, nor even abused or battered, much though you deserve it. But you'll bear the marks on your skin for the next few days so you can meditate on what I am going to say now. Stop that crying and listen."

Marguerite continued to cry, but gradually she steadied, got her breath and crawled across the bed away from him. Rolling on to her back hurt her bottom, so she opted for getting to her feet on the far side of the bed. She felt ridiculous in her lovely underwear, now twisted and useless around her. The look on Eugene's face was more than she could bear, and she started crying again, but this time in silence.

"You are my wife, and you will behave as such," he said bleakly. "I will not have you bringing dishonour to me, to yourself or to our family name. You are part of Dunnings and its reputation. I will not let you ruin it. Divorce is not something that will happen in this family. Do I make myself clear?"

Marguerite didn't even realise he had asked a question until he repeated it. "Oh yes, I'm so sorry."

He looked at her with contempt. "If I ever have cause to even suspect a repeat of this behaviour, I will have you declared mentally unsound and ensure that you never see the outside of an institution again. I trust you understand I'm serious." He paused. "I thought better of you, Marguerite. I find myself ashamed to have loved you. What a waste of that most precious of emotions."

He turned to the door. As he opened it, he turned back. "Why, Marguerite? For God's sake, why?"

He paused a moment, as if waiting for her answer, but all she could do was sob and shake her head. She had no coherent answer, so how was she to explain what she had done to him?

He left.

Marguerite threw herself face first across the bed and cried with all the intensity of a broken heart. She knew, with real bitterness, just what it was that she had thrown away for a fling with David. The pain in Eugene's eyes was more than she could bear, and she herself had put it there. He was a proud man. That he should have been cuckolded by a young, scruffy artist must be intolerable.

Marguerite felt she cried for hours. Eventually she ran out of tears. If death, or sudden disappearance were options, Marguerite wished for them. She pushed herself to her feet and forced herself to walk to the bathroom. She ran herself a hot bath and climbed in, seeking the warmth of the water as a comfort. The hot water on the welts made her cry out. She stood and looked at the stripes in the mirror. They were raised and ugly on her fair skin, a couple already turning purple as the bruising came out. She felt herself tearing up again.

She made it downstairs, albeit stiffly, and found there was no sign of Eugene.

Max came in. "Would you care for tea?"

She was about to refuse then decided it might be a good idea. She was shaky and cold and aware her eyes were red and swollen in spite of her efforts to cool them with a cold flannel. She prayed Max had been out throughout the whole scene upstairs. Anyone present in the house would have heard her cries and been aware of her shame. She accepted the tea and drank it standing up by the window. Her hands were cold on the cup, and she couldn't stop shivering. Eventually she told Max she was feeling ill and would miss dinner that night. She took herself back upstairs to the bedroom, drew the curtains and shivered her way into bed. She couldn't seem to get warm, in spite of the tea.

It was a long time before she slept.

The next morning she woke up and for a moment everything seemed normal. Then she rolled over onto her sore buttocks and remembered the day before. The surge of shame and desolation hit her like a punch in the abdomen.

Eugene had not slept in the bed. In all their years together, he had only ever been away at night a handful of times and always because of business. Usually she travelled with him. She saw proof of his absence and cried again. Would he ever come back, let alone forgive her? She assumed he'd been at his club. If he had stayed overnight with one of their friends, what would he have told them? Marguerite saw endless social humiliation stretching in front of her.

It took all her courage to roll out of bed and start the day.

She organised a lunch meeting with Peggy, desperate to tell her friend everything.

Peggy listened, enthralled, to the details. "I don't know whether to be appalled by Eugene, or to admire him," she declared at last. "His reactions are deliciously primitive, aren't they?"

She saw Marguerite was hurt. "Darling, I know he was a beast, but at least he cared enough to react. Half society's toffs wouldn't care. They either bat for the other team or have mistresses of their own. You just happen to have married a Neanderthal." She looked at Marguerite's strained face and became thoughtful. "I have to tell you, sweetie, I don't think you're a woman made for infidelity and affairs. Not like yours truly. Your qualities are more the loyal, supportive sort. Sure, you've tasted forbidden fruit, but you've paid a high price for it. I suggest you make it up with your husband if you can. You'll be the happier for it."

Eugene was away for three weeks. Her bed felt emptier each night, and she had no choice but to carry on as if nothing was wrong. Max asked her nothing, and Marguerite wondered if it had been he who had betrayed her.

Marguerite telephoned David and told him the affair was over. He was shocked, having been convinced that he had won her. She was surprised by how small her own distress was. David was an episode she would excise from her life as thoroughly as she could.

Eugene returned home as if nothing had happened. He made no

reference to the events of their last explosive meeting and treated her with dispassionate courtesy. At night he slept beside her in their bed. Marguerite lay sleepless, night after night, listening to his quiet, deep breathing. In the morning it was apparent he had slept well, while Marguerite was pale and tired.

After a couple of weeks Eugene reached for her in the night. Marguerite went to him gratefully. If the sexual transaction was quick, impersonal and silent, at least it was a sign that things could perhaps improve in time.

She was still of this view a couple of months later. She came downstairs to find Max was going to be out. Eugene, he said, had given him the evening off.

Marguerite was surprised but hoped an evening alone together might help the healing of their marriage. Cook had left a salad already prepared with a Chicken à la Reine. Marguerite planned an intimate dinner.

Eugene arrived home at five o'clock, which was unusually early for him. She greeted him with shy politeness and offered him a drink.

They sipped their sherry in silence, deep in their own thoughts. Marguerite thought he looked tired and strained. She was afraid he would name her as the cause.

Eventually she asked, "How was your day?"

Eugene sighed and sat staring into the depths of his glass. "There's something I have to tell you."

Marguerite froze. Perhaps Eugene had changed his mind and wanted to divorce her after all. She'd been worrying about this since their quarrel.

She had told her mother about her disastrous affair and its aftermath, and Edith had been appalled. "You stupid, stupid girl! You're a barren wife, and your husband has been understanding and kind. You enjoy a lovely life. Why throw it all away and have an affair? Eugene could divorce you tomorrow, and there'd be no defence at all that you could muster. Is that what you want? The courts aren't very kind to adulterous wives."

Now, waiting for Eugene to speak, Marguerite felt her world crumbling.

"I have something to tell you," Eugene repeated. He gazed at her, his looks haggard. "When I left you *that* day, I went to Bristol to work up there on the store. I was angry, distraught."

Marguerite started to speak, but he put his hand up. "No, listen to me, please."

"There was a woman, one of our consultants. She was sympathetic. She saw I was in distress, and she was kind. She let me talk. One thing led to another." Eugene raised his eyes to hers. "I'm not going to dignify this with any excuse. I was drunk and ended up in her bed that night. Also for a few other nights, until I pulled myself together and realised that she was no solution to our problems. The affair has ended."

Marguerite nodded numbly. There was nothing she could say. She realised she was mindlessly pleating her skirt, tidying the mass of material into thin, folded lines. She couldn't look at Eugene. Far from being angry with him, his admission added to her own guilt. All of this was her fault.

As if reading her mind Eugene said, "There's something else. I haven't told you this to make you feel bad, or to make myself even with you or anything else." He paused, and drew a paper from his pocket and unfolded it. "I received this letter from her today. She tells me she is pregnant, and the child is mine. She wants nothing from me, but thought I had the right to know." He looked away from his wife. "I also thought you had the right to know," he said quietly.

"Oh Eugene!" said Marguerite involuntarily before she forced herself to silence. The pain when he'd beaten her was nothing to this explosion of anguish. She was screaming inside. She tried to come to terms with Eugene having an affair, tried to understand that he would have a child, a firstborn, from some other woman.

Eugene's head was bent as he twiddled his sherry glass between his fingers.

They sat for a long time in silence, not meeting each other's eyes. There was nothing to add to the conversation.

Eventually Marguerite got to her feet. "If you would excuse me, I think I will go and lie down for a bit."

Eugene rose politely and opened the door for her. As she

passed through he reached out as if to touch her shoulder before withdrawing his hand short of touching her.

She thought she heard him sigh as she left the room.

She lay curled in a foetal position, her arms crossed over her belly as if to protect herself from pain. She was cold and shaking, beyond tears in her shock and grief. She had no doubt it had been her own actions which had caused this.

Whatever feeling, passion or lust, she had felt for David had long gone, burned away in the repercussions.

Eugene came to bed several hours later. He didn't switch the room lights on when he entered but stripped and climbed into bed in the dark. Her back was turned to him, but she could feel his presence beside her on the bed.

After a few minutes she felt his hand move towards her and cup her hip. She took a shuddering breath as she felt his touch. She reached her hand down to cover his.

"Marguerite?" he whispered.

She didn't answer but rolled over towards him and lay on her back. They lay for a long time in the quiet darkness just holding hands.

"I am so sorry. God, I am so sorry," he said at last. His voice was cracked with emotion. It sounded very unlike her usually urbane husband, his quiet voice racked with pain.

His fingers gripped her hand tighter for a moment before withdrawing.

She rolled towards him. It would be unfair for him to apologise alone. "No," she said. "I started this with my stupidity. I'm the one who is sorry. I didn't mean to cause harm. I didn't think." Was there any pain more excruciating than knowing she had brought this ruin on them both? She heard him draw a ragged breath.

"I've never stopped loving you," he said. "I was just so angry and jealous and out of control with it all. Partly in revenge I allowed this thing to happen, and the result is something we will both have to live with."

"I know," she said. "I don't blame you. I was bored, and he flattered me. I was childish and foolish, and I betrayed you, and it's so stupid because I love you so much."

She rolled towards him. "Oh Eugene, I am so sorry." And now the tears came.

He pulled her into his shoulder and let her cry. His arms were round her tightly.

Sometime later when she quieted, she pulled away, sniffing, and reached for a handkerchief. Marguerite was certain, although she couldn't see in the dark, her husband had been crying too.

She blew her nose and returned to his arms.

"I swear we can do better. We need to heal this thing between us, and I believe we can," he said.

Marguerite nodded. "We will do better," she agreed.

In the days that followed they treated each other with kindness and gentleness, aware of their individual shame and determined to expiate it.

Month followed month, and year followed year, and if time couldn't erase the past, it did help them heal.

It helped that the nineteen sixties were a pivotal time for Dunnings. England and its capital had become fashionable. The lessons Marguerite had learned during her friendship with David were not wasted. She was determined Dunnings would prove just as much a drawcard as Carnaby Street, and forced the store to keep up with new trends.

Gone were the full skirts and elegant suits that were her style. Instead there were geometric designs, slight shifts, trouser suits, tunics and caps. Colours, hairstyles and makeup palettes changed. By the mid years of the seventies, Dunnings was a very different store.

Marguerite was so wrapped up in the business she barely noticed when her periods stopped. Assuming it was a precursor for the change, she shrugged and ignored her symptoms. The discovery that she was five months' pregnant was an overwhelming shock.

CHAPTER
THIRTY SIX

London, 1973.

"DARLING," SAID PEGGY, A FEW WEEKS after the delivery, in that smoky voice she used now, "I love your little girl, of course, and I'm sure once she's grown up she will be lots of fun, but I'm not a maternal woman. I don't know what to do with small babies." She handed Tamara back to her mother as fast as she could.

Marguerite chuckled. "I thought you might like to play with her."

Peggy grinned at her old friend. "Not me. You look after her now, and I'll play my part as fairy godmother when she's sixteen. At least I'll know what to talk to her about then. I'm not fluent in goo and gaa."

Marguerite snorted. "I'm not sure I'll let you near her when she's an adolescent. You might not be good for her moral guidance, godmother or not."

At which Peggy just stuck her tongue out at her in a very unglamorous way. Her career was at its peak, and there was no way Peggy was going to give it up for marriage or motherhood.

Marguerite smiled at her friend and knew that she was the luckier woman.

"Where did the name come from?" asked Peggy.

"We wanted to retain a vestige of her Russian ancestry, and we liked the name." Marguerite shrugged. "At least it's more exotic than Jane or Mary."

Marguerite's only disappointment was that she failed to conceive again. Eugene adored Tamara, but she knew he'd wanted a legitimate son and heir. Somewhere out there was another child growing up who could call Eugene 'Father'. Marguerite could only hope that luck would strike twice and she would produce a son.

In the absence of such a happy event, Marguerite threw herself into decisions about which school the little girl should go to.

"Send her to boarding school," she was advised. Marguerite wouldn't even consider such an option. Memories of Katya's misery at the Reading orphanage were far too vivid. Her little girl had been born with a silver spoon in her mouth, and Marguerite intended she grew up never knowing need, fear or poverty. Her protective instincts shocked her, they were so powerful. If she could spare Tamara pain or grief, she'd move mountains to do so.

Tamara was a happy-natured girl with a strong will for such a small child. Once she made her mind up, it was almost impossible to get her to change it

"Yes," teachers would affirm to Eugene and Marguerite, "Tamara is intelligent, maybe even highly intelligent, but she refuses to concentrate or work at her academic studies," or alternatively, "Tamara talks too much and doesn't listen."

After carrying the responsibility for Katya's education, and the misery it had brought, Marguerite wasn't inclined to turn Tamara's education into a drama. As long as Tamara obeyed her, Marguerite was content.

Eugene, though, took the feedback from the teachers seriously. He was an indulgent father, but he had high personal standards, and no child of his would be allowed to be lazy or underachieve. Tamara was likely to be the only child they had. It would not do for the eventual heir to Dunnings to be an uneducated and overindulged woman.

They had been to yet another school meeting.

"It's a plot to make adults feel like children," grumbled Eugene when they got home. "We pay that school enough, why do we have to sit on infant seats when we go to parent-teacher meetings? And then they tell us our daughter is underperforming. You'll have to have a stern word with her, Marguerite. Tell her she can't ride her bicycle for a week or something until she improves her grades."

Marguerite nodded noncommittally. "I'll talk to her," she agreed.

These were prosperous years for the Dunnings. The financial risks Eugene had taken investing in Oxford Street proved to have been shrewd judgement. The store had a life and entity of its own. People would casually refer to Dunnings in conversation as in 'If you can't find it anywhere else in London, you'll find it at Dunnings'. It was even trendy amongst the young set.

The seventies were less innocent than the swinging sixties, and drug and hippie culture had become mainstream. Eugene confessed he had no idea what young people wanted any more.

Marguerite smiled at him. "Probably what they've always wanted. Sex, love and rock and roll – just modern versions of what we wanted. The trouble with us, my darling, is that we are older parents. You can't expect us to be as up to date as we should."

It was a thought that had occurred to her recently. She was now in her forties, Eugene a few years older. They were a generation older than the parents of Tamara's contemporaries.

"Have you ever thought how we are going to cope with Tamara's adolescence?" she asked him.

Eugene stared at her. "She's not going to have one, even if I have to put her into a convent for her own safety. She'll be kept on a very tight rein."

"Well, that's a good plan," said Marguerite sarcastically. "Let's hide our heads in the sand and ignore all the potential issues." Still, she thought, they had muddled through a lot in their lives; they would work the future out as well.

Tamara was out of the house, having a sleepover with one of her friends. It took Marguerite most of the day to sort out what she needed for the visit, deliver her across town safely and tidy up afterwards. When she came downstairs from organising her daughter, it was almost six o'clock. She poured herself a drink.

Eugene arrived home promptly. Standing beside him was a young boy. Marguerite thought him somewhere in his early teens. Before Eugene spoke she had seen the resemblance between them: the fine facial features, the feral expression in the eyes, a similar mouth.

"Marguerite," said Eugene formally, "may I present Clive to you. Clive is my son."

Marguerite, who had been standing to greet Eugene, sat down rather hurriedly. "Clive, may I present my wife, Marguerite Dunning. She'll be caring for you and acting as your mother from now on. Your half-sister is away tonight, but you will meet her tomorrow."

Marguerite was used to acting as a hostess, and that discipline forced her through organising a bedroom for the boy and a suitably courteous reception. She felt she could hardly discuss the matter while the dark-eyed boy was with them, and it was well past nine before he was sent to his room.

Marguerite rounded on Eugene. "Who the hell is he? What do you mean he is your son? How long have you planned to bring him here?"

"You know who he is, Marguerite. He is my bastard son, from a relationship twelve years ago, which you would have good cause to remember. He's lived so far with his mother. She's now remarried and thinks it is best if he moves in with his father."

"He can't," said Marguerite. "I'm not having a bastard son of yours here. Think of Tamara," she wailed. "How can you do this?"

"The new stepfather won't have the boy, so I am his only option. I only heard about this myself today so don't accuse me of planning this to hurt you. I can't imagine how damaging this must be for the boy. Clive can, and will, move in with us and will be recognised as my natural son. You will treat him with every courtesy and affection."

"Over my dead body!" Marguerite was fairly spitting with fury. "I won't have it. No bastard child is going to grow up with Tamara." She felt so angry she could have hit her husband.

Her anger lit a reciprocal rage in Eugene. He stood up and moved quickly until he was standing over her. He grabbed her chin and forced her head up to face him. His eyes were blazing. "Don't you try and tell me what will or will not happen, Marguerite. I say he will come to live here, and he will. As it happens, he attends boarding school, so he won't be here during term time. He's only here at the moment because he was released from school to attend his mother's wedding. He returns on Monday."

Marguerite writhed in his grip, but he simply tightened his fingers until she was sure bruises would show on her face.

"You'll do as I command in this, my dear," said Eugene. "Don't you ever give me cause to suspect that you are playing at being a wicked stepmother. Do I make myself clear?"

Marguerite hissed at him through her screwed-up mouth. He softened his grip on her face, rubbing his thumb over the areas he had bruised. She stepped back, rubbing her mouth and chin, and glared at him.

"Come on, Marguerite. Show some kindness. This boy has been abandoned by his mother and her new husband. The least we can do is help out."

"Don't you realise that every time we look at him he's a reminder of the worst time in our marriage?" she cried. "How can I welcome him here?"

Marguerite rose, intending to storm out to the bedroom. She flung the door open in her rush to escape and found Clive standing on the other side. It was quite clear he had heard the interchange. She acknowledged him curtly before pushing past him and up the stairs. She could swear there was malicious amusement in the look he gave her.

CHAPTER
THIRTY SEVEN

London, Present Day.

PURDIE WAS ESCORTED TO A ROOM further down the hall. She baulked in the doorway.

"Your room, Miss Davis. We hope you will be very comfortable for the duration of your visit." He spoke for all the world like an hotelier, Purdie thought.

She decided on the straightforward approach and refused to enter the room. "I am not a guest, and I insist, again, that you let me leave."

"Please enter the room, miss; your luggage has already arrived," he replied.

Honestly, it was as if he hadn't heard her.

Purdie wheeled, determined to make it down the staircase. Immediately he transposed his body between her and the rest of the lobby. There ensued a couple of minutes of jostling where she feinted right and left, to be matched by him each time. He wasn't going to let her past. Nearer to the stairs another man in a suit had entered and stood watching.

"Please, miss, accept our hospitality. The room has been

prepared for your use."

Purdie glared at him, but accepted defeat. She didn't want to provoke anyone into using force if she could avoid it. She wasn't sure if this was prudence or cowardice, but it seemed best to save herself for a genuine opportunity for escape rather than waste time and energy in a situation she wasn't going to win.

She entered and heard the door shut behind her. Her luggage had been placed on a chest at the end of the large bed. She checked it. It had obviously been searched, and her handbag had been rifled. Her makeup was no longer in its usual compartment and her travel documents disarranged. She checked her passport and tickets. All seemed to be present, as was her notebook.

A thought occurred to her, and she rechecked her bag. Her old phone was missing. She'd kept it for the data that hadn't been transferred. Now it was gone. She swore long and fluently.

There was a bowl of fruit on the table, flowers in a vase on a lacquer dresser, and when she visited the bathroom there were towels, bathrobe and all the amenities in place. This was either an upmarket hotel or a seriously impressive guest bedroom. Five minutes later there was a knock on the door, and a maid entered with a pot of tea, a pot of coffee and biscuits.

As soon as she had left, Purdie tried the door but found it locked. She hadn't heard a key turn when the maid entered, so she presumed it was some sort of electronic lock. Plans of standing behind the door and coshing the next visitor over the head occurred to her. Often the best moves are the simplest, she thought, and looked around for something heavy enough to use.

If she succeeded in leaving the room, there was still the problem of getting as far as the front door of the apartment, let alone through it, down the lift and through the external doors. Purdie suspected her captors owned the whole building. Even if she got outside, where would she go? She had no idea where she was, so she would have to use Google maps and call a taxi.

She felt the weight of her smartphone on her hip. No one had frisked her person, and the light jacket she wore fell to hip level over her jeans, hiding any sign of the phone. Thank heavens it was slim and was set on silent.

Her fear of being drugged or white slaved had eased slightly. It seemed, from the chairman's comments, that their objectives were simple. Regain, or rather find, a treasure to which they believed they had a claimant's right. Purdie didn't have the treasure, so she dismissed this as irrelevant. Her problem was loss of freedom, and she didn't like being a pawn in someone else's game.

She looked at the fruit and wondered which would be the easiest to dose with mind-altering drugs, then realised that both tea and coffee were potential hazards and sighed deeply. She was truly very hungry and tired.

She grabbed a cup from the tray and entered the bathroom. She drank several cups of tap water and felt better as the cool liquid poured down her throat. She would know in a few minutes if she had made a terrible mistake. In the meantime she was tired, travel-grimed and stressed.

She unpacked clean undies, jeans and a T-shirt and entered the bathroom, locking the door behind her. So far she had been treated with courtesy, but it made her feel even more vulnerable. A simple thug after instant gratification she could understand. But how was she to get a handle on this elaborate charade? Would they bow politely before they slit her throat? It was hard to imagine they could ever let her go, not with such a story to tell to the news.

Would her grandmother be interested in dealing with them anyway? She cursed her curiosity which had led her into this mess.

She turned the shower on, used the loo and flushed it so the noise filled the room, and then started texting.

Nick: Kidnapped by Chinese. High rise in city, London. No joke, please help instantly. Phone on, follow GPS if poss, call police. Repeat, not a joke, urgent.

Sophie: Kidnapped, Help. Make Nick ph. police. Contact Peter Harris for details of Grandma. Let her know. Need rescue NOW.

She sent both texts and waited to see whether there was any action from her captors. Was it too much to hope they hadn't noticed she had a phone? It showed the texts had been delivered. She hoped her friends would respond soon.

When it was still quiet a few minutes later, she stripped and entered the shower. It was bliss to have water pour over her, and she took the opportunity to use the expensive brands of shampoo, conditioner and moisturiser she found.

She revelled in feeling clean and fresh although she was still hungry. She dried herself and used the hair dryer to tame her hair.

When she emerged half an hour later she felt much more courageous. She checked out her room, especially the door, food and bed, and opted for the latter. She replaced the phone in her back pocket, once again muted, and went to bed fully dressed, deciding she felt less vulnerable clothed. She didn't want to experience a dawn raid in her PJs.

CHAPTER
THIRTY EIGHT

London, Present Day.

MARGUERITE CONSIDERED PURDIE'S DISAPPEARANCE IN THE hours that passed. While she could see that a girl, unknown in her character and motivations, might take advantage of a free fare to the UK to pursue her own agenda, the security footage of Purdie's interception told a different story.

She accepted, for the moment, that Clive didn't know what had happened, so who had taken the girl, and more importantly, why?

Kidnapping would usually result in a ransom demand. Dunnings was a high-profile company, but she wouldn't have expected it to be targeted. Was this a personal attack on her, or was it corporate orientated?

She tried to control the rage she felt, aware of its pointlessness. She'd been looking forward to meeting her granddaughter, and her disappointment was immense. She was incredibly anxious for the girl.

It was late afternoon when the phone rang. Max answered it.

Marguerite, watching his face, saw the change in his expression. Silently he flicked the phone to speaker for her to listen in.

"This is the Dunning residence. May I help you? Mrs Dunning? I'll check whether she is available. Who may I say is calling?"

Quietly Marguerite switched her mobile to voice record and placed it beside the phone.

She nodded when Max asked her, with raised brows, whether to put her on. She took the phone but indicated he should stay.

"Hello, Marguerite speaking."

The voice was educated and courteous, but there was an elusive accent which Marguerite couldn't pick. "Mrs Dunning?"

"Yes."

"Your granddaughter, Miss Perdita Davis, is a guest of ours. She is, of course, being treated with all the respect we can offer to a daughter of your house. You may rest assured of her comfort and well-being."

There was a pause, as if the disembodied speaker expected her to say something.

"You have a treasure in your family's possession which we would like in exchange for the return of your granddaughter. Would you be interested in discussing such a trade?"

Marguerite gasped in surprise.

"What treasure? What nonsense," she replied. "Please put my granddaughter on so I can talk to her and be assured she is unharmed."

"I am afraid that is impossible at the present time," said the voice. "Your granddaughter is asleep, and it would be inconsiderate of us to disturb her after her long flight. The treasure involved is part of the legacy your grandfather brought from Russia in 1915. It has been traced to you."

"I know nothing of any such legacy," replied Marguerite. "My family fled as refugees. Refugees tend not to have treasures, or at least not for very long," she said drily, remembering their impoverished beginnings in London. "You have the wrong person."

"No," said the voice. "We know that we have neither the wrong family, nor the wrong person. You had a great uncle, Ilya.

We know the truth from him."

Marguerite tried to recall anything her grandfather had said about a brother. She remembered the time he had spent with her, telling stories of the past and how she had loved him. Had he mentioned a brother? She rather thought he might have, but she couldn't recall.

"I think there was a brother, who, I suppose, would be a great uncle, but I know nothing about him. I think my grandfather said he fled east as the rest of the family moved west. If he found treasure, then I know nothing about it. Clearly it must have occurred after he separated from the family, otherwise there would be stories about it."

She was aware of Max standing across the other side of the table.

"Do you require a ransom?" she asked. "What sort of figure are you asking?" Talk of treasure wasn't going to bring her granddaughter through this safely.

"We require the Fabergé Eggs, Mrs Dunning: the Imperial Eggs and nothing else. You might say our family takes a particular interest in them."

Marguerite frowned at the phone. "What eggs?" she asked. "Yes, yes," she added testily, "of course I know who Fabergé was. I assure you that if we owned Fabergé Eggs, we'd have sold them long ago, just to survive the early years."

The voice on the other end of the phone went silent. Marguerite imagined her counterpart at the other end of the phone turning and seeking guidance. She raised her eyebrows at Max. He put his finger to his lips and gestured that she carry on listening and recording.

Eventually the voice on the phone returned. "I am sorry to have kept you waiting, Mrs Dunning," he said. "We understand these eggs were never something you could have sold casually. They were entrusted to your family by a man who was dead a fortnight later. Had they been sold, either on the open market, or quietly, without publicity, then we would still know about it. These eggs have never been sold. They are too famous for such a thing to have happened without news leaking out to those who are interested in such artefacts."

Marguerite sighed. She was certain her father had never said anything to her about such a trust, or treasure. The memory of the last day she saw her father was particularly clear. Pain had etched it so deeply into her consciousness that she could have recited in their entirety the words spoken that morning.

He had urged all of them to stay indoors and not venture out. There had been no last-minute words, no final farewell. Charles had simply gone. If there had been a secret treasure, he had not told his eldest daughter about it. Marguerite doubted he would have told his wife – Edith wasn't the sort of person you shared important secrets with. She tried to sift through anything her grandfather may have told her.

"Whatever information you believe you have, there is no record, either verbal or written within my family of such treasure or resource. My father was murdered in the war. If there were stories to pass on, he failed to do so. I truly do not know what it is you seek, or why you think my family is involved. There is no information I have which could help you. I just want my granddaughter. What is your price?"

The voice at the other end grew cool. "You understand that your granddaughter's happiness and safety may depend on your answer?" Marguerite strained to hear any background noise to aid her in identifying the caller. "I'll leave you for now, Mrs Dunning, but I must advise you to research your history. It would be a tragedy if the house of Dunning failed, or was subject to a hostile takeover by your stepson. I will call again when you have had time to reflect," and he hung up.

Max clicked off the record button on the mobile.

They stared at each other.

Marguerite collapsed onto the sofa. "What do you think, Max? Is this some elaborate hoax? I have no idea what he's talking about. All I am certain of is that he has my granddaughter."

"Call the police," advised Max. "You can play them the tape and let them analyse it. I'll pour both of us a drink. Incidentally, do you know anything at all about what he is looking for?"

"Nothing," she said incredulously. "Absolutely nothing."

It was late after dinner that evening when the phone rang again. Marguerite answered it herself, making a careful note of the number on the display.

"Hi," said a male voice. "May I speak to Mrs Dunning?" She pressed record on the machine.

"You're speaking to her," said Marguerite. This voice was accented as well, but it wasn't the one that had called earlier.

"I'm a friend of Purdie Davis. I believe she is staying with you? May I speak with her?"

Marguerite thought quickly. "I'm sorry, I didn't get your name?"

"I'm Nick, calling from New Zealand. Is Purdie there? May I speak to her?"

"I'm afraid Purdie isn't here," said Marguerite. "May I know how you got this telephone number?"

There was a pause. "As I said, I'm a friend of Purdie's. She told us she was coming to meet you. She didn't give us much in the way of contact details, apart from her own phone number, which she said would be on roaming until she got set up. I got a very strange text from her a few hours ago."

"Go on."

"I'll read it to you. *Kidnapped by Chinese. High rise in city, London. No joke, please help instantly. Phone on, follow GPS if poss, call police. Repeat, not a joke, urgent'.*"

"Shit," swore Marguerite.

"I wasn't sure if it was someone's sick idea of a practical joke. I tried the police at our end, but they insisted I had to make contact with Purdie. I didn't want to do that directly, because if she really has been kidnapped, we don't want a phone going off alerting everyone she still has it. For the last couple of hours we've been trying to find your details so we could phone. Is Purdie OK? Has something happened to her?"

"Purdie disappeared from the airport earlier today," said Marguerite. "Someone else picked her up. They must have been able to convince her I had sent them. I got a phone call, not three hours ago, with a ransom demand. The problem is that I don't have what the captors want, or any idea of how to get it for them."

Nick's voice was cool when he replied, "I would have thought that, as her long-lost grandmother, you would have been prepared to pay anything to get her back, particularly if she is in danger. I understood Dunning's was a wealthy organisation."

Marguerite flushed with annoyance. "That's the problem," she said tightly. "They don't want cash. They think I have a treasure that they're after; some Russian Fabergé Eggs. And I don't have them."

There was a silence at the end of the phone. "I'm sorry. I thought they would have wanted money. I didn't mean to be abrupt. Did you know that someone sent Purdie exotic presents while she was back here in New Zealand? One was a jewelled egg. We looked it up on the Internet because it looked valuable, wondering if it was a Fabergé Egg made for the Tsar, but then decided it wasn't quite as ornate as those in the pictures."

Marguerite gave a little gasp. "The lawyer from New Zealand phoned to ask if I had been sending Purdie presents. Was that what he meant? And what does it signify?"

There was silence while Nick thought. "I don't know. I think you'd better contact the police at your end ASAP. We don't know how long her phone will keep a charge, or whether it will be discovered."

"I know the commissioner. I'll phone him straight away," said Marguerite. "Now that we have something concrete to go on it makes a great difference to our credibility. Thank you for your call. May I have your details?" she asked, thinking of everything the police would ask.

Nick gave them to her, then added, "I'm coming over immediately. I can get on a flight tonight and be in London tomorrow. My phone number is 0064 ... 274 ... 832 ... 791. I'll give you a ring when I arrive at Heathrow so you can fill me in on progress."

"Give me your flight details and Max will meet you," said Marguerite.

"I'll email them through. Thanks."

"Well, that was a bit abrupt," said Marguerite after he had

hung up. "What do you think, Max?"

"I think he's right. You had better get the police onto this before she loses signal," he replied. "Do you want me to make up a room for this man if he is coming over?"

"I suppose so. He's a friend of Purdie's. It makes sense for us to work together."

Marguerite phoned the commissioner. Reassured London's police resources would be brought to bear on the problem of locating her granddaughter, Marguerite poured herself a large glass of wine and sat down to think.

CHAPTER
THIRTY NINE

London, 1989.

MARGUERITE AND EUGENE ORGANISED A BIRTHDAY party to celebrate Tamara's sixteenth birthday.

"All your friends from school will come of course," said Eugene, "and I've asked Clive to pick some suitable boys he knows and invite them to make up the numbers." Eugene was enormously proud of Clive who was now at university studying economics.

Tamara winced. She would have been happy with a small party of just her friends and family but didn't like to tell her father so. She couldn't tell him there was something about Clive that made her very uncomfortable, and she didn't imagine his friends would be any better. He had bullied her all through her childhood, although he'd been cunning enough to keep that hidden from Eugene. Recently his attention had turned sexual.

Tamara was beginning to show signs of growing into a real beauty. She had inherited her father's intense blue eyes and dark colouring. From her mother she had a curvaceous body of which she was still self-conscious.

Edith, who adored her granddaughter, laughed at her concerns. "My darling, you have a beautiful, womanly figure," she said. "You are a very lucky girl and will grow up to be a lovely young woman. Don't worry about being a little podgy still, it's only puppy fat."

Tamara sniffed. "Who wants to be told they have a 'womanly figure' with 'puppy fat'," she said to her best friend Elizabeth. "It's like describing the char lady." Tamara wanted to be slim and svelte, and be able to wear a shift dress that fell straight from shoulder to knee without unseemly bumps on the way down. Her long hair should have fallen straight down her back; instead it sprung into natural and unfashionable curls. Nothing seemed to match the teenagers in the *Seventeen* magazine the girls read. Compared to the models photographed poolside at a party, even her skin colour was wrong. They all had tanned legs and faces.

Tamara's self-consciousness wasn't helped by her growing awareness that Clive watched her covertly. She could feel his eyes on her breasts. She would be reading in the drawing room, apparently alone in the house, and suddenly become aware he was there, staring at her. Something about his look was malicious, and she felt powerless to stop him. It wasn't the sort of thing she could bring up with Eugene. If she told Clive to go away, or stop looking at her, she knew he'd simply deny anything offensive, tell her it was her imagination and laugh at her, making her feel small.

She tried to raise the matter with her mother, but her complaint was vague and left out Clive's involvement and her nervousness round him. Marguerite misunderstood her and assumed Tamara's misery was simply adolescent confusion. She did her best to reassure her daughter.

"You must remember, darling, that in an odd way, it is a compliment to a young woman for a man to look at her."

"I don't feel complimented," snapped Tamara and stomped off, her problems unresolved.

Marguerite watched her go, fondly trying to remember how awkward being her age had been.

By the night of her sixteenth birthday party this sexual

harassment had been going on for two years and had entered a new phase, with Clive brushing up against her whenever possible. A few times he had managed to manoeuvre close enough to brush an arm, oh so casually, against her breast, which filled Tamara with horror. She was becoming increasingly afraid of him and used every strategy she could to avoid contact with him.

The party was in full swing by ten o'clock. Edith was enjoying herself talking to Mr Schwartz; Auntie Katya had sent a telegram from Australia where she had emigrated a few years earlier; Peggy was dancing with Max; and Marguerite was charming the young men whom Clive had brought.

Tamara's schoolfriends were happy. The presence of the young men had livened up the occasion. At that curious age of not being truly adult but too old for children's activities, they welcomed the opportunity to try out new skills.

The musician was loudly playing covers of top-twenty hits, interspersed with Elvis Presley, the Beatles and Neil Diamond for the older folk. Girls danced in the courtyard under the lights. There was no alcohol present, but Marguerite had organised a fruit punch which was proving popular. She would have been mortified if she had seen the bottle of vodka one of Clive's friends poured into it when her back was turned. Some of the girls were already getting a little giggly on the mix.

The boys had retreated to the back of the courtyard where hip flasks were being surreptitiously passed around. As the evening darkened you could see a row of cigarette ends glowing along the fence line where they stood and puffed. Most were scornful about attending a sixteen-year-old's party and had only been induced to attend by Clive, with the promise of, as he put it inelegantly, 'plenty of plonk and plenty of young pussy'.

They had, of course, also come to see how the Dunnings lived. It was an opportunity to meet the founder of the well-known company in a casual environment. Most were determined to dance with Tamara as a means to advance their job prospects when they left university. That she was easy on the eye was another inducement.

Eugene, playing the part of genial host, circulated among

them all. He danced with everyone he could, both young and old, although he complained noisily about modern dancing. "What's the point," he asked, "of just jiggling around like a St Vitus victim?"

Marguerite laughed at him in passing. "You're getting old," she teased.

Eugene grabbed her and pulled her onto the dance floor. "If I am, then so are you, and all the better for it, my darling," he murmured as he foxtrotted her neatly and improbably round the floor to a Bee Gees number.

Marguerite smiled up at him. Their marriage had survived her attempted affair, Clive's existence and the stresses of running the business. It seemed their love was built on too strong a foundation to be destroyed. Tonight, the celebration for their much-loved daughter was an endorsement of all they valued. Marguerite rested her head lightly against his shoulder as her body moved in the easy rhythm.

Tamara, as birthday girl, had responsibilities. Not only was she there to accept presents, compliments and affection from her family and friends, but she was a quasi-hostess. As such, she accepted any offers to dance, either from Mr Schwartz, Max or the younger crowd.

She fended off some of the over-amorous and slightly drunk boys and ensured that at least three people were between her and Clive at any moment. She was having fun. The public nature of the event meant Clive had to behave, and Tamara was enjoying being the belle of the ball. She watched her parents dancing, their affection very obvious. She smiled at them before accepting yet another dance from some young man.

She had been introduced to them all and vaguely remembered there was a Peter and a Simon. The names escaped her, but it was pleasant to dance with her friends, and having real boys as dancing partners was a considerable improvement on the single-sex dancing lessons her school organised.

The band had just struck up again after their break when a chill on her skin made her aware Clive was approaching. She saw him in her peripheral vision, clearly intent on dancing with her. He had just got within speaking distance, to ask for the next dance, when she panicked. Pretending she couldn't see him, she almost threw herself at the nearest boy who sportingly hauled her onto the dance floor. She was aware of Clive's fury as she danced away. Clearly he wasn't fooled by her pretence. Neither Marguerite nor Eugene noticed.

When she returned after the set, Clive wasn't around. She relaxed and kept her senses tuned, but he didn't reappear.

The party finished at midnight, to the amusement of the university crowd. The girls were picked up by their families or their drivers and escorted home. By one o'clock the house was free of guests, and Tamara and her parents headed for their beds. Tamara, who had only had a couple of glasses of the spiked punch, was feeling a little giddy and happy.

She entered her bedroom, stripped off her dress and stockings and headed for the bathroom. She was about to leave her room when the door opened and Clive entered. She gasped in apprehension. He had never done this before.

"Get out," she whispered angrily. "Get out of my room."

He ignored her, grabbed her hand, switched off the light, and she found herself struggling against him. She tried to scream, but he put his hand over her mouth as he hauled her over to the bed. She fought desperately, trying to bite his hand. He shook her, and her head smacked against the bed head, knocking her senseless.

"You little bitch," he snarled as he dragged her onto the bed. "Do you honestly think you can treat me like that and get away with it? You fucking little cunt, I'll show you who's who."

He took his hand away from her mouth for a moment and she tried to scream, but the next second she found something forced into her opening mouth. It was her stockings, and they formed an effective gag, half choking her as she struggled to breathe. There were tears streaming down her face as she felt him rip her knickers off.

Clive forced his weight onto her. He was a big man, and playing rugby had developed his muscles. Tamara fought desperately but made no impression on his weight and strength.

He let his grip on her wrists go, and she tried to rake his face. He grabbed them back before they had done more than put a slight scratch near his eye.

"Don't you try that on me, you fucking bitch," he said, before slapping her soundly across the face.

Tamara knew her parents were only a few doors away. Surely she could get their attention, get their help. She kicked Clive hard with a free leg and was slapped soundly again. This time the blow was so heavy it knocked her out for a moment. When the world steadied, she found him pushing his knee between hers, his flies undone and his penis stabbing at her thighs.

"Just take it and enjoy it, you cunt," he said.

She felt her legs being forced apart. Try as she might, she couldn't get away. He was stabbing now at her cleft. She thought he wouldn't be able to enter her, that she could buck and writhe too much for it to be possible, but her resistance excited him.

"Oh yes, you feel it now, don't you, you little whore?" he gloated. He lowered his head to her lips and bit them viciously. She moaned deep under the gag. She felt a tearing pain and writhed again, frantic, as he filled her. The pain was indescribable as he forced his way in. The gag made breathing difficult, and her involuntary cries of pain meant she was nearly suffocated.

He rode her viciously, stabbing again and again into the pain. Finally, after what seemed like forever, she felt him shudder. He gave a grunt and eventually rolled off, leaving her in a mass of pain. One of her eyes was half closed from the blow he had dealt to her face.

"If you ever tell anyone what happened here, I'll make sure it happens every night from now on. Do you understand?" he hissed at her. "You led me on tonight, flirting with all the other men, so no one will believe you anyway."

He stood up and looked down at her. She was a shaking, sodden mess of sobs, shock and terror. He pulled his trousers up and moved back to stand beside the bed. Tamara cringed in fear.

"You little bitch," he said again, and deliberately filling his mouth, he spat down at her pubic area. She could feel the coldness of the spittle on her hair and trickling against her thigh.

"I'll make sure you're ruined for anything, you shop-soiled tramp. Don't ever try and act superior to me again. You try, and I'll tell everyone about this, about how you moaned and begged underneath me." He made the words convey a depth of salaciousness that appalled her. He watched her shaking and laughed.

"Make sure you remember me, darling," he said sarcastically.

He left, leaving Tamara sobbing on the bed.

CHAPTER
FORTY

London, 1989.

TAMARA LAY ON THE BED FOR a long time. She was dizzy and then too frightened to leave her room for the bathroom in case Clive was lurking on the landing. Eventually the need to scrub herself clean of him forced her to her feet. Wrapping herself in a robe, she opened her bedroom door and looked out, but the landing was clear. She hobbled to the bathroom. She could barely walk, and the swelling over her eye made it difficult to see.

She locked the door, ran a bath and did her best to scrub Clive off her skin. She felt she could taste him and smell him even after she had given herself a thorough soaping. She scrubbed at herself with the nail brush and pumice stone. She was bruised and battered between her legs, and a continuing trickle of blood on her thighs suggested there was internal damage as well. She felt she would never feel clean again.

Tamara was terrified he would return. Even with the door locked she no longer felt safe. She knew she would never sleep in her bedroom again, she couldn't bear it. She considered calling for her mother but abandoned the idea. Clive's threat to say she'd led him on halted any urge to involve her parents. She didn't want them to know.

The thought of Marguerite's anger and grief were more than she could bear. Better just to deal with her own emotions than worry about her parents'. She would have been too ashamed to talk to her father anyway. In the meantime, she couldn't stay here when Clive could repeat the attack at any time.

She returned to her room, dressed, grabbed a bag into which she thrust her savings book and purse, some underwear and a sweater. She couldn't think of what else to take. She listened for any sounds of movement outside her room.

She crept down the stairs to the front door. Max looked after security, and it took her some time to open all the locks, particularly with trembling hands and non-responsive fingers. She felt guilty about being unable to lock the house again as she left.

She had no idea where she was going as she walked down the street. London at four o'clock in the morning was a strange place for the sixteen-year-old girl who'd lead such a protected life. She wandered aimlessly, taking side alleys as they came up, with no sense of direction. Her sole purpose was to disappear where no one could find her.

A couple of cars passed her, a few cabs and a police car. She shrank into the shadows when she saw it, and it passed without noticing her. A square she walked across was noisy with rubbish collectors emptying bins in the chill morning air. One saw her and looked at her with suspicion.

"Oi, darling, what you doing out at this time?"

She ignored him and kept walking.

"Hey you!" he called out.

She could hear them discussing her behind her back, but she kept going, turned a corner and felt safe from interference again.

Dawn was approaching, and she was getting tired. She ached everywhere, and her head felt stuffy and unclear. There were a few more people around now, and she got a few startled looks as they saw her and the state of her face. One woman, clearly a cleaner, stopped to ask if she was all right. Tamara pushed past. She was beginning to realise she had to find somewhere to rest.

The streets she was walking were no longer residential. Without noticing it she had come into the heart of the city itself. The area looked rougher and the street she was on was lined with small businesses and shops. Outside one was a planter box on a plinth. Tamara sat down wearily. Even sitting hurt. She wondered how far she had come. She hadn't really noticed her feet among all her other aches, but now she realised they too were tired. She slumped back on her perch, too tired to get moving again. She was woken by someone shaking her shoulder.

Tamara woke with a start and opened her mouth to scream. The grip on her shoulder felt like Clive's.

The woman shaking her was young. The jeans and T-shirt were ubiquitous and told Tamara little, but the woman's accent gave her away immediately as cockney.

"What're you doing here, luv?" she was asked.

Tamara stared back blankly.

"Jeez, you ain't 'alf got a shiner. What bastard did that to you?" the girl asked.

Tamara just shook her head wearily. Her head ached unbearably. She shut her eyes.

"Now, don't go off to sleep again," said the girl. "Where're you staying?"

"Don't know," muttered Tamara.

"Well, you can't stay here. Mr Khan will be along in a moment, and he won't want you cluttering up his doorway," said the voice. "Ain't you got a 'ostel or summat?"

Tamara shook her head.

"Jeez," muttered the girl to herself. "Come on then. There's a 'ostel just round the corner. Cheap and cheerful, just like me." She pulled Tamara up.

Tamara groaned as her body shifted itself to vertical. The girl looked at her. "Some of that damage on the inside as well, right?" she asked, then didn't wait for an answer. "Bloody bastards. All the same. Men!"

She half led, half dragged Tamara round the corner to a

doorway. The sign said: Hotel, Rooms by the hour. Terms: Cash in Advance.

There was no one at the counter. The girl rang the bell, and when that failed, knocked on the office door. Eventually it opened.

A man in a vest and trousers ambled out, a cigarette dangling from his mouth. He was about to tell them to leave when he recognised Tamara's companion.

"Hello, Susie love, what you got here?"

"Girl who needs a room," she said. "Someone's given her a hiding. If she doesn't lie down soon, she's going to croak it, and then we'll have the cops all over the place."

The man grunted. "Orright. You got cash?" he asked Tamara.

She gave a small nod.

"Go on, Susie, I'll take it from 'ere." He came round from the counter. "Upstairs with you," he said to Tamara and led her up to a room on the second floor. It was tiny, dismal and run-down, with a bed, a small desk and chair. There was nothing whatever to recommend it apart from it being where Clive couldn't find her.

"Bathroom down the hall, communal kitchen downstairs. Most people eat out. Cash up front daily," he said.

Tamara found her purse and paid him.

He left.

She collapsed onto the bed.

She woke in the late afternoon, used the bathroom and returned to the room. She climbed back into bed and slept until morning.

CHAPTER
FORTY ONE

London, 1989.

WHEN TAMARA FINALLY WOKE, SHE REALISED she had to confront her situation.

God, she thought, her parents would be frantic. They would probably have called the police, which was the last thing she wanted. There would be a real fuss if Eugene Dunning's daughter suddenly disappeared. She would have to call home.

She was hungry as well and found a greasy café, a block away, with a pay phone, ordered egg and chips and with the change put through the call.

Max answered. "Please can I talk to Mummy?" she said.

"Oh my God, where are you?" Max exclaimed. "What's happened?"

"Please get Mummy," she repeated quietly.

A second later Marguerite was on the line. "Tamara, where are you? What's happened? Are you all right?"

Tamara asked, "Is Clive at home?"

"What? No. He's out. Where are you, I'll come and get you."

"Come and meet me, but please don't tell anyone where.

Not anyone. Please promise." She extracted the promise from a troubled Marguerite and gave her the address of the hostel.

"Max, tell Eugene that Tamara is found," Marguerite instructed. "She was very specific that no one knows where she is. I'll fill him in when I get back." She and Max stared at each other. "I don't know what's gone wrong," she murmured.

Half an hour later Marguerite was sitting down beside her daughter. She had seen the bruises on her face, the purple more dramatic now than twenty-four hours earlier. Marguerite was white with shock. Her beautiful girl! "What happened? Who did this to you?"

Tamara started crying.

Marguerite held her closely and rocked her. "My darling girl, what happened to you? Who did this?"

"I don't want to say," she sobbed. "Please don't make me."

"But you must, darling," said Marguerite. "You must say what happened. This is a serious police matter. Who would treat you like this? Why did you leave the house? Did this happen out in the street?"

Tamara just cried harder and shook her head.

"Come on then," said Marguerite, standing up decisively. "Come with me; I'll take you home. We can sort this out when we get there."

Tamara shuddered. "No," she whispered. "I can't go home."

Marguerite stared at her, puzzled. "Why ever not? Please, darling, we need to make you safe. You may need a doctor for that face."

"I can't ever go home," sobbed Tamara. "Don't make me," she begged.

"What happened?" breathed Marguerite, thinking back.

"We were there that night and we saw you go up to bed," she said slowly. "All the visitors had gone – I know because I checked there was no one left. Max checked as well." She considered the sobbing girl. "Did something happen later that night? Dearest, you must tell me. I promise not to tell anyone unless you allow me, but you must let me know."

Still Tamara said nothing. She wiped her nose on her sleeve. Out of habit Marguerite fumbled in her handbag for a handkerchief and passed it to her. A nasty suspicion was forming in her head. "Were you attacked by someone at home? A burglar?" she asked. "The house was unlocked that night, although Max swore he bolted the doors himself after everyone had gone."

Tamara shook her head.

"Not a burglar then," continued Marguerite. She already knew that Eugene couldn't have done this. He had been with her the whole time. That only left … "Clive?"

There was a fresh burst of weeping.

"Was it Clive?" Marguerite asked again.

Tamara nodded slowly.

"Oh sweet Jesus," said Marguerite. "What happened? Did you have an argument?"

Tamara started crying again. The handkerchief wouldn't last long.

"What did that bastard do to you?" Marguerite asked fiercely. She looked at her daughter's bowed head and shaking shoulders.

Surely her suspicions were wrong? But deep down, she knew. She could see it on her daughter's face, in the shame and pain. "Did he rape you?" she asked quietly.

She read affirmation in the way Tamara flinched. Tamara, who was her joy, alive with vitality and laughter, reduced to this crumpled, crying girl. Marguerite thought the pain and grief would kill her and held her daughter tightly. "Tell me," she coaxed. "This is something you can't keep to yourself, my darling. It's too big."

So Tamara told her. She left out the worst details, but Marguerite could imagine them for herself all too well. Her heart ached. She was overcome with guilt that she hadn't seen the risk sooner, hadn't protected the girl. For God's sake, Clive was Tamara's half-brother. This wasn't just rape, it was incest.

Gradually she began to understand the hold Clive had on Tamara. "No one will believe you led him on, darling," she soothed. "We all know that's not the case. We know you don't even like him. You didn't ask for this, or invite it." She made the girl look at her. "Tamara, you must listen. This is *not* your fault, do you understand?"

"But Daddy might believe Clive," whispered Tamara. "I think Daddy would rather believe him than me. He mustn't know," she begged her mother frantically. "Please, you promised. He mustn't know."

Who indeed knew what Eugene would think? Marguerite had never fully understood his attitudes towards sexuality, but the rape of his only daughter would surely be devastating. Would he believe her innocence, though? Would he be inclined to accept that Clive had been led on? What would he make of the incest? Tamara was barely more than a child herself. The police must be told. She hoped Clive would hang for the crime.

Then, horrifyingly, she realised she could never put Tamara through such public humiliation. The police couldn't keep it confidential, and the gossip magazines would have a field day. Whatever happened, Tamara's life would be ruined, even if Clive were convicted and sent to prison for life. Marguerite groaned and hugged her daughter.

When they were both calmer, she got Tamara to agree to visit a doctor with her. "We aren't going to report anything to the police without your agreement," Marguerite said firmly, "but you must be checked by a doctor. I want your injuries recorded by a professional. You don't have to tell the doctor who attacked you, or that it was your half-brother. But I won't have you threatened by Clive again. If he ever tries, there will be evidence to use against him."

Reluctantly Tamara agreed. The doctor, shocked at Tamara's state, scolded Marguerite for not bringing the girl in before she had cleaned herself up after the rape.

"Evidence," he said.

Marguerite looked at him in silence. He listed the injuries. None were physically serious, as they would heal naturally, but there were contusions and abrasions both internal and external.

"If you won't report this to the police, and I think you should," he said kindly to Tamara, "then you must understand, trauma takes time to heal, a lot of time. Both physically and mentally. In the long term, time is the only thing that will heal you."

He was a fatherly, older man and managed to make the experience tolerable for the girl. Later, as Tamara got dressed, Marguerite asked, in an undertone, about the possibility of pregnancy.

The doctor shrugged. "It's too soon to say," he said. "I hope not, for your daughter's sake." He shook his head. "This is a bad business, a bad business." He handed Marguerite a copy of his notes.

"I've read about some 'morning-after' pill?" asked Marguerite.

"In a few years, no doubt there will be one. I've read they've been doing studies of a prototype with animals. At best there are a couple of trial products. Such treatment has to be started directly after the sexual act. In your daughter's case, forty hours have gone by. It is too long a period."

"Can you not at least try?" begged Marguerite.

"It would go against all good practice," he said sharply. "There is no good medical evidence to support such an action."

Marguerite sighed.

Tamara refused point-blank to return to the house and was equally adamant her father was not to know what had happened to her. Uncertain what the right thing was to do, Marguerite elected to let Tamara make the decision.

Eventually Marguerite phoned Peggy. She didn't go into detail, but she knew her old friend would only have to look at Tamara to have a shrewd idea of the problem. It was agreed Tamara could stay with her godmother for the next few weeks while things were sorted out.

By the time Tamara was settled at Peggy's and Marguerite made it home, she was exhausted. Ahead of her lay the burden of concocting an explanation that would suit her husband. And of course, Clive would have to be encountered and dealt with one way or the other. She decided to relay the information that Tamara had been mugged and the injuries treated by a doctor.

She hoped the veiled truth would satisfy her husband and explain why Tamara had been missing for two days. She also hoped that Clive, reading between the lines, would know there was firm evidence of rape and that it had been documented by an independent witness. She wondered if she was being wise. Apparently increasing age didn't automatically grant wisdom.

As it turned out, she need not have worried. While she was away, Clive had told Eugene he'd found an apartment with other students, and moved out. He would be back to pick up anything else he needed. Eugene was torn between pride that Clive was, as he put it, 'really becoming an adult', and the knowledge he would miss him around the house.

Marguerite delivered her expurgated report on Tamara, omitting the rape and focusing on the assault. She implied the assailant had been unknown to Tamara and adjusted the time and circumstances of the incident to being part of an early-morning walk by their daughter. Eugene was horrified for his daughter but agreed with Marguerite's assessment that involving the police would, unfortunately, expose the girl to press attention which could cause her more stress and reflect badly on her and the family generally.

Marguerite explained Tamara would have to have a couple of weeks off school and would stay at Peggy's in the interim. As it was nearly the end of term anyway, Eugene made no comment.

Although he hadn't discussed it with Marguerite, he had sufficient concerns of his own to keep him occupied. The economy was buoyant but jittery. Doomsayers were everywhere, talking about a forthcoming crash. No one could pick when the bubble would burst, and corporate spending was still on the rise. There was a much larger gap these days between rich and poor. Highfliers were more likely to be doing their shopping in New York or Paris, whilst the poor were struggling at Marks and Spencer. Dunnings, which was in the centre of the market, was suffering.

As Marguerite assured him his daughter was now safe and all right, he was content to leave matters in her hands.

CHAPTER
FORTY TWO

London, Present Day.

IT HAD BEEN AGREED THAT PYOTR should seek an interview with Marguerite Dunning while the delegation was in London. He had wondered how best to ask for this meeting and how to couch his questions. It seemed a little blunt to simply phone her and ask, "Where are our missing Fabergé Eggs?" Something more diplomatic was needed.

After some research he discovered Marguerite Dunning was interested in art. A search of the Internet showed photos of her attending various London galleries. It was arranged that she be sent an invitation to preview a small exhibition of Russian iconographic art due to open in London. Pyotr planned to be introduced to her and then take the discussion from there. Unfortunately, this event was scheduled to occur the day Purdie was due to arrive in London, and consequently the invitation had been declined.

This left Pyotr with no alternative but to contact Marguerite directly. He telephoned and was surprised at the speed and urgency with which the phone was answered.

"May I speak with Mrs Dunning?"

"Speaking." Marguerite was making urgent signs to Max to listen in on the speaker phone.

"My name is Pyotr Karolan, Mrs Dunning. I am a researcher with the State Historical Museum in Moscow, currently in London as part of a delegation to discuss repatriation of art works. I was given your name as a contact. I understand your family were originally Russian. I wonder if you would be prepared to speak with me?"

Marguerite, who had been expecting another phone call to negotiate Purdie's return, was caught by surprise. "Well, yes, my family were originally Russian, but a generation or two back. I don't know much about Russia myself," she replied. "I can't imagine why anyone would have given you my name."

"I would very much like to meet with you, Mrs Dunning, as I have a matter I would like to discuss. Is that possible?"

Marguerite screwed her face up in irritation. She wanted him off the line in case the kidnappers phoned again. "May I know what this is in relation to?"

"We believe your family may have information we are seeking about items which disappeared from Moscow at the beginning of the revolution. I would appreciate the opportunity to talk to you about this."

Marguerite looked at Max, who raised his eyebrows. "What items, exactly?" she asked.

"If I may, I would like to discuss that with you in person," said Pyotr.

"What do you mean by items that disappeared? Are you accusing my family of theft?" Marguerite's voice hardened.

Pytor was shocked. "Certainly not," he hurried to say, "but I have reason to think your family may hold the key to information we need."

"I should think that's extremely unlikely," said Marguerite. "My grandfather, who *was* Russian, died in Poland during the war years, and so did my father. I know very little of my family history. I don't think I can help you."

"Nevertheless, I would appreciate an interview, if you could spare me the time," he persisted.

Marguerite thought fast. It was too much of a coincidence that a second person was referring to mysterious Russian items.

"All right," she said. "When would you like to meet?"

It was agreed he would visit that evening. Max had been assigned to pick Nick up from the airport, and Marguerite hoped he would be with her during the interview. It might be that his knowledge of Purdie could add some detail she was missing.

"Well, well, well!" exclaimed Max.

Marguerite was looking puzzled. "I don't know what these people are talking about! I'm perfectly certain there's no treasure or anything valuable in my family. We wouldn't have been so poor during all those wretched refugee years if we'd had something valuable with us. We'd have sold it."

"Still," said Max, "it looks as if there must be something, for two different groups to be contacting you. Fabergé Eggs were what the first lot were after. What exactly do you remember from your childhood?" he asked curiously.

"Virtually nothing," she replied. "It was during the Second World War. I knew we were Russian, and my grandfather told stories of having had a factory, and being well off. But there was no mention of anything valuable. They had been prosperous when they lived in Moscow but left it all behind when they fled. They planned to get to England but stopped in Poland because my grandmother was very ill, and they ended up staying there. Grandfather became a tailor, and so did my father. When we heard the Russians were invading, my father was in a real hurry to leave Poland. Maybe there's some significance there, but if so, I don't know what it is." She picked up the phone. "I think it's time to phone my little sister."

Katya, in Australia, knew nothing at all about any treasure. Edith had never mentioned anything, and Katya thought it unlikely they could have had anything of real value with them. Marguerite cast her mind back and could think of nothing either.

It was later that night, thinking about her granddaughter, presumably alone in a strange bed, that she remembered the boarding house, and the first night she'd had her own room.

She'd used her father's tin box as a table. Come to think of it, they never had opened it. The key had been missing for so long, and there was never any urgency to see inside. It had become a family joke – the unopened box. Katya said once, on one of her visits home, it was sort of a 'To the Island' box. When asked what she meant, she had said vaguely that it was more fun to wonder what was in it than go to the effort of getting a key cut to fit.

Marguerite supposed she was right, though she wondered if the real reason no one had opened it was they suspected it contained papers from the businesses in Poland and Russia. They might be useful for a family archivist but not compelling enough to make an effort over.

Now, the insistent queries from the Russians and Chinese raised the question about exactly what had been in it. It was imperative she find out quickly. The problem was, she had made a sentimental present of it some quarter of a century earlier.

CHAPTER
FORTY THREE

London, 1989.

MOVING IN WITH PEGGY WAS THE best thing for Tamara. Peggy, sympathetic to whatever catastrophe had occurred, showed no tendency to carry on about it or make a drama of the events. This soothed Tamara. She was terrified of encountering Clive again, but at Peggy's she was well sheltered; Peggy moved in a very different circle.

Unused to caring for children and without other standards to guide her, Peggy treated Tamara as an adult. If she was having a cocktail, she assumed Tamara would want one. If she was going to a party, she assumed Tamara would come. Tamara began to see the joys of independent adult life.

A week after Tamara's arrival, Peggy had to fly to New York to attend the opening of her latest film, *Love Through Eternity.* She left Tamara with full use of the apartment and, topping that off, left her with the keys for her MG.

Tamara had barely got her driver's licence and had never been allowed independent access to a car. Peggy's casual trust was a wonderful balm. Tamara was terrified of driving in London, but the challenge of being able to do so meant she took the car out each day and grew in confidence and competence. By the time Peggy returned, Tamara had clocked up several hundred miles of valuable driving experience.

The bruises on her face faded to yellow smudges, and Peggy insisted she help make up Tamara's face to hide any remaining damage.

Peggy giggled. "It seems like yesterday I was performing the same service for your mum," she said with nostalgia. "Look at yourself now," she commanded, turning the girl towards the mirror, and was gratified by Tamara's cry of pleasure.

To Peggy's surprise she found she enjoyed having the younger woman around. Tamara hero-worshipped her and imitated her as much as she could, a fact not lost on Peggy.

After Tamara had attended a couple of parties, she started making friends. She was a good listener and genuinely interested in the talented people she was meeting, so they warmed to her. She missed the circle of friends she'd had at school and the casual camaraderie of daily contact with them. Several times she picked up the phone to call Elizabeth, but each time put it back in its cradle. No power on the planet would make Tamara divulge what had happened to her, and she knew her friend would have endless questions.

Her new friends were very different to her schoolfriends. They spoke differently, their accents unashamedly regional. Tamara, reared to use the Queen's English, was fascinated. They might not know how to set a table, or address a bishop, but they were canny with practical matters about which Tamara had no clue.

They met for coffee during the day or attended concerts at night. It seemed everyone she met had just come back from Morocco or from crewing a boat round the Greek Islands. If they hadn't just returned from some exotic place, they were just about to go.

Mandy, a cheerful girl and the lead singer for a folk trio, was about to set off in a Kombi van on the 'hippy trail', which turned out to be driving across Europe and Asia, stopping in various countries on the way, and ending up in Australia. Tamara was green with jealousy. Oh for the freedom to do such a thing!

She fantasised about travelling. Mandy and her friends made it sound very accessible and easy. They had a relaxed attitude towards money, simply assuming that they'd earn enough on the way, either by busking or doing any work they could get. Tamara said wistfully that the trip sounded wonderful. A week later Mandy phoned to say there was a place available in the van if she wanted it.

She hadn't had her period since the night with Clive, and the weeks were passing. She knew stress could alter menstrual patterns, and she had never been regular anyway. TV had convinced her a normal pregnancy involved vomiting every morning, and fainting gracefully. As Tamara felt well and had no sign of either symptom, she pushed the thought to the back of her mind.

When she visited her parents, she was aware of the unspoken question in Marguerite's "How are you dear?"

She wiped all sign of makeup off before these visits and moderated her language while she was at home. Marguerite had always made clear that saying 'damn' in public was the height of profanity and unacceptable for her daughter. Tamara could only imagine what she would make of some of the words she and her friends used so casually.

She mentioned this to Peggy, who stared at her in disbelief for a second, before dissolving into hoots of laughter. "Let me tell you, your mum can swear like a trooper if she wants to. She may restrain herself around you, but I remember her before she was married, when she wasn't quite as refined."

Two months passed, and Tamara could no longer ignore the probability she was pregnant. She made an appointment with the same doctor who'd examined her before. This time she went alone.

The doctor broke the news gently. Tamara had expected it, but even so, it was devastating. What was she to do? The doctor wasn't prepared to offer his opinion and urged her to discuss the situation with her parents.

Tamara shuddered, imagining her father's reaction. Other

families might be accepting, but she was certain he would hold the opinion that only 'bad girls' got into trouble and scorn her accordingly. It never occurred to her she could speak to him openly.

"Can I get rid of it?" she asked the doctor.

"Not legally, not unless you are prepared to testify to the rape," he replied. "Also you have to ask yourself whether you'd regret it later. Taking a life, even an unborn one, is a big issue."

"I just want things to go back to the way they were," she said desperately.

"I know, my dear, but time doesn't go backwards for anyone. What I can tell you is that you are healthy, and your baby is growing normally. You *must* discuss things with your parents. Your mother knows what happened. Many girls get pregnant; some opt for adoption. Most families do survive an unplanned pregnancy, you know, and in your case, being the victim of a rape will surely mean your parents are sympathetic." He read her opinion of that statement on her face and sighed. "There are no perfect solutions to this, my dear. You simply have to try and do the best you can. You may come to love the baby and want to keep it. My best advice, though, is to be open with your parents."

How could she even think of keeping the baby? This was a child of rape and incest. Tamara wondered if it would be evil, simply because of its violent conception. She was crying as she left the doctor's office and took a cab to her parents' house.

She braced herself to follow the doctor's advice and tell her parents the news. Unfortunately, Eugene had that morning seen a photo of her attending a party after a rock concert. The headline in the paper stressed the drunk, drugged and disorderly goings-on of the young at the after-party function. Tamara, innocent of any such behaviour, just happened to have been captured in the forefront by the photographer. She was clearly identifiable both by the reporter and by her father. Tamara's name and family connection spiced up the story.

Eugene was nearly apoplectic. His worst fear was having his family name dragged through the gutter, and that this could occur, at a time when he was under enormous financial pressure, was unforgiveable. He overrode his daughter's explanation and insisted she return at once to the family home.

"That woman," he declared, referring to Peggy, "has allowed you far too much leeway. You should never have been allowed anywhere near such an occasion. How dare you sully our reputation by behaving like a tramp? Imagine what would have happened if you had been arrested."

Marguerite tried to intervene. More empathetic than Eugene, she clearly saw Tamara was already distressed. "Eugene, dear," she tried diplomatically, "listen to Tamara. She is explaining that this wasn't her fault."

Eugene was adamant. This was the sort of behaviour that could only lead to trouble. Tamara was coming back into the family home and under his thumb. Changing times had put pressure on his business and now invaded the inner sanctum of his home. He wouldn't tolerate it and was going to lay down the law now, before the rot set in. He set about demolishing his daughter's character.

"You've just proven you can't be trusted being treated like an adult. You've behaved like a silly, irresponsible child, allowing yourself to get caught up with such a crowd, and at such a function."

Tamara tried to imagine telling him she was pregnant. Her courage failed. She felt such fury at his stupidity and unreasonableness that she could hardly speak. Tears poured down her face, and she broke into sobs.

"That won't help you, my girl," said her father brutally. "Get on the phone to Peggy and get her to send your things round."

Tamara was furious with the tears that made her look so weak. Her temper snapped. "I won't," she said furiously. "I am not coming back to live here ever again. I'm going travelling."

Eugene stared at her in disbelief. "Don't be stupid," he declared. "You're far too young. You need to get back to school straight away. I've been much too lenient with you."

Tamara shook her head. "I'm not going back to school," she declared. "I'm going away."

"You'll do what you are told, my girl," he said. "What in

God's name has got into you? What sort of attitude do you think this is?"

"One that is a good deal more reasonable than yours," shouted Tamara, who turned and walked from the room, slamming the door hard behind her.

She grabbed her coat and headed out the door. Never, never again, she swore, would she be pushed around by other people.

Back in the drawing room Eugene moved to rush after her but was stopped by Marguerite.

"Let her go," she urged. "You can see she's really upset. You can't talk to her now. Really, dear, I do think you were a little harsh. She said she hadn't done anything wrong. It wasn't fair of you to keep shouting at her. Let her be now. She'll be back."

It was six months before Marguerite saw her daughter again.

CHAPTER
FORTY FOUR

Travelling 1989.

TWO MONTHS LATER, IN THE PIAZZA high above
the sea in Sorrento, Tamara passed the hat around the
audience. Mandy and the group had paused for a drink,
and in the interval Tamara was working the crowd. "*Grazie,
grazie,*" she said as the lira fell into the hat. Each of the quartet
had equal rights, but they had divided the labour up. Tamara
cooked most of the meals, collected the money when they were
busking and was the minder of the group's finances when they
were performing.

Lewis was frontman, the violinist and main decider of material
they used. He also fronted negotiations for gigs, and terms.
Mandy was lead singer and PR person. Her lively personality
and charm attracted the crowds as much as her deep musical
voice.

Dan sang harmonies, played lead guitar and sang the male leads.
He was their agreed driver and the oldest, most experienced of
the four. He never put himself forward, or attempted to dominate
a conversation, yet he was the person they all turned to when

making decisions. Each had input into where they travelled, but Dan had the final say. So far, these decisions had led them through France, northern Italy and down the coastline.

In England it would be cold, foggy and murky, but here the only sign of autumn was a slight softening in the daytime temperatures, which made it all the more comfortable.

The sun had tanned Tamara's face, and she had small freckles on her nose. She smiled to herself as she took the money. She was happy just being here and enjoying the 'Italianness' of it all. The baroque Chiesa del Carmine and the Palazzo were across the piazza. Life was close to perfect.

Earlier she had bought herself a fresh lemon juice and the bartender had warned her to keep a lookout for gypsies targeting tourists. In her loose smock top and ankle-length skirt she looked much like a gypsy herself. Her clothes comfortable, practical and concealing her slightly thickened waist.

The girls had slept in the van at first, and the boys outside in a small tent, but in the last few weeks an understanding had developed between Mandy and Lewis. Nothing was said, but the glances they exchanged spoke of a degree of intimacy. Sexual tension was running high.

A couple of nights ago Tamara had gone to bed before the others and had been startled an hour later to find Dan opening the door of the van and climbing in with an armful of bedding.

"Sorry," he said apologetically. "I hope you don't mind, but I got the feeling I was in the way out there. I didn't fancy being a chaperone. I promise not to bother you, although I might snore."

For the first half hour Tamara lay awake, bracing herself for an advance, but soon the steady rhythm of his breathing relaxed her and she fell back to sleep herself.

From then on, the group divided its sleeping arrangements so Mandy and Lewis had the tent, and Dan and Tamara bunked together companionably in the van.

Tamara liked Dan. He was a great performer onstage but self-effacing at other times. He generated enthusiasm and participation from the audience like a real pro, and when he and Mandy sang their duets, the crowds cheered, stamped and applauded.

She felt safe around him and content not to be on guard all the time and just be herself. She began to treasure their evening chats in the van before they fell asleep.

It was light and casual, but this was the nearest she had come to finding a confidant since she had parted with Elizabeth. She sent a few postcards home, but with no fixed address received none back. She wondered how her family were. She knew her mother would be worried and assumed her father would still be angry.

As a young child she'd adored her father, but as she grew older, nothing she did seemed to please him or meet the high standards he set. She wondered whether her gender was the issue. He seemed to approve of Clive.

"The only thing I can't stand is causing others deliberate pain. That seems to me to the real immorality," said Mandy, philosophising over a glass of wine.

She was seconded by Dan, who added quietly, "First do no harm."

If only the rest of the world could be like them, thought Tamara. She hadn't decided what to do with the baby. Any product of Clive's seemed doomed to be evil, but part of her wondered what a baby of hers would be like. Would it be someone she could love, cherish and look after?

The group headed north again, this time on the east coast, to Venice. Tamara knew she was now five months' pregnant. Soon she wouldn't be able to keep this private. Her breasts were sore and swelling, and she would shortly have to buy a new bra.

They had been discussing where to go after Italy. Tamara kept quiet, not knowing how much longer she could stay. Lewis wanted to carry on driving.

Dan suggested they sell the van for what they could get, fly to Egypt, then head north, taking in Jordan, Lebanon and if possible, Israel, as they went. There was some question over Israel, as the political situation was volatile. When this was pointed out by Tamara, Dan shrugged.

"Well, half the scenic stuff is in the Arab countries anyway.

I only want to see Israel because I've read *Exodus*," he grinned shamefacedly.

Mandy agreed, in spite of her allegiance to Lewis. "Yeah, *Exodus* was a great book. I want to see the kibbutzniks," she said enthusiastically. "All those tall, tanned, hard men … Bring it on." Lewis rolled his eyes.

Tamara was doing mental calculations. She reckoned she could stretch things out another few weeks at most before she'd have to chuck travelling and settle down for the birth and whatever came after. She had been well throughout her pregnancy and was sensible about what she ate and drank.

"I'm for Egypt and the rest," she said. "I may have to go home in a month or so, and I want to see as much as I can. The pyramids, the sphinx, the Nile."

Dan glanced at her.

She smiled at Lewis. "Driving does take a lot of time."

Dan went back to studying maps. "Then there's Sinai, not to mention Petra, Jerash, and if we went to Lebanon, all those cedars."

They agreed to mull things over until after they'd finished with Venice.

Venice was overwhelming: the history, the crowds, the colour, the culture. They separated during the day to take in the sights.

Mandy and Lewis went to Burano; Dan opted for a quiet day after all the driving of the last week. He had seen Venice before. "It's charming, but a tourist hotspot. Today is going to be a scorcher, and I could do with a break," he decided.

Tamara wanted to buy a present of Murano glassware for her mother and went exploring on her own. By the time she got back to the van she was overheated, her feet swollen and her head ached.

Dan put down the guitar he was tuning and looked at her with sympathy. "Come on," he said. "I'll buy you a cold drink from that café over there."

Tamara opted for an iced lemon. It was cold and fresh.

"You were right, it's a wonderful place, but so oppressive! I can't imagine how they managed in medieval times with long gowns and robes, in all those tiny streets and alleyways."

She smiled at him. "At the moment I'm a bit over sightseeing. Floating down the Nile with no effort on my part is beginning to sound good." She stretched her legs out in front of her and relaxed back in the chair. Suddenly she gave a little jump. She had definitely felt something move inside her. She glanced at Dan. He was watching a Vespa rider on the opposite side of the street. Cautiously she let her hand rest on her stomach. Yes, there it was again, a sort of squirmy, fluttering sensation. Her baby was real, and it wanted to move around.

She bit her lip. She had been pretending the baby didn't exist or wouldn't make a difference to her. Now she'd have to adjust to the child inside her having a life of its own.

Dan was looking at her, or rather at her hand on her belly. He met her gaze for a second and looked away again, but in that moment she understood that he'd already known her secret.

"You know, don't you?" she asked.

He looked back at her. "I thought I knew a few weeks back."

Tamara cast her mind back. "How?" she demanded. She had been careful to keep herself modestly covered so her increasing waistline wasn't obvious, and she couldn't see any other difference.

"Your breasts are bigger," he said. "I share the van with you. I don't mean to offend you, but I couldn't help noticing. Also you've got that glow about you. I wondered."

"Why didn't you say something?"

"Well, I could ask you the same thing," he retorted. "It was no business of mine. If you'd wanted to talk about it, you would have. You didn't, so I thought you probably had your reasons." He looked embarrassed. "I didn't want to upset you by raising the subject, or ruin our friendship by making it awkward, or by you becoming self-conscious."

Tamara mulled that one over. "Do the others know?"

Dan snorted. "At the moment they've only got eyes for each other. If you turned into a frog they wouldn't notice, as long as you turned out a nice pasta and salad for dinner with a decent red wine."

Also, Mandy and Lewis weren't observant people. Tamara had noticed before that Dan seemed to see his way into things other people missed.

"An eye for detail." She could hear Marguerite's approving voice. Her mother would have been talking about dress designers or art works, of course. Still, she thought, Marguerite would like Dan.

"I haven't spoken about it because I don't really know how I feel, or what I want to do."

Dan asked, "Do you want to talk about it? I mean if you don't, it's OK. I won't press the matter."

"No," said Tamara. "Now you know, there's not a lot of point in pretending it doesn't exist." She hesitated, embarrassed about how to begin. Dan would surely think her loose or just foolish to get caught in this way.

"I didn't mean to get pregnant," she said haltingly. "I was forced." She saw he looked blank. "I was raped," she said bluntly. "It only happened the once, but I got pregnant. I've been running away ever since." She saw the look of horror on his face and felt her eyes tearing up.

"I just wanted to get away from England, from everyone who knew anything about me, and try to cope with it all." To her embarrassment she suddenly found herself in real tears. The café proprietor was staring at them. She dropped her face into her hands, mortified that everyone could see her.

She felt an arm on her shoulders. Dan had moved and was crouching down beside her, his arm around her. "Come on," he said. "Let's get you back to the privacy of the van and we'll talk there." He helped her up, and she leaned into his shoulder, crying uncontrollably. After a while the tears dried up a bit. She sniffed, found her handkerchief and allowed him to take her arm and lead her from the café. He put his arm round her shoulder again as they walked across the street, and she leaned into him.

"I'm sorry, I'm so sorry," she said, shamed by her tears.

"Shush," he said. "Of course you needed to cry. God help us! You've been carrying such a terrible burden all this time on your own. Of course you've got to let it out."

He sat beside her on the bunk. Gradually she calmed down enough to tell him the details more or less coherently. He tensed when she told him about Clive, particularly when she said he was her half-brother.

"Fucking bastard," was his muttered comment.

"I suppose now you won't want me to come with you to Egypt," she wept anew.

"Why ever not?" he asked, surprised.

"I thought you'd send me home," she confessed. "I don't want to be a nuisance, and a pregnant woman is more hassle than a free-and-easy girl."

"You're not, and never have been, a nuisance," he assured her. "You contribute as much as anyone, and it's largely because of you everyone has got on so well for so long. You never fuss or moan. Of course you're not going to be sent home by any of us. It's up to you, and you alone, what you decide to do."

CHAPTER
FORTY FIVE

Travelling 1989.

THEY FLEW INTO CAIRO AT NIGHT. As the aircraft circled over the lit-up pyramids, Tamara felt a thrill of delight. What more perfect sight could there be? She knew enough history, and had read enough, to be looking forward to King Tutankhamen's treasure and the mighty Nile River. It stood out among the lights as a dark snake through the glow of the town itself. She hugged herself with excitement.

Well, nowadays she hugged herself and her unborn baby. There had been a few more flutterings since the first surprise. She wondered about its gender. She could envisage a pretty little girl, with dark curls like her own; someone she could protect from life's evils and love with all her heart.

They stayed that night in a YHA hostel. Cheap, cheerful and divided firmly on gender lines. Tamara and Mandy were left in no doubt that this was a Muslim country: enlightened and liberal, but one where unmarried women were wise to be modest, virtuous and self-effacing. Tamara decided to buy a cheap gold ring so she looked married, in case anyone took an interest in the shape of her body. She mentioned the idea to Dan, and that afternoon, as they wandered the bazaar, he bought her a ring.

For the first time she began to think about her future. Eugene's stress on qualifications and Marguerite's message of independence for women had left their mark. Tamara wondered if archaeology might be the career path for her. She'd always been interested in history, and Italy and Egypt had been eye-opening.

She was thinking about it a few days later as they boarded a felucca to go upriver to Aswan. Fourteen passengers were on board, all sharing the same basic conditions. There were no bathrooms, so comfort stops were taken when the boat pulled up to the shore. Mandy and Tamara went together into the desert and sheltered each other.

The only accommodation was the deck, sheltered by an overhanging canvas sheet. During the day they lay, dozed or watched the sights from the comfort of the cushioned deck. At night, they made their beds in the same spot, and slept foot to foot, seven aside under the stars. The first night, the creaking of the rigging, the bright moon and nighttime noises kept Tamara awake. After that she adapted and snoozed away, both day and night. Dan slept beside her, and on the second night she awoke to find she had inadvertently rolled over in her sleep and ended up in the crook of his arm. He smiled at her when she tried to disentangle herself.

"Relax, sweetheart," he advised. "I enjoyed it. The nights get cold, and you made a great hot-water bottle at two in the morning."

She smiled at him shyly. "I hope I didn't snore."

He grinned. "Only soothing deep breathing, I promise." He kissed the tip of her nose. "Did you also know you talk in your sleep?"

She looked at him, appalled. "Oh Lord, what did I say?"

"You told me you loved this chap. What was his name? Oh yes, Dan." He grinned, adding, "Must be quite a guy."

She gasped then picked up her pillow and thumped him with it. "What a load of rubbish. I even believed you for a moment."

"You are so easy to rile," he laughed. "But actually, you do mutter in your sleep. It was just that I couldn't get a coherent sentence out of you."

"You should have woken me," she said.

"I would have, if I could. But you slept like the proverbial log. And then you looked sooooo peaceful," he murmured.

Tamara thumped him again before flinging herself back onto her own pillow. "This is just so beautiful," she said. "I can't believe it's our last night on the river tomorrow. I could live like this forever."

Dan flexed his arm. "I'm going to have to get some exercise in this arm to sustain the weight of your head if it's going on forever." He just laughed as Tamara glared at him. He reached across. "I'd better get started now," he said, pushing his arm back under her shoulders. For a moment Tamara stiffened, then relaxed and curled closer into his arm.

"I think you're right," he said, pulling her closer. "I, too, could live like this forever."

They stayed together throughout Egypt and Jordan. By the time they arrived in Amman, Tamara was seven months' pregnant, and even beneath loose-flowing peasant dresses, long skirts and smock tops, her shape was clearly visible. Dan had taken on the role of husband to protect her from gossip and harassment as they crossed borders and checkpoints, simply saying there had been no time to get her new passport updated in her married name.

Late in the Egyptian part of the trip Tamara became aware of Mandy's suddenly sharpened gaze on her body, and had smiled, a little sheepishly. "I guess you had to know sometime," she said.

"I had no idea," confessed Mandy. "Is it Dan's?"

"No, I was pregnant when we started travelling. It's why I am travelling, in fact." She forestalled further questions by shrugging. "It's complicated, OK? I don't really want to discuss it."

Tactfully, Mandy didn't bring the subject up again, and Lewis, after a self-conscious moment when Tamara caught him staring at her belly, said nothing at all.

Petra was a long bus drive south. Tamara began to feel the pregnancy slowing her down. Her back ached from the three-hour drive, her bladder filled with untimely haste and she was getting tired of travel. There was a long walk downhill from the coach drop-off point before they came to the ancient valley. The gradient was easy, but Tamara felt she had started, as she put it to Dan, 'to waddle'. He smiled and pointed out the horses and carriages that could take her back up at the end of the trip.

That night, back in Amman, she told her friends she would be flying to London. "It's time to go," she said. "Even geese know when it's time to migrate," she added.

"I suspect all of us will be going our separate ways soon anyway," said Mandy. "We can't earn anything doing gigs in bars or cafés here because there aren't any, and busking isn't too popular with local traders either. I know I'm nearly broke."

Lewis nodded, "Yeah, we have to make some decisions of our own." He looked at Mandy. "We've talked about seeing if we can get jobs here, or in the Lebanon, as English teachers. That way we can refinance ourselves for the next step of the journey through to India."

The group looked at Dan. "I think I'll be going back to the UK soon myself. Let's go to Jerash tomorrow; have a celebratory dinner to mark the good times we've had, then go our separate ways. It's a small world, we may all meet again."

They exchanged contact details and swore eternal friendship.

"I doubt we'll ever see them again," Dan remarked privately to Tamara. "People come together and then part. It's the way of things."

Tamara looked at him wistfully. "It's been the best of times for me," she said. "I'd hate to lose contact with everyone."

Dan smiled. "I promise you won't lose contact with me."

Tamara braced herself to phone home, carefully doing the maths about time differences. She timed her call for two in the afternoon in England, when Eugene would be at work and her mother at home.

When Tamara broke the news of her pregnancy there was a long silence at the end of the phone. "Oh God, it's Clive's, isn't it?" asked Marguerite.

"Yes."

"I've wondered, every single day, since you've been gone. It's been a constant ache. I knew when you left that something was terribly wrong. Not just the attack you suffered."

"I need to come back; it's time," said Tamara.

"Of course," said Marguerite. "Oh God, darling, you have no idea how much I've worried."

"I'm sorry," said Tamara, feeling guilty. "I didn't know how to tell you, let alone Daddy. I needed to get away from everything."

"I'll meet you at the airport."

It was hard saying goodbye to Lewis and Mandy. Harder yet saying goodbye to Dan. He volunteered to come with her, but she refused. "Secret woman's business," she said wryly. "I think you need to let me get through the next bit on my own."

Dan argued, but Tamara refused to yield, conceding only that she would love to see him after the birth. Her sole focus now was the child.

In the end Dan abandoned the fight. "I'll be back in England in only a few weeks. Give me all the ways of contacting you, and I'll look you up as soon as I get back," he promised

CHAPTER
FORTY SIX

London, 1990

MARGUERITE MET TAMARA AT THE AIRPORT and took her to a quiet hotel. Her first sight of her unmistakeably pregnant daughter was a shock. Marguerite had mentally prepared herself, but the reality of her daughter's big belly so jarred her she was in tears as she hugged her. She was grateful that no intrusive reporter had witnessed Tamara's arrival.

Tamara was tanned and glowing with health. "Oh God, it's good to have you back," said Marguerite as she embraced the girl again.

"It's good to be back," replied Tamara, laughing.

Marguerite studied her and saw the changes in her face. The childlike softness had gone, her cheekbones more defined, her mouth and chin firmer. She looked, thought Marguerite, a happy and relaxed young woman, notwithstanding the pregnancy. As she helped her with luggage, she noticed the ring on Tamara's wedding finger. Tamara saw her looking at it and smiled. "Dan gave it to me," she said. "It's much safer to be some man's 'wife' when travelling in Arab countries."

She didn't add anything more, and Marguerite was left wondering who precisely 'Dan' was and whether he was important. He wasn't travelling with Tamara now, she noted, so she shrugged her shoulders and let it slide.

They talked long into the evening simply catching up. Tamara gave Marguerite the Murano vase and told her about her travels. Marguerite brought Tamara up to date with what she knew of her friends, and Eugene. She cautiously told Tamara that Clive had joined the firm and was working for her father. The last news brought a frown to Tamara's face. She looked so distraught that Marguerite regretted bringing his name up at all and apologised.

"I don't ever want to have to see him again," Tamara said. "Keep him away from me. I try not to think of the bastard."

"I know he lives in London and that Daddy is fond of him. Well, as I haven't told him why he shouldn't be, I can't blame him. I just don't ever want to be in a situation where I have to encounter Clive again." She gave a grim little smile. "I guess I won't be shopping at the family store anytime soon."

Marguerite snorted. "He isn't working on the shop floor, darling. Don't you think you should tell your father what happened? God knows what Eugene would think of me keeping it from him. There doesn't have to be adverse publicity, but maybe you should tell him the truth, otherwise you will be avoiding Clive for the rest of your life."

"I have thought about it," replied Tamara reflectively. "Sometimes my head seems full of nothing else. The thing is, Daddy didn't want to listen to me last time we met. What would happen if I told him and he didn't believe me?" Her eyes filled with tears. "I know I can't do anything right as far as he is concerned, and Clive looks like a goody two-shoes. Suppose my own father thought I was being malicious."

"We've got the doctor's report, sweetheart," said Marguerite. "You made a complete statement at the time. It would be hard for Clive to refute that."

"And then what?" asked Tamara. "Clive would lose his job, but it would destroy my father in the process. There's no guarantee, even with the doctor's statement, that Daddy wouldn't think I had contributed to the situation. I'm pregnant, he's bound to assume I'm immoral in some way. You know what Daddy's like."

"I do," said Marguerite sadly. If Eugene couldn't be trusted to listen, then he couldn't be trusted with this information. Marguerite sighed, wondering how life had become so complicated. "Tell me about Dan," she said to change the subject.

Tamara made an appointment for a check-up.

"I'm very pleased to see you again," the doctor said. "I wondered how you were getting on." He checked her and the baby over, pronouncing both mother and baby to be in fine health. "What have you decided to do when the baby is born?" he asked.

Tamara braced herself. "I want to give it up for adoption. I can't keep the child. I'm not ready to be a mother myself, and there are reasons why this child can't fit into my family."

"You mean the rape?"

"That and other things," said Tamara evasively. She wasn't going say this child was the result of incest as well as rape. She wanted to protect it, even though she wouldn't keep the baby. It would be unfair for it to start life with such a tarnished reputation.

The doctor sighed. "Well, my dear, you're the only one with the right to make the decision, and I know it isn't an easy one." He organised the appropriate forms to be sent to her. "Think long and hard," he advised.

The weeks before delivery passed quickly. Tamara kept a low profile, careful to keep out of the way of anyone who might recognise her. She met frequently with Marguerite, but at places neither would normally go.

Once she said the baby would be adopted, neither Tamara nor her mother talked about the future. No discussion of gender, no name choices, no speculation about who the baby would look like. Conversations now were carefully anodyne. It was like trying to avoid jabbing at a sore tooth with your tongue, thought

Marguerite, something impossible to achieve.

She should have been busy buying layettes or helping set up the nursery. She remembered how excited Edith had been in the weeks leading up to Tamara's birth. She cursed Clive for the misery he had caused.

What would her father have felt about his own granddaughter giving up her child? Or about a Komarov being wrenched from its family?

She wasn't prepared to discuss this with Edith, who would certainly demand the child stay with its mother. Marguerite wanted to spare Tamara the pain of other people's opinions, but she constantly questioned her own wisdom and advice to the girl.

Tamara went into labour early on a Wednesday morning. The ward was an uninviting green, the beds utilitarian and comfortless, privacy and dignity nonexistent. There was an implicitly censorious attitude from the staff, which made Tamara uncomfortable. It wasn't her fault she was an unmarried mother. Worse, the contractions that had started out so promisingly, refused to strengthen and commit to full labour.

"False labour," said the ward sister disparagingly as she came past on her ward visit. "This could take days yet." She looked as if she were about to discharge Tamara but changed her mind when she saw her expression.

The sister shrugged. "Try walking up and down the ward. See if that will help move things along a bit," she advised.

For the rest of the day Tamara walked the corridor. The contractions came regularly eight minutes apart, but never increased. It was as if the baby didn't want to be born, thought Tamara, exhausted. The pain was unpleasant but not impossible, and she was getting tired.

She passed a cubicle with the curtains drawn. Quiet sounds of weeping were coming from inside. When she had circled the ward and was back outside the cubicle again, the person inside was still crying. Curiosity and pity for anyone in distress in this comfortless place led Tamara to open the curtain.

"Excuse me," she said tentatively, "but I can hear you're upset and wondered if there was anything I could do for you. Are you all right?"

The woman on the bed was young, only a few years older than herself. Her face was red and blotched with weeping.

"Sorry," she said. "I didn't mean to have someone else hear me and be distressed."

"What happened?" asked Tamara. The woman's belly looked a bit too flat for her to be in labour.

"I lost my baby this morning," said the woman, her eyes brimming over again. "I really thought this time I could carry her through. It was a little girl, and she was 32 weeks. I thought I was safe."

"Oh God," breathed Tamara, "I'm so sorry. How terrible for you."

"It's the third time," sobbed the woman. "I get pregnant, but I can't carry them for some reason. They put stitches in and everything, but it just didn't work. I still went into labour too early. It's as if my body just doesn't want to do the job properly. I don't think I can go through this again." She blew her nose. "My husband and I so want a family, but I don't think it's going to happen for us."

She turned away from Tamara. "I feel such a failure," she cried, her tears renewed.

Tamara sat beside her and held her hand. "The world's so terribly unfair," she said. "Here am I not wanting my baby, and you, who really want one, can't have one. There's no justice."

The woman stared at her. "Why on earth don't you want your baby?"

"I was raped," confessed Tamara. "So being pregnant isn't exactly a joyous event."

"You might feel different after the baby is born," said the woman. "Once you hold it yourself ..."

"I won't ever hold it," said Tamara curtly. "I'm adopting it out at birth. If I'd known how to set about it, I'd have had an abortion, but the doctor wouldn't let me, and I didn't know where else to go."

She suddenly realised what she had said and that she had been tactless with a grieving woman. "I know it's different for you," she said. "How lovely that you and your husband really want children. That must be so nice." She cursed Clive again for what he had taken from her as another contraction gripped her belly.

"Are you in labour at the moment?"

"Yes," panted Tamara. "It's just not getting anywhere. I assumed when you started contractions, the baby was there in a couple of hours. My body doesn't seem to want to get on with the job."

"So unlike mine," sighed the woman. They looked at each other in a moment of comradeship.

"Hi, I'm Tamara."

"And I'm Nora."

They smiled at each other.

"Life's a cow, isn't it?" said Nora.

"You can say that again. Oh well, I'd better get walking again."

"Good luck!"

From then on, she stopped in every time she passed Nora's cubicle until later that afternoon when Nora's husband came in. She left them to their grief, her heart sore for her new friend.

When Marguerite came to visit, she told her about Nora. They both agreed how unfair it was.

"She and her husband seem like such nice people," said Tamara. "Why do awful things have to happen to nice people? There are plenty of horrid people in the world who need to be dealt to. It's not fair."

"No one ever said life was fair," said Marguerite. It was a phrase from Tamara's childhood, so she smiled.

"Do you think they'd be interested in adopting your baby when it's born?" suggested Marguerite.

"Do you think I should ask her? I thought of it this afternoon but then wondered if it would be tactless and unkind of me."

"I don't know," said Marguerite frankly, "but you've said these seem like nice people who really want a child. If they were agreeable, it would mean you'd have some control over where your baby goes, which you won't have with the social welfare system."

"I'll talk to her next time I see her," said Tamara. "The way things are progressing I'm going to be pacing the floor for hours."

When she approached Nora and Paul she tried to find a time when the corridor was quiet, but there were always staff or visitors wandering around.

"Hi," she said nervously.

"Hi again," said Nora, and introduced her husband. Tamara braced herself to say the words. "Please don't be offended," she began, "and I don't want to upset you by asking, but I wondered if you'd considered adoption? I have to give my baby up, and you've just lost yours. I wondered if you would be interested in having my baby." She faltered as they both stared at her in disbelief. "I'm sorry, it was probably a stupid thing to ask," she said, "but you seemed so kind and to want a baby so much ..." She trailed off, embarrassed.

She turned and bolted out of the door, only to be seized by one of the strongest contractions yet. She stopped, leaning against the wall of the corridor while it passed.

"Are you all right?" Paul said behind her.

Tamara straightened up, gasping. "Yes, fine, thank you. Just another contraction." She smiled weakly.

"Did you mean what you said?" he asked. "I mean about offering your baby to us?"

Tamara nodded. "I can't keep my baby, but I want to know it goes to someone who really wants it. If I go through welfare I won't get to choose the people who adopt, and who knows who they will be? At least with you, I'd know my baby would go to good people. It seemed like such a simple solution. I guess I wasn't very tactful, though."

"Can you come back and sit down?" asked Paul. "We need to talk this through."

Paul and Nora agreed to the adoption almost immediately. Tamara could see the excitement in Nora's face and felt shamed by the woman's hunger for a child.

Tamara said Marguerite would be in charge of the arrangements and legal requirements. Her own involvement ended at the moment of birth.

"This way we get, at least partly, what we want. You go home with a baby, I go home without one. I promise I won't be a nuisance in the years ahead."

Nora looked at her gratefully. "I think you must be an angel from heaven. I can't thank you enough for your gift or think of a greater honour that you could have shown us. We promise to bring your baby up as our own, in every way, and to give it all we can."

Tamara felt tears welling and stood up with her eyes brimming.

"Well, I've got a job to do now," she said. "I won't see you again. Thank you for helping me out. I feel much better now. My mother will bring you the baby as soon as it's born."

She walked back to her own bed. Marguerite phoned her lawyer, Donald McCrae, whom she had been using for some of her personal transactions. She knew him to be ambitious and very aware that looking after Marguerite's affairs satisfactorily was a good way of achieving those ambitions. A man who knew which side his bread was buttered, thought Marguerite, who liked him all the better for it. If he was startled by her request, he didn't comment, merely advising her that private adoptions were illegal in the United Kingdom.

"There must be some way to organise it, though," argued Marguerite. "It's in the best interests of everyone."

Donald thought for a while. "There may be a form of guardianship that would be possible. It's wouldn't be as binding as adoption, but it could be a legal option, where the child is looked after by a new family. It might be possible later on for it to be transferred to a full adoption. I'll have to look at ways of making the arrangement legal and binding on both parties. You'd better give me the details of the prospective adopters. They need a lawyer, if they want to go ahead with this, and we will have to sort out the details."

"Can you come in and see them this afternoon?" asked Marguerite. "Tamara is in labour now, and this couple need to be able to take the baby home when it is born. It's got to be sorted now."

She got a cautious affirmative from Donald but not before she'd heard his sudden gasp as he took on the dimensions of the task.

Marguerite left him to his paperwork and concentrated on her daughter.

As though the arrangement with the Davises cleared the way, Tamara's contractions grew steadily stronger. Shortly she was in full labour. Even gritting her teeth and trying to be brave, she still moaned with pain. She'd had no idea it would be this painful. They wheeled her to the delivery room and put her legs up in stirrups. The process was too painful to be embarrassing. Two hours later she gave birth to a small, perfectly formed and healthy daughter.

Checked, cleaned and wrapped, she was handed to her grandmother who left the room with her. Tamara lay in the last phases of the birth, tired and tearful. The saga that had started less than a year ago was finished. She was three months short of her seventeenth birthday.

She heard the gynaecologist murmur to the sister, "The mother is only a child herself, for heaven's sake."

Tamara turned her head away and cried.

Halfway down the corridor Marguerite stopped to gaze at the granddaughter in her arms. There was a fuzz of dark brown hair on her head and a pair of unfocused, dark blue eyes. Marguerite bent her head and kissed the child.

She smiled at the couple through her tears. "Your daughter," she said proudly, carefully handing the baby to Nora.

Her reward was Nora's joy. She transformed from the tear-drenched woman of earlier in the day to a glowing madonna.

"I can't and won't stay," said Marguerite. "I've organised the paperwork, and for the birth to be registered properly. The baby is yours from now on, as far as my daughter is concerned. I ask, though, that you allow me to make her a small present, through my lawyer. If you would be prepared to accept it for her, when she grows up, she'll know she was loved from the moment she was born. That she wasn't adopted out because her mother and her family didn't want her." Marguerite felt her voice give a betraying quiver and stiffened her spine.

"Of course," said Paul gently. "That's a nice thought. We can't thank you enough, and we promise she will be a true daughter to us."

Nora smiled at her mistily.

"How shines a good deed in this naughty world," murmured Paul softly.

"I beg your pardon?" said Marguerite confused.

Nora gave a little laugh. "Oh, don't mind him," she said. "He's always quoting something. It's a measure of how much I love him that I put up with it. It's infuriating sometimes." She smiled radiantly at her husband.

Marguerite dropped her head and kissed the baby goodbye before turning and walking firmly back down the hall to Tamara. If tears broke through once she had passed out of the Davises' sight, then that was her business and no one else's.

A few days later Donald completed the legal paperwork. Marguerite thought hard about what to give the child. She wanted to give her a sense of her birth family, without intruding on the new family's rights to the child. Eventually she remembered her father's old metal box, still unopened, which connected the baby right back to old Grandfather Komarov. It was the only remaining part of her Russian heritage.

If it contained family papers, she thought, then so much the better. At some time the child was bound to ask questions about her background. The box could guide her search for her origins. She had it brought down from the attic and couriered to Donald to pass on to the Davises.

CHAPTER
FORTY SEVEN

London, 1990.

TWO DAYS LATER MARGUERITE BROUGHT HER daughter home. Tamara initially protested but eventually gave in, accepting it was the only option in the short term. She would have to face her father sometime. He might be difficult, rigid and authoritarian, but she'd missed him. She loved him, particularly if she didn't have to spend too much time in his company.

Max was thrilled to see Tamara. If he thought she looked tired and a lot older than the last time he saw her, he kept his observances to himself. Tamara hugged him then went to the kitchen to see Cook, who was equally delighted by her return.

Tamara had wondered if her bedroom would trigger nightmares, but felt nothing. Her room was an insight into the girl she had been less than a year ago, with dolls on the dressing table and a unicorn poster on the wall. A little girl's bedroom, she thought, amused. Her schoolbooks lay on the shelf, a memory of what life had been like. She was touched her parents had left the room unchanged.

It was nice to see her feet again and be able to lie on her tummy if she wanted. She had squeezed herself into a pair of jeans when she left the home. Worn with a loose top, the bulge of post-baby flesh at the top wasn't really noticeable and was shrinking fast. Her breasts were still large, sore and heavy, which made her feel out of proportion. To her annoyance she couldn't fit into a 12B cup and had to wear maternity bras.

She felt she could pass muster and doubted anyone would know she'd just had a baby.

The reunion with Eugene was unexpectedly touching. Both Tamara and her father approached the meeting with caution. Eugene was so pleased to see his daughter, and so relieved she was well and safe, in the end he simply hugged her hard. Tamara melted, her prickliness and antagonism evaporating in his obvious joy at seeing her.

Marguerite wondered again about her wisdom in keeping secrets from him but decided the die was cast. Anyway, she thought, trying to justify her decision, it was Tamara's right to decide who she told.

Eugene, on his best behaviour, asked what Tamara had been doing over the past few months and refrained from commenting on the suitability of a girl not yet seventeen jaunting around Europe and the Middle East.

Tamara, relaxed and happy to have a non-judgemental father for a change, told them about her adventures, the people she had travelled with and the experiences they had shared. She was light in tone, wry in her descriptions of people and events, and very funny. Even Marguerite forgot for a while, as they laughed together, that the story rested on a bedrock of tragedy and pain.

Inevitably the subject of Tamara's future plans came up but, Marguerite noted, Eugene was careful to ask his daughter what her intentions were, rather than issue a diktat.

"I don't really know," said Tamara. "Wandering round Italy and Egypt gave me such a taste for history. I wondered about studying archaeology." Her expression was sheepish. "I threw away my schooling last year, so I'd have to do a catch-up, maybe at night school, to get the qualifications to go to university. It's just a thought at the moment, but it's going to take a while to find my feet. In the interim I need to work. I'm a bit broke at the moment."

Marguerite saw Eugene start to open his mouth, and got in smartly. "Well, you've time to think things through now you're back." She knew her husband well enough to know he had been about to suggest Tamara work at Dunnings.

Quite apart from the problem Clive presented, she had a shrewd idea that Tamara would never again place herself in a situation where she yielded her independence to Eugene.

"Have you thought about where you want to live?" Marguerite continued. "Your home is always here, of course, but I did wonder if you might have other plans now you've been away from home for so long."

Tamara smiled, relieved it had been her mother who brought up the subject. "Again, I haven't thought it through yet. I thought I might give Aunty Peggy a ring and see if I can board with her for a while. It worked out well before, and she's got lots of contacts in all sorts of fields. Who knows, she might even be able to find a bit part for me in one of her films!"

Eugene's face was getting progressively darker but he kept his mouth shut. At least he'd learned something, Marguerite thought. It was probably best to get these tricky subjects out in the open now, before he built up a set of expectations around Tamara which weren't going to be met.

The conversation moved to safer ground as Tamara prodded Eugene to talk about how Dunnings was going. The fact that he could happily talk forever about his passion helped the evening finish on a good note.

Two days later Tamara moved to Peggy's; Peggy had been delighted to get her call. She'd missed Tamara and was very pleased to have her surrogate daughter home. Not many women admired Peggy with the whole-hearted regard she received from Tamara.

She kissed the girl when she arrived and looked her up and down shrewdly. "You're looking lovely, of course," she said, "but what have you been using for moisturizer and sunscreen? Your skin looks as if it needs a bit of help." She observed the new maturity and the subtle changes in her body, but made no comment.

Tamara laughed and hugged Peggy back with enthusiasm. It was good to be back, if only for a short time, in a girly world of pampering and preening. "I've used absolutely nothing," she assured her honorary aunt. "I was much too busy having fun and adventures."

CHAPTER
FORTY EIGHT

London, 1990.

DAN CALLED TWO MONTHS LATER, HAVING first phoned her parents' place and been given Peggy's number by a curious Max.

Tamara was shy when she met him. They had travelled together for so long that she'd thought herself comfortable with every detail about him and was surprised to find herself meeting him like a stranger. He was well dressed, his hair cut, and he looked like an urbane Englishman rather than a tatty travelling hippy.

Then again, several weeks of Peggy's influence had seen her own hair trimmed, conditioned and styled. She wore urban clothes rather than travelling gear and felt like a slightly different person.

They embraced nervously, but it didn't take long to break the ice. Dan asked about the delivery, checked out her new post-baby figure with approval and was tactful in asking about the infant.

Tamara simply said the child had been a daughter and had

gone to a good home. She heard herself sounding like a breeder selling a puppy, and winced, though she kept her face neutral. Dan, who knew her a little too well, made no comment.

It had taken him longer than he expected to leave Jordan. He tried to get into Israel to complete his travels but hadn't been able to obtain the necessary documents. His enquiries had been met with hostility by Israeli authorities.

Tamara asked about Lewis and Mandy. They had stayed on in Amman looking for teaching work, or anything else that English speakers could do to earn a living. They'd get by easily enough, commented Dan. "So, what are you going to do now?" he asked.

She laughed. "Everyone keeps asking me the same question, and the truth is, I don't know. I'm footloose, fancy-free and not certain what I want to do. If I give it time, I'm sure something will come up. I still feel sort of jangled after everything that's happened. What about you?"

It occurred to her she had never asked much about Dan's background before they joined up as a travelling group. She knew, of course, that he was musical, with a fine voice and guitar skills. She also knew, from comments he'd made, that he was university educated. What his qualifications were had never come up. She believed he was about 25. There had been no need for sharing confidences on their travels, and she'd been too busy guarding herself to be concerned about anyone else's background.

"Well, that sort of depends," said Dan. "I could go back to the hospital, I suppose. ... As a registrar," he replied, to her questioning look. "I might be a bit rusty after twelve months off, but it's an option. Or I could look at getting into private practice somewhere. The NHS is a bit of a tricky system, but there would be a place for me somewhere."

"I didn't know you were a doctor," exclaimed Tamara.

"I didn't know you were the 'daughter of Dunning's'," he retorted. "Seems there were a few things we didn't know about each other."

Tamara looked a bit self-conscious. "I guess, on the trip, I liked that people took me as I was. I've always been my parents' well-behaved daughter, taught not to make waves or get any bad publicity. It was great to have people not care who I was, or who my parents were. It was real freedom."

Peggy came in and was introduced, and set out to charm Dan herself.

Later, she remarked, "I like your young man."

Tamara coloured. "He's not my young man!"

Peggy smiled at her. "Whatever you say, darling. Do you want to bring him to the wrap party we are having next Friday? You are very welcome to. Everyone will be there."

So Dan escorted Tamara. She was amazed at how easy his manner was. He was relaxed with star and groupie alike, carrying his share of conversations and listening to others when they spoke. He was a good raconteur, and the groups that formed round him were usually lively and laughing. Tamara took pride in having brought such a charming companion. More than one young hopeful was giving Dan the glad eye.

"I felt I ought to provide you with a chaperone," she said later. "The girls were all over you."

Dan grinned. "It's only because I was one of the few young, straight males in the room. Surprising how many artistic types are gay, isn't it? Anyway, you were getting a few admiring looks yourself."

Tamara smirked back at him. "I'm hot stuff, that's why."

Dan said something below his breath. Tamara wondered if she had heard him right.

"Most people are only interested in me because they think it will give them access to my aunt. It's as bad as being with my parents. Folk think that by being nice to me they'll make contact with my parents. It never works, of course, and it's mostly annoying."

Dan just smiled lazily. "Come for lunch Sunday?"

He had moved into a flat in Nottinghill. It was bright, airy and welcoming.

"Do you want me to cook?" asked Tamara. "Or help?"

"Just set the table," he replied.

He'd cooked a decent roast. "I thought we would go for a traditional Sunday."

They drank wine and talked through the afternoon and into the evening. Later, much later, he said, "Do you want me to escort you home, or …?"

Tamara looked at him. "Or?"

"Stay the night," he urged softly.

Tamara tried to suppress a sense of panic. Could she do this?

She thought rapidly. A call to leave a message on Peggy's phone, and the decision was made.

She was shy about her post-baby body. Her breasts, less sizeable than they had been, were still large, and she felt her waist was too big.

Dan kissed her worries away. "Silly girl," he said. "You really haven't a clue about how beautiful you are, have you?"

She tensed with worry, memories of Clive intruding.

Dan caught her movement and looked at her tight little face. "Are you all right?" he asked gently.

"Just a bit nervous," was her shaky reply.

He pulled her down to the bed, holding her cuddled against his shoulder. They lay quietly together while Tamara felt herself relax. "It's like being on that boat on the Nile."

"This is making love, sweetheart," said Dan. "Don't be afraid. You're the one who's in control here. Nothing happens that you don't want and allow."

Tamara nodded. His hands and mouth soothed her fears. He took his time and gentled her, his lips soft against her eyelids and her neck. Her back arched to meet him as he made his way leisurely downwards.

She found herself moaning with need. "That is so good," she murmured. For a long time she allowed him to give her pleasure, her body's natural responses reassuring her and easing her tension. She looked down at him between her legs. "I could do the same for you," she said softly.

He looked at her questioningly. When he saw she was serious he moved round so their bodies curled into each other. She began to pleasure him, his immediate reaction adding to her own building release. Eventually they readjusted their positions and he entered her. She had been so afraid of this moment, but Dan made it easy. It didn't take very long for her to reach a peak. Her cry came as he reached his own climax.

After, he pulled her to him so her head rested on his shoulder. "All right?" he asked.

"Very," she said softly. "I didn't know it would be this good."

She felt rather than saw him smile into the darkness.

"It was very good for me as well," he said. "You have no idea how long I've fantasised about having you in bed with me."

"Really?" said Tamara surprised. "Why didn't you say so?"

"Well, it would hardly have been right, would it?" he said indignantly. "The last thing you needed was someone else taking advantage of you."

Tamara relaxed against him. "Any time you want to take advantage of me, just feel free," she said lazily as she drifted off to sleep.

She woke early. For a while she lay there, remembering the night before. Dan was spread out beside her, snoring. She studied him while he slept and wondered whether he would be embarrassed this morning and if she should get up and go. She wasn't sure of the etiquette of this sort of situation.

She slid out of bed and went to the bathroom. No toothbrush or toothpaste for her here. She satisfied herself by putting toothpaste on a finger and rubbing it over her teeth. It wasn't quite proper hygiene, but it felt better. She returned to the bedroom and was wondering where her clothes were before she realised Dan was now awake and watching her.

"What are you doing?" he asked.

"Just trying to find my clothes," she said. She was too shy to lift her eyes to his.

There was a swirl of bedclothes, and he was beside her. "You're not thinking of leaving, are you?"

She nodded. "I thought ..."

"You didn't think," he said sternly. "Everyone knows you can't leave a party before you've said goodbye to your host ... and thanked him," he added.

She looked up at him to see his eyes laughing at her. She blushed. Their gaze lasted for what seemed like a lifetime.

"Don't go," he said quietly. "Come back to bed." He pulled her gently back and climbed in beside her.

"You haven't said thank you for having me, yet," he said sternly. Her eyes widened at the double entendre. "Now, how are we going to solve that problem?"

He was kissing her throat, nuzzling the sensitive line that ran down the side of her neck.

"Oh," breathed Tamara.

"Oh indeed," mumbled Dan. "But I think we can do better than that, don't you?" and he proceeded to show her how.

CHAPTER
FORTY NINE

London, 1990.

TAMARA MOVED INTO DAN'S APARTMENT THREE weeks later. She told her father she'd gone flatting, without being specific about the nature of the other flatmates. Eugene accepted the news at face value and asked no further questions.

Tamara was more frank with Marguerite and Peggy.

"You're sure this isn't too soon?" asked a concerned Marguerite. "This isn't some sort of emotional rebound?"

"Well, it seems soon to you, but we've lived together, in a manner of speaking, for months," answered Tamara. "We know each other very well, and now we want to be together."

Peggy, more practical or more tactless, said, "Well, let the course of true love run smooth, I say. You are taking precautions, aren't you, sweetheart?"

Tamara nodded.

"Just checking!" grinned Peggy, quite unabashed. "Gosh, isn't it a different world nowadays, Marguerite, to when we were girls? Can you imagine what people would have said if we'd shacked up together with young men like they do today. The effect of the pill is just amazing. Do you remember all those douche things we used to have to use?"

Marguerite, aware of Tamara's burgeoning interest, brushed the comment aside. "It wasn't what either you or I would have done," she said stiffly.

"You speak for yourself, darling," said Peggy, amused. "I certainly would've, and who knows," she smiled secretively, "maybe I did."

Marguerite looked at her with a fond smile. "You're a shocker, you know! No wonder the Lord Chancellor thought actresses are depraved. What I'm concerned about is what both Eugene and Edith will say when they discover the true nature of Tamara's living arrangements."

"Times move on," said Tamara. "We can't all live as Victorians nowadays. Anyway, we've got the pill."

"Many a slip ..." said Peggy in warning tones.

Tamara gave her a grin.

Marguerite warned, "Be careful, darling. Be discreet. The paparazzi haven't seen you in a while, but that doesn't mean they aren't there."

Tamara nodded, and with that her mother had to be content.

Tamara brought Dan round for afternoon tea and introduced him to her father. Marguerite had prewarned her husband to be on his best behaviour. Eugene shook Dan's hand and eyed him up and down. He allowed afternoon tea to be passed around before asking, "What line of business are you in, Dan?"

"Medicine," Dan replied. "I qualified last year but then took some time off to go travelling. I've just accepted a post at the Royal Brompton & Harefield."

"Ah," said Eugene, pleased. "What department?"

"Hepatology. The liver is my field of interest, and they've got good facilities. In recent years there's been such a growth of knowledge. It's a very exciting area."

Eugene looked even more pleased. "So where did you travel to?"

"Same places that Tamara went," said Dan easily. "We were all part of a group that travelled together." He smiled. "As Tamara has probably told you, we had a lot of fun. We did some busking along the way, and we saw an awful lot of places. All on the cheap, of course, as none of us had much money."

Max ensured that sandwiches and cakes were passed round. He was under orders from Mrs Ferguson to report back on 'Tamara's young man'.

Tamara could tell Dan was making a good impression. He really had a knack of speaking to anyone, she thought. Maybe it was part of his bedside manner, which got her thinking a little too intimately about the recent bedside manner she had enjoyed.

She was miles away but came down to earth when she heard her father ask, "And what are you doing with yourself, darling?"

"I've been doing some secretarial work for Aunty Peggy," she replied. "She gets fan mail, and she's hopeless about following it up. So I'm doing that and it's working out well. And I'm taking extramural courses in history so I can get a degree eventually. I've got to finish off my A levels of course. But so far I'm doing OK."

All in all, thought Marguerite, it was a very successful meeting. Eugene appeared genuinely taken with Dan and accepted Tamara's news, that she was studying, with equanimity, without trying to persuade her to attend some special school or facility he could set up for her. Altogether it had been very satisfactory.

*   *   *

Tamara and Dan had three years together. Three years of happiness, years in which Tamara completed her schooling and enrolled at university and Dan began research into the chemistry of the liver. He published a paper on liver disease which brought him attention and official approval. Life was sweet for them both. Dan was Tamara's rock. He didn't dominate her, tell her what to do, or control her; but his constant, quiet support, his demonstrated pride in her achievements and successes, and his unfailing love gave her the fertile ground she needed in which to grow and develop.

They had begun talking about marriage. Dan was now 28, Tamara 20. They celebrated her birthday with a trip to Paris. They both grinned as they walked the streets they had walked years before when they were first travelling together.

"It's like time-lapse photography," said Tamara. "I keep expecting to see the younger me still here, like a ghost. If you ran a film of this spot alone over the years, you would see me flickering in and out. It's like a part of me is always here."

Dan kissed her. "And me too," he said. "We flicker together, my darling." They were very much in love. "When I'm gone," he said, "you can walk down the same road, and I will be here still."

"Don't be silly," she giggled. "That's either stupid or morbid."

"Well, it's probable you will be on a Zimmer frame by then yourself," he said cheerfully, "but it's a nice thought."

They were back in London. Christmas had been and gone, and it was April. The weather was still cold, changeable, murky and depressing, in spite of it being spring. Tamara was at home catching up on studies neglected over the holiday period. Dan had gone into the central city to meet an old friend from his university days.

Tamara wrote diligently for an hour or so then got up to turn the lights on. She stretched, made herself a cup of coffee and switched on the TV. Headlines proclaimed there had been an explosion in Bishopsgate. "Suspected IRA attack," the reporter suggested. Tamara suddenly focused. She hadn't paid much attention to Dan's plans for the day but knew they included strolling through the City. Dan's friend was down from Birmingham and wanted to see the sights.

She hoped Dan was all right, but she also knew if there was an emergency, he would have stopped to help. She resolutely pushed her concern to the back of her mind over the next couple of hours, even though he was now overdue.

Marguerite phoned to ask whether she had heard about the bombing, and whether they were all right.

"I don't know," said Tamara, feeling her agitation growing. "I haven't heard anything from Dan. No news is good news, isn't it?"

As she spoke there was a knock on the door. Tamara opened it, saw the police and knew the news was bad. They were professional, kind and devastating. Forty-four people were injured in the blast, but only one man had died – Dan.

With her parents' help Tamara stumbled through the funeral. She thought she was coping, all things considered, but then found she had put the toothpaste in the freezer, or salt in the washing machine.

Dan's parents came down from Manchester for the funeral. She tried to speak coherently to them, recognising the pain they were in, but she had no words to say.

His funeral was held at the Church of St Mary Abbots where Dan and Tamara had planned to have their wedding. The church was packed with reporters and the public. Hospital colleagues, musician friends, university mates from years ago all squeezed in to say their farewells. The eulogy was given by Dan's younger brother Matthew.

The day was a series of tasks, and Tamara felt like a circus animal moving on command. Trained never to display emotion to the newspapers, she held herself in rigid control throughout the service and the gathering afterwards.

Marguerite watched her with concern. When she had lost her father violently all those years ago, she had been able to cuddle up to Katya. Tamara had no one now, and she refused offers of help or company from both her own family and from Dan's.

She retreated to the apartment where she could still see signs of Dan's presence. She hadn't changed the sheets on the bed yet, fancying she could still smell his head on his pillow. His clothes were still in the laundry basket. His favourite blue vein cheese, which she would never eat herself, was still in the refrigerator. A part of her brain knew at some point she would have to tackle these things, but she was incapable of it.

She prowled the flat in the early hours of the morning, talking to him. She wondered if a part of him still lingered with her, and thought it did. She felt his presence, but however hard she peered into darkened corners, or reflections on window panes, she never caught a glimpse of him.

Her days passed listlessly until the morning that Peggy arrived, practically forcing her way into the flat. Over Tamara's pleas, she insisted on providing food and practical help. The bed, now messed and dirty, was stripped. Washing was folded, dishes done, along with dusting, mopping and vacuuming.

"You can't live like this, Tamara," said Peggy firmly. "I'm not here to be unkind, but Dan wouldn't have wanted to see you this way. You know that perfectly well."

Tamara nodded.

"And," added Peggy, "I need you back at work. My paperwork is piling up. There's this new computer the studio has forced on me, sort of like a typewriter, but not. I need you to sort out what I'm supposed to do with it. My accountant has been talking about spreadsheets. You need to come in tomorrow and try and see if you can make head or tail of it."

Peggy left, after she had dragged an agreement out of Tamara.

The next morning, at 7.30, Tamara's phone rang. She let it ring until it annoyed her enough to get out of bed and cut it off. Before she could slam it down, there was a squawk from the earpiece.

It was Peggy. "Don't hang up, don't hang up," she kept repeating.

Eventually Tamara put the handset to her ear. "Yes?" she mumbled.

"It's Peggy. Are you coming over?"

Tamara began to launch into a series of excuses, when Peggy cut in again.

"Either you say yes, and mean it, or I'll come over myself and bring you back here to work."

Reluctantly, Tamara agreed.

Peggy refused to let her slack – if anything, piling more work on to her. At least, supposed Tamara, it passed the time.

Her evenings were spent with the lights out, curled up in bed doing nothing, or in a flurry of activity, where she would wear herself out making the apartment spotless, cleaning it within an inch of its life, in an attempt to wipe out any sign of occupation.

Eventually Peggy insisted that she accompany her on a visit to her agent. "I need you to take notes dear. He's talking about a new project, and I never remember what he says," she said airily.

So Tamara sat and took notes. Outside she was surprised to see a sunny day. Somehow the season had changed to summer while she wasn't looking.

How strange, she thought: a summer without Dan in it. She bowed her head with grief and was only brought back to the present by Peggy finishing the meeting and rising to leave.

Peggy forced Tamara to accompany her more and more. Meetings, casting calls, photo shoots; apparently Peggy required Tamara's support at all of them. Peggy was writing her memoirs now, and there were hours of dictation. It was slow work, made bearable only by the fact that a lot of the gossip involved her mother as a young woman, and more recently, the famous men whose lives had crossed with Peggy's.

"Richard Burton, Laurence Olivier?" she queried.

Peggy gave a slight smirk.

Tamara raised her eyebrows, wondering whether the stories would get past Peggy's legal team before publication.

Slowly Tamara began to return to sufficient functionality to do her job. She kept in touch with her family now, going round for dinner most Monday evenings. Tamara had never been a big girl; now she weighed under ninety pounds. Food had become a chore, only to be undertaken when the body simply wouldn't function further without fuel.

Eugene was appalled by the profoundness of his daughter's grief. His heart went out to her. He was a practical man, so it was agony to find a situation he couldn't fix, or find a way to make his daughter happier. He found her pain scraping along his own nerve endings.

If he'd thought her lightweight in her approach to life, she was refuting it now. He'd liked Dan greatly and had looked forward to him being his son-in-law. He had never got used to Tamara living with a man outside marriage, but it gradually dawned on him that no one else seemed bothered.

Eugene had kept his feelings to himself and accepted that Dan was a decent man and Tamara a happy and lucky girl. That it should end in such terrible tragedy was a travesty.

CHAPTER
FIFTY

London, 1993.

PEGGY REQUIRED TAMARA'S COMPANY AT AN after-premier party. She dressed carefully – a black sheath dress, once firm on her curves, but now loose. The dress came with its own cropped, lapelled jacket. She was lighter than when she had worn it last, but the effect was still pleasing. Her slenderness gave the outfit additional sophistication, her hip bones clearly visible beneath the sheath, their narrowness balanced by width at the shoulders of the jacket and its wide lapels.

She was less concerned with how she looked than presenting a respectable background for Peggy. She had never been vain but had learned she was less visible in Peggy's world if she dressed with style and sophistication. The rich and famous were familiar to her now. People were there to see and be seen. There was nothing surprising about finding a billionaire talking to an actress, or a director chatting up a young starlet. The three pillars of beauty, sex and money had propped up show business since Adam first invented it.

Peggy was past master at navigating such parties. Tamara was not but ensured her safety by effacing herself at every opportunity. It was purely misfortune that, as Tamara eased herself back into an alcove, she bumped into a man attempting to do the same. He turned to apologise to her, then took a second look.

"Well, if it isn't the long-lost half-sister!" Clive smirked at her. "Fancy bumping into you here. I mean literally, of course." He eyed her up and down. She felt his hostility like a physical presence between them. "All grown up then, are we? You've managed to stay in hiding a long time, little sister."

"Excuse me, I must go," she muttered as she tried to manoeuvre herself past him.

"Not so fast," he said. "There's a lot of unfinished business between us. I've heard you live alone now." His tone was resonant with innuendo and threat.

"I believe I have your address in my Filofax. Recently widowed, I heard, but never a bride. What a real shame. We must get together sometime soon. Your daddy would like your big brother to lend his support, now wouldn't he?"

Tamara gasped in dismay and tried to push her way past.

Clive stepped back, apparently allowing her room to move, but at the last moment he stopped, so she was wedged against him. She couldn't get past without shoving him, which she found she couldn't do. She revolted against touching him in any way. He looked down at her, enjoying her horror. "As I said, sister, unfinished business." His hands started to move up to her shoulders.

They were interrupted abruptly by Peggy who, blessedly, had noticed Tamara's absence, and gone searching for her.

"Oh, I'm sorry," she continued in confusion seeing Tamara with a man. Then recognising Clive, and interpreting the look on Tamara's face, said calmly, "I'm sorry, my dear, but I do need you right away. Can you come now?"

She followed Peggy across the room, thankful for the reprieve, but knew Clive wouldn't quit now. He had picked up on her fear and enjoyed it. She had read it in his eyes.

When the cab dropped her off at her apartment she entered

rapidly and locked the door behind her. She checked the rooms nervously, afraid to find him there already. Her refuge now felt like a danger zone.

Again she felt the touch of his hands on her shoulders and lived the rape anew. She was so frightened, so very, very frightened. It never occurred to her to call for help.

She realised her life was going to be dependent on whatever mercy Clive chose to extend. Or else she'd spend it trying to evade his games. Dan had been a present and total safety net. No one had troubled her while Dan was her love and her protector. With him gone she was vulnerable, not just bereft, and she found she couldn't stand it. She rebelled against being a victim.

Death was something she could control. In death she would be free. Free to join Dan, if heaven granted that, and free to defy Clive's twisted plans. She felt she had lost her right to mercy when she gave up her little girl. She was a sinner, and she'd have to pay the price. Muddled school catechisms came back to her.

Almost absentmindedly she cleaned the apartment. When finished, it was as impersonally clean and tidy as a motel room. She let herself out of the front door and locked it behind her. She knew where she was going. Hornsey Lane Bridge was notorious.

'Archway' was such a non-threatening sounding locale, she thought. Something like *The Archers*. Her mother had always listened to The Archers. Well, Archers … Archway; either way she was writing her own story tonight.

She stopped in the middle of the bridge. Others had stood here before, and that comforted her. There was a safety in numbers. She had read once about an Indian woman committing suttee, who placed her red palm print on the wall amongst prints of earlier victims before she went out to face the fire. Tamara felt a sisterhood with those who'd stood in this place before her.

For a moment on the pavement she gathered her small frame together and climbed up. It was quite a stretch, she noted, but her young, fit body managed effortlessly. Others had also managed. It was a mark of attainment, like joining an exclusive club. Tamara smiled, she was of course, quite mad. The thought amused her. There was no sorrow, no loss and no tragedy as she faced the morning wind and then, quite calmly, stepped forward into it.

CHAPTER
FIFTY ONE

London, Present Day.

WHEN PURDIE WOKE, THE LIGHT FILTERING through the curtains told her it was early. She consulted her phone, self-set to local time, and it confirmed that it was 5.30 am. She felt rested and energetic.

She crawled under the duvet and covertly checked the phone for messages. Both texts indicated they had been received, and there was a return message from Nick: *Police called, spoke 2 yr Nan. Will be on nxt plane, Luv N*

She thought back to the farewell party at the flat. Nick had made her feel wanted, desired and safe. She wondered how many men would have left her alone that night, after her very clear invitation into her bed. Not many, she suspected, and surely not on a point of principle. She missed him and felt warmed and comforted by the thought of him coming to London. For a while she lay in her bed, letting her mind drift over endless possibilities with Nick.

Eventually her bladder forced her from the bed. She padded to the lavatory, shut the door and checked her texts again. The battery was worryingly low and would fade quickly now it was down to five per cent. She daren't recharge it in front of her captors in case they confiscated it and could only hope the Metropolitan Police had already tracked her signal.

She showered again, wondering whether prisoners in a secure wing were allowed two showers a day. She had watched *Bad Girls* on telly. There was something about a good hot shower that washed the feeling of imprisonment away.

There was no sound of activity, that she could hear, within the building. As a matter of course she tried the door again, but it was firmly locked. She got her wallet out and tried using a credit card to slide through the lock, without success. Eventually she gave up, exasperated by her failure.

There were several fashion magazines on the coffee table, and she settled down to read about scandals involving the rich and famous. She was forty pages into the *Tatler* when she was startled to find an article about her grandmother. Written after her husband's funeral, the reporter had interviewed Marguerite about the future of Dunnings and Marguerite's own take on fashion in the new millennium. Purdie studied the photos. It was encouraging to find her grandmother was actual flesh and blood, and she tried to get a sense of her personality from the article.

Purdie was starving by seven-thirty, when there was a discreet knock on her door. It opened, and the same girl who'd waited on her the night before came in. She started to clear away the plates and food. As it became obvious that Purdie had neither eaten nor drunk anything, she become increasingly distressed and voluble in her speech before giving a sharp exclamation of frustration and leaving the room. Purdie reflected that taking Mandarin or Cantonese at school might have been a better option than Russian.

There was a cursory knock at the door and both the girl and the man who had shut her in there last night made their entrance.

"Nan Xi has noted that you haven't had anything to eat or drink," the man said accusingly.

"I don't wish to eat food provided by my captors," Purdie said. "I understood that the sharing of bread and salt was a guarantee of friendship, but you've imprisoned me and stopped me in my perfectly lawful attempt to find my grandmother. I don't break bread with my enemies."

All of which was fine, if her tummy hadn't actually been rumbling. She suppressed it firmly. How long could the human body survive on a starvation diet? She had a feeling that, with water, the survival period was several weeks. She tried not to feel daunted at the thought that she might have to be brave for that long. She could kill for toast and marmalade at the moment.

The man stared at her for several minutes then exchanged a quick fire of words with the Chinese girl who nodded and left the room.

He approached Purdie. She stepped back. She saw he noticed her retreat.

There was a shrewd look in his eye when he next addressed her. "You are afraid we are trying to drug or poison you? I have asked Nan Xi to bring us a shared meal. I will eat first. Then you will eat. We don't need to harm you; you are only a means to your grandmother, so you are quite safe."

In a short time Nan Xi returned with both Western and Chinese food.

"This is Western food," the man explained. "Toast, cereal, preserves and fruit."

She nodded.

"This is Chinese food: Congee and trimmings, savouries of a Chinese type. Fruit."

Again Purdie nodded her understanding.

"Please, choose what you wish to eat," the man said. "I will then take some of it and eat it before you have to taste it. Then you may be assured that the meal is safe. OK?"

Purdie agreed this was possibly so and indicated the cornflakes, milk, sugar, toast, marmalade and butter.

"This takes me back to my university days," said the man cheerfully, and he proceeded to eat.

Eventually, and cautiously, Purdie followed his example. It was capitulation, but she figured she wasn't a lot of use to them dead, and if they wanted to drug her and send her to sleep, well, she had already been comatose for the best part of ten hours, with no ill effects.

She felt much better as food and coffee flowed into her system.

After the man had finished he watched her with a satisfied smile on his face. "Good. Eat, and keep up your strength," he said with approval.

"So what is the plan for today?" asked Purdie when she had polished it all off.

"Your grandmother will trade for you," he said cheerfully.

"What happens if she doesn't?" said Purdie rather crossly. "I've never met her, so why would she trade anything for me."

"You'd better hope she trades for you." For a moment he looked grim, then he smiled. "This is a successful businesswoman. Of course she understands the meaning of a good trade. You need have no worries there. Your grandmother was probably Chinese in a previous life," he chuckled.

CHAPTER
FIFTY TWO

London, Present Day.

NATHAN PARSONS KNOCKED ON THE DOOR of Clive's office.

"Come in!" snapped Clive.

"Sorry, sir, just reporting on that information you wanted."

Nathan was intimidated by Clive – never a good response to a bully.

It amused Clive to have that effect on vulnerable subordinates. He liked to watch them squirm. "Well?" he asked.

Nathan handed him a sheaf of papers. "I managed to find an entry for 1990," he said nervously. "A daughter, born to a Tamara Edith Dunning. The father's name wasn't recorded."

Clive stared at the papers. "Fuck," was his sole comment.

He hadn't believed Marguerite. Her story was so convenient and pat that when she'd trotted it out at that staff meeting, he'd assumed it was a ploy.

"I couldn't get too much other information," apologised Nathan. "I dug up what I could, but as I wasn't a relative, they wouldn't give me much more. I tried to trace whether she was adopted, and it seems not. At least," he amended, "there's no record that I could find near the birth date. The child might have been fostered, I suppose, but if so, I couldn't track anything down."

Clive dismissed Nathan with cursory thanks and settled down to study the birth certificate. He was busy doing calculations. Tamara would have been very young in 1990, he reflected. There had been a time when she had disappeared overseas, backpacking. Was the child a product of a casual fling while she was travelling?

Clive racked his brain, but couldn't remember how long she'd been gone. He knew she had left soon after her sixteenth birthday because he'd been worried about the consequences of his actions that night. Tamara's disappearance had been a relief.

The wave of anger which fuelled the attack had gone by the next morning, and the repercussions if Eugene had found out could have been catastrophic.

If, of course, Eugene sided with his daughter. Clive could have said the girl led him on, could claim she seduced him, but even *he* couldn't ignore the fact that what had happened was incest.

In the months that followed, however, Eugene had never referred to the matter, simply venting his frustration occasionally at his daughter's hippy ways and irresponsibility.

Clive looked again at the date of birth on the certificate. The most hideous possibility swirled through his brain, one which had never occurred to him before.

CHAPTER
FIFTY THREE

London, Present Day.

MAX RETURNED FROM THE AIRPORT WITH Nick an hour before Pyotr was due to arrive. Marguerite liked the man she saw, even tired and rumpled from the hastily organised trip.

Nick was nicely dressed, well spoken, thoroughly presentable and a professional as well. If he was serious about Purdie, then he looked to be a good catch. She wondered what her granddaughter thought of him.

"What is the situation with the police?" he asked.

"They've cautioned me to wait for more instructions, even though they now know where she is," she replied. "Apparently they feel the risk to Purdie would be much higher if they go rushing in, than if we reach an agreement with the kidnappers. Negotiation, rather than force. I suppose they know what they are doing."

"I hope so," said Nick. "Are you able to pay the ransom? Have you had any more thoughts about this treasure?"

"Only one, I'm afraid," said Marguerite. "It's a long shot, but if I'm right, then Purdie is the only one who can solve this. I gave something away, many years ago, to her adoptive parents, to be kept for her. I don't know whether she still has it, or even if the parents passed it on to her." She sighed. "The worst thing is that I don't even know if it contained this valuable egg, but it's the only possibility left."

"Purdie never mentioned anything," said Nick. "She seemed as surprised as the rest of us when the presents started to arrive."

"So either she never opened it, or there never was an egg in it," said Marguerite.

"What did you give her?" asked Nick.

"An old box that had belonged to my father," explained Marguerite. "We never opened it."

"Let's hope there is an egg," said Nick grimly, "and that Purdie still has access to it. If her captors were determined enough to grab Purdie, they aren't mucking about."

"Which would suggest," interjected Max, "they have some very serious reasons to think you do have the item they want, Marguerite."

There had been no contact from the kidnappers for twenty-four hours now, and the stress was beginning to tell. Pyotr's arrival was a relief. Marguerite left it to the Russian to introduce his mission.

"As you know, Mrs Dunning, we have reason to think that your family was involved in retrieving at least one, and maybe more, of the eggs made for the last Tsar by the jeweller Fabergé. Our research has shown that the most likely way this occurred is by way of a General Mirov."

Marguerite looked blank, so Pyotr pressed on.

"Mirov was known to be a Tsarist officer, loyal to the imperial family and famous within Russia for his exploits in the First World War. It is believed that, as a hero of the imperialist regime, he may have been responsible for attempting to safeguard Russia's treasures in the days after the arrest of the Tsar and his family.

"We believe Mirov, like others, was trying to find a safe hiding place for at least one of the eggs. It is known that your grandfather, on the night he was to leave Moscow, met with Mirov and left with a large parcel, although there is no further record of what was in it. This meeting was documented by an informer. We believe that parcel may have contained two of the Imperial Eggs, and maybe some other less valuable trinkets."

He looked earnestly at Marguerite. "Please understand, there is no suggestion at all your family was involved in looting or theft. We believe that if he accepted guardianship of these eggs, it was as a custodian. We know Mirov's reputation for integrity and have no reason to doubt your grandfather's."

Marguerite stirred. "What makes you approach me now?" she asked. "I mean, at this point in time particularly. Has something changed to make you research this now?"

"We've been aware of your family for a long time. Right back in the 1940s an attempt was made to contact your mother, but history and politics made this difficult. The world is freer now in some ways, so my sitting here with you has become possible."

Marguerite looked at him thoughtfully. "The reason I ask, is that you are not the only person to approach me this week. Another party is also convinced I have an Imperial Egg in my possession."

Pytor looked shocked. "Did they say who they are? I wouldn't have thought it possible anyone, outside a few people in Russia, would have had access to this knowledge. Are they bidding for the treasure?"

"In a manner of speaking," said Marguerite. "I believe them to be of Chinese nationality."

Pyotr looked flabbergasted. "How would any Chinese know of this?" he asked.

Marguerite shrugged. "I don't know, but they do," and she told him of Purdie's kidnap and the ransom demand.

"I must make it clear," she said, "that I know nothing about eggs, Imperial, Fabergé or otherwise. There is, as I have explained, only one possibility where it could be, and if it is not, then I don't know where it is. My grandfather may have hidden this thing years ago, back in Poland. It might be buried at the bottom of our garden there. It might be stored in the vaults of the local bank. The possibilities are endless, even if we accept my grandfather had such a treasure at one time."

Nick, who had listened quietly throughout, now asked, "What was your intent regarding this egg, if Mrs Dunning had been in possession of it? Is it the Russian state's intent to purchase it, or lay claim to it in some way?"

Pyotr looked embarrassed. "My interest, and that of my colleagues, was academic only, I'm afraid. We want to know where all the eggs are. There were fifty-two made, and we know where most of them are now. Some are in private hands, others in museums. Eight are still unaccounted for, and we don't even have pictures for six of them. Because of their importance to Russia culturally, we want to know their fate. Eventually, of course, we would like to repatriate them all to their native land, but such things are complex. When people have bought them, or inherited them, it's not something we can force." He smiled. "My interest was to see if we could establish exactly whether you did have possession of an egg or eggs. It would have been wonderful if it were so," he said wistfully.

He drew out papers and showed them photographs of several of the Imperial Eggs. Some were in black and white, but the most recent were in colour, each one a testament to the jeweller's skill. It wasn't just the opulence of material, or the ingenious nature of the design, but the charm and whimsy that made them irresistible. Each egg, Pyotr explained, had contained a 'surprise'.

Marguerite imagined receiving one each year. Presents for adult children, she thought, and wondered at the amount of wealth involved.

Nick and Max had both stood up to look at the photographs over her shoulder.

"They are magnificent," said Max.

"Of course, we now know that most of these are well cared for and valued by responsible collectors or museums." Pyotr smiled. "I would love them all back in Russia, but if they were, so many other people would not be able to enjoy them."

"What about the missing ones?" Marguerite asked. "Do you know what they would look like?"

"Fortunately there were detailed notes made about each one," replied Pyotr. "Fabergé documented them extremely well. We even know their names," and he went on to list them.

"The Danish Jubilee; the Alexander III Commemorative; the Hen; the Necessaire; the Cherub; the Mauve Enamel."

"Mrs Dunning, you must understand that, if you were to have one of these eggs, it would be enormously exciting."

"I am afraid, Mr Karolan, that if we find, as I am concerned we will, that I do *not* hold one of those eggs, then things are likely to get even more exciting. And my granddaughter is in the middle of it all."

CHAPTER
FIFTY FOUR

London, Present Day.

PURDIE FELT REJUVENATED AFTER BREAKFAST. SHE wasn't the sort of girl who thrived on starvation. Whatever vices she had, anorexia wasn't one of them.

The maid cleared up and after she had checked that the door had indeed clicked back into its locked position, Purdie was left to her own devices. Her Kindle kept her amused for a short time, but she found it hard to concentrate on the novel she was reading. She decided eventually she had little alternative to charging her phone, even if there was a risk of it being confiscated. She picked a wall socket on the far side of the bed, so not visible to anyone entering the room, and thanked *Lonely Planet*, as she plugged it in, for reminding her to buy international adaptors for her trip.

After a couple of hours she was thoroughly bored. She abandoned the novel and worked through the magazines on the table. *Harper's Bazaar*, *Tatler*, *The Spectator* and *Vogue* were all amusing enough for a while but no compensation for her lack of freedom.

The maid returned mid-morning with pots of tea and coffee

and some biscuits. Purdie watched her as she hurried her way into the room. It seemed that rather than some remote locking system, the maid had a swipe card to activate the door.

As the maid's grasp of English was lacking, she mimed her request for extra magazines. The woman looked harassed, but it seemed that she understood, and left.

A few minutes later she returned, this time with two other women. Purdie shrank back before realising they were cleaners. Between them they made the bed, cleaned the bathroom, vacuumed and then left, bowing formally at the door. Neither had shown the slightest interest in the phone plugged in and charging. Purdie inclined her head as they left. She could become used to this level of service, she thought.

She made a point to listen to the lock on the door. It seemed to take a brief period of time to actually click into place after the women had exited. Presumably it didn't 'catch' until its weight had brought it into the correct position. There were possibilities there, thought Purdie.

The maid was back two hours later with a fresh batch of magazines and lunch. The magazines were more eclectic, as if grabbed in a hurry: *Woman's Day*, *National Geographic*, *The Economist*, *New Scientist* and *Punch* amongst them. Purdie grinned. Well, it was one way to catch up on the latest news.

It took the maid two entrances to get everything into the room: first with the magazines, and second, with the lunch tray, which had presumably been placed on a table outside the door. Seeing her so burdened, Purdie instinctively got to her feet to help with the door. Not that she got any thanks for it. The maid glared at her as if it was all her fault, before bolting off again.

Purdie didn't push her luck, but over lunch she thought about the door and its lock. She thought she had heard people in the passage outside the door. The maid had looked harassed and rushed. It seemed she had other demands on her time.

Purdie made a leisurely lunch. It made no sense, she decided, to be paranoid about food now. As her companion had observed this morning, food gave her strength. She had already eaten in captivity and would die of starvation if she simply refused to eat at all. She would need all her strength this afternoon.

She positioned herself so she was in easy reach of the door and repacked her handbag with the items she thought she might need if she managed to escape – her recharged phone, Kindle, purse and passport. She could abandon the rest of her stuff if she had to, but she needed her documentation and her wallet. She set her bag within grabbing distance of her perch on the sofa.

The next time the maid entered to clear lunch away, Purdie was sitting casually on the arm of her sofa, with a leg tucked underneath her, apparently reading. The tray was piled, not just with the remains of lunch, but with all the extra magazines Purdie had been able to find. As she suspected, the maid was unable to carry the whole tray in one go. She could almost hear her sigh as she stacked up the magazines on one side of the table, picked up the tray and exited with it. Purdie exclaimed loudly and indicated that the used magazines were to be taken as well. The maid nodded and left. Just as Purdie had almost given up, the maid re-entered, grabbed the magazines and removed them as well.

It took Purdie all of a second to grab her bag and move from the arm of the sofa to the door. She grabbed the handle before the lock could click into place and held it firmly, just short of a closing position. She hoped, from outside, the door would look as if it was locked into place. To be on the safe side, she counted out five minutes – one thousand and one, one thousand and two … all the way to the five-minute mark – and then eased the door open.

She couldn't hear anything, so opened it further and peered into the hallway. It was deserted. The tray with the remains of her lunch and the magazines still sat on the table outside.

She slipped from her room, letting the door close behind her. Her heart was beating faster than she thought it could go. As she passed the table, she almost gasped aloud. On the lacquer table was a security card. Presumably the maid, running out of hands, had dumped it when she returned for the magazines. Purdie grabbed it and shoved it into her pocket.

The door to the meeting room was shut, but she could hear

raised voices as she tiptoed past. If there were a lot of people at the meeting, then with any luck, the household staff would be busy caring for their needs.

Once downstairs she faced a problem. Would the maid's pass card be adequate to open the front door? To give herself time to think, she wedged herself into the corner behind the lacquered dresser to work out her next move. She knew she couldn't linger. Presumably there were cameras that would track her progress. She'd been in luck so far, so perhaps the guards were relaxed at the moment.

She was about to risk the walk to the doors when they opened. Purdie shrank back. Peering round the side she saw a porter wheeling in luggage on a trolley. He wedged the doors open before going back for a second trolley. The porter was joined by two other men from a door on the far side of the room. A series of orders and comments in a mixture of Chinese and English established that their job was to carry the cases upstairs.

To Purdie's relief, the porter was part of the team doing the carrying, and after a few moments the panting men disappeared upstairs, leaving her in the foyer, with open doors leading to the lift.

Working now purely on instinct, Purdie grabbed one of the trolleys as camouflage, wheeled it to the lifts and found one was already on the floor. Its doors opened as soon as she pressed the button. She pushed the trolley in and closed the doors. Her hands shook as she pressed the down button, but nothing happened. There was a swipe card arrangement below the lift controls, so she swiped her card over the sensor. She pressed the ground floor button again. This time the lift lurched into action.

She watched the floor numbers slide downwards on the monitor. They reached the ground with a slight bump. Pushing the trolley in front of her, Purdie exited the lift. There was no one around, but she remembered the concierge from her arrival. She hadn't been able to tell whether he was the same man pushing trolleys upstairs, so she was decidedly wary.

There was only one barrier left between herself and freedom. The door. She prayed her card would work, as it didn't open to her push.

To the left of the door was a swiping contraption, with a green button below it. She pushed the button; nothing happened. Then she tried the card. Still nothing. She found herself panicking, pressing the button again and again. The door simply would not open.

Suddenly she heard a slight buzz. She straightened and ran in front of the door. It opened, to admit another woman. Purdie mimed acute surprise as in 'I was just opening the door myself' type actions, and stood back politely to let the woman through.

The woman looked as startled as Purdie but held the door courteously for her to exit. Purdie didn't give her time to think twice, smiled politely and stepped briskly through the door. She walked quickly to the nearest corner, rounded it and began running. She turned deliberately at every corner she encountered to make her route as complicated as possible.

She had absolutely no idea where she was, but anywhere was better than being a prisoner. She needed help, and quickly. Although she had escaped without incident, it was too much to expect that people who had gone to the effort of detaining her in the first place would give up easily.

She found herself in a service alley. A couple of dumpsters lined the lane. She was mulling over the possibility of hiding between them and making some phone calls, when she looked over her shoulder and saw a police car driving slowly past the entrance to the alley. She turned and ran back to the street. The car had stopped to give way at the corner. Gathering her last strength, Purdie ran the twenty yards to it, and, before it made its turn, managed to hammer on the window.

The car lurched to a stop. Purdie slumped against the side of the vehicle, thoroughly exhausted. A policeman got out, prepared to read her the riot act for slamming into his vehicle.

Telling her tale later, Purdie had to admit the PC did well. Her story tumbled from her, completely incoherent and jumbled. The only thing that must have been clear would have been her joy at seeing a policeman.

He took his time, but once he realised her actions were not

malicious and he'd got the gist of her tale, he put her in the vehicle and drove her to the station.

CHAPTER
FIFTY FIVE

London, Present Day.

THE POLICE TREATED PURDIE WITH efficient courtesy and kindness. She gave her statement to the female police officer and listened as it was read back. It sounded different when stripped of emotional content, but Purdie supposed it told the facts effectively enough. She signed the document and was then free to leave.

Outside in the foyer she found Nick waiting for her. His smile when he saw her lit up his face.

"Purdie," he said, and then grunted as she flung herself into his arms. She had never been so pleased to see anyone.

"I can't believe you got over here so quickly," she gasped. "You must have travelled all night." Personally she thought the slightly dishevelled, unshaven look suited him well. He looked bigger and more impressive than she'd ever realised back in their flat.

"I did," said Nick, grinning. "I should have known you couldn't find your way across London without stuffing it up. I thought I had better come and act as your guide dog."

"Dog would be about right," mumbled Purdie in an indignant tone, but she had a smile on her face.

Nick gestured towards her grandmother and stood back. Purdie suddenly realised there were other people with him. "Mrs Dunning," he said formally, "may I introduce Purdie, your granddaughter."

Purdie gave him a startled glance. The two women embraced.

"Grandma," said Purdie politely.

"My dear, it may take a while for me to earn that name," said Marguerite. "I have waited a lifetime for this moment," and hugged her again. They both stood back and studied each other. Purdie saw an elegant older woman, well dressed and groomed. She had a certain grandeur and authority, more evident in the flesh than in the photos she had seen in the magazine. Marguerite's elegance made her aware of her own untidiness. What Marguerite saw when she looked at her, she couldn't imagine.

There was a pause, then Marguerite smiled, a genuinely warm smile, and gave a little nod, as if confirming something to herself. She turned to the man beside her, who had been waiting quietly. "And this is Max," said Marguerite, "a long-time friend and assistant."

Purdie shook hands with the slight, greying man. He stood straight and shook her hand firmly.

"Pleased to meet you," he said, giving her a warm smile that made her feel welcome.

The PC was still hovering. "May I just have a quick word?"

"I have Miss Davis's statement, and a complaint she has laid about being detained unlawfully. We will assess this ourselves, but I need to know whether you intend to pursue this as a formal complaint?"

Purdie started to open her mouth, but Marguerite stepped in. "We have to discuss all this between ourselves and the circumstances leading up to this kidnap." She handed her card to the PC. "My lawyer handles most of my affairs, but if you need me in the meantime, I can be contacted at those phone numbers."

The group assembled in Marguerite's living room. Max kept the occasion fuelled with tea, cakes and later, drinks. There was such a feeling of relief. Later there would be time to discuss everything else. In the meantime, it was good for grandmother and granddaughter to talk and learn about each other. It was more than wonderful to see Nick.

The first that Marguerite, Nick and Max had known about Purdie's escape was when the police had phoned to say a person of Purdie's description, claiming to be Marguerite's granddaughter, had been picked up by a patrol car. They had rushed down to get her.

Pyotr had been unceremoniously evicted from the house, his only consolation was permission to phone the following day. The poor man was equally excited and downcast by Purdie's release. He had hoped to be part of a negotiation process involving Imperial Eggs. Now there was no need for his presence.

Marguerite finally spoke. "Firstly," she said, "this is a very moving and important moment for me. I want to welcome both Purdie and Nick here. In particular, of course, Purdie, who is the daughter of my daughter. I last saw you my dear, when you were less than a day old." She blinked back an uncharacteristic, sentimental tear. "I remember handing you to your adoptive parents. I thought my heart would break."

"I hope this doesn't prove tedious for Nick and Max, but I will simply tell the story as I understand it, then Purdie can fill in what she knows."

They all nodded agreement, with Nick saying, sotto voce, "If you think the last few months have been tedious, then your standards for boredom are set extremely high in England," which made Purdie give a snort of laughter.

Marguerite began her tale.

From what she remembered of her grandfather's stories, she recreated a merchant's life in Moscow at the turn of the twentieth century. "I understand they were very wealthy," she said, "not as wealthy as the Tsar or the nobles, of course, but wealthy enough to have a large Moscow house and a dacha, or holiday home, away from the city. My grandfather's younger brother, whose name if I remember rightly was Ilya, or Ilyitch or something similar, had a horse brought into his bedroom as a surprise on the morning of his fourteenth birthday. So the house must have been pretty impressive. They had a family business, saddlery making, and an imperial patent by the Tsar. There was a factory, which employed many people."

"The Russian Revolution was not kind to businessmen. My grandfather was forced to flee, closing the factory and taking his family out of Russia. I don't believe the younger brother went with them. I don't know what happened to him; I'm not sure if I ever heard of his fate."

She became aware of Purdie nodding her head vigorously.

"You know something about this?" she asked, surprised.

"Yes. Thanks to the guys who invited me to stay last night," said the girl, "I can fill that in for you now."

"Ilya went east and eventually ended up in Shanghai. He fell foul of some local toughs and the Li family helped him out. Later he was murdered by a criminal gang, but before he died, he was tortured and revealed that his family had been entrusted with two of the Imperial Fabergé Eggs. There were some other relatively minor items he had with him. The Chinese family told me it had been his will that his possessions be returned to his family or its heirs. They left China themselves immediately after Ilya's death. I got the impression they had been too scared to stay." She paused, then grinned at Nick. "The presents I got were Ilya's things. I know they looked fabulous to us, but apparently they were just the bits and pieces. The real value was in the Imperial Eggs, and of course, he didn't have them.

"The way the Chinese people spoke, they had looked after Ilya and honoured his wishes for the bequest to be passed to his family, namely me (although how they traced me is hard to fathom). In return, they wanted information about the Fabergé Eggs. I knew nothing about them of course," said Purdie.

"Up until the moment they decided to hold me in that room, I had been grateful for the story they told me of my ancestry. Unfortunately, their intentions were more complex than just honouring an ancient family debt."

"We had a Russian envoy here today, talking about the eggs," said Max. "He put the individual value of the eggs in the vicinity of $30 million US dollars each. If you have two of them, that's an incredible fortune."

"Wow!" said Purdie.

"Let me continue the story," said Marguerite. "My grandfather, grandmother and their son, my father Charles, left Russia the same day Ilya did, but they went west instead. Unfortunately, my grandmother became seriously ill shortly after the journey began, and the family, who had intended to reach England, had to stop in Poland while she recovered.

"I was only a child when my grandfather told me these stories, so I only have a very fragmented memory of what he said. I think my grandmother had TB, because he mentioned her going to sanatoriums in Switzerland back in the days when they had money. It was a couple of years before my grandmother recovered enough to contemplate further journeying, and by that time the family had started to put down roots where they were.

"Eventually my father married a local girl, and they accepted that they were settled in Poland."

Marguerite paused to take a long sip of her wine. "Then the war came," she said bleakly. "We focus now on what happened to the Jews, gypsies and others whom they called deviants, but life wasn't very good for anyone else in Poland either. The Germans were extremely hostile and brutal with us ordinary Polish people.

"We were hungry all the time, and my sister and I weren't allowed to leave the house unless we had an adult with us, and even then it wasn't often, mainly to go to school or church. I've ended up neither well educated nor religious, so maybe those trips were a waste of time." She smiled ruefully.

"We stayed throughout the war. My grandfather had started a tailoring business when they first arrived, and my father carried it on. It probably saved us because he was useful to the Germans. Otherwise, with our Russian name, we would have been in trouble.

"Then we heard the Germans were retreating and the Russians were coming." She smiled. "My father insisted immediately that we had to flee. I accepted it at the time, of course, as I was only fourteen. Now, I wonder if we had to run because my father had a specific reason to fear the Russians.

"We left Poland. On the way, my father was shot by the retreating Germans." Her face hardened as the group gasped. "Some things you never forgive, not ever," she said bitterly. "I had to identify his body. We travelled to England without him. The Resistance were wonderful. They ferried us from one fishing boat to another for months. I don't know how we made it. There were patrols and seaborne mines around all the time.

"We arrived in England and made it our home. Eventually I married, and that is how I am here," she said simply.

"The rest of the story only involves Purdie, and I will tell it to her another time. The issue we have to deal with now is that both the Chinese and the Russians think we know about these eggs and where they are."

There was a silence while they considered the story she had told.

Eventually Purdie laughed. "Well, if Max is right about his valuation, it looks like we won't ever need to work again." She looked at her grandmother. "So, where are they then?"

Nick, who had been looking thoughtful, suddenly gave an exclamation. "Stop right there," he said urgently.

They gazed at him in surprise.

"Did Purdie have a chance to tell you," Nick asked Marguerite, "that we found a couple of bugs in our old flat in Wellington?"

Marguerite shook her head, and then frowned. "The lawyer from New Zealand said something about bugs, I think, but he was also asking if I had been sending presents, which I hadn't. I didn't really concentrate on what else he said. I was looking forward to seeing Purdie, and it all sounded like nonsense."

"Well," said Nick, "it might be relevant. Someone had been listening in on our conversations."

"What are you trying to say?" asked Max.

"If I'm right, it was only after your husband died that the

presents started arriving for Purdie?" he asked.

She nodded. "Possibly. The timing sounds about right."

"And it was after that," continued Nick, "that suddenly someone became interested in Perdita Davis, previously an anonymous New Zealander."

Max looked thoughtful.

"Did you mention the existence of a granddaughter to anyone before your husband died? Particularly anyone in this house?"

"No, never," said Marguerite. "She was never discussed with my husband."

"In that case, the only way anyone could have known about her was if they had heard it from you, after his death. I'm picking this room is bugged too."

Purdie said urgently, "It's true, Grandmother. Nick's right. We should search before we say anything else."

The two men turned the room upside down. It took very little time for them to find the first electronic device stuck underneath the phone table.

"Bingo," said Nick. "Let's keep looking."

Careful searching failed to find anything apart, as Max pointed out tartly, a few dead flies. "I'll be having a word with the charlady," he tutted.

The bug disposed of, they regrouped.

"Where were we?" asked Marguerite.

"You were about to tell us where these fabulous eggs are," said Purdie comfortably.

Marguerite looked at her granddaughter. "The truth is, my dear, that I don't know the answer to that question. I only have a conjecture, and if I am right, then you, Purdie, have the eggs."

CHAPTER
FIFTY SIX

London, Present Day.

"WHAT?" EXCLAIMED PURDIE. "NO, NO, I assure you. I certainly don't have any imperial treasures sitting around. In fact," she said tartly, "I don't even have a change of clothes, thanks to the people who grabbed me."

"If I'm correct," said Marguerite, "then the only place I can think of where these eggs might be, is in my father's tin box that we carried to England after his murder. By the time we were unpacking in London, we realised we didn't have a key to it. Yes, we could have had a locksmith create a key, I suppose, but it always seemed to be a bit too much trouble, so we never got round to it."

She looked directly at Purdie. "When I gave you to the Davises, I gave them that box as a keepsake for you. I explained it wasn't valuable, just a sentimental link to my father, but that one day you might want to have some contact with your birth family, and it was the best I could do. We always assumed it would have business papers from Poland or Moscow." She shrugged. "They accepted it and said they would give it to you when you were older, if you started asking questions. I take it they never mentioned it?"

Purdie stared at her grandmother. She was aware of Max and Nick looking at her. Thinking about her parents always triggered a surge of emotion. It was coming up two years since their death, but it still tore at her when she allowed herself to think of them too closely. She turned her head away. "I don't think we ever discussed my adoption that much. Mum assured me once, when I asked, that my mother had been a respectable girl, forced to give her child up because she couldn't keep her."

She glanced up shyly at Marguerite. "It was a happy adoption, you see, and I didn't probe too deeply. I sensed my adoptive parents were uneasy about my past, and I didn't want to hurt them. It didn't seem that important. Now they are dead, and it's too late to ask them about it, and of course, I have you now to fill in the details." She smiled at Marguerite.

"Yes, but do you remember any box?" Nick prompted.

"Nothing significant. When they died I had everything packed up into the attic of our house. There were boxes of family memorabilia, photos of me growing up and of my parents' childhoods. There were lots of boxes. Cardboard boxes, old cigar boxes, old tins of buttons, you name it. My mother was a hoarder. What did it look like?" she asked Marguerite.

"It was a black and battered metal box with a handle on top of the lid and a lock on one side. The lid hinged open."

Purdie thought some more. "Yes, I think there was a case like that," she said at last. "My father said it was the sort of box soldiers were issued during the First World War, which is the only reason I remember it. We'd been doing a project on Gallipoli, so it stuck in my mind. I never examined it. There was too much to do sorting everything after the accident. Is that really the only place you think these eggs could be?" she asked in amazement.

"If we have them, then yes," said Marguerite. "They aren't here, nor with my sister, and Mother would have mentioned if she'd found them. She's dead now, of course, but there was nothing in her estate, and I did go through it all. There were a few family pieces from my father, and naturally she inherited my grandmother's jewellery. Some of that was quite fine, but again, nothing of value or even the size of a Fabergé Egg. If they really left Poland with our family, that box would be the only unexplored place left. We were refugees and had very little when we arrived in England."

The four of them sat for a while in silence, considering the situation.

Finally Nick stood up. "Well," he addressed them. "On that note, I am going to turn in for the night. I'm bushed. Thank you both for the bedtime story. I look forward to the next instalment." He smiled as he left them.

Tired as she was, Purdie lay in bed that night considering her grandmother's tale. Was it possible, unknown to anyone, that Imperial Eggs were resting in her old home? There were often stories in the news about people finding Gainsboroughs, or a first edition Shakespeare shut away in attics.

The next morning Purdie thought she was the first up and into the kitchen, only to find Max there before her. He offered her coffee and said he would be serving breakfast in the dining room. Purdie was about to leave him in peace when he said, "Have you had any more thoughts about what was discussed last night?"

"Only the obvious, I suppose," said Purdie. "We need to investigate that box. I guess that means a quick trip back to New Zealand. I can't say I'm keen at the moment. I've only just got here."

Nick had just joined them and chipped in. "I know what you mean, but it occurred to me last night that it's a miracle no one has turned your parents' old place over, searching for these things. There's more than one lot of people on the trail of these eggs. It would be wise to get moving and find them yourself before anyone else does."

"And if they're not there?" asked Purdie. "It would be one hell of a chore going all the way back to discover the box contained manifests for leather bits, or whatever saddlery making involves. I'm sure it's all interesting historically, and I look forward to exploring it. Just not tomorrow, if I can avoid it."

Nick laughed and followed her into the dining room where Marguerite was sitting. They served themselves and ate for a while in silence.

Purdie relayed their conversation to Marguerite. "What do you think I should do?" she asked.

"I've been thinking along the same lines," said Marguerite. "The only alternative to you going back is if someone you trust, and I mean really trust, could go and retrieve the box for you and get it couriered here."

"That's not an easy ask," said Max, who'd joined them. "First of all, they have to get the tenants to agree, and then climb round an attic, find the box, get it packed up and sent here. They couldn't open it of course."

"Plus, you have the problem of what Customs might make of it," said Nick. "Sorry," he said as they turned to him, "it's just a reality nowadays. Is there anyone you know who could do that for you, Purdie? What about that farming family you know?"

"I was thinking about them," said Purdie slowly. "I could ask them. They're old family friends," she told Marguerite. "They are sort of an honorary aunt and uncle. And yes, I would totally trust them. When I left New Zealand, I left the items the Chinese had sent me with them."

"Well," said Nick, "don't leave it too long before you ask them. If the Chinese don't have you as a bargaining tool, they'll probably try something else. They were prepared to bug our flat, so lawfulness and scruples aren't going to be a problem for them."

"I suggest you phone your friends as soon as possible," said Marguerite, "because we need to get you fresh clothes and other necessities. It's lucky I happen to know someone who owns a store and would be delighted to help. And, talking about the store," she continued, "I wonder whether we import from New Zealand?" She saw the question on Purdie's face. "It occurs to me that, if we do, the box could be added to the manifest," she said. "It might be the safest way for it to travel. I'll make enquiries."

Left alone after breakfast, Purdie looked at her watch. Nine o'clock. A respectable hour in the evening to phone Barbara and Tim.

"Purdie, how are you?" Barbara answered. "How lovely to hear from you! Is everything all right? You got there safely?" Purdie could hear the concern rushing through her aunt's mind.

"Yes, yes and yes," she replied laughing. "A lot has happened, and I'll fill you in about it later. I'm with my grandmother now, and she's very nice and hospitable. I'm actually on the scrounge for a favour from you and Uncle Tim."

"Of course, love. What can we do for you?"

"You remember when I was with you last, we talked about whether my parents knew my birth family?"

"Yes, indeed I do," said her aunt. "Are you saying I was right?"

"You were very right. It seems my birth family left me something, which my parents kept for years. The trouble is, I never looked at it, and it's in the attic of the old house. I need it urgently. I wondered whether I could ask you and Uncle Tim to do a run into Wellington and fossick around in the attic? I know it's a big chore, but the stuff I need is in a tin box. I need it sent to me as fast as possible. I don't want to come back to New Zealand for it, seeing as I've only just got here, but I need it urgently." She let the plea in her voice speak for itself.

"Well, now you've really got me curious," said her aunt, amused. "You'll have to tell me all about it when you can. I am sure Tim would be happy to help. We've got to go down to Wellington next week anyway, and I don't mind poking around in the attic for you. You'd better describe this box to me. Do you know where it would be in the attic?"

Purdie gave her as many details as she could. "If there's anything else you want to know, just text," she said.

"We'll be in touch to let you know if we find it," said Barbara. "You're sure you're all right though, aren't you? It's not like you to be so mysterious."

"I promise I'm fine. I'm finding out about my history," she said. "But it's all good, I promise. And Nick is over here; he won't let anything bad happen to me."

"Nick?" she heard her aunt exclaim. "Really?"

"He's a friend, just a friend," said Purdie laughing. "Give my love to Uncle Tim."

"I'll let you speak to him," said her aunt.

"What's this I hear about you wanting a favour?" growled her uncle a moment later.

"Pretty please," teased Purdie, and proceeded to fill him in with some of the details.

"It'll cost you, girlie," said Tim.

"A big sloppy kiss when I get back to New Zealand?" laughed Purdie.

"Get away with you," said Tim. "You always could get round your old uncle. Don't fear, we'll get this box for you."

Purdie hung up, feeling warmed by their affection.

CHAPTER
FIFTY SEVEN

London, Present Day.

THE WOMEN WENT SHOPPING. PURDIE FELT awkward at first with Marguerite's great generosity. She was acting as Purdie's own private fashion consultant. Eventually, realising how much her grandmother was enjoying herself, Purdie let her get on with it.

"I've never had a personal shopper before," she remarked appreciatively. "I feel as if I'm on one of those makeover TV shows."

She could see people respected Marguerite. When she spoke it was with courteous authority, and Purdie admitted her suggestions were good. Stylish, but not over the top, and age appropriate for Purdie. She'd been afraid that Marguerite would make her look middle-aged, but her fears were groundless.

They chose jeans, shirts and tank tops (Purdie's choice); a couple of formal gowns, some pretty frocks and a smart business suit, (Marguerite's choice).

Purdie queried the need for smarter clothes. She was on holiday and only needed casual gear. She tried to explain that her lifestyle didn't lend itself to formal wear and tried to imagine wearing posh clothes around the flat in Wellington, before realising those days had gone, the flatmates dispersed.

Marguerite smiled. "Well, you might as well get these things now, while you've got the chance. If you buy classic pieces they'll last you for years. Besides which while you are my guest I'd like to show you round. Take you to a musical or two, go to Covent Garden and see some theatre. You can't come to London and not enjoy its culture. And," she added slyly, "I think that boyfriend of yours would brush up nicely. I imagine he would like to see you looking glamorous."

Purdie blushed. "He's not really my boyfriend," she tried to explain.

Marguerite cut her off tartly. "Well I don't know how many men you know who'd drop everything to travel round the world because they hear you're in trouble. I suggest you value him for his concern and at least give him a fighting chance."

They went shopping for underwear, or lingerie as Marguerite insisted on calling it. Purdie would have been happy with plain cotton, but Marguerite vetoed it in horror and coaxed her into lacy bras, knickers and camisoles. Purdie had to agree she looked really sexy in the mirror.

She giggled. "Ah, so if I'm run over by a bus I don't have to worry about my undies?" she asked.

Her grandmother looked at her in despair. "No, it's so you don't have to worry about your undies, as you put it, when you take a lover. Anyway, most women wear nice underwear to please themselves. There is something very comforting about knowing that, underneath the sackcloth you might have to wear, you look stunning."

Marguerite gave a quiet grin to herself when she saw Purdie's face.

Clothes and lingerie dealt with, Marguerite swept the girl to the cosmetics department.

"I don't wear a lot of makeup," protested Purdie.

"I don't want you to wear a lot of makeup either," said Marguerite, "but while you have the opportunity, let's get some advice from Estelle here, who is a wonder with colours. She can get you set up with cosmetics for casual and formal occasions."

By the time they had finished, she was the proud owner of a large Bobbi Brown makeup kit, more brushes than she had known existed and the recipient of some extensive training in skincare routines. "I can't believe there's so much to know," she marvelled.

Marguerite organised the parcels to be delivered, leaving them free of shopping bags.

"Let's lunch," she said, leading the way into a small brasserie. The dark, traditionally stained wood of the little café opened out into an inner courtyard. Soft London sunshine filtered through the branches of a plane tree onto the tables beneath.

Purdie sat down gratefully. "I thought I was fit," she said ruefully, "but shopping does take it out of a girl. I'm not used to it. I'd never make it as a character in *Sex in the City*."

Once the food came and they were alone, Purdie repeated her thanks for the morning's experience. "I've never had such nice things," she said.

"It has given me a great deal of pleasure to be able to do this for you," said Marguerite. "I didn't realise how much I enjoyed shopping with Tamara until I lost her. She wasn't particularly fashion conscious either, but she did enjoy pretty clothes."

"Tell me about her," urged Purdie. "How did she come to have me; what sort of person was she?"

Marguerite smiled. "When we get home," she said. "This isn't a story for a public place,"

Marguerite led Purdie to the living room, sat on the sofa and patted the seat beside her to indicate Purdie should join her. She picked the photo of her daughter up off the table and smiled at it before handing it to her granddaughter.

"You asked me what Tamara was like? She was intelligent, beautiful and a little wilful," Marguerite said. "She was our only child, so when she went, it was like all the sunshine disappeared out of our lives for many years. You are very like her in some ways – your colouring and looks."

"What happened?" asked Purdie.

"It's time you knew," agreed her grandmother. "I just don't know where to begin."

"How did she come to get pregnant? Did she have a boyfriend? Why couldn't she keep me?"

"There's no easy way to tell you about your mother, my dear. A lot of problems started with her father. Eugene was a lovely man, and he adored Tamara, but he was very old-fashioned in his attitudes. He worried that she was interested in so many different things, so vivacious and social in her behaviour; wanted her to be serious and scholarly and follow him into the family business. He became very upset with her school reports; they used to say things like 'Tamara could do better if she tried' or 'Tamara talks too much'."

Purdie laughed. "Well, so did mine."

"Tamara was very young then, probably no more than seven or eight, but Eugene was a serious-minded person so it caused friction in the house and between us as well. I thought, as she grew older and found out what she wanted the situation would take care of itself.

"You've asked why she couldn't keep you. She wanted to, I know, because I was with her. Eugene was very conservative when it came to sex, and in particularly about children born outside marriage. He had an affair which resulted in a child. In those days that was quite a big disgrace, especially for the girl. Eugene never got over that. He felt he'd betrayed himself and his honour. Eventually he brought the child into our home."

"So, he would be an uncle of sorts to me? I've always been an only child. It's nice to find I've got a family."

"We aren't close," said Marguerite abruptly. "Anyway, after Clive's birth, Eugene became extraordinarily circumspect about sexual relationships. The reputation of the family and the firm's name meant everything to him."

Marguerite smiled. "I think it had always been part of him. Even when we were courting, he was conservative about such things. He wasn't going to make mistakes. When Eugene and I founded the Dunnings store, the founding document, our will, so to speak, was specific. If Eugene and I died, then in the first instance, only a legitimate child of our marriage could inherit the company, regardless of age or gender. If there was no such child, then illegitimate children, other members of the family and so on could inherit as second best. Tamara was the child of our marriage, which made her the heir apparent. Eugene's older, illegitimate son couldn't inherit."

Purdie was trying to put two and two together. "So when my mother found she was pregnant, she couldn't tell her father?"

"That's right," said Marguerite. "Eugene would never have forgiven her, nor the child. You," she added, as if she had just realised who she was speaking to. "Our family name was high profile, and the paparazzi were a pest. We knew if her pregnancy were revealed, it would be widely publicised."

"Couldn't my father help?" protested Purdie. "My mother didn't get pregnant by herself. Was my father her boyfriend?"

Marguerite went quite still. She knew she had to handle the next few minutes very carefully. "No, Tamara didn't have a boyfriend. She was only just sixteen when she got pregnant. She was attacked, molested."

Purdie went white. "You mean she was raped?"

Marguerite nodded.

"Oh my God. Am I the result of that? How horrible. Jesus, I never expected that." Purdie found she had clapped a hand over her mouth. She withdrew it slowly and took a deep breath.

"I'm sorry, my dear, but I thought you should know now," said Marguerite, reaching out to pat Purdie's hand. "It doesn't reflect on you in any way, but it was a terrible, terrible time. My poor daughter."

"Did you go to the police?"

Marguerite shook her head. "To do so would have dragged Tamara through the gutter press. The man who did it threatened her – if she reported it, he would say she'd led him on, that she had consented. The police process isn't very kind to rape victims, even today. Back then it was even worse. Because of her name, and the public profile of the company, it would have been Tamara on trial, not the man. She was seen by a doctor and it was all documented, but that was as far as it went. We never let Eugene know."

"In God's name, why not?" Purdie glared at her grandmother. "Surely he was entitled to know?"

Marguerite took a long time answering. "I will never know whether we made the right decision or not," she said slowly. "Tamara didn't want him told, and I wasn't sure that he wouldn't blame her for having contributed to the situation in some way. He was always so hard on her."

"Yes, but surely," blurted Purdie, "being hard on someone because of school grades is one thing, but your daughter being raped is rather different. Of course he'd have believed her. Any father would."

Marguerite smiled sadly. "You obviously had a very loving adoptive father." She took a deep breath. "You see, complicating the issue was that the man involved was someone her father knew, loved and trusted. Eugene would have been in a very difficult position.

"You may well think we were wrong, and you might be right. Hindsight is a great thing," she sighed. "At the time, though, it did seem the best thing for both you and Tamara was to give you up for adoption. Tamara was torn about it but she knew she didn't have the resources to bring up a child. She was virtually a child herself."

She gazed away from Purdie, who could see that Marguerite had unshed tears in her eyes. Purdie didn't know whether she ought to console her grandmother or abuse her for what she'd just been told. What a horrible nightmare this was. She just wanted to get away from it all and think through what she had been told.

Marguerite braced herself for Purdie's inevitable next question. She had no idea how she was going to explain the relationship between Clive and Tamara. The girl was badly shaken already.

Marguerite could barely contain her relief when the question never came. Later, she told herself; she would deal with that bit later.

After a few moments' silence, Marguerite turned back to

Purdie. "I'm sorry, my dear, this must be a horrible shock for you, and it was a terrible time in our lives. In the nursing home, when Tamara was in labour, there was another young woman, your adoptive mother, who had just lost her third baby. Tamara and Nora became friends. Nora and her husband were desperate for a child but couldn't have one, and Tamara had a child she didn't feel she could keep. Eventually they agreed that the Davises would take you and love you as their own."

Marguerite sighed. "It wasn't ideal, but then, what is? It was a solution, and it gave some hope of happiness to good people who hungered for a child. We knew they would give you everything they could. I think you told the lawyer in New Zealand it was a happy adoption?"

Purdie nodded. "The best. They truly acted like my real parents. I knew I was adopted but I never understood the ins and outs of it. Then my parents died before I got round to asking them."

Marguerite nodded. "Even in those days, it wasn't strictly legal just to hand your child over to another person. I suppose the authorities wanted to make sure no baby farming went on. Private adoptions were a no-no." She smiled reminiscently. "There was some fairly complicated guardianship type document that was signed allowing your release to the Davises, then later on a formal adoption was possible.

"You haven't asked me yet why I insisted you buy a business suit," said Marguerite.

Purdie glanced up. "I assumed it was an all-purpose go-to-funerals, go-to-christenings and see-the-bank-manager sort of garment."

Marguerite laughed. "Well, all of the above. But no, I had a more specific reason."

"I described the nature of the document which founded Dunnings? Well you, my dear, are more than just my long-lost granddaughter. You are the heir apparent of the family business. When Eugene died, he left no other legitimate children, so you, as Tamara's daughter, are next in line."

"I thought the children had to be born to a married couple," said Purdie, confused.

"That was an oversight when the original document was drawn up. I've no doubt that was Eugene's intent, but it never occurred to him any child of his would have children out of wedlock. The original document is quite specific that only a legitimate child of Eugene and I could inherit in the first generation, but it doesn't have that clause when it comes to future generations. So you, my girl, are it."

Marguerite stirred her coffee thoughtfully. "Isn't it awful that I'm sitting here talking about illegitimate children, when both of us know there's no such thing." She smiled. "Maybe parents are illegitimate, but children aren't."

"Are you telling me," Purdie said incredulously, "that I stand to inherit the entire company of Dunnings?"

"Yes," said Marguerite. "I've no doubt Clive will try and contest the will, but I don't believe it can be broken, and I've had it checked over by several lawyers."

"Is that the Clive who is my uncle, or would it be half-uncle?"

Marguerite nodded.

"Wow," said Purdie. "Um, what happens if I don't want to inherit a store? I mean it's not exactly in my ten-year plan, if you know what I mean."

Marguerite chuckled. "As long as I don't shuffle off this mortal coil, you don't need to build it into your current planning, my dear. What you do need to do is spend the time thinking about options that would be available to you. That's all I ask. And getting back to that business suit, I do need to present you to the upper management of Dunnings. I told them about you and half thought I was delusional, and you were just an old woman's fantasy. Whatever the future, we need to consolidate the present. Eugene's death has created a power vacuum, and it's important that everyone knows you exist and there is a future for them. Please let me do that?"

Purdie agreed. "OK, for the time being, while we consider options. I suppose it will be all right."

"And that," concluded Purdie, "is my report on my shopping day with Grandmamma."

She was sitting with Nick in the little garden at the rear of the house. The brick walls were overgrown with climbing roses bursting with the first flush of summer colour. The walls contained warmth, and the garden was protected from the light, cool summer breeze that tossed the clouds around in the sky above. It was a pleasant place to linger for a pre-dinner drink.

Purdie had poured her heart out to Nick as if he was in some way judge and jury.

"How are you feeling about everything now?" he asked cautiously.

It wasn't like Purdie to blurt out heaps of personal information. That she had meant she was too deeply distressed to be discreet or, more promisingly, she trusted him enough to confide in him. He liked the latter option and hoped he was right.

"Honestly?" Purdie pushed her hair back from her face and gazed at him. "I truly don't know. I mean, it's a horrible story, and in a sense it's about me, but at the same time it doesn't really seem to involve me either. I was gutted when I heard I was the product of assault and rape. My childhood fantasies were that I was the daughter of the gypsy king who was kidnapped, or that I was a changeling. You know, exotic, fantastic, romantic stuff. Not this gritty drama."

"I think your mother and grandmother probably did make the best decision for you, after all," said Nick. "You ended up with a fantastic family who loved you, and you were taken out of what was a very squalid situation so it could never affect you."

Purdie considered that thought. "Yes," she said, "I really was lucky, wasn't I? I just wish, though, my parents hadn't died."

"Any family scenario has the possibility of loss. I'm sorry for you too, but some families never have the closeness you had, even if it was cut short. And you'll carry that with you through to your own children. Parenting is as much learned behaviour as anything else. Your people did well by you."

Purdie smiled at him shyly. "I didn't mean to dump on you, though."

It was Nick's turn to smile. "I am happy I'm here for you to do so," he said softly. "I was really afraid when you said you'd been kidnapped."

"Too many white slavery films?" she asked.

"Too many all sorts of things," he replied. "I couldn't bear being half a planet away from what was happening. Not that I was very much use in the end."

"It was a bit of an anticlimax, wasn't it," replied Purdie. "I thought I could be Lara Croft. Instead I just walked out of captivity without a hassle. Still, I scored a couple of meals and a free night of five-star accommodation in London. That's got to be worth something." She looked up to see him watching her and raised her eyebrows questioningly.

He held her gaze. "There's unfinished business between the two of us, you know."

Purdie's expression was mischievous. "You mean some more dishwashing?" she asked, gesturing towards their glasses. She could feel her heart starting to speed up again, and for some reason she had gone breathless.

He gave a choked laugh. "Something like that." He stood up and pulled her to her feet. "Maybe we could try something else this time."

She went to him willingly. Her grandmother's words came back to her. *Well, at least I have appropriate lingerie,* she thought briefly, before the sensations his lips were causing stopped her thinking about anything at all.

Later that afternoon the phone rang. Marguerite was surprised when Max handed it to her while waving a 'caution' sign with his free hand.

"Hello," she said.

"Mrs Dunning? This is John Li. I head the family responsible for the kidnap of your granddaughter the other day."

"Why are you calling?" asked Marguerite, her voice icy.

"I am aware that my family and I owe you and your granddaughter a most humble apology for their outrageous behaviour. I am phoning to ask for an opportunity to make those apologies in person, and I'm requesting a suitable time for this, perhaps tomorrow morning at eleven o'clock?"

Marguerite felt her jaw drop. "You mean you wish to come here?"

"Yes," said the voice. "I am requesting that. I believe a formal apology is owed to you, and I would be grateful if you would allow me to deliver it appropriately."

Marguerite thought it over and agreed.

"What do you think their purpose is?" she asked as she put the phone down.

"I imagine this is damage control," said Max. "Abduction is a serious offence. You got Purdie back only because she was plucky enough to get herself out of a bad situation. Things could have gone very differently."

Marguerite looked at Purdie.

"We might as well hear what he has to say as long as it doesn't pose a risk to us. Maybe he has more information to share."

Marguerite nodded. "I agree," she said absently, "but it needs to be formal, you understand?" She exchanged glances with Max, who nodded.

When the entourage arrived, Purdie was unashamedly gawking out of a window. "Why are there two cars? I thought only Mr Li was coming."

"Security, I suppose," said Marguerite.

"No," said Purdie. "Look, the first car is full of flowers."

The men from the first vehicle were laden with an enormous floral display and followed their leader up the steps. By the time they arrived at the front door, Max had opened it to receive them.

"Mrs Dunning is expecting me."

"This way, sir," said Max calmly. "Your companions?" he queried.

A couple of phrases were exchanged before Mr Li announced, "They will remain here. The flowers are for Mrs Dunning if you would receive them for her."

"Certainly, sir," said Max. "If your entourage would remain here in the hall, I will show you through."

Marguerite and Purdie had been waiting in the drawing room and rose when Mr Li was escorted in.

Purdie didn't recognise him from any previous meeting. He appeared to stiffen his spine as he approached the waiting women. "Thank you for seeing me, madam," he said, bowing deeply to Marguerite. "I am grateful that, after my family's bad behaviour, you are so magnanimous as to allow me to apologise to you and to rectify this fault."

Purdie watched silently as Marguerite smiled graciously. "Please be seated. Would you care for tea or other refreshment?"

Marguerite, Mr Li and Max discussed the merits of jasmine, pu-erh and oolong teas. There was small talk as it was prepared, before Max re-entered the room with the tea trolley.

Finally, with the cups of delicate tea poured, Max stood behind Marguerite's chair. There was something about Max's quiet presence that made Purdie feel safer than if a host of crack SIS troops had been protecting her.

Mr Li began. "I regret, Mrs Dunning, the dishonour paid to your family, and I wish to make amends and apologise for this incident so there may be peace between us from this time on."

Marguerite inclined her head. "My granddaughter tells me that in a previous time, my family owed yours a great debt for the care it gave a relative of mine. I was unaware of this debt, but let it weigh in the scales between us."

"You are most gracious, madam. I believe your granddaughter met my grandfather." Li smiled. "He is an honoured elder of our family, but times move on. I understand he perceived an opportunity for our fortunes to advance, and that blinded him." Mr Li smiled again. "Grandfather is now aware that he made a mistake, and those subordinates who should have advised him appropriately are undergoing some re-education in the principles of our family's business."

John Li smiled a genuine, warm smile. "I am sure you appreciate the delicacy of the situation, madam. My grandfather has been the absolute ruler of our clan. His wisdom and guidance have ensured our growth and current prosperity. I don't want to diminish these things. I intend to base my own reign on his values, but he is ageing."

He sighed and paused in his pacing. "I believe he met your great uncle, madam. The story he told your granddaughter is one we have all heard as part of our inheritance, viewed amongst us as a story of virtue well rewarded. Our clan used your great uncle's funds to stake their claim when they got to Hong Kong, and the rest, as they say, is history."

"No one anticipated that the historical story would be hijacked to create not a story of virtue, but of crime. Abduction, extortion – these are not values my family support, Mrs Dunning." He brought forward the cushion he had carried in. "I would ask you to accept these tokens of our sincere respect and regret. For you, madam." He presented an elaborately decorated and boxed parcel to Marguerite.

Then turned to Purdie. "And for you, also. You were the main victim of this crazy plan. I ask your forgiveness and request that, as a sign of our regret and our continued respect and engagement with your family, you accept this gift."

The parcel he handed to Purdie was hardly less beautifully packaged than the one Marguerite had received. Purdie wondered if it was appropriate to open it and was relieved to see Marguerite carefully unwrapping hers. Marguerite paid due attention to each layer of wrapping, she noted, and Purdie ensured she did the same.

Inside the parcels were two exquisite jade bracelets. For Marguerite, a wide bracelet of vibrant green jade set with a gold hinge. Marguerite held it to the light and the piece glowed.

Purdie's bracelet was a pale, light jade cuff. The colour was delicate, the carving beautiful. A simple scene of willows, graceful ladies, a bridge and two birds wound around it.

Purdie put it on. "It's beautiful," she breathed. Then remembering what the occasion was, she volunteered her own comment. "Mr Li, I was afraid when I was kidnapped, but I could not fault the care your people took to make me comfortable. Had your grandfather not caused this, neither my grandmother nor I would ever have known a large part of our family's history. I thank you for your gift."

Marguerite smiled at her approvingly. "I, too, am pleased with your gift. Do I understand that you are now the leader of the Li family?"

"I am. We are a successful clan with a portfolio of businesses. Kidnapping, extortion, bugging and covert surveillance of innocent people are not among them."

Mr Li rose, followed by Marguerite and Purdie.

"Thank you both, ladies, for your time and courtesy," he said formally. "If you will excuse me, I need to return to my family and enforce the changes my presence has effected." He grinned at them both. "It has truly been a pleasure to meet you, and I hope to do so again under more pleasant and appropriate circumstances." He left with his entourage trailing behind him.

"Well," breathed Marguerite, "that was quite an apology. The flowers alone will keep Max in work trying to get sufficient vases for them all."

CHAPTER
FIFTY EIGHT

London, Present Day.

THEY GATHERED AGAIN IN THE BOARDROOM. "Another day, another meeting," said Tony Manners cheerfully to Nathan Parsons. Nathan, he noted, had been a little subdued recently. For a man previously bullish and a little pushy, Nathan's manner seemed suddenly reserved. "Are you OK?" asked Tony, a little concerned.

"Yes, fine," muttered Nathan.

"What do you suppose this bunfight is about then?" asked Tony.

Nathan cast him a harried look before remarking sourly, "Well, I assume it's the presentation of the little princess. Then all the fairy-tale bits will be in place, won't they? Just be grateful you backed the right horse."

Tony stared at him. "I beg your pardon?"

Nathan reddened. "Sorry, mate," he muttered.

Puzzled, Tony watched him move to the opposite side of the room – exactly, thought Tony, as if he was avoiding friendly contact.

After a second he ignored Nathan as Samantha came up beside him. The last month or so had been wonderful for Tony. Samantha Merilees was cool, efficient and merciless when it came to her professional life, but her private life was a very different story, and Tony had been privileged to share it. It had started as a professional interaction after Marguerite had redefined their roles but rapidly turned into something more rewarding. He still couldn't believe that a creature as beautiful as Samantha would find him fun to be with, let alone take him to her bed.

He smiled at her and took his place beside her at the table. She grinned at him and, below the level of the tabletop, slid her hand across to stroke his leg. He gave a soft gasp of surprise then allowed himself to relax while her fingers stroked a steady pattern on his thigh. He glanced at her and found she was talking to her partner on the other side. He assumed she was talking intelligently, which was impressive and more than he could hope to do – the touch of her fingers was hypnotic.

As far as he could see, the only outward sign she gave of the activity beneath the table, was a faint smile curling her lips.

A few minutes later Clive arrived, which curtailed Samantha's game. He was followed by Donald McCrae and Marguerite. A slight young woman entered between them.

They settled at the table. A movement at the edge of his vision made Tony glance at Clive; the tension in his body language was palpable. He leaned, his head thrust forward, staring at the young woman.

Tony looked round. While others at the table were observing the girl with curiosity, Clive looked like a wolf about to eat her.

"Good morning," said Marguerite once everyone was sitting. She ignored Clive.

"Thank you all for attending today. Firstly, I want everybody to know that I am pleased with progress since our last meeting. I know you and your various departments will have received a number of reports tracking the success of the changes we introduced. I am happy to say that, with very few exceptions, the results have been exemplary. So, well done everyone.

"If you all carry on with the same degree of excellence for the rest of this year you may find a pleasant bonus in your Christmas stockings. I am sure Clive will have some words to say to you at the end of this meeting concerning trends in our financial status, our budgets and our goals for the next trimester.

"Before that, though, I have a very pleasant duty to perform. At our last meeting I disclosed the template Eugene and I developed all those years ago for handover of control in the company from one generation to the next. As I mentioned then, according to the terms of that agreement, my granddaughter will, in the course of time, be my successor. She hasn't long been in England, being from New Zealand, so I ask you to all show a warm welcome to Perdita Davis."

There was a formal ripple of applause from the seated delegates as Purdie stepped forward. If she was nervous, she didn't display it, thought Tony. He searched for any resemblance to her grandmother but could see none.

Clive, he noticed, was riveted. The man's face had paled, and there was sweat across his forehead.

"Good morning," said Purdie. "Thank you all for your welcome. I am very proud to stand here today as one of the Dunning family. As my grandmother said, I have been in London for little over a week, so I haven't had much time to find my way around. I am happy to say that one of my first trips out in London was to Dunnings, where I had a wonderful time experiencing the best you have to offer."

Her voice was pleasant, thought Tony, pitched low and musical with its slight New Zealand accent. She looked good as well, although Clive didn't seem to be appreciating the sight.

"I hope to meet you all over the next few months and look forward to strengthening my bonds with my grandmother and with the company she heads. Thank you all once again," she concluded.

The room applauded as she sat down beside Marguerite.

Tony wondered what a New Zealand granddaughter really made of the whole affair. She remained attentive throughout the rest of the meeting, smiling as required and attentive to her grandmother. Perhaps Nathan's cynicism was right. The little princess had indeed been formally presented.

Tony wondered if this was a PR job to ensure they all felt secure about Dunning's future, and if so, whether the presentation of a young Kiwi woman as the future look of Dunnings was really going to achieve that end. Clive, who had the most to lose by this woman's presence, looked ghastly. The rage and fury he had demonstrated at the last meeting had evaporated. As it was never Clive's style to give in gracefully, Tony assumed he must be ill.

Afterwards, Tony, along with everyone else, shook hands with Purdie as he left the meeting. She murmured a few words as she took his hand, her grip surprisingly firm for a young woman, and he thought he saw a glimpse of humour in her eyes as the line filed past her.

Tony was waiting in the foyer for the lift when, looking back, he saw that Clive had arrived in front of Purdie. He stared hard at her for a few moments without taking her proffered hand. Purdie, Tony saw, was slightly disconcerted and withdrew her hand, inclining her head in apparent dismissal. Clive said something to her briefly before moving past and entering the lift in front of Tony. Purdie's head snapped up, and she stared at him as he left.

The men shared the lift as it descended to the fifth floor. Clive leaned back against the wall, his eyes on the ground. He looked so ill that Tony was moved to enquire if he was okay.

"Mind your own business," snapped Clive ungraciously and barrelled his way past Tony as the lift doors opened, disappearing down the corridor.

Tony shrugged. Good luck to the little princess, he thought, if she could keep that monster in his place.

Alone in his office Clive paced in front of the window. The girl was the living image of Tamara. Yes, a bit older of course, but clearly Tamara's daughter. He hadn't expected to feel shocked, but he was. Deeply, fundamentally unsettled and unbalanced in his thinking. There was a divide between his brain and the way his stomach was lurching uncontrollably. It wasn't a condition he was used to. There were few situations where he wasn't able to push his way through, either by rational argument or by bullying the opposition.

Perdita. What a stupid name. Who called a child that? Presumably her deceased adoptive parents.

There hadn't been any awareness in her eyes when she looked at him. So she didn't know who her father was. He had never been certain about what, if anything, Marguerite knew. She hated him, of course, but that had been true from the first time she had met him. Surely, if she had known at the time who raped Tamara, she would have tried to destroy him then.

There was an irony, not lost on Clive, that he had the power to destroy this girl by revealing she was the result not only of rape, but of incest. Wouldn't the media just love to run with that all over the news? He considered the possibility briefly. A clear and positive outcome would be if it caused the old bitch, Marguerite, to have a heart attack. Regrettably, it would destroy Clive as well. He rejected the notion. All it would achieve would be a lengthy stay at Her Majesty's pleasure. Clive Hannah was not going to spend a large chunk of his life behind bars, not for a silly girl.

He stared at the view beyond the window. He'd always loved the view over the river, loved to watch the traffic move up and down on its ebb and flow. It made Clive feel the long trade history of London, of which he was a part. He'd given his life to Dunnings, built it to where it was today, and for what? What possible future did he have, now that this girl had turned up?

God curse Eugene, he thought viciously. Curse him for his stupid insistence on legitimacy and family. He'd admired and loathed his father equally. All his life Clive had been no more than a bastard in his father's eyes. He had recognised the importance of pleasing Eugene and had dedicated his young life to achieving just that goal.

While he'd sweated, grovelled and placated his father, that spoilt little princess, Tamara, had floated through life on a happy cloud of privilege. God, he'd hated her. She'd had it coming, he thought, recalling the night of her birthday. Someone had to bring her down a peg or two, and by good fortune he'd been the one, he thought with satisfaction.

Ironic that it was that act which generated the daughter

who was now wrecking his plans. Since getting Purdie's birth certificate, Clive had done the maths over and over again. There was a slight possibility, he supposed, that Tamara had become pregnant while on her travels, but she'd have had to do so within a fortnight of the rape. Not that it was really a rape, of course. Tamara had been flaunting herself all that night. If it hadn't been him, one of the other young men there would have been at her.

He had been prepared to demand DNA tests and force the issue before he saw the birth certificate. Now he'd seen the girl, the family resemblance to her mother was very strong. All a DNA test would achieve would be to confirm the identity clearly demonstrated by the legal documents Nathan had dug up for him. God, what a nightmare. He considered a spot of murder but rejected the idea as too risky.

Eugene had used him, but he'd given him opportunities as well. Clive was a wealthy man in his own right. Another man might have been content, but for Clive, it was intolerable that he be forbidden, by chance of birth, from taking his place at the head of the company. There was no way that he, Clive Hannah, was going to play second fiddle to a little colonial girl. Not in this lifetime. Nor was he prepared to leave the company and seek another future. He had invested too much in Dunnings.

He poured himself a full glass of Chivas Regal and downed it in one draught. "Here's to the end of it all," he toasted bitterly as he tipped the glass back.

That evening, Marguerite made good on her promise to take Purdie to the theatre. She had obtained four tickets to Peggy's latest stage performance, *Mrs Cooper's Last Stand*.

Purdie was beside herself with excitement. "I've heard it's the most marvellous play," she enthused. "I saw a write-up about it in a magazine while I was a guest of the Chinese. Dame Peggy is supposed to be magnificent."

"Well," said Marguerite. "Peggy claims it'll be her last performance. She says she's getting past it, and it's too hard to learn lines at her age."

"I don't know how you learn lines at any age," remarked

Nick. "Beats me how they remember them. I'm sure I couldn't."

"Well, that's reassuring," mused Purdie. "All your patients will be thrilled to know you can't remember stuff. It will be a case of 'poor old Dr Nick, what a brilliant mind is here o'erthrown'."

Nick stuck his tongue out at her.

"I didn't realise you knew your Shakespeare," commented Max, ignoring the byplay.

"Oh, that was my dad," said Purdie. "My adoptive dad," she amended hastily. "He loved his Shakespeare. Well, look at what they christened me, for heaven's sake. It's not your everyday Sally or Mary is it?"

The play was as good as the reviews had promised. It played to a packed house, and Dame Peggy was given a standing ovation. They loved her and knew this was her swan song. The majority of her audience hadn't even been born when she first trod the boards. She was an institution in her own right, and more than one theatregoer was in tears as they left the auditorium.

Peggy joined them for a late supper. Purdie and Nick were enthralled. Late-night dining with celebrities of this calibre didn't occur in Wellington.

Peggy was her usual charming, cynical self. She admired Purdie's beauty and inevitably commented on her resemblance to Tamara. "I loved that girl so much," she said. "Having you back here in London has given us old fogies a new lease of life."

"You speak for yourself," murmured Marguerite. "I'm not the one who's planning on retiring."

They arrived home late and were just separating for the night when Max picked up a message on the answerphone. "Marguerite, it's for you," he called. "Donald wants you to call him, any time, day or night. Says it's urgent."

Marguerite phoned, apologising for the lateness of the hour. She listened for a few moments then thanked him and put the phone down. She stood in silence for a moment. Her expression, Purdie thought, was hard to define.

She turned to them all. "Clive is dead," she said. "He was found a couple of hours ago. He committed suicide this evening. Jumped off a bridge."

Neither then, nor at any time later did she or Max see fit to tell Purdie that the bridge Clive had chosen was the same one Tamara had jumped from so many years earlier.

CHAPTER
FIFTY NINE

London, Present Day.

UNCLE TIM PHONED FROM NEW ZEALAND. He'd retrieved the metal box, packed it up and had managed to convey it to the company which handled Dunning's New Zealand purchases. It would be included in the next manifest and sent by premium delivery. The parcel would be traceable every step of the journey. He was happy to report that the tenants had Purdie's house in good order, and everything looked shipshape.

Purdie grinned as she thanked him. She knew her uncle. Without being obvious, as part of his visit, he would have cast an eye over her roof and guttering, automatically checked for any structural issues around the house and scanned the garden. He was one of the most practical men she knew, and he liked things nice and tidy.

"I just hope we don't have any problems getting the box through customs," commented Marguerite. "While we have nothing to hide, it would be a very complicated conversation if we had to explain what was inside it – or why we didn't know."

It took ten days for delivery. While they waited, Marguerite showed Purdie and Nick the sights of London. They did the usual touristy things – the Tower, the Globe Theatre, St Paul's, the Eye. One day they took a ferry trip down the river to the Thames barrier and Greenwich.

Purdie lapped it all up. Her parents had spoken so often of England, and the names and places were familiar to her from listening to their conversations as she was growing up.

There was a tacit agreement that Nick and she would stay with Marguerite, at least until such time as the parcel arrived and the mystery of the box was cleared up. Purdie had heard Nick trying to persuade Marguerite to let him pay his way while he stayed, only to be firmly rejected.

"I don't charge my guests," he was told.

"Yes, but," protested Nick, "I'm not exactly a guest. I invited myself. It's not quite the same thing."

"What it has been is a pleasure," said Marguerite. "I want no further discussion on this point, please. Just seeing my granddaughter happy is more than enough."

*   *   *

They attended Clive's funeral, and Purdie's suit did come in handy, as she pointed out, to Marguerite's amusement.

There was a decent turnout at the funeral. A man of Clive's position had to be honoured and seen off respectably, whatever people's personal opinion of him had been.

Purdie was intrigued to discover there was an ex-wife and two teenage children present, none of whom seemed particularly grief-stricken by his death. There were few close friends, and it was the vicar who gave an impersonal obituary. Marguerite had been asked if she would speak at the service but declined. She made no further comment about Clive's death since hearing the news. The pallbearers were management staff of Dunnings.

They had been to another company meeting where Marguerite appointed Seth Hampton as acting general manager until such time as a general board meeting could be held.

Marguerite had spoken simply to the meeting about the gap Clive's death made in their ranks. She expressed conventional regret but was careful to point out that there were now many opportunities for the future.

Purdie finally plucked up the courage to ask Marguerite something that had been troubling her. "Do you think it was meeting me that made him commit suicide? It happened on the same day I met him."

Marguerite sighed. "I wondered if you would think that. Yes, as it happens, I think there was a direct relationship between Clive meeting Tamara's daughter and his decision. Now," she said, "I have a question for you. What did Clive say to you when he shook your hand?"

Purdie said, "I've been wondering about it. He said 'a life for a life'. It made no sense to me. I assumed at the time it was a threat."

"Well," said Marguerite cautiously, "he was an unusual, difficult and complicated man, and I suppose that could have been what he meant. There were things in Clive's past that, thankfully, have died and are laid to rest with him."

Purdie looked at her keenly but didn't pursue the matter. She had thought Clive a creepy character the only time she'd met him and had no particular feeling about his death. She knew from Marguerite that he had been fully aware she was coming to London, so it was hardly the shock of her presence that triggered his decision to jump.

Nick and Purdie enjoyed exploring London. Being on holiday together was very different from sharing a flat and the domesticity of working life. It was fun being a tourist. The parks were amazing. Purdie had never realised how large they were. They shopped in Oxford Street and Harrods and argued over purchases and where they would go next. Each day brought them closer together as a couple.

"It's only a holiday romance," teased Purdie. They were in Regent's Park, and she was lying beside him on the warm grass with her head on his shoulder. It was a perfect summer's day.

Nick snorted. "Yeah, right. If you think I'm going to let you go now I know you're a wealthy heiress, you've got another think coming. I fancy a rich woman who can keep me in luxury. I'm developing a taste for the high life." He started singing, "*She's a rich girl, she don't try to hide it, diamonds on the soles of her shoes. He's a poor boy, empty as a pocket ...*"

Purdie rolled towards him and pushed herself up on one arm. "That's one of the things that worries me," she confessed. "I'm Purdie, a registered nurse from New Zealand. I can't get my head around all this other stuff. I mean, what if my grandmother expects me to run the company?"

"You'll have to talk it over with her," replied Nick. "She doesn't strike me as the unreasonable sort. After all, there's a distinction between being her heir and actually being involved in the business. That's what boards and managers are for."

"I don't want to disappoint her. She's been very good to me, and it's nice having a family again. I wasn't enjoying being an orphan that much. At the same time, I'm used to looking after myself. I don't want to get swamped."

"You won't disappoint her," said Nick, cuddling her back into the crook of his arm. "As for family, you may have to do with me in the interim, at least; that is, until you run out of money and I have to find another meal ticket."

Purdie reached over and thumped him.

* * *

The parcel was delivered. Max, Marguerite, Nick and Purdie stared at it sitting on the table.

Eventually Max broke the tension. "I'll get a pair of scissors, and we can at least unpack it."

"It's like looking at a little bomb," said Nick. "I don't know whether I want to know what's inside."

"I think that's why we never opened it," said Marguerite. "Sometimes not knowing is better than knowing, but we don't have that option now."

They had agreed there would be a formal opening of the chest to ensure that there were no further questions from interested

Russians, Chinese or other parties.

Marguerite had invited Pyotr to attend and extended a similar invitation to John Li. She had also organised Donald McCrae to be in attendance. "There probably won't be anything in it," she had said to him. "But if there is, I imagine we would be wise to establish provenance and document the occasion."

The locksmith was booked, and the guests gathered in the drawing room.

"It's got a very simple old lock," he said. "Probably any old key could have opened it." He oiled the lock and turned the key.

He was about to open the lid when Marguerite stopped him. "Thank you," she said. "As long as we know the lid will lift for this presentation, that's all we need."

Max showed him out.

"Before we start," said Donald, "I believe we need to set the terms for this meeting. Whatever occurs here remains private and confidential until Mrs Dunning or Miss Davis gives their complete consent for information to be released. I have produced a short document for you all to sign to confirm your agreement of these terms."

The men signed, and Donald gathered up the papers. "Who gets to do the honours?" he asked.

"It should be Purdie," said Marguerite. "After all, it is her property."

Purdie moved towards the table and looked at the box. She smiled at Nick. "Here goes," she said, lifting the lid.

She stood staring down into its contents. "There's just a pile of old cloth," she said doubtfully.

"Lift it out," said Marguerite. "Carefully."

There were several layers of felt, a few small bags and an envelope, then underneath, a couple of much larger items wrapped in soft leather. Purdie lifted one out and slowly unwrapped it. "Holy shit," was all she could say.

"Oh my God," breathed Marguerite. "We had this all those years and never knew."

There it was, gleaming with the sheen of old gold, still rich and undiminished by its years of seclusion. An awesome relic of a different age and time.

The egg was gold with a timepiece in it. "It's a clock," said Purdie. "A clock egg."

Carefully she handed it to her grandmother.

"I'm picking the bright shiny stone is a diamond?" asked Nick, peering over her shoulder. "I could get to like the idea of winding a clock up with a diamond."

"What's the other thing?" asked Max as Purdie unwrapped it.

"That's the pedestal the egg sits on," explained Pyotr.

Even the roses on the pedestal were decorated with diamonds and sapphires. When assembled, the egg stood about eight inches high.

"I can see why my family were so determined to get this," said John Li. "It is magnificent."

Donald was busy with his camera. "I think we need a photograph of the box, the egg, and also the people here today," he said.

"I agree," confirmed Pyotr. "I've brought mine as well. May I?" he asked Marguerite, who nodded.

"What else is in there?" asked Nick, as Donald and Pyotr circled round, snapping their cameras.

Purdie put her hands in and lifted out more felt, then one more package. "It's a chicken," she said as she slowly unwrapped it. "In a nest?"

"A basket, certainly," said Marguerite. "With an egg." She turned to Pyotr. "Do you think these are authentic?"

It amused her to watch the play of emotion on his face as the wide-eyed enthusiast strove for professional distance and control. "They will have to be studied, of course," he replied. "But given the circumstances surrounding your possession of them, yes, I would hazard a guess they're the real thing. But you must keep everything. The wrappings, the material, everything. Please."

They put the eggs on their stands and stood back to admire them. They gleamed with light and colour in the drawing room.

"Talk about having all your eggs in one basket," quipped Nick.

Purdie groaned.

"I'm sorry," he said. "Opulence makes me nervous. Who knew that until today?"

"They must be worth a fortune," murmured Donald. "It's wonderful to see them close up, but I must say it makes me sick with nerves to see them here and not in a vault or museum."

"That's somewhat ironic really," said Purdie, "seeing as they've spent the last few years stashed in an attic."

"And before that they were lugged all over the place," commented her grandmother wryly. "I even used that trunk as a small table once. Who would have guessed?"

Purdie was folding up the wrappings neatly and putting them back in the trunk. She picked up one of the small bags and undid the cord. She tipped it up over one of the bits of felt and a stream of stones fell out. She opened the other little bags. There were stones she assumed were diamonds and others of various colours. There were some gold and other coins, and one other small egg, pretty, but not of the same quality as the others.

Purdie looked at it. "This looks like the one I received in New Zealand," she said. "From your people, Mr Li, I assume?"

He nodded.

"I think I feel like the person who discovered Tutankhamen's treasure," she said. "This can't really be happening, surely?"

"Look at those precious stones," said her grandmother staring at them. "I can't believe how hard it was for us when we first came to England and had nothing, and there was all this treasure just sitting in this box."

"The question is, what are you going to do with it now?" asked Donald.

Purdie picked up the envelope and pulled out the document inside. She unfolded it. The paper was brown and stained with age.

"Careful," said Pyotr, watching her, horrified. "You don't want to damage it."

Purdie handed the document to her grandmother. "I can't read it," she said. "I guess it's in Russian?"

"May I?" said Pyotr. "It's on letterhead, but I don't recognise the crest.

"Dated March 15, 1917.

In the name of the Tsar, I have this day charged Kyril Gregorovitch Komarov to conserve these two Imperial Eggs, property of the Romanov family. They are to be removed from Russia and held safely against the day they can be returned to our nation.

In payment for his service he has received a fee made up of precious stones and gold.

May he go with God.

General Mirov."

"That was my grandfather," said Marguerite. "Kyril Komarov. He never said a thing about this to me. I suppose my father must have known, otherwise he wouldn't have taken the box with us when we fled Poland. What an extraordinary saga."

Purdie turned and hugged her grandmother. "What an extraordinary *family*," she said. "I never expected anything as exciting as this when you first contacted me."

"I also would like to know what you will do," asked Pyotr.

"That," said Donald repressively, "will be discussed by my clients later ... alone."

"It's just that ..." began Pyotr.

"We will discuss it," confirmed Marguerite, "and we will inform you of what we have decided. There is a lot to think about in this situation. Our decision will take a while. I know you have already signed agreements, but I just want to remind everyone not to talk about this. I think there will need to be a press release, and Pyotr, your embassy may wish to be part of that. These are, after all, part of Russia's history, whatever our eventual decision is."

And with that Pyotr had to be content. He continued taking photographs of the treasures from every angle but agreed not to disclose or discuss anything he had learned that afternoon.

A similar pledge was made by John Li.

The guests left soon after. Donald lingering just long enough to reiterate that no decision about the treasure should be announced or finalised in any way until he had been consulted.

"This is a unique situation," he reminded them. "Ownership of those eggs is an open question, at the very least. And you have already encountered some very determined collectors. There will be plenty more when this news gets out. And it will," he said cynically. "Please keep those eggs very, very safe."

Marguerite assured him they would be locked in Eugene's old safe in the house.

Finally they were left alone. Purdie retired to a seat with a drink and studied the bag of jewels. "I'm picking that these, at least, are ours?" she asked.

"I suppose so," said Marguerite. "That seemed to be the intent of the letter."

Purdie poured them out and pushed them round for a while. Nick went off to help Max with some chores.

After a while Marguerite looked over at Purdie. "You know something that's odd? We are all avoiding actually looking at those eggs, now that they are here. It's as if we are scared of them."

Purdie smiled. "I think that hits the nail on the head. We're all terrified of them, of the responsibility and risk they represent."

"Have you any ideas about what you want to do with them?" asked Marguerite.

"Me? I don't know. It was your grandfather who was given them. It has to be your choice."

"Hm," said Marguerite. "It was your great-great-grandfather who was given them, so it's as much your responsibility as it is mine. Plus, I gave them to you when you were born."

"But you had no idea what you were giving," said Purdie. "You can't make that gift stand now, you know."

"Yes I can," said Marguerite. "I didn't know what I was giving away, that's true, but it's still yours. I intended to intrigue you enough to hope you would explore your family's history."

"Intrigued is one word for it," smiled Purdie. "You certainly succeeded there!"

"The eggs are going to be your decision," said Marguerite. "I'm happy to discuss it with you, and I am sure Max and Nick will put in their two pennies' worth as well. But the final decision is yours. And yes," she smiled, "I'm sure the stones and the gold are yours as well, so you can get some nice jewellery made up if you want."

CHAPTER SIXTY

London, Present Day.

IT WAS A QUIET QUARTET ASSEMBLED that evening for a light dinner. The excitement and drama of the day had drained them all. The eggs were in the safe, and Max and Nick had done double duty checking locks and bolts and setting the alarm.

"I can't live like this permanently," complained Marguerite. "I thought I knew what it was like to be wealthy, but treasure like this makes me paranoid."

"I think the sooner you decide what to do, the better," said Nick. "I know they were a charming little Easter egg game for the Tsar and his family, but they are too much for simple mortals. Just thinking about them in the same house gives me the heebie-jeebies."

"I think the decision on what happens to them is quite simple," said Purdie. "They were given to our ancestor as a trust, and I think we should honour that. They need to be given back to a museum in Moscow for the people of Russia."

The rest of the table sat quietly.

"Well," asked Purdie nervously, "doesn't anyone agree with me?"

Again there was that strange silence until Marguerite broke it. "I think you are right, my dear. I would have been disappointed if you had felt differently. But this has to be your choice, and only yours. You are the next one in the family to pick up the challenge. They were a burden laid upon my grandfather, and he may or may not have wanted to carry it. I agree with you that it's our job to finish the task."

Nick said, "I would second that."

"And I," said Max.

"Good, that's decided then," said Purdie with relief. "Please could you organise Mr McCrae to sort out the details? I agree with your statement about a press release as well. The news that these have been rediscovered is a seriously 'good news' story, and we can use it, both for your store and for building relationships with Russia. Had you thought part of the deal might be to put them on display for a while in Dunnings? It would generate a lot of interest, I think. That is, if we could organise the right security, of course."

Nick looked at her with surprised approval. "Go, girl! You might be an entrepreneur after all!" Purdie blushed.

*   *   *

Purdie stood beside Marguerite on the podium in the main hall of Dunnings. The Russian Ambassador greeted them and thanked Purdie for her generous gesture in returning the treasures to the people of Russia. The world's press was ready as Purdie took a step forward and grasped the cord of the screen which hid the eggs from sight. As she slowly pulled on the silken cord, the velvet drape dropped from the glass case and there was an intake of breath from the audience before every photographer in the room was snapping pictures for the press.

Purdie stepped back to rapturous applause.

She heard someone in the audience say, "I thought they'd be bigger. They're only about seven or eight inches tall," and smiled to herself. She caught her grandmother's eye.

Marguerite, who had clearly heard the same statement, leaned forward to her. "If they weren't that small, they'd never have remained safe and hidden all those years."

Purdie smiled at her, a warm glance of affection before they were both surrounded by media.

*   *   *

Many months later Purdie stood beside Nick in Moscow's Kremlin Armoury Museum, and Max was escorting Marguerite. It was time for the eggs to come home.

Purdie, Marguerite and their companions had been invited as honoured guests to view the ceremony. The eggs had been displayed at Dunnings in Oxford Street for four months before travelling to New York, as part of a display of Russian artefacts in the Big Apple.

The press had been keenly interested throughout the exhibition. The story of how the eggs were saved, lost and then found had been retold in every paper in the world.

Purdie, young, beautiful and generous, returning the eggs to the Russian people, was a heroine. Even when she laughed the tag off, pointedly saying that she had had little to do with the story, she couldn't avoid the publicity. Her face was nearly as well known as that of the Duchess of Cambridge, to whom she had been introduced.

Having made the decision to return the eggs, Purdie had been prepared to glide gracefully through all the hoopla the decision engendered, although, as she said to Nick, she would be glad when it was all over. She'd surprised herself with her ability to cope with crowds and media.

Marguerite was very proud of her. They had agreed that Purdie would have little to do with the Dunnings business empire on a day-to-day basis but would remain as a family representative on the board so the Dunning line was still involved. If she ever wanted to increase that involvement, she had that option. In the meantime, the governance was in the hands of an experienced board.

Marguerite herself had slowed down. "Age, my dear, catches up with all of us in the end, but I'll still be able to dance the night away at your wedding."

Nick and Purdie's engagement had been announced two months earlier, and Nick had taken a job at St Ormond's. They had agreed to base themselves in England in the short term, but, observed Nick, "We all know New Zealand is the best place in the world to raise kids."

Purdie grinned at him mischievously.

Marguerite, hearing the statement, rolled her eyes and said, "Please, at least get a ring on her finger first."

They watched the eggs unveiled yet again, this time placed reverently into a glass case in the museum. Seeing them in context with the other ten eggs was a revelation.

"You know," said Nick, "just two of those eggs in a house looked ostentatious. Once you see them en masse, though, they start to become almost ordinary. Maybe we need a few more?"

Purdie nudged him to shut up. He put his arm round her and pulled her into his side. "Happy?" he asked.

"Very," she said, leaning against his shoulder. "Like those eggs, I feel I've come home."

Marguerite, standing close enough to hear, smiled at her. "I think you have as well."

Please continue reading for a bonus excerpt from Penelope Haines's second novel –

HELEN HAD A SISTER

PROLOGUE

IT IS PLEASANTLY COOL ON THE terrace. The balustrade and pillars hold the warmth of the day's sun and press comfortably against my back as I sit on the railing here in the twilight. Beyond, in the shrubbery, I can hear the susurrations of little night creatures starting to go about their business. The scent of jasmine hangs in the still air and it is magically beautiful. Moonrise will be early tonight. Last night it was full and lit my room with its silver light.

The palace is hushed. The usual domestic sounds of food preparation, children wailing and slaves readying the house for the night are missing. Many of the servants have fled. Charis came in a while ago bringing a shawl, spiced wine and sweetened cakes, setting them out on the table as if laying places for guests. Perhaps she is. I would have refused the food, but I knew it kindly meant.

When she had finished, she came and knelt at my feet. "Lady, let me stay with you," she pleaded.

I looked at her kneeling form, reached out and touched her soft, dark hair. I love this girl, she is all I have left of my eldest daughter. "You cannot stay. This is for me alone, Charis. If you stay, you will be killed. You must go."

She looked up at me, her eyes red and swollen. "Lady, please, I beg you."

"Go, Charis." I was firm. "I need no innocents on this journey. Don't weep for me. All here is as it should be."

She sighed, but eventually left.

Aegisthus died some hours ago. The screams first alerted me. I sent Charis to investigate the uproar, and she came running back, white with shock, to report his bloody body lay in the forecourt. The slaves, after their initial outcry, faded from the scene. They will have found some safe place to hide and tomorrow will emerge to serve whoever survives the night.

My murderer is in the palace already. I wonder what he's been doing in these hours. Has he gone to the bathhouse to pay his respects to the shade of his father? Does he pray? Is he afraid of what he has come to do? He must know I will not resist him. Of all who ever lived, he is the one man forever safe from me.

I have loved him most truly, treasured his embraces, valued his opinions and rejoiced and shared in his goals. He left me seven years ago, and the pain of missing him has been the greatest grief to me.

I feel Aegisthus's presence, and it comforts me. He will wait until I join him so we can walk the dark road together. It won't be long now. I try in these moments to steady myself. I seek some pattern or meaning in the skein of my days, but my mind is restless, its processes near inchoate. I remember myself as queen, lover, mother and avenger. How did I become murderer and monster; hated by my children and reviled? At the end I will die as a victim. If there was some plan or working to make me what I am, I cannot see it. Truly, we may simply be the gods' playthings.

The sun set an hour ago, and I watched as its edge dipped below the horizon, knowing I saw it for the last time. I will not be alive when it rises tomorrow.

DEAR READER,

Thank you for reading *The Lost One*. I hope you enjoyed it.

Much of the storyline of the novel is based on my own family's history, so writing it was a very moving experience for me as I tried to put myself into the situations and thoughts of those who suffered during war and its repercussions in twentieth-century Europe.

When I launched *The Lost One* I got many letters from fans thanking me for the book. Some had an opinion about Nick and Purdie. Many had formed quite a virulent hatred of Clive. Others had questions about various historical facts.

As an author I love feedback from my readers. You are the reason I write, so tell me what you liked, what you loved and what you hated. I'd love to hear from you.

You can write to me at penelope@penelopehaines.com.

Finally, I need to ask a favour of you. If you're so inclined, I'd love a review of *The Lost One*. Loved it, hated it – I'd just enjoy your feedback. As you may know, reviews can be tough to come by. If you have the time, leave a review on Amazon.com or Goodreads.com. You, the reader, have the power now to make or break a book.

Thank you so much for reading *The Lost One* and for spending time with me.

In gratitude,

Penelope

ACKNOWLEDGEMENTS

This work is entirely fiction, but in writing it, I have drawn heavily on my own family's history. The views expressed in the novel are mine, not those of family members, and although I have done my best to present their story as accurately as possible, any faults or failures in this regard are entirely my own responsibility.

I am especially indebted to the Nanowrimo movement, which inspired me to record the story. Their disciplines taught me a good deal about the requirements of becoming a novelist.

To each of you who helped me write *The Lost One*, some in small ways, others hugely, my heartfelt thanks.

First in line are those tolerant souls who read the earliest drafts and guided me into forming the whole into a coherent narrative. To my beta readers, Renee van de Weert and Kelly Pettitt, I owe an inestimable debt for their frank but constructive criticism during the various revisions of the original draft document. They were unrelenting, patient and diligent in their revision and advice. In particular, I would like to thank Sue Reidy and Tina Shaw, who provided invaluable criticism and guidance. Every writer should have a mentor as focused and generous as them, to aid their creative efforts. I owe thanks to Debbie Watson for checking my spelling and to Vanessa Garkova for the cover artwork. Finally my deepest thanks to Adrienne Morris who proof read and edited the final manuscript.

My gratitude to my husband Cavan who sustained me, helped in a thousand ways and never failed to encourage me.

Finally, my thanks to Reilly for spending the long hours with me and who wagged encouragement, Pascal who lay on my lap as I typed away at the keyboard, and Cash, on whose broad back I cantered away from the frustrations inherent in the creative process.

ABOUT THE AUTHOR

Penelope came to New Zealand as an eleven-year-old after a childhood spent in India and Pakistan. As an only child, reading was her hobby – she read everything that came her way, a habit which has continued throughout her life.

On leaving school she trained as a nurse, without fully considering that a brisk default attitude of 'pull yourself together and stop whining' might not be an ideal prerequisite for the industry. Conceding, at last, that nurturing was not her dominant characteristic, she changed career path and after graduating with a BA (Hons) in English Literature, moved into management consultancy, which better suited her personality type.

After some years of family life she worked as a commercial pilot and flight instructor, spending her days ferrying clients into strips in the Marlborough Sounds and discouraging students from killing her as she taught them to fly.

Penelope lives with her husband, dog, cat and horse in Otaki, New Zealand.

Death on D'Urville is the first novel in her *Claire Hardcastle* series.

Straight and Level takes place some three months after *Death on D'Urville*.

Stall Turns, the third in the series, continues to follow Claire's adventures.

Helen Had a Sister is her second novel.

All novels are available in various formats from Amazon. com.

Paperback editions can be purchased within New Zealand from Paper Plus, Unity Books and other reputable book stores and suppliers. Alternatively, they can be ordered from Penelope's website - www.penelopehaines.com, and you can visit Penelope on Facebook @penelopehainesbooks.

Made in the USA
Coppell, TX
29 November 2020